Other books by Gordon Ryan

Dangerous Legacy
Threads of Honor

SPIRIT OF UNION

DESTINY

GORDON RYAN

Deseret Book Company
Salt Lake City, Utah

Library of Congress Cataloging-in-Publication Data

Ryan, Gordon, 1943–
    Spirit of union : destiny / by Gordon Ryan
        p.   cm.
    ISBN 1-57345-215-7 (hardcover)
    I. Title.
    PS3568.Y32S65   1996
    813'.54—dc20   96-27285
                                                            CIP

Printed in the United States of America

10   9   8   7   6   5   4   3   2

For my beautiful wife, Colleen,
a modern-day pioneer woman,
who taught me that handcarts are not always visible.

Acknowledgments

To my loving daughter Kate, who served as my chief plot strategist as we walked through the streets of Paris.

To Jan Molloy, a fair dinkum Kiwi, a true friend, and a most compassionate, caring woman, who provided the character example for Sister Mary Theophane.

To Richard Peterson, my editor and friend, sincere appreciation for his (oft required) patience, his clarity, and his ability to bring the characters to life.

To Kent Ware, Senior Art Director, for visually capturing the essence of *Spirit of Union*.

To Emily Watts, editor at Deseret Book, for her thoughtful and incisive critique.

To the Oakridge Women's Book Club in Farmington, Utah, who gently led me through the emotions of a woman in distress and the travail of losing a child at birth. Though I understood the agony firsthand from a father's point of view, I truly lacked the compassion to see it from a mother's perspective until this thoughtful group of women held my hand.

And to Sheri Dew. Again.

Introduction

Get gold. Humanely if possible, but at all costs, get gold.

King Ferdinand II of Aragon. 1452–1516

On New Year's Eve, 1995–96, I sat with my wife, Colleen, and several friends in the upper gallery of Abravanel Hall in Salt Lake City while the Utah Symphony Orchestra entertained us in a midnight concert. It was the beginning of what would be a year-long centennial celebration of statehood throughout Utah. Under the direction of Maestro Joseph Silverstein, the orchestra performed brilliantly, and I was thoroughly enjoying the music. I have always felt that just as good literature has the ability to touch the heart, good music has the ability to touch the soul.

Sitting there, I was struck by the thought that in spite of the harshness of the environment, the original Utah pioneers highly valued the performing arts, and as the settlement process began in earnest, and immigrants by the thousands arrived to help tame the wilderness, they sacrificed much to ensure that culture was part of the civilization they were establishing.

Three hundred and fifty years before the Mormon pioneers entered the Great Basin, Spanish Conquistadors

1

set out under a commission from King Ferdinand to explore the area. Moving north out of Old Mexico, they crossed the desert in search of gold. Along the way, they founded such communities as Mazatlán, Albuquerque, and Los Angeles.

They succeeded in their task. The Spanish invaders returned stores of gold to the thrones of Europe, and others would make additional discoveries over subsequent centuries.

But not until 1847 did other European immigrants, some of them already third-generation Americans, find the real treasure, which the native Ute Indians already knew existed—the land itself. Laboring to cross the Rocky Mountains, then descending into the Valley of the Great Salt Lake (where previously only sagebrush and reptiles had thrived), these hardy Mormon trailblazers were able to establish a virtual oasis in the desert. Irrigation transformed the land, and the barren landscape that had greeted the pioneers gave way grudgingly to the tree-lined streets and shady parkways of modern-day Salt Lake City.

Among these early pioneers were some who sought to push on to California in search of the traditional gold that King Ferdinand had sought. But to those faithful who followed Brigham Young's admonition to settle in the less hospitable place and labor to make the desert blossom came the "true gold." Demonstrating the "Midas touch," these intrepid settlers transformed the scrub brush landscape of the Territory of Deseret into a fruitful and productive place to live.

National political affiliation took longer. Following heated debate, discouraging setbacks, misunderstanding, and even a military invasion, statehood was finally bestowed in 1896. Utah, forty-fifth in line, took her place among those original thirteen colonies that had banded together to form the political confederation known throughout the world as the United States of America.

The formerly forbidding wasteland, described by the conquistadors as desolate and unworthy of further exploration, is today thought of by many as one of the most desirable places to live in America. Getting gold, such as that sought by early explorers, was indeed a short-sighted goal; and in their blind pursuit of such treasure, the early comers had overlooked the true value of what they had discovered.

The Mormon pioneers weren't the only ones who worked to settle this land. Others came to help and to build our communities. People of various faiths—Roman Catholics, Protestants, members of the Greek Orthodox Church, and Jewish people—were part of the mix, in some cases nearly from the beginning. Ethnic minorities, including Hispanics, Blacks, Native Americans, Asians, and Polynesian peoples have enriched the culture. Each group has contributed something unique to the diversity of the once predominantly Mormon settlements—especially in Salt Lake City. Many of these people have given not only their toil, but sometimes their health and often their lives, to help turn the wasteland into a golden paradise. This book gratefully acknowledges their contributions.

As we commence the second century of Utah statehood, it remains for us to build on our excellent beginnings and to expand the vision that helped found our state. We must instill in our children the knowledge that the gold that needs refining is not so much the precious mineral as it is our quality of life and the freedoms we enjoy.

If we are able, in the face of changing times, to retain these values—values for which so many have sacrificed so much—then our great-great-grandchildren who attend the

New Year's Eve concert and participate in the Utah Bi-Centennial celebrations in 2096 will reap the reward.

This book begins shortly before statehood, at a time when the now verdant Salt Lake Valley was no longer a haven solely for those of like belief. In this book, a variety of religious, political, economic, and social mergers take place. They are the events that have enriched our history and make Utah an increasingly interesting and desirable place to live.

Learning to live together in peace and share the bounty in the beautiful high mountain valleys of Utah has not always been easy. *Destiny* celebrates our diversity and describes the struggle that has often taken place as Mormons and Gentiles have struggled to accommodate each other. It is an ongoing challenge—one that has always required a "spirit of union."

Gordon W. Ryan
Salt Lake City, Utah
August 1996

The author would be pleased to receive E-mail correspondence from readers who wish to communicate. He can be reached at screen name GordonRyan@AOL.com

It took Tom Callahan nearly a week to walk the hundred miles from Tipperary to Cork. Traveling mostly at night, to avoid any chance meeting with a curious constable, he arrived foot sore and hungry at his destination on the southern tip of Ireland. Once there, he had saved the expense of renting a room by rigging a makeshift shelter out of the crates of sea freight stacked on the wharf.

The morning after his arrival, the *Antioch* arrived and moored nearby, and, having decided upon his course of action during his walk through Ireland, Tom booked passage on the steamer. Then for two days, he slept on the docks and kept to himself while waiting for the ship to sail. It was April, 1895, and he was anxious for a variety of reasons to leave Ireland behind him.

The young Irishman spent part of those days amusing himself by watching the comings and goings of a very pretty, blonde young woman. From his hiding place on the wharf, he had been able to observe her without being seen. What he saw intrigued him. She was in the company of an older man and woman, whom Tom took to be her parents, two young girls, probably her sisters, and a young man who Tom guessed was an older brother. They were all apparently going to be passengers on the same vessel as Tom, and he had watched with interest as the young woman and her family busied themselves on and off the ship.

One morning, after a half hour or so of activity on the ship, the family had walked down the gangway and past Tom's hiding place. They crossed the wharf and went into one of the streets that led to the waterfront in Cork. Tom had only been close enough to overhear a snatch of their conversation, but he had enjoyed listening to the young woman's laughter and watching the graceful way she made her way up and down the gangplank and around the wharf.

Tom was intrigued. They were clearly not Irish or even English. He guessed they were speaking a Scandinavian language. Tom knew the young woman could speak English, though, because he had heard her asking directions of the ship's First Officer. Whatever language she spoke, it had been pleasant to observe her and entertaining to imagine somehow being able to meet her once they were on board the ship and under way. The idea of sharing the sea voyage with a pretty lass made the prospects of spending nearly two weeks on the water less daunting.

There was no doubt that Tom took a certain pleasure in observing a pretty face and a shapely figure. At nineteen years of age, he had already wooed his share of Irish "Colleens," but there was something about this young lady that piqued his interest in an unusual way. While he was watching her, the sunlight broke through the overcast Irish skies and the light glinted off her blonde hair. She was tall—taller than most Irish girls—and had the figure and the carriage of a mature young woman, but her girlish laughter and the playful way she behaved with her little sisters made Tom wonder if she might not be younger than she appeared. No matter, he decided. She was certainly pretty enough to merit his attention and might provide some diversion during the voyage.

It did occur to him that meeting her might be something of a problem. It was obvious that her family was wealthy. She and her mother wore full-length, high-necked dresses and tailored, dark wool coats. Tom noticed, too, that the ship's captain behaved deferentially toward the young woman's stern-looking, well-dressed father. Considering the steerage rules that had been explained to him when he purchased his ticket, Tom thought it might prove difficult to arrange a meeting. His passage provided only limited access to the upper decks of the ship, but it pleased him to think of making the attempt.

The morning of the day the *Antioch* was to sail, Tom had a brief encounter that made him even more determined to meet the pretty, blonde woman. There was a good deal of noise and activity on the wharf as the sailors and dock hands made final preparations to embark. Hoping to buy something to eat before the ship got under way, and shivering from the cold, Tom stepped out onto the dock from his dank sleeping place and nearly bumped into her. She was with her brother. It was an overcast, chilly morning, and her face was flushed. She had plaited her thick blonde hair into a single, heavy braid. She wore no hat, but the two ringlets that curled down in front of her ears framed her fresh, young face in a way that struck Tom as very becoming. The thing that held his interest, though, was her eyes. They were a deep green color and even though she was momentarily startled by Tom's sudden appearance in front of her, she smiled prettily and held his gaze for a moment before glancing away. The young woman's brother greeted Tom with a nod and taking his sister by the arm, steered her around the crates and cargo toward the gangplank. Tom had not responded to the greeting except to instinctively scrape his cap from his head and stare at her as she passed. Now, as she and her brother walked away from him, he stood gazing after them. Those eyes and that face had been something to see, no matter how young she was. The challenge of finding a way to meet her, Tom decided, would make an interesting diversion on his first sea voyage.

Later that day, the gangplank would be hauled in, the giant ropes loosed, the ship's massive horn would sound, and under an umbrella of noisy gulls, the *Antioch* would be under way. Tom had never been on board a ship, though he had seen many of them depart Ireland. This time, however, he would not watch it sail out through the breakwater nor observe the plume of smoke from the double stacks disappear over the horizon. Instead, standing at the railing on separate decks, Thomas Matthew Callahan, born October 5, 1875, in County Tipperary, Ireland, and Katrina Hansen, born June 15, 1878, in Horten, Norway, whom Tom had not yet had the pleasure of meeting, would be bound for America.

The short voyage across the North Sea from Oslo to Aberdeen, followed by the long train ride through Scotland and England to Liverpool and the half-day sail from Liverpool to Cork, had been particularly tiring to Mrs. Hansen. But the ocean voyage across the Atlantic would begin tomorrow, and so Katrina had convinced her mother and sisters to take one last opportunity to walk about the village.

There wasn't much of interest to see in Cork. The seaport looked and smelled like the harbor in Oslo. Gulls screeched overhead, and the buildings as well as the seamen, who were moving about on the quay, seemed equally salt-encrusted. Katrina couldn't, of course, remember it, but the port resembled, too, the one in Horten, the village located about eighty miles down the fjord from Oslo, where she had been born. Indeed, most harbors were alike— some bigger, some smaller.

In the mid 1890s, the activity on the waterfront in most Norwegian cities was much diminished from the bustling days of whaling. In those more spirited times, ships would line the quay and hordes of people were always greeting or saying good-bye to family as the men of coastal villages put out to sea in pursuit of the great whales. By the late nineteenth century, however, the heyday of whaling had long passed. The discovery of oil in Pennsylvania in 1859 had caused a sharp decline in the industry. As the population of whales also declined, there was an international reduction in the chase, the sea hunt became harder, and voyages took seamen away from home for years at a time.

As the whaling industry wound down, Lars Hansen had struggled to keep a ship's chandlery business in operation in Horton, a business his father had started following the loss of his leg at sea. Realizing, in light of the declining ship's traffic, that it was a losing battle, Lars had moved the family to Oslo and converted his shopkeeping and woodworking skills to furniture making—household necessities that he felt people would always need regardless of the changing economy. The Oslo enterprise had succeeded far beyond his expectations.

In 1890, Oslo, Norway, was a bustling city, the center of the Norwegian struggle to wrest independence from Sweden. Ruled for centuries by Denmark, Norway had been ceded to Sweden by the Treaty of Kiel in 1813, following the Napoleonic wars of the early nineteenth century. On

May 17, 1814, shortly after the treaty was effected, Norway elected a king and its own parliament. By the time Lars Hansen arrived in Oslo in 1890, Norway was being governed under a constitutional monarchy in domestic matters, but Sweden still controlled foreign policy, and the Norwegians persisted in fomenting for complete independence.

By 1893, Lars had established ties with cabinet makers across the Baltic Straits in Copenhagen, and it was on one of his buying trips to Denmark that he crossed paths with the man who would ultimately change his life and that of his family. Harold Stromberg, a young Mormon missionary from Salt Lake City, Utah, serving in the Scandinavian Mission of the Church, impressed Mr. Hansen with his forthright presentation on religion. Lars invited Mr. Stromberg, should he ever travel to Oslo, to visit with his family and to share his beliefs. Late in 1893, as the mission grew and new territories were opened for proselytizing, Lars Hansen answered a knock on his door one crisp winter evening to find Elder Stromberg and another young man smiling at him and shaking snow from their overcoats. Within two months, the Hansen family, under Lars's guidance and firm direction, had embraced the new faith and, to Lars's way of thinking, a new future.

During their initial visit in Denmark, Stromberg had told Hansen of the throngs of Mormon converts who were leaving European countries for America, a new land where equal opportunity was available to all its citizens and where like-minded people who wished to serve their God could do so in harmony with their neighbors. Such an idea appealed to Lars, and the rejection he experienced at the hands of former friends in the family's Lutheran Church, once they learned of his conversion to an upstart religion, solidified his decision. The Hansens would sell the store and immigrate to America. Mrs. Hansen found this a hard decision to accept, but the recent death of her elderly mother, whom Mrs. Hansen had been nursing, eased the transition. Propelled by the strong determination of Lars, the Hansens prepared to migrate to Zion.

Strong religion was not a new thing to the Hansens. Lars's father, Wolf Hansen, had been a devout Lutheran, adhering to the tenets of the state-sponsored Church all of his life, and involving his family from the day of his wedding. As a young lad, Lars's earliest memories were of his father's condemnation of the "papists," as he called all Catholics, and of his father's vitriolic hatred of the "ignorant Spaniard," also a Catholic, who had, as a deckhand on the *Jenny Tollefsen* where Wolf served as first mate, caused the accident that resulted in the loss of Wolf's leg.

Nurtured in such a parochial environment, Lars Hansen easily formed the opinion that Catholics were "the spawn of the devil." When Lars finally took a wife and began his own family, the tradition continued. The new Mrs. Hansen lacked the will to oppose her husband in any matter, and so acquiesced in every instance to her husband's wishes. It would never have occurred to Lars that it should be any other way.

By April of 1895, the business and family residence sold, the Hansens found themselves at the last stop before the great leap across the ocean toward what Lars had begun calling "their destiny." Ensconced aboard the *Antioch*, Lars and Jenny Hansen had the main cabin; Anders, the oldest child at twenty, a small cabin to himself; and Katrina, together with her two younger sisters, shared a room with two double-tiered bunks, one of which was used to house the younger girl's large collection of dolls.

11

In later years, during the height of upper-class travel in the early twentieth century, such accommodations as the Hansens had would come to be designated "POSH," referring to the "Port Out, Starboard Home" placement of the cabins, which allowed the wealthy occupants to be on the equatorial or sunny side of the ship during both passages. The Hansens, however, on a one-way voyage to their new life, required only the port side.

On this last day before sailing on the *Antioch*, Katrina and her brother had gone ashore to stretch their legs and explore the quay in search of diversion before the long trip to America.

Through either coincidence or destiny, Tom Callahan and Katrina Hansen had been brought face to face. Each was seeking in their own way to throw off the yoke of a domineering father, and both were on the brink of a great change in his and her lives. The brief, early-morning encounter on the docks of Cork had greater import than either could have known. Two young people had cast their lot to the winds and were about to embark on life's voyage, ignorant of the part each would soon play and the impact each would have in the life of the other.

———&———

Walking the length of the quay, as he had done most evenings since his arrival in Cork, Tom found himself in a melancholy mood as he contemplated his last night in Ireland. His week in Cork had been spent working at odd jobs and trying to conserve his meager funds. For entertainment, he had only indulged himself in a nightly pint or two of beer. Though he enjoyed a brew, he had imposed on himself a limit to how much he drank. As a boy and young man, he had seen too much of a truculent father who routinely stumbled home after the pubs had closed, demanding that his wife reheat his dinner and attend to his other needs, and becoming physically abusive when she took too long to be about it. Tom's older brother had stepped in one night to prevent their father from assaulting the frightened woman and absorbed a fearful beating for his trouble—an event that provided the impetus for the older boy to leave home forever. Tom, who was thirteen at the time, had weathered his share of heavy blows and over the years had been conditioned to never interfere when his father came home inebriated.

At sunset, on what was to be his last evening in Ireland, Tom stood at the end of the quay, watching the clouds on the horizon turn from pale pink to gray and thinking of his home. He loved his mother, and during the times when his father wasn't drunk, their home had been pleasant enough—especially when he was young. Memories of happy times spent in the village and the cottage where he had been raised flooded his mind and evoked a wave of nostalgia. He thought of the mournful Irish songs his mother had often sung to him when he was a lad, and the memory created an ache in his chest, the likes of which he had not experienced. His favorite time when he was a boy had been this very time of day—evening, after supper, when the lamps were lit in the cottage and a fire glowed in the hearth. To think of never seeing that again filled him with a sense of loss he would not have been able to describe.

As the sun dropped into the sea, beyond the horizon, the evening stars began blinking through the occasional break in the gathering cloud cover. The tide was out, releasing the pungent odor of the sea, and Tom watched as birds swooped in during the last light of day to feed off the exposed floor of the bay.

Earlier that day, Tom had wandered through the waterfront district of Cork. What he had seen there had shocked him and contributed to his melancholy frame of mind. On the public board, he had seen a wanted poster. "Thomas Callahan," it had read—"nineteen years old, black hair, six foot, one inch tall, weighing between thirteen and fourteen stone. Wanted for questioning with regard to an assault in County Tipperary." Seeing the poster had startled Tom, although he had expected such a notice to be posted at any time. He was pleased that no reward was offered. He took it as his good fortune, too, that the notice had arrived in Cork just one day before his planned departure.

Once his decision to leave Ireland had been formulated and he had booked passage on the *Antioch*, Tom had not spent much time considering the impact of his hasty departure from home, nor his even more bold decision to sail to America. This night, however, as he stood on the quay gazing out over the ocean, Tom thought more seriously than ever before about what it would mean to flee his homeland.

A light rain began to fall, and Tom turned up the collar of his coat against it. Glancing back at Cork, he could see the gas street lights beginning to flicker on, while out to sea, an occasional flash of lightning illuminated the thick band of dark clouds that hung over the horizon.

The gloom that had descended over the ocean matched his mood. Leaving Ireland to go to America seemed a sensible thing to do. He had heard that life in the United States was filled with opportunities. But what they were, he found it difficult to imagine. Doubts and fears crowded into his uncertain mind. His uncle John, gone the same path these past six years, had written only once, and the letter— posted from Alaska—was not full of tales of riches.

Walking slowly back toward his lonely nest on the

wharf, Tom began the process his mother had taught him so many years ago to counteract the despondency that besets so many Irish. *"Count the good, Tom, and you'll see it always outnumbers the bad,"* she'd said. He hadn't always seen the merit of it, and as he grew older, he found her optimism hard to emulate.

In his experience, there had often been more evil than good in the world and bad things had the greater power to hurt you. That was what he was leaving in Tipperary—a cruel father who had compelled him to work for little or no wages as a clerk in the family store. The older Callahan justified the forced labor by saying, *"I feed and clothe ye, lad. Be grateful in these hard times ye found work."* He had a mother who, he knew, loved him but who had many younger ones who required her care and a husband who demanded constant attention. The parish priest had called her a "compassionate soul," but Tom could see she was a woman in who, at forty-one, the life was ebbing.

He thought also about the police who were pursuing him. That was the part that made leaving easy.

Reaching his hovel, Tom squeezed between the wooden freight containers he had arranged into a shelter. The one wharfie who had discovered his quarters, after ordering Tom away, had relented, *"but only for a couple of days,"* when Tom had explained that he was bound for New York and his ship would shortly sail.

Lying on the bed of old rags and straw, full dark now upon him, Tom wondered if the good did indeed outnumber the bad and if his plan to go to America was sound. The vision of his seven younger brothers and sisters, and the memory of his mother's desperate hug at his departure, crowded his thoughts as he drifted uncomfortably toward sleep.

15

As the memories played through his mind, a few rain-drops angled their way into his shelter and mingled with the tears on his cheeks. Tom would have been ashamed to have admitted he was capable of crying, but lying there in the cold and far from home, the nineteen-year-old boy/man surrendered to his emotions. Ignorant of the prayers his mother said for him, and filled with sadness, Tom wondered what his future held.

Three days at sea passed before Tom caught another glimpse of the young woman from the quay. For the first two days, he'd stayed strictly in the areas marked for steerage passengers. But on the third morning, he saw her standing at the rail on one of the upper decks. She was alone, and Tom determined to approach her. Taking a chance on being caught, Tom ducked under a chain and climbed a flight of stairs to the deck where she was standing, looking quietly out to sea. Three times Tom casually walked by, trying to think of something to say. If she noticed him, she didn't let on. By the fourth pass, Tom had worked up the courage to make his approach.

"'Tis a vision of loveliness I see this morning," he said, stopping behind her to gaze out over the ocean.

And you're even lovelier up close, he thought.

Katrina, hearing but not comprehending his comments, turned to face him, confusion on her face. "Uh, excuse me?" she replied in English.

Tom smiled his best and most friendly greeting, hoping Katrina would respond with an openness of her own. Disarmed somewhat by his cordial demeanor, she seemed willing to converse with him. "I said, it's a vision of loveliness

16

I see this beautiful morning," nodding toward the expanse of ocean.

I mean you're the most beautiful girl I've ever seen and can I hold you in my arms?

Unsure of his meaning, Katrina once again hesitated. His forward manner was a little unsettling, but she did not want to give offense or appear foolish, if, indeed, he was not speaking of her. She and her brother, Anders, had been sent for schooling to Great Britain, something their father thought necessary if his children were to move easily in polite society. She therefore spoke and understood English quite well, but she was sometimes confused by the conflicting meanings of words. She was uncertain now about what this young man was trying to convey. Standing before her, he continued to grin broadly and looked to be friendly.

"Do I know you, sir?" she asked politely, making certain to smile, so as not to offend.

"I don't believe so, miss, but we could remedy that situation if you're of a mind," he said, continuing to smile.

Embarrassed by what she now perceived was his forward manner, Katrina began to blush. She drew herself up to her full height and, dipping her head slightly, said, "That would not be proper, sir." Then, reaching down to gather up her skirts, she excused herself. "Perhaps I should return to my cabin. It's getting on toward *middag*."

"*Middag?*" Tom asked.

Blush rising from her neck to her cheeks, Katrina quickly tried to cover her unintentional retreat into her native Norwegian. "Lunch, sir. I meant lunch. Please excuse me now, I really must go."

I'd like to fall into those green eyes, ya lovely lass.

"Are you bound for New York, then," he persisted, trying to prolong the conversation. Being able to look into her

17

face from that close a distance confirmed what he had seen in their brief encounter on the wharf. It truly was a face filled with freshness and loveliness, such as he had not seen. He stared unashamedly at her green eyes, her curly, thick, long blonde hair, and her lovely mouth, which at this moment had taken on something of a determined look.

She didn't immediately answer, but instead moved toward a nearby hatchway.

Still smiling, Tom moved quickly to open it for her, startling her by the suddenness of his movement.

"No, sir," she replied, stepping daintily toward the inner stairwell. "We're, uh, my family that is, are going to Utah," she said.

"Ah, Utah," Tom said, feigning awareness of American geography. "Lovely place, Utah." Then tipping his fingers to his button-down cap, as a field hand might to the landed gentry in Ireland, Tom held the door as Katrina exited, stealing one last confused glance at Tom.

In a way, he was relieved to have her gone. His heart was thumping so loudly in his chest he was quite certain she must have heard the bloomin' thing. He was sure also that the lump that had risen in his throat would have made it impossible to say another thing to her.

As the hatch closed, Tom turned back to the railing and stared out over the ocean, listening to the wash of the sea against the hull of the great ship. He couldn't help smiling. *A bit more stuffy than the Irish girls*, he thought. But still, all things considered, she'd looked back at him as she departed, and according to Tom's old mate, Paddy O'Rourke, ladies' man extraordinaire in Tipperary with a reputation as far as Limerick, when a lass looked back, it was a sure sign. A sure enough sign.

25 April 1895

Dear Nana,

We are at sea now, Nana. I hope you don't mind that I have started writing in English, but since we are going to America, Poppa thought that we should use less Norwegian and practice our English. I know you'll understand.

I think I miss you more now than when you first left. Our family decision to leave Norway has brought much pain to my heart and Momma cried for days after Poppa declared his intention. I don't know what we would have done if you had still been with us. I know it would have been hard for you, too.

I think of you often, Nana, and especially since Elder Stromberg told us about the Celestial Kingdom. I know you are there, Nana, and that you have been joined again with Grand Poppa. The gospel message has brought me so much understanding, and I am now happy for you, even though I cannot have you with me longer, I know you watch over me, and I feel your presence often.

On this trip, Nana, I will need your strength and your love with me, please. It is so comforting to converse with you each evening, but I have not told Poppa or

Momma of my diary. It will just be between us, as when I used to sneak into your bed at night and you would tell me stories. I'd best get to sleep now. All my love, Nana.

Oh, one more thing, I met a young Irish boy today. You would have sent him away. He tried to speak with me alone, without having been introduced. I think I behaved like a foolish schoolgirl, but I remembered your words: 'a proper young lady . . .' remember that? He has the deepest blue eyes, Nana, and a smile that makes me smile too. Bedtime!

Yeg elske deg,

Your Trina

The moon had barely risen above the horizon as Tom stood aft by the port side railing, looking at the moon's broad reflection shimmering on the black surface of the ocean. For two nights, since talking briefly with Katrina, Tom had been restless and unable to sleep more than a couple of hours at a stretch. Restricted by the ship's rules to the lower steerage decks by day, Tom had felt liberated to be able to walk at night on the upper decks of the steamer.

Even if his mind had not been full of this new woman, Tom would have found it difficult to sleep in the hot, steamy, steerage compartment. Situated immediately above the main engine room, fifteen three-tiered bunks provided sweltering accommodations for forty-five smelly, often lice-infested, European immigrants, all bound for America and the opportunities they envisioned would open to them there. That, at least, was the bill of goods many of them had been sold by those who advertised the trip. Fleeing poverty and sometimes more sinister things, each was casting aside traditions, homeland, and cultural legacy for a new life in a new land. Speaking little English, and bringing few resources other than hope, most would struggle to be assimilated into American life. Tom at least spoke English, though he would find in the coming months that his thick Irish brogue would attract as many detractors as admirers.

For the first three nights of his nightly escape to the upper deck, Tom had without thinking drifted toward the stern of the great ship. Standing there, gazing back over the wake, he contemplated his former life in Tipperary and the role his father had imposed on him. Tom was the second of nine children and the eldest at home. His older brother had endured a final beating from his father and already run away. That meant that it had fallen to Tom to leave off his schooling to attend to his father's shop. Treated more as an apprentice than a family member, Tom had resented his father and as a show of independence had taken up with a gang of hooligans that made it its business to wreak nightly mischief if not havoc on the countryside. Their raids took them to the hamlets and villages within a couple of hours by horseback from Tipperary. Wherever they went, they almost always managed to foment a donnybrook and raise the hackles of the Guarda, the local constabulary.

It was on one of these nighttime forays that Tom made the mistake of striking the wrong individual in the person of the son-in-law of a town mayor. When word came that a constable was on his way to arrest him, Tom had taken only long enough to scoop up the weekly cash proceeds from his father's shop—a sum of twelve pounds nine—before scurrying home to quickly grab his extra pair of pants, two shirts, a heavy coat, and the two and six pence he had hidden under the floorboards of the sleeping room he shared with his four brothers and the family dog.

He paused only to kiss his mother good-bye. It was a scene she had already played. Tom's older brother had done the same thing—left home in a rush to escape his domineering father. She gave her second child a knowing look and a desperate hug. "Thomas," she said through her tears, "whatever happens, promise me you'll not forsake the faith."

"I promise," he said, pulling impatiently away from her and striding off. He left the road, climbed over a rock wall, and walked quickly over the green hills, scattering a flock of sheep as he went. She knew his route. It was one that would lead him permanently away from Ireland and from her.

Striding out through the fields, Tom made his way over and around the maze of ancient rock walls built nearly two centuries earlier to impede British military advances as they ventured "beyond the pale." Not yet sure of what he would end up doing, he finally chose the road to Cork, traveling mostly at night and hiding out during the day. Upon reaching Cork and spying the first ship at the quay, his plan was instantly formulated. Thomas Matthew Callahan, formerly of County Tipperary, Ireland, would head west. *Far* west.

As he stood looking over the fantail of the *Antioch*, his thoughts drifted back to the reckless decisions he had made throughout his early life, most of which had resulted in harm to himself, or, more often, to those who had gotten in his way. How this would play out in America he didn't yet know, but, as he looked ahead, the memory of the struggle he had made to merely stay above the fray of life in Ireland, somewhere back there over the ocean, was steadily diminishing.

This particular evening, his thoughts were more of the young woman. *Utah*, she had said. Tom didn't even know what or where Utah was, or how far it might be from New York. But the fact that she was going there had made the place immediately intriguing. There was no doubt that she was a beauty, but there was something more about her that piqued his interest. As of yet, he hadn't quite been able to put his finger on what it was that appealed to him so. Most of the girls Tom had known weren't so reticent to accept his attentions. She was different. She didn't seem so much *shy* as *proper*. That was the word. But not in a snooty way. Her smile had not been flirtatious, but certainly open and friendly. Perhaps lady-like would be a better description of her response to their encounter. And she *had* looked back.

For the first time since the ship sailed, Tom had worked his way forward as far as passengers were allowed, and he found himself staring ahead into the darkness at the unbroken sea and the course the *Antioch* was taking on her voyage to America. His thoughts were interrupted by the sound of a man crying out in pain. The voice came from the starboard side lifeboat station, and it startled Tom. As he moved to investigate, the man cried out again. It was a sound that rang all too familiar to Tom's ears. Rounding the forward bulkhead, Tom saw three roughly dressed youths standing over another young man who was pinned face down to the deck by the foot of one of his assailants. Surprised by Tom's sudden appearance, the men turned quickly to confront him. Tom said nothing, but quickly surveying the scene, he decided which side to take. The downed man obviously hadn't had much of a chance, and Tom felt a need to balance the scale.

"'Ere, what's with you, mate?" the larger of the three men said. Tom smiled slightly and held the eyes of the belligerent man.

Nothing that giving you a good boot in yer teeth wouldn't cure, mate.

"Aye, not to worry, lads. I was just takin' me breath of air, so I was."

"Yeah, well, be on with ya. 'Tis none of yer doin' here."

Taking care to keep his back to the bulkhead, Tom continued to smile disarmingly at the three, a ploy that had usually given him the element of surprise in previous

24

confrontations. Agitated by Tom's reluctance to leave, the larger man of the threesome stepped toward Tom, threatening by his posture to give Tom a bit of the same.

"So, ya want a piece of the action, do ya, mate?"

Ya think ya can handle it, ya great oaf?

"Not at'll," Tom responded. "As me pappy used to say, 'It'd be most unfair.'"

"Eh?" The large fellow stepped threateningly toward Tom, revealing in the dim light a severely pock-marked face.

"Well, if me ear bids me right," Tom said, continuing to smile disarmingly, "it's only three from Liverpool we've got here, and being only an Irishman meself, I wouldn't be wanting to take advantage of the situation."

The leader turned to his cronies and laughed. "'Ere, Alf, we got us a Mick with a mouth on 'em. What say we let 'em join the Norski on his face. Seems he needs a bit of a lesson hisself, though I don't believe he'll have the money this bloke's carryin'."

Didn't yer Pa tell ya, mate, never take yer eyes off the other lad?

Before he had fully turned back to face Tom, a blow to the side of his head had rendered the large man mostly senseless, and he fell to his knees. As he tried to regain his feet, Tom delivered a quick kick to the man's ribs, then, planting his boot on the back of his neck, slammed the man's face and nose against the steel plates of the deck, where he lay without moving. Shocked by the speed with which Tom had dispatched their leader, the two cronies stepped backward, away from the no-longer smiling Tom.

"Now, lads," Tom began, maintaining control of his voice and nodding to their victim, "I'd be helping this young man to his feet if I were you, and then your pal's likely going to be in need of the ship's doctor. He seems to have injured his nose rather badly in a fall down the gang-way—or perhaps you'd rather tell the ship's officer that one scrawny Irishman stepped in while you were trying to put the squeeze on one of their first-class passengers. What say ye?"

The two glanced nervously at each other. The forward man immediately lifted his foot from the shoulder of their victim, bending to help him to his feet. Tom slowly lifted his foot from the large man's neck, still keeping the bulk-head to his back. The two rowdies moved to assist their companion, lifting him to his feet and heading off down the passageway, leaving a trail of blood behind them.

"Oh, and lads," Tom called out, "it's not a good idea to stroll these decks of an evening unless you've good inten-tions. Never can tell when you might run into an Irish ruf-fian, don'tcha know." Smiling politely as the two departed, carrying their injured leader on wobbly legs, Tom turned his attention to the young man he had saved, who was now standing unsteadily.

"Can I help you there, lad? Tom Callahan's the name. And who might I be addressing, sir?"

Wary that perhaps he had escaped one incident only to fall victim to another, the young man remained cautious. Tom noticed his fear and smiled gently at him. "Not to worry, lad. And what might your name be?"

As the shaken young man stepped forward into the light, Tom recognized him immediately.

By all the saints, it's her brother, he thought.

He was about Tom's age, and unmistakably the man he'd seen walking with the young lady on the quay in Cork. Tom had chosen the right side, a decision that now filled him with an immense sense of satisfaction.

26

"Hansen," the man said. "Anders Hansen, and highly grateful to you, sir, for your intervention." He spoke with a decidedly proper British accent but something about the tone eluded Tom. Not British, he thought, but well-schooled in English.

"And where might ye be from, Mr. Hansen?" Tom asked.

"My family is from Norway, sir, uh, Mr. *Callahan*, was it?"

"That's right. Tom Callahan. Here, let's see if we can clean up some of the blood before your mother goes over the side with shock," Tom said, reaching for the handkerchief in Anders' pocket and handing it to him. "Seems the lads," Tom said, nodding toward the direction the three had departed, "were out for a bit of your money. It's kind of late to be up on deck all alone."

As Anders wiped gingerly at the blood under his nose, he began to grin—a response to Tom's being there alone also. "Aye, well, the Irish are used to being alone, even in a crowd," Tom laughed.

"Mr. Callahan, this Norwegian is most thankful you chose tonight for your solitary stroll. And how might I repay your kindness, sir?"

A broad grin crossed Tom's face. "We'll come to some agreement, Anders Hansen. Indeed, we will. Tell me a bit about your family," Tom said, leading the way back toward the port side railing and the rising moon, now well above the ocean and reflecting off the waves that stood between the *Antioch* and America. "Now would ye be having a sister, Mr. Anders Hansen?" Tom laughed.

And would she be interested in a formal introduction to a handsome, young, Irish lad?

27

The following evening, the one-week anniversary of the *Antioch*'s departure, Tom invaded the crew's quarters, and by exercising a bit of subterfuge, cajoled one of the crew to let him use the shower facilities. It felt good to remove a week's accumulation of salt spray and the Cork dust left over from his forced march through the southern tip of Ireland.

Dressed in the one good shirt he owned and the better of his two pair of trousers, Tom climbed the stairs to the upper decks. He was careful to avoid the crew members who were likely to forcibly remind him that steerage passengers were not allowed on deck until after nine P.M. Anders had said seven-thirty, and no crewman, nor three for that matter, were about to deter this Irishman, who was headed for a formal introduction to the vision that nightly danced in his head.

That thoughts of Katrina continued to occupy his mind confused Tom. For most of his life, at least since girls had become of interest, Tom found he could take them or leave them. In fact, when Molly O'Reardon, the one girl with whom he had formed a close attachment, advised him she intended to marry Patrick Lynn, Tom had casually wished her all the best and gone his way. Molly had bristled at the ease with which Tom had said good-bye. Of course when Tom told his mother about Molly, she had said that one day, he'd not find it so easy to move on, but that required the right girl, she'd counseled. Now, not only had Tom schemed to find ways to meet this unnamed woman, he found himself thinking about her during the rest of his waking hours.

Standing port beam, forward of the mid and upper deck passenger dining area, Tom leaned against the rail and fidgeted with one of the buttons on his shirt. It was loose and about to fall off. When he looked up from his inspection of the dangling button, she was standing not two feet in front of him, a slight smile playing at the corners of her mouth.

"Good evening, Mr. Callahan," Anders said. "It's a pleasure to see you again. May I introduce my sister, Katrina Hansen. Katrina," Anders said, turning to face her, "may I introduce my new friend and rescuer, Thomas Callahan."

She's already figured it out, Andy. But it's worth the humiliation. She's the prettiest thing a man could imagine.

Tom smiled the broad grin of a man caught with his hand in the cookie jar. Katrina had obviously figured out that she had been set up, and that her brother was in cahoots with the man who had tried to ignore formal courtesies only two days before. Still, she didn't seem anxious to depart on this occasion, as she had on his last attempt. Perhaps Paddy O'Rourke was right.

I didn't listen to ya before, Paddy, but this time . . .

"So, it's off to Utah, then," Tom laughed, bringing a bright smile to Katrina's face, which started Tom's heart to thumping once again. He felt as if the tongue in his mouth was beginning to swell larger than the container God had given it.

"Yes, Mr. Callahan," Katrina responded, her demeanor courteous but hesitant. "And it's still New York for you?"

New York's dead, Katie. I'm for Utah, if you'll just give me the sign.

"Aye, that it is," Tom replied, shaking his head slightly, as if to indicate that his destination, not matching hers, was fast becoming a disappointment to his plans.

Sensing the attraction between his sister and his new friend, and not quite knowing what to make of it, Anders interrupted: "So, Mr. Callahan, what takes you to New York?"

Tom was taken aback—a condition in which he had seldom found himself when it came to verbally explaining his position. It was the Tom Callahans of the world that had given rise to the Irish myth that if one kissed the Blarney Stone, in Blarney Castle near Cork, one would quickly develop a silver tongue and never be at a loss for words. In this instance, not having even considered for himself what he intended to do in New York, Tom stumbled. Raising his arms in mock ignorance, Tom replied, using the phrase his mother had frequently used as her children asked foolish questions, "Trust in the Lord's good graces."

Anders raised his eyebrows while Katrina continued to observe this new associate of Anders. Earlier in the day, she had been required to listen patiently for most of the morning while Anders described in detail the assault he'd endured at the hands of several British wharf rats and how he might have lost his money and even his life, had it not been for the intervention of one Thomas Callahan. She just *had* to meet him, Anders had cajoled, and finally, with little else to do on board ship, Katrina had given in to her brother, only to discover that the one and only Tom Callahan was in fact the same brash, young Irishman who'd so brazenly approached her two days earlier. Only her diary knew that for the balance of that day, and since, Tom had occupied her thoughts.

"Well, sir," Katrina said, "if that is indeed your plan, then you shall be in good hands, although I have it on good authority that the Lord's servants now reside in Utah." She smiled brightly, pleased with her newfound knowledge and, not yet seventeen, unaware of the impropriety of flaunting it, especially with regard to religion.

"Aye? And would the Pope be knowin' about that?" Tom teased.

"He'll be aware soon enough, Mr. Callahan," she replied, slightly miffed at his taunting tone.

"Thomas," Anders said, intentionally changing the subject from religion, "I've spoken to my father about your actions last night."

"Aye?"

"Well, he may wish to speak with you about the possibility of temporary employment once we arrive in New York," Anders added.

"I thought you were going on immediately to Utah," Tom said.

"Yes, we are, but we have a shipment of equipment coming after us, and Poppa thought perhaps you could see to its transfer to rail for forwarding to Utah. Would you be interested?"

Tom looked at Katrina briefly, smiling before answering. "Aye. That I would," he replied, not taking his eyes off Katrina as he spoke.

Embarrassed, Katrina turned to Anders. "We'd best be off to dinner, Anders. It's nearly time for first seating."

Anders shook Tom's hand again. "Thank you, Thomas. Perhaps we'll be seeing you on the morrow. I'll tell Poppa you're interested in speaking with him about the job."

"Good, Anders," Tom replied. "And Katrina Hansen," he said, raising his fingers to the brim of his cap, "it was indeed a pleasure to be *formally* introduced to you this evening. Perhaps we, too, shall meet again."

The following morning, Tom carefully evaded the crew members and snuck onto the upper deck, where he found Katrina sitting on one of the deck recliners and reading. When his shadow fell on her book, she looked up and

31

smiled. He nodded toward the deck chair next to her and, sensing no objection, assumed the seat.

"We're halfway there," he said.

"*You're* halfway there," she replied. "We have another two thousand miles by train, with even less opportunity to move about."

"Aye. Still, if Utah is as lovely as you say, it's a trip worth taking."

"Oh, yes, indeed. It's the land of our people—our new home."

"Your people?" Tom asked. "You mean many Norwegians have settled there?"

Katrina laughed and turned the book she was reading for Tom to read the title. "No, not Norwegians. Mormons. This is the Book of Mormon."

Tom reached for the book, quickly flipping through its pages. "What's a Mormon?" he asked. He took no interest in the book and set it down on the small table between their deck chairs. He was grateful, however, for any excuse to speak to her.

Katrina smiled brightly and turned toward him in her seat, excitement radiating from her face. "Elder Stromberg told me I'd have an opportunity to teach the gospel. I didn't know it would be so soon," she laughed. "A Mormon, Mr. Callahan—"

"Just call me Tom," he said.

Katrina furrowed her brow.

"We *have* been formally introduced," he said. "By your brother, no less."

Katrina allowed a smile to cross her face. "How about a compromise? May I call you Thomas?" she offered.

You can call me anything you want, lass. Just keep calling me.

"I've heard Andy call you Klinka, but I'll call you Katrina and we'll remain on a semi-formal basis, if that will make you more comfortable," he replied.

Katrina furrowed her brow again. *His vocabulary and accent have improved and he doesn't sound so . . . so "country,"* she thought to herself. "Yes, Thomas, I think that will be acceptable. Now, where were we? Oh, yes, a Mormon. Might I presume you are Catholic, Mr. Calla . . . , Thomas?" she smiled.

"Aye, that ye may."

"What would you say if I told you the true Church has been restored to the earth?" she said brightly, her enthusiasm returning.

"I didn't know it had been lost," he laughed.

Katrina pursed her lips and retrieved the book from the small table next to her. "Mr. Callahan, this is not a laughing matter. You asked me a question, and I am trying to offer an honest answer. I can assure you, sir, I take my religion very seriously, and if it is not your intention to listen with equal seriousness, then I am wasting my time."

"Whoa, lass," Tom raised his hands. "I think we've jumped off the deep end. This older gentleman, Elder Strummer, I think you said, did he take such offense at your questions when he taught you his religion?"

Katrina laughed out loud. "Elder STROMBERG," she said. "He's not much older than you. But you're right, Thomas," she said, her pleasantness returning. "I apologize for my abruptness. After all, I'm sure you have heard nothing about the marvelous works that the Lord has brought forth in this century. Mormonism, Thomas, is the Lord's true religion, restored to the earth through a prophet."

"You mean like Moses?" he asked, trying to keep a straight face.

"Well, somewhat. A prophet is someone who talks with God, Thomas. We have such a man at the head of our Church today. Isn't that wonderful news? Someone who talks directly with God."

Tom leaned back in his chair, reaching for the book again, being careful not to stifle what he perceived as Katrina's determination to tell him about the Mormons. "You mean like the Holy Father?"

"Well, I'm sure he means well, Thomas, but he doesn't have the authority to speak for God."

Tom's eyebrows raised slightly, and he continued to thumb through the book, looking up occasionally at Katrina. "Who gives this authority?" he asked. "I've always thought the Pope could talk to God and our Priests could as well. In fact my mother always told me to pray to God and my prayers would be answered."

"Oh, yes, they will, Thomas," Katrina responded with glee, leaning forward and nodding her head to confirm his statement.

"But you just said that a person needs authority to speak with God."

"Well, I didn't mean exactly that, Thomas. I meant, oh, it's so simple, yet so confusing. A Prophet, like President Woodruff, is ordained to the priesthood and is called of God to preside over his Church."

"Like the Pope," Tom repeated, enjoying watching Katrina's animated expressions and listening to her enthusiastic explanations.

"No. Oh, Thomas, I want so to tell you what's right, but I feel I don't have the knowledge to do so."

Tom smiled and leaned toward Katrina. With both of them sitting sideways on their deck chairs, their faces were only inches apart as the conversation became more animated. A delicate lavender fragrance filled Tom's nostrils as he took in her scent, and he admired again the way her blonde hair framed her lovely, young face.

"Perhaps I could read a bit in this book and we could talk more about it later," Tom suggested.

"Oh, yes!" Katrina exclaimed, clapping her hands together. "Let me show you some important passages, and then you may borrow the book for as long as you like. I can always use my mother's copy."

She showed Tom two or three lightly marked scriptures, and told him that the answers to many of his questions would be found in those areas. Suddenly aware of their close proximity, Katrina leaned back on her chair and swung her feet up into the resting position, resuming her gaze out over the ocean. They sat quietly for a few moments as Tom thumbed through the book, stopping to read some of the marked passages.

"Katrina," he said. "Have you always been Mormon?"

She remained still. She had taken those moments to consider the propriety of launching into the teaching of religion to a stranger. She was fired by the unexpected opportunity but was also slightly embarrassed to have revealed so much enthusiasm. "No. My family was Lutheran, but about two years ago, a young missionary, the Elder Stromberg I have referred to, met my father in Denmark. Later, when he came to Norway, he visited with us and taught us the gospel. We were all baptized into the Church and are headed for Salt Lake City, which is the Church's headquarters."

"You said this Elder Stromberg was about my age. When you first mentioned him, I pictured someone quite a bit older. Isn't that a bit young to be teaching religion?"

Katrina thought for a moment, her intention now to go more deliberately, trying to be certain of what she said. "I don't know, Thomas. They send their young men, and also older men, out into the world to teach others about the Church God has restored. He was very knowledgeable and most considerate of our thoughts and questions."

"I see," Tom answered. "And this religion—this *Mormonism*, I think you called it—is obviously important to you."

She sat up in her chair, turning again to face Tom and looking earnestly into his eyes. "It has become the most important thing in my life, Thomas."

Tom studied her for a moment before answering. Her cheeks were tinged with redness, the effect of the brisk morning air and the agitation she was feeling. In her enthusiasm for their discussion, she had cast aside the blanket she had used to wrap her legs and her movements were very animated. Tom was pleased to also note that she seemed to have taken to the sea voyage with ease, unlike many of the passengers, some of whom had begun complaining of sea sickness even before ship had cleared the confines of Cork harbor.

"And you believe it is a true Church of God, even though it's only just started?"

Katrina reached for the book in Tom's hand. "This book, Thomas, was my teacher. Elder Stromberg answered my questions and helped with my concerns and those of my father and mother, but as I read this book, and prayed about it as Elder Stromberg said we should, God bore witness to me that the things written in here are true. He can do that for you, too, Thomas." She nodded vigorously as she said so and then smiled triumphantly.

"But I have a religion, although, I must admit, I haven't attended all that much since I was a child." He smiled sheepishly.

"I had a religion, too, Thomas," she said, handing the

book back to Tom and again leaning back in her chair. "And I *did* attend. But when the Book of Mormon spoke to me, I just . . . I just knew it was true. Will you read it, Thomas?" she asked, angling her head to look into his eyes again.

"I will, indeed, Katrina. If . . ." he paused, waiting for her attention, "you will answer those questions I have the next time we meet."

She smiled and started to gather up her things. "I will do the best I can, Thomas. I'm still learning myself, but I will try to help you if you have questions. But . . ." she paused, "the best answers will come if you also pray about the book as you read it."

"Well, we shall see." She was standing now, and he smiled up at her. "I think I'll just sit here for a while and browse through it," he said, holding up the book. "Thanks for the loan."

"Thank *you*, Thomas," she replied. "You're my very first student."

"Shall I call you teacher, then," he laughed.

"Not yet, but I will be someday," she answered, instantly serious.

"Well, I'll read through this a bit, Katrina, and return tomorrow to see if you have come up with the answers."

"Perhaps, Thomas, if you follow *all* my instructions, you'll come back to *me* with the answers."

"Aye," he said, lying back down on the recliner as she departed.

"Oh, and Thomas," she said as she reached the hatchway, "I'm sure the Pope is a good man and means well. But we *do* have a Prophet now, and he *does* speak with God."

Tom smiled at her as she stepped through the door.

Keep teaching me, Katrina. I'll listen every day if that's what it takes to spend time with you, he murmured to himself.

28 April 1895

Dear Nana,

I am so happy tonight, Nana. I had the chance to teach the gospel today for the first time. The young Irish boy I told you about sat and listened as I told him of the restoration of the Church. Anders told me that Poppa has offered Thomas a job in New York to wait for our store equipment and see that it is shipped on to Utah. Poppa was not pleased with me for teaching him the gospel, preferring that I just give him a Book of Mormon and let him contact the missionaries in New York after we arrive. He thinks Thomas is coarse and common—and Catholic. Of course, you know how Poppa is.

Thomas, oh, that is his name, Nana, was polite, but I couldn't tell if he was really interested in the Church. He seems a nice boy, Nana, but I wish you were here to give me advice. I think I like him, but Poppa has cautioned me and insisted that Anders be present when I speak to him again. Becoming a young woman is hard, isn't it? Was it hard when you were a young girl, too?

Yeg elske deg,

Your Trina

Shortly after ten that evening, earlier than his usual midnight appearance, Tom was once again up on deck for his nightly stroll. Climbing to the uppermost level of the ship, he walked alone. A cool breeze dictated that he turn his collar up and pull his cap down over his eyes. Not ten minutes into his walk, he heard the faint strain of a woman softly singing, almost humming, below him, and he made his way to the railing to discover the source of the sound.

One deck below, lying back on one of the deck recliners, was a woman holding a young child against her breast. The child was wrapped in a down blanket, and the woman was singing softly to the toddler.

For nearly half an hour, Tom stood leaning on the rail, silently listening to the singing below and enjoying the gentle rocking of the ship as it plowed ahead through the sea. Unheard, one of the ship's officers came up behind him and joined him at the railing.

"Sounds comforting, doesn't it?" the officer said, startling Tom.

"Aye. Reminds me of my mother," Tom said, taking out his pocket watch, the one family possession given to him by his grandfather, to check the time and determine whether he was legally on deck. Assured that he was, he smiled at the officer and said, "But that would be the case for most of us, wouldn't it?"

"It's well after nine," the officer laughed, confirming to Tom that the officer knew it was quite legal for Tom to be on the upper deck. The officer leaned over the railing, and looked at the woman below. "She'll be gone soon," he said to Tom. "She's up here nearly every night, helping young Mrs. Peterson with her young'uns."

"It's not her child?" Tom asked.

"Hers?" the officer smiled, glancing again toward the

lower deck where she was sitting. "No, she's only a young kid herself. That's the Hansen girl. She's been helping out because Mrs. Peterson's traveling alone with her children, and when one of the kids can't sleep, Miss Hansen there takes the child on deck to allow Mrs. Peterson some time to catch a bit of sleep. That is, if her other baby will allow it. I keep an eye on Miss Hansen whenever I have the watch," he said, offering Tom a polite warning. "Well, have a good evening, lad," he commented, heading for the ladder and the lower decks.

Tom looked again at the couple below, wrapped securely in blankets, the singing now ended as the child apparently slept. Tom envied the child, snuggled as it was against the body of the girl/woman he now knew to be Katrina Hansen. Tom continued his unofficial watch until fifteen minutes later, when Katrina rose from her deck chair and carried the child below. Tom remained on deck, thinking about this woman whom he had mistaken for a mother—an older woman—gently nurturing her child.

You're nothing but a slip of a girl yourself, Katie Hansen, but if I was to put words to it, I'd swear you're a natural born mother. "Will ya never stop surprising me, Katie, me darlin'," he voiced quietly to himself.

3

Three days later, with two additional deck-chair meetings behind them, at which the Book of Mormon was the primary subject of conversation, Tom had discovered this young woman was headstrong and fiercely independent in most things. That's why he was surprised at how completely she submitted herself to her father's will. It made Tom wonder when, and if, she might ever find the courage to assert herself with regard to Mr. Hansen.

Tom's discussions with Andy, late one evening as Tom had gone for his nightly stroll, had enlightened him as to the forceful nature of Lars Hansen.

"Ya, Klinka is headstrong in most things, Tom, but she has always been an obedient child and followed our father's wishes," Andy had said.

"And you?" Tom said.

Andy smiled. "I have often felt the need to go my own way, Tom," he laughed. Growing serious again, he continued. "But not Klinka. I think she finds it hard sometimes, especially as she grows older, but Father's word is still her rule," he said, leaving Tom with an increased concern about his ability to reach out to Katrina over her father's objections—something that was beginning to appear necessary.

It was clear from what Katrina and Anders had to say about their father that Mr. Hansen would never approve of one of the Tom Callahans of the world making a play for his daughter.

With the final day of the voyage at hand, a dinner party for the upper-class passengers was planned for the last night on board ship. With Tom having accepted Mr. Hansen's offer of temporary employment in New York, Andy said he considered Tom a member of his father's staff, and he took the liberty of inviting his young Irish friend to attend the final dinner with his family. Tom was reticent to accept, but since it would provide one further chance to be with Katrina and because time was running out for him, he thanked Anders and said it would be his pleasure to dine with the family. Tom sensed he would be somewhat out of place, but rationalized he could somehow make it through the meal and entertainment without embarrassing himself.

When Katrina joined them on deck and Andy advised her that Tom would be coming to dinner, her surprised look told Tom all that he needed to know. It wasn't that she didn't want him to come, he hoped, but Tom sensed that she felt he would be uncomfortable and that his sitting down as a hired hand to eat dinner with the family would not meet with her father's approval.

As evening approached, Tom grew more and more apprehensive regarding the dinner. He met Andy in a pre-arranged spot, and they entered the first-class dining room together. The rest of the Hansens were already seated, and the moment Tom sat down at the table, he knew he'd made the wrong choice and that he should have paid more attention to Katrina's unspoken warnings.

You were absolutely right, Katie. Maybe I'd better pay more attention to your instincts next time, he reflected.

The steward who served their table went immediately two tables away to whisper to the First Officer, who then held a prolonged stare in Tom's direction. Mr. Hansen peered disapprovingly over the rim of his pince-nez spectacles at Tom's attire. He flapped his table napkin dramatically and coughed to register his disapproval and tucked the corner of his napkin into his shirt collar, all the while staring down his nose at Tom. Mrs. Hansen seemed embarrassed by the situation, and Tom hoped her sickly smile was an attempt to ease his discomfort. Katrina avoided eye contact while Anders, seemingly undisturbed by the drama of the situation, reached for the rolls and butter. The two younger Hansen girls, their heads lowered in conspiratorial adolescence, giggled continuously at the handsome new addition to their dining ritual.

Lars Hansen's English wasn't as well-practiced as Katrina's or Anders's, and he spoke in the typical sing-song rhythm of Scandinavian speech. "Ya, Mr. Callahan, Anders say you go alone to New York. Your Momma and Poppa go before?"

I'm a big boy now, Poppa, and I'm off on me own.

Tom glanced around the dining salon, aware that the First Officer continued to occasionally look his way. "No, sir. My family is still in Ireland."

"Ah," Hansen nodded, "then they come soon?"

They'll not be coming at'll, Poppa.

"No, sir. I believe it is their intention to remain in Ireland," Tom continued.

Hansen's eyebrows went up slightly, his glance at Mrs. Hansen informing Tom that he didn't approve of the situation. "You go to stay alone, Mr. Callahan?"

Tom glanced quickly at Katrina, who kept her eyes

lowered. *There is one other possibility, Poppa, so's I wouldn't have to go it alone.*

"Aye, sir. But it's a big land, so I've been told, and many of me forebears have gone before me."

"Ya, ya, Mr. Callahan. Quite so. But they find no work, I think. After you finish the shipping job for me, do you have a trade, Mr. Callahan?"

I've done me share, Poppa, and I'm twenty-five years younger than you and have plenty of time to find one. Where were you at nineteen, Poppa?

Tom could see Mrs. Hansen's discomfort. But she was obviously reluctant to intervene or say anything that would stall her husband's interrogation of him. Tom interpreted her thin smile as a weak attempt to make the situation more tolerable. He could see, however, that she was not about to confront her husband in any way.

Thank you for your kind thought, dear lady, but I'm afraid the man's got his stamp on you, too, and if Katie doesn't get out soon, he'll break her spirit as well.

Angered by Hansen's insistent badgering, Tom began slurring his speech, intentionally playing the "Paddy." "Sir, me Pappy owned a wee shop in Tipperary, and I've worked there since I were but fourteen. Aye, it's a bloody harsh life, 'tis," Tom answered.

And ye bloody fool, you'll be losing all yer children while yer out mending the fences of yer corral. Look to yer wife, man, and patch that fence while ya still have the chance.

Katrina looked up briefly, her ears perked by the change in Tom's brogue and his demeanor. Offended by Hansen's obvious disdain, Tom determined to stand up to the proud Norwegian's provocations. No matter that his lovely daughter was there to see it all. Tom would not brook being pushed around by this haughty, rich man. Tom continued the dialogue in his thickest Irish, a ploy that confirmed Mr. Hansen's low opinion of the upstart, uncouth Irish lout. Tom did not consider that his behavior would likely offend Katrina. He was too stubborn and proud to let it go.

Mrs. Hansen finally took advantage of a lull in the conversation to speak. "Mr. Callahan, Lars and I are so happy for you to help our son with the, the thugs. We thank you. Ya, *tusen tak,*" she smiled.

And if I'd known who he were, ma'am, I'd have arranged for the Brits to attack, so's I could rescue him, just to meet Katrina.

"'Twere nothing, ma'am. I was glad to be of assistance."

"Umm," Anders mumbled, his mouth full of food. "He saved my bacon, that he did."

"Ya, we are most grateful," Mrs. Hansen repeated. "Isn't that right, Lars?" she said, turning to her husband.

"Ya, ya, of course. Fine thing, young man. Fine thing," he said, removing and cleaning his glasses, replacing them on his nose, and looking again at Tom. "And you have work in New York, Mr. Callahan, after the shipping job, or family to help you?" he repeated, much to Mrs. Hansen's dismay, who now lowered her head and folded her hands in her lap.

No, ya bloody fool. I've no money, no job, and no family in America. So what, then? Lie down and die, should I?

"No, sir, now there's the rub of it," Tom drawled, "and not a farthing to me name," he lied, having retained about six pounds twelve from the money taken from his father's shop, after subtracting steerage passage on the *Antioch,* and the cost of fruit and potatoes purchased for his larder during the crossing. "'Cept of course, I have me natural Irish charm," he added, glancing at Katrina and reading in her eyes the disappointment over his coarse behavior.

Though Anders attempted to introduce some levity at

45

their table, the Hansens and Tom took their meal in relative silence. Ignoring their father's disapproving glances, the younger girls continued to giggle at the slightest provocation. In Tom's judgment, which was based on vastly limited experience, the food and service were astonishing. For two weeks, he had eaten only the food he had brought on board, except for a few items smuggled to him by Anders in the last few days. Given the level of his hunger and the amount and quality of the food, he should have enjoyed his meal immensely, but Mr. Hansen's interrogation had made him too angry. Sitting there was an ordeal he wished were over, but he felt trapped and didn't know how to leave.

The sound of a small bell from the Captain's table broke the awkward silence at the Hansen table, and all in the room turned to look toward the sound.

"If I may have your attention, please, ladies and gentlemen. We are indeed pleased to be with you this evening," the First Officer commented. "Traditionally, on the *Antioch*, we have offered a small entertainment following our final dinner at sea. As you all know, we shall enter New York harbor tomorrow and our voyage shall conclude. It has been a pleasure having you on board, and we hope that, should business or pleasure take you back to Europe at some future date, you will once again sail on British White Star Line."

Not bloody likely, Tom thought to himself.

"Tonight, we are to be favored with a reading from Shakespeare by Mrs. Morgan, and a medley of favorite songs by Miss Katrina Hansen. I'm sure you'll enjoy the evening. If there is anything the captain or crew can do for you on our last evening, please let us know, and again, thank you for sailing on British White Star Line. Mrs. Morgan, if you please?"

A polite round of applause accompanied Mrs. Morgan

to the front of the room, where a large, floral wreath, somewhat the worse for its two weeks at sea, was on display. Tom noticed a distinct embarrassment on Katrina's part, and understood her additional reason for being concerned when she had learned Tom had been invited. Certainly, she had not known he would be present when she agreed to sing.

Twenty minutes into Mrs. Morgan's presentation, Tom felt the Bard of Avon was turning over in his grave, or at the very least, resolving never again to sail British White Star Line. Nevertheless, polite applause accompanied her conclusion, which to Tom's way of thinking came more from relief than appreciation.

Katrina rose and walked quickly to the front of the room. A gentleman from another table also got to his feet, and seated himself at the piano in the corner of the room. Katrina's first number was a Norwegian lullaby by Edvard Grieg. Tom recognized the tune as the one she had been singing to the young child on the evening when he had spied her on deck, comforting the youngster.

Watching Katrina perform, Tom once more had occasion to reflect on the variety and depth of Katrina's abilities. Her knowledge of literature had become apparent during their daily talks regarding religion. She had not intended it, but Tom felt inferior in the face of her education and his lack of one. He had also seen her capacity for compassion in her service to a young mother and her children. And now she was singing beautifully, in a mature and resonant lyric soprano's voice—a voice that might have been found in a much older woman. Tom sat transfixed, not only by the clear sound she achieved, but also by her poise and beauty. All that reinforced the feelings he had developed for Katrina over the course of the voyage.

Once, several years before, a small opera company from

Dublin had toured the countryside, and Tom had attended a performance in Limerick. It too had filled him with appreciation for the music and the God-given talents some were fortunate to possess. Katrina's voice, surprisingly rich and full for a woman of her age, delighted those in attendance. Even Mrs. Morgan dabbed at her eyes as the young girl sang.

Concluding her lullaby, Katrina nodded to the piano player, who reached for a page of sheet music resting on the piano top. As he began to play the introduction, Tom immediately recognized a tune that had recently become a favorite in Ireland. Originating in a New York stage play, the tune had been taken to the collective Irish bosom, and it had become wildly popular in the Emerald Isle. Recalling home, Tom listened intently as Katrina sang. At one point, she briefly locked eyes with him, but the spell was broken when Mr. Hansen coughed softly and Mrs. Hansen began to fidget.

"Sweet Rosie O'Grady," Tom thought, would forever remain in his heart as having first been heard—truly heard—that evening on the steamship *Antioch*, sung by the voice of an angel, whom Tom, at that moment, knew he loved. This was the woman his mother had spoken of years earlier. This was the woman who would permanently claim his heart. In that deeply emotional but private moment, listening to her sing "Sweet Rosie O'Grady," he vowed that whatever the cost and however difficult the road, he would make it to Utah. Katrina Hansen was the one.

Later that evening, after the farewell dinner, having avoided two crewmen in order to make his way above decks, Tom found Katrina standing at her usual spot by the deck chairs. He quietly slipped next to her, leaning on the railing without speaking. For several moments they stood silently together. Finally, Katrina broke the silence.

Having endured her father's outburst in her parents' cabin following dinner, Katrina had come on deck rather than return to her own cabin. Anders was still in their parents' cabin, continuing to receive his father's tongue lashing.

"My father reprimanded Anders for inviting you to dinner, and told me I was not allowed to see you, Thomas," she said softly. "He also told Anders to tell you that he would no longer require your services in New York. I'm sorry, Thomas."

I know it's our last night, Katie, but tell me you're not going to obey him. Please, tell me quickly.

Tom remained silent. "I'm sorry too . . . ," he finally said. Katrina turned to face him and Tom looked into her eyes, ". . . both for his instructions to you, and for the way I behaved at dinner."

Katrina returned her gaze to the ocean before responding. "You were both . . ." she hesitated, groping for an appropriate word, "well, *foolish*. And you, Thomas Callahan," she said, looking intently at him, her tone now reproving, "took offense at a father's protectiveness."

"Aye," was all that Tom could muster. They both fell silent again for several awkward moments. "And will you follow his instructions?" Tom asked, without daring to look at her.

Say it girl, say it—"No, Thomas, I'd rather be with you for the rest of my life." Tell me, lass, please tell me.

Katrina didn't answer immediately. Stepping back from the railing and gathering her skirts around her in a manner Tom had come to recognize, she formed her face into the little pout Tom had noticed the first time he had confronted her.

49

"Father says you're nothing but an Irish ruffian and that you'll not amount to anything in life," she smiled.

Aye? Well, perhaps he's not as stupid as I thought, Tom thought but didn't say.

"I see. And does he forget that his Viking ancestors came knocking on me great-great-great-grandmother's door and for all he knows we're already related," Tom taunted.

Katrina allowed a small laugh to escape her lips at this historical revelation, and then immediately assumed a more serious countenance.

In the few days they had been acquainted, Tom had recognized that his interest in Katrina was larger than passion or youthful conquest. Consequently, he had refrained from his usual "steal a kiss" approach. Yet, on this final evening prior to their arrival in New York, Tom wanted desperately to tell her his feelings, to confide in her the love he had come to feel in his heart. He refrained, however, and remained content to stand with her, silent as to their respective feelings.

After a few moments, Katrina placed her hand on Tom's arm on the railing and turned to smile at him. "Thomas, tomorrow we will arrive in America, and we shall be required to go our separate ways."

Oh, ye can't be telling me good-bye, Katie, I've just . . .

"You are a good man, Thomas Callahan, in spite of my father's opinion to the contrary," she continued, exhibiting, to Tom's way of thinking, a wisdom beyond her years. "And I," she paused, lowering her eyes, "shall be sad as we part. I want to give you something, Thomas." She reached up her sleeve to retrieve a small photograph. "This was made a couple of months before we left Norway. I would like you to have it, Thomas."

Tom accepted the picture, looking at it quietly for a moment and then placing it in his shirt pocket.

This can't be all I'll have from the trip, Katie. I can't let you go that easily, he quickly thought, startled by the ache that throbbed in his chest.

"Katie, me darlin' . . . ," Tom softly replied, speaking aloud for the first time the term of endearment he had come to apply to Katrina in his private thoughts, and from which he meant no insult or improper familiarity. In truth, hearing it for the first time, it instantly became rather endearing to her although no sentiment had yet been expressed by either of them in their brief association.

" . . . parting is sweet sorrow," he smiled, "or so the Bard has told us. Mrs. Morgan forgot that excerpt tonight."

Katrina laughed again.

"I know we've had but a short time together," Tom continued.

"But, Thomas . . ." she began, but he placed his finger over her lips and smiled.

" . . . and in that short time I've come to care for you, Katie. I know your father doesn't think I'm worthy of you, and," he paused and smiled, "aye, the truth be known, he's probably right. You've told me a bit about this new religion of yours, and your father's feelings toward Catholics. But I don't really know how *you* feel, and," he said, looking out over the railing toward tomorrow's landfall, "we don't have the time to consider it now. But this I want you to know, Katrina Hansen." He turned to look deeply into her eyes. "I'll ask you but once to consider my proposition. If you are willing, I shall find a way to this Utah—I don't know how or when yet, but I shall come. You have my word on it. And I ask ye, Katie," he paused, once again looking back out over the sea, " . . . I ask ye to wait with any marriage plans you

51

may be considering till the end of the year. I will find you within that time and we will see what fate, or the Lord, has in store for us." He looked back into her eyes and took her hand in his.

For several minutes they stood there silently, listening to the wash of the water against the hull of the ship and looking west, toward the reflection of the moon and their anticipated landfall the next afternoon. A bank of clouds hung low on the horizon, and the late setting sun splashed them with a kaleidoscope of colors that stretched the length of the sky, north to south. Birds had appeared earlier in the day, but with the coming of darkness they were now gone.

Finally, after what seemed to Tom like an eternity, his question hanging in the air, much as the waning moon, Katrina strengthened her grip on his arm and turned to face him.

Katrina Hansen, two months short of seventeen, stood five feet, six inches tall as she gazed up at Tom Callahan's six-foot-one stature. With her free hand, she lightly brushed back his black, unruly hair and rose up on her toes, gently pulling his face down toward hers. Placing her cheek softly against his, she felt the warmth of his skin, and stood that way for several moments. Then her lips sought his, and, keeping her eyes closed, she kissed him tenderly.

Tom was startled by the boldness of this wisp of a woman, who, with a touch of her hand, a sparkle in her eye, and a crystal in her voice, had brought the Irish larrikin to his knees. He took her in his arms, holding her for the first time, then releasing her to look into her eyes. She smiled at him once again, her eyes dancing, with determination etched on her face.

"The end of the year, Thomas Callahan. I'll wait till the end of the year."

29 April 1895

Dear Nana,

Tonight was a most unusual night, Nana. After dinner, Poppa got very angry and has forbidden me to see Thomas, but I have disobeyed him.

There's just something about Thomas that makes me feel warm all over. It is a new and confusing thing, but I can't talk to Momma because of what Poppa instructed. I wish you were here, Nana. Is this how it feels when someone is falling in love? Can someone fall in love in only a few days? I don't know what to do, Nana, but then, as I read back over my letters to you, I never seem to know what to do, do I?

Should I follow my heart or my father? Do all young girls have this problem? Questions, questions.

Yeg elske deg,

Trina

Tall and majestic, her eyes serene, and her countenance weathered by nearly a decade of greeting those who came to partake of her promise, she stood at the entrance to the harbor, her arm raised high to light their way. As the *Antioch* glided gracefully past her small, island home, Tom stood at the port railings with the other passengers. Class rules had been suspended during the approach to New York harbor, and immigrants, first-class, and steerage passengers alike stood shoulder to shoulder and three-deep to gape at the Statue of Liberty and the approach to the busy port of New York. For many passengers, those escaping tyranny in its many forms, it was the beginning of a dream come true, and they wept.

In their joy, they were blissfully unaware of the living metaphor being played out by the mingling of upper and lower classes on that bright, sunny day. They would soon learn that in this new country, economic differences were more significant than proper social birth, and that given the right combination of luck and perseverance, within a generation, even the lowliest of immigrants could provide for their children the right to occupy the same first-class cabins their parents had been denied while coming to America.

The Statue of Liberty, France's gift to the people of the United States of America, stood towering above the harbor entrance and welcomed the three hundred forty-two people aboard the *Antioch*. Slowing, the ship turned slightly to meet the government boat that would ferry this latest cluster of immigrants to Ellis Island, the port of entry where, to date, nearly two million immigrants had arrived to begin their new lives in America.

Tom's excitement at the arrival was tempered by the knowledge that he would soon have to endure the departure of Katrina. Rather than the end, Tom had determined, it was going to be only a brief interlude in what he had come to hope would be the beginning of the rest of his life—a life to be lived with Katrina Hansen at his side.

30 April 1895

Dear Nana,

I saw the Statue of Liberty today, Nana, as the ship entered the harbor. Hundreds of the passengers lined the deck of the ship to look at her. Some people were crying.

We are on a small island in the harbor of New York, and Poppa has arranged our train passage to Utah. It is two thousand miles further, and we will stop to see Uncle Arthur and Tonta Jessie. Sorry, Nana, I still think in Norwegian some-times... Aunt Jessie in Chicago.

Nana, I must confide in you tonight. I have come to like Thomas Callahan very much, and in spite of knowing how Poppa would feel, I have seen him on several occasions during the voyage. Always with Anders present or nearby, Nana. Well, just once without.

He asked me to wait for him till the end of the year, when he will come to Utah to find me. I don't know why, Nana, but I agreed to wait. There's just something in my heart. I know you would understand. He doesn't know much about our Church yet, and I am concerned. But the gospel is true and he will believe, won't he? As I know you and Grand Poppa now understand.

Did your Poppa approve of Grand Poppa, Nana? Is it always necessary to go against one's parents in these things? I do not wish to be disrespectful, and I love Poppa, I really do. But he seems, well, he just seems afraid that I am becoming a woman. It must happen Nana, mustn't it?

I am excited to be in America.

Yeg elske deg,

Trina

The afternoon of his third day spent on Ellis Island, Tom stood in line with dozens of other immigrants waiting to speak with the immigration officer who was seated at a table, processing the applicants. Tom resented the cardboard name tag he and the others were required to wear, hanging from their lapels by a piece of string, as though they were so many pieces of luggage rather than human beings. While being subjected to the medical review the previous day, Tom had been made all too aware of the nature of his status—similar to the sheep in Ireland that merely followed those ahead as they calmly went to their shearing, or in some cases, to their slaughter.

Continuing to scan the vast room, he was momentarily startled to catch a final glimpse of Katrina as the Hansens were escorted through the barrier into their new life as Americans. Citizenship was some time off, and in fact where the Hansens were heading, citizenship was at present, denied, even to those born in Utah.

On the final afternoon of their voyage, after the ship had been intercepted by the immigration authorities, Anders Hansen had found Tom on the middle deck, where the Irishman had been watching the first-class passengers being boarded on the launch that would take them to Ellis Island. Anders said his good-byes, thanking Tom once again for having rescued him from his three assailants. He handed Tom a small, wrapped parcel and said he hoped they'd have the chance to meet again someday. Then, wishing Tom the best of luck in New York, he quickly moved down the stairway to rejoin his family. Unwrapping the parcel, Tom felt a twinge of pain as he read Katrina's short note.

"Thomas, this book is my most prized possession. I pray that you will come to understand its meaning and the truth it contains. The Lord's blessings be with you, Thomas. Till the end of the year, Sincerely, Katrina."

Now, waiting in line for his turn to become an American, with the Book of Mormon tucked into his hip pocket, Tom's final look at Katrina was as she adjusted her bonnet, preparing for the windy harbor ride to New York City and the train west. She didn't see him as they parted, but the sweet sorrow of which William Shakespeare had written, centuries earlier, was as present in Tom Callahan's heart as it was the day the Bard penned the words.

"Name?" the gruff voice called, breaking Tom's reverie.

"Thomas Matthew Callahan," Tom replied, Katrina's departing vision firmly etched in his mind.

"Mick, is it?" the man grinned, looking up at Tom.

"Thomas . . . Matthew . . . Callahan," Tom repeated slowly, drawing out each name, his eyes firm in the man's face.

Slightly cowed by Tom's stare, the man assumed an officious posture, harrumphed, and returned to his paperwork, beginning the tedious process of filling out the forms to admit another hopeful, ignorant, immigrant.

"The Irish are all 'Micks' here," he spat out. "Get used to it."

Never had Tom seen anything to match New York City. On the one occasion when his father had taken him on a buying trip to Dublin, Tom thought there could be no larger city and no more people clustered in one place. New York City quickly dispelled that illusion.

For two days, Tom had walked the streets of New York and had not passed the same place twice. If the map he'd found in the park was right, he'd barely scratched the edge of the city, remaining well within the confines of lower Manhattan.

Spending the first two nights sleeping on the ground in Battery Park, near the south end of Manhattan, Tom quickly came to discover just how many people were without homes or employment, and the enormity of the task he faced trying to break through that mass of humanity. By the morning of the third day, he'd found day work in the fresh vegetable market, partly because of the lessons his father had drummed into him had provided a knowledge of fruits and vegetables, and partly because the floor boss at the market was also Irish.

Finding living accommodations proved harder. Given his memory of crowded conditions back in Tipperary, he hadn't expected fancy, but he found himself surprised by the squalor of the flop house and the stench of the mattress he was provided for fifteen cents a night. He quickly learned from the other tenants not to leave anything of value around during his time away, which didn't prove much of a problem, since he wore most of his clothes on his back, and carried his shoulder kit with the rest, every place he went.

Within a week his routine had been established. He rose at three o'clock to be at the marketplace long before dawn. Finishing his work by noon, he spent the rest of the day looking for work more likely to provide the kind of money he would need to fund his trek to Utah. Always Utah.

Thoughts of Katrina flooded his mind while he worked, and it became an obsession to find a way to move in that direction. Though his job was sufficient to pay for his abysmal accommodations and meager food, his wages were not enough. Something else would have to be found in order to obtain funds to move west.

The hardest part was the loneliness he felt each night as he lay on his mattress on the floor, listening to the myriad sounds emanating from his rooming house. The photograph of Katrina was becoming tattered from constant review, and even the Book of Mormon, especially the early parts about the two brothers, was dog-eared. Lying there in the dark, he struggled to picture her lovely face and he recalled again and again the kiss she had given him. He remembered her mannerisms, especially the earnest look she would get on her face while struggling to explain her newfound religion. The images were sweet to contemplate, but also a kind of torture.

He was frequently overcome by fear—that his chances of actually making it to Utah were minimal and the likelihood of her waiting to marry were even less. Still, rather than abating, his determination grew stronger. He *would* get to Utah.

Eight hundred miles to the west, on the far side of Chicago, the train pulled out slowly, gathering speed as the Hansens settled in after a full week and a half of resting, bathing in Lake Michigan, and obtaining sleep lost during the previous several days traveling from New York. Lars Hansen and his family had stopped in Chicago to visit with relatives who had immigrated several years earlier, and to explore the prospects for his business ventures in Utah. A furniture maker by trade, Lars had arranged with the Chicago branch of his family to obtain necessary materials and to ship additional orders and specialized cabinetry that would be needed to establish his new business in Salt Lake City.

Katrina and her sisters had used the time to refresh themselves and to purchase some new American clothes. Her mind was filled with constant thoughts of Thomas and how, or perhaps *if*, he would indeed come for her. In a way, the promise she made to him on the *Antioch* was thrilling, but there were times when she panicked thinking of actually being married to a man she had only briefly known. It didn't help that her father had such strong views on the topic. She'd heard him express his pleasure to her mother that they had finally gotten the Irish lout out of Katrina's life and that as soon as they got to Utah she'd find some suitable Mormon boy from a proper family and settle down. "Ya, Momma, it is time," Mr. Hansen had said to his wife, "she's coming to be a woman."

The train trip west proved mind numbing. For a time, the scenery west of Chicago was green and lush and the rail line frequently ran through small communities. Then, the number of towns thinned out, and the landscape became more open, dry, and dusty. Advised that they were approaching the Mississippi River, which she had learned about in world geography, Katrina brightened some, but in the main, each clickity-clack of the train wheels only served to reinforce the image of the miles opening up between herself and young Thomas Callahan, the handsome Irishman who continued to permeate her thoughts and dreams.

19 May 1895

Dear Nana,

Oh Nana, what a wonderful time we had in Chicago with Uncle Arthur and Aunt Jessie. The entire Norwegian neighborhood celebrated our arrival, and we had a good old fashioned Norske party.

We are on the train now, and will have many days of travel. I will tell you about America as we go.

Jeg elske deg,

Yours, Trina

As June stretched into July, Tom found the stifling New York heat almost unbearable. He had taken to stopping at a reasonable facsimile of an Irish pub on his way home from an evening job he had located as a night janitor for the New York Transit Authority. Cleaning horse-drawn trolleys at night, after spending ten hours at the produce market, wasn't the most enjoyable thing Tom had ever done, but it did provide another seventeen dollars and fifty cents a week to add to his growing savings. He had accumulated slightly over a hundred and twenty dollars, much of it acquired from one-time odd jobs. Tom had found he wasn't afraid of work. Thinking back, he thought it ironic that the one thing his father had taught him was to work hard, and that ability was the thing that was enabling Tom to survive.

His visits to the pub, however, were beginning to sop up an ever-growing portion of his earnings, and his tendency to brawl after drinking was bringing Tom to resemble the typical "Paddy" many New Yorkers despised. Feisty, belligerent, and downright mean-spirited when drinking, Tom was quick to confront anyone who dared to voice an opinion contrary to his. Luckily for him, he was handy with his fists and more often than not came out on top in the fights he provoked or accepted. But the course he was on was leading him toward exactly what Katrina's father had warned her about and—what frightened Tom the most—to becoming a replica of his own father. Whether he acted out of depression over the seeming impossibility of ever catching up to Katrina or in response to his native Irish temperament, the result was the same. Tom was fast becoming a typical, hard-drinking, hard-fighting Irishman who bore little resemblance to the man that Katrina continued to harbor in her dreams.

Quietly listening to the piano player bang out the latest hit tune, "Sweet Rosie O'Grady," Tom sat in the pub one evening, staring morosely into his pint of Guinness, his mind and spirit back on the *Antioch* the night Katie sang to him, when he had felt the confirmation of his love for her. He didn't notice the man who approached the table until he spoke. "Mind if I join ya, lad?"

Tom looked up from his stein, over which he'd been brooding, toward the kindly face of an older man. Looking pointedly around the room, Tom gestured to several empty tables, and returning his gaze to the man, responded in a surly tone, "I prefer to drink alone."

"Aye," the visitor responded, "I've noticed, but conversation, now that's another thing entirely, and I'm in desperate need of someone for a palaver." He smiled affably as he pulled back the empty chair and seated himself. The man's hair was sparkling white and thinning, and his face was ruddy, showing a number of small, broken capillaries around his nose and cheeks. Tom was in no mood to notice, but the lobes of the man's large ears turned up, almost as though they were folding over on themselves, providing a somewhat comic look. He held Tom's gaze with a pair of eyes that were a deep brown color, and continued smiling as he made himself comfortable.

Tom returned his gaze to his beer stein. "Suit yourself, old man," he said.

"I notice you're coming in more often than at first," the old man stated, forming a question.

Tom continued to stare at his drink, unsure how to handle the intrusion. Most with whom Tom had dealt in the bar had been young Irishmen, like himself. After an initial meeting, either a discussion or a confrontation resulted, but the old man—that was a different story. "What's it to ya?"

Signaling to the bartender for a pint of Guinness, and continuing to smile, the old man just stared at Tom for several seconds. "Everything, lad," he said softly. Then leaning forward and folding his hands in front of him on the table, he said, "Let me tell you a story.

"I met a young lad not too long ago. Much like you, he was. Came in here nearly every night, he did. Sat mostly by himself but occasionally got involved in a bit of a donnybrook. One night, three of the lads were waiting for him outside the pub, and in the fight, he picked up a piece of cobblestone and bashed in one of their heads." The old man paused to take a drink of his beer, before continuing.

"I sat with him once more after that, not long ago, upstate, as he waited to meet our Lord. He was more subdued by then, frightened you might say, as was I. You see, lad, the jury found him guilty of murder. I sat with him for hours, heard his confession, and prayed with him. I walked with him down a long corridor and read to him from the Holy Book as they strapped him in the chair. He's gone now, lad," the old man continued, looking up at Tom. "He was electrocuted in New York State Prison, not yet turned twenty-one."

"What's that got to do with me, old man," Tom asked, his voice angry and accusing. "What are you, anyway, a do-good Yank?"

The old man laughed. "No lad, just an Irish immigrant like yourself, only I've been here over forty years now. Came over in '52 as a young man about your age."

"And you spend your time in pubs bothering the rest of us with scare stories?"

"No, I spend most of me time down the street at St. Timothy's. I'm the parish priest there, lad."

Tom was surprised. The man wore ordinary work clothes, with no visible sign of his calling. "So, are ya looking for contributions then, Father?"

65

"You could say that, lad," the priest acknowledged, "but not so as you'd think. I'm after saving souls, lad, not money."

"Humph," Tom snorted, "ya missed yer mark this time, Father. I'm not in need of saving this fine evening. I got troubles enough of my own, and you'd do better looking for someone's soul who needs your services."

"Oh, I think you missed the point, Mr. Callahan," he said, surprising Tom with the knowledge of his name. "It's not *your* soul I'm after saving, it's me own that needs help, lad. Ya see, the other lad I told you about—I saw the trouble coming for months, and I just sat back and let it happen. It wasn't *his* soul I was worried about up there in the prison cell, for he'd seen the error of his ways. It were me own soul I feared for."

"Well, I'm not the one with the collar around me neck, Father, so's I can't give you absolution. Go see yer own priest."

The old man downed his pint and slid his chair back, continuing to stare at Tom as he started to stand. "I have, lad. I have that, indeed. But I'll not stand by and let another walk down the same path he did without trying to help. You been here what, two, three months? You look to be about twenty, Mr. Callahan, and might have a long life ahead of you, if you but find your way. I'll give you my oath on it, lad, the next six months will tell the tale. You might indeed live a long and adventurous life, but in the next six months you'll determine how it'll play out. I'd like to be of help, but you've got to be willing, lad. Father O'Leary's the name, and you can find me at St. Timothy's just down the street. Anytime, lad, anytime."

He stood to leave but then paused for a moment. "One more thing, lad. If it's a young lass you're brooding over, you'll not find her in the bottom of that beer mug." He stood quietly, until Tom looked up at him briefly, "And if she knows *you're* in there, she'll not be wanting you, either. Think on it, lad, and come see me."

After Father O'Leary left the pub, the bartender came over to replace Tom's drink. "He means well, son," the bartender said. "He's just burdened with his load, like the lot of us. He took young Patrick's death hard, that he did."

Tom returned his stare to the fresh glass as thoughts of Katrina began to run again through his mind. *Till the end of the year, Thomas Callahan*, she had said. *I'll wait for you till the end of the year.*

Eventually finding his drunken way back to his dingy one-room flat, Tom lay fully dressed on his mattress, unable to sleep and thinking about the old priest's words: "The next six months will tell the tale, lad." *In more ways than you think, Father. In more ways than you think*, he mumbled to himself.

5

The early morning fog swirled around the harbor and the wharf in Copenhagen giving a ghostly appearance to the small group of young men waiting to board the steamship, which was already crowded with other passengers who had boarded the evening before in Bremerhaven.

After shaking hands with a well-dressed, older gentleman, Harold Stromberg, leader of the six men boarding the ship, carried his belongings up the ramp, with the rest of the group following quickly behind him. After stowing their gear in their cabins, the young men returned to the main deck and stood at the railing, watching as the crew singled up all lines. As soon as she was released, the vessel began drifting away from the pier, aided by the harbor tug pulling at the stern of the great ship.

Stromberg hailed from Salt Lake City, Utah, and held the honor of being the grandson of Magnus Stromberg, one of the early pioneer settlers of that arid desert. By the time Harold's father had been born, the economy of the Utah Territory was thriving and already had drawn thousands of Mormon converts from the eastern states and the British Isles to the high mountain valleys. When his father, also named Magnus, had been called to serve a mission in Wales, young Harold was already six, and it was standing by his mother's side, holding back the tears, that he had watched his father leave with a group of men for their fields of labor. In the Mormon tradition, their service and sacrifice (including their extended absence from the family) was viewed as both an obligation and an honor—a necessity to further the Lord's plan on earth. Elder Harold Stromberg was, then, a third-generation Mormon and the third in his paternal line to complete a mission for the Church. He was intelligent, somewhat more sophisticated than the other elders, and possessed of a strong sense of duty. In short, he was the product of a strong intellectual and spiritual heritage and had represented himself very well.

The older man, who had remained on the wharf, was Charles Ogleby, president of the Church's Scandinavian Mission. He had come to say farewell to the six young men who had served under his leadership, but who were now going home. The elders waved good-bye to their president and spiritual leader, until the fog completely obscured him. With land out of sight and the ship entering the harbor's main channel, Harold Stromberg allowed the memories of the three years he'd spent in Denmark and Norway to play through his mind. Both countries were part of the Scandinavian Mission of The Church of Jesus Christ of Latter-day Saints, a mission territory that extended as well to Sweden, Finland, and Ireland. One thought above all others occupied his mind, as it had since first meeting Lars Hansen's family and his daughter Katrina. Stromberg knew that the Hansens had emigrated and were by now living in Salt Lake City, Harold's final destination. And the letter from Lars Hansen, posted from Chicago and received only two days before Stromberg's departure, advised that his return would be a welcome occasion and stated that he was heartily invited to call on the Hansen's, where, Mr. Hansen had assured him, Katrina would be most happy to receive him.

It had been a long and arduous three years, and Elder Harold Stromberg, aware of his family heritage and imbued with the spirit of his calling, had worked hard to ensure the Lord would find his service acceptable. But now, as he turned his thoughts toward home, he was just as sure the Lord had a multitude of future blessings in store for him. Katrina Hansen stood at the head of that list, and in less than six weeks, he hoped to reap the most important reward of his service.

The young lad carrying the flyers wasn't more than ten by Tom's reckoning, but like hundreds of other children Tom had seen since arriving in New York City, he was out earning his portion of the family's income. Tom accepted one of the posters from the lad and glanced at it as he boarded the trolley, bound for his evening job. The notice took his immediate attention.

In 1868, John Augustus Roebling was commissioned to build a bridge that would span the East River, from Manhattan to Brooklyn. With ferry service the only way across, the river had long served as an inconvenient barrier, and Roebling had long dreamed of building a bridge that would span the river. He had worked for many years to see it established. Unfortunately, early in the process that started in 1869, Roebling died in a construction accident.

His son, Washington Roebling, a Civil War veteran, continued the work, though he was at one point incapacitated by diver's sickness, or the "bends" as the decompression ailment came to be called. Bedridden during much of the construction period, the younger Roebling nevertheless continued to engineer the building of the world's first cable-wire, steel suspension bridge, a true engineering marvel.

The first task, however, designed to facilitate the building of the bridge, was the fabrication of a caisson, or floating construction dock. An engineering marvel in its own right, the caisson was a device that employed a pressurization system to remove water from its lower compartments, enabling construction workers to work below the surface of the water. The use of the caisson was fraught with dangers and a number of mishaps and deadly accidents dogged the massive project. When the bridge was completed fourteen years later, in 1893, the construction had been costly in terms of both money and human life.

Folding the flyer and putting it in his pocket, Tom found himself astonished at the wages, exceptional by any standards for skilled tradesmen, much less general labor. Unknown to Tom, ten years earlier, the original bridge laborers had earned only two dollars and fifty cents a day. The peril involved in working within the pressurized caissons had made it difficult to keep good men and had driven the wages up.

Applicants were directed to apply in person to the foreman, Stanicich Construction, 236 East River Road, between six and noon for the following three days.

At five-thirty the next morning, Tom arrived to find a large number of men already standing in a line outside the warehouse facility. The applicants ranged in age from kids no older than the young man who had passed out the flyers, to men the age of the priest Tom had met in the pub. At six sharp, a man opened the door to the warehouse, and the line began to slowly move. Tom could tell from the men coming out that the old and the very young were being rejected for the work, raising his hopes for acceptance. Finally his turn came and he entered a small room where two men were seated behind a table. A stocky man, with a two-day growth of beard and chewing on a cigar, looked up.

"What's your name, son?"

Tom removed his cap and held it in his hands in front of him. "Callahan, sir. Thomas Callahan."

"How long you been in America, Callahan?"

"Three months, sir."

"Any experience working around the harbor or on bridges?"

Tom hesitated, not wanting to eliminate himself on the basis of lack of experience, but not wanting to be caught out in a lie. "No, sir," he replied, "but I'm a quick learner, sir."

The man glanced up at Tom. "It's not a job for the faint hearted, Callahan. You got the stomach for a dangerous job?"

"Aye, sir," Tom replied, beginning to wonder what kind of job would pay such wages with no experience necessary.

"All right, Callahan, sign here, and be back at six o'clock tomorrow morning. Six sharp, Callahan, and sober.

Miss one day's work, drunk, and you're through. Understand?"

"Aye, sir. Thank you, sir," Tom said, backing out of the room quickly.

Outside again, Tom fell in quietly with a cluster of men who had also apparently been hired. He mingled with the group, hoping to find some clue as to the kind of work they would be doing. He saw a man about thirty years old, who was talking to several younger men, seeming to give instructions.

" . . . ten per caisson, two hours a shift," he was saying as Tom joined the group. "Three hours topside on the labor crew and then back down for another two in the hole, three topside again, and that's it for the day. Any questions?"

No one spoke up and Tom held his peace. As the group began to break up, Tom took stride with a couple of the younger men leaving the warehouse yard, listening to their conversation and discerning several dialects.

"Six tomorrow for you, too?" Tom said to one he took to be Irish.

"Aye," the other replied, continuing his Irish brogue, which Tom had recognized earlier as the more clipped, staccato speech common to Belfast. "And you?"

"Yeah. Any idea what we'll be doing? I didn't hear what that fellow said."

"Working on the pilings on that there bridge," he said, pointing to the bridge that now spanned the East River between Manhattan and Brooklyn. "She's barely ten years old, the man told us, but some work needs to be done on the pilings. We're gonna' have to go down to do it."

"Go down?" Tom asked.

"Yep. In a tube of some sort—with ten men in it. They pump air into it, and it keeps the water out."

Tom's eyes widened. "You done this before?" he asked.

"Nope. But for five bucks a day, I can learn," he grinned back at Tom.

"Aye, I guess you'd be right. See you then," Tom added, heading off for the nearest trolley to return to the produce market.

The next morning at a quarter to six, Tom stood waiting outside the warehouse entrance with a small number of men whose names appeared on a roster and who had been allowed inside the gate. The line of new applicants was already formed as it had been the day before, all ages once again represented. Tom had convinced his boss at the produce market to give him a couple of days off for some personal business, not inclined to quit before he knew the job at hand would be permanent. By ten minutes after six, the crew of about forty men were loaded on several horse-drawn wagons and were en route to the construction site, located on the Manhattan side, under the main bridge abutment.

Tom and some others were told that for the first three days, they would be on a topside crew becoming familiar with operations, and then he'd be assigned to a diving crew and begin to work his two shifts a day beneath the river.

By noon of the third day, Tom had heard the stories of men who had been injured or simply quit once they had been assigned to a crew. "Even the guy who built the bloody thing, got crippled as a result," one man said.

At least two of each new ten-man crew quit after their first two-hour shift underwater, often the result of panic at being confined in the restricted space inside the caisson and beneath the waters of the East River.

Tom's first assignment was to work on a platform suspended beneath the main bridge, about fifteen feet above the water line. Some of the men on his crew managed the air lines, suspension cables, and the compressor unit and mechanical equipment used to support the submerged caissons. Tom was given a job mixing the mortar being used to strengthen the bridge pilings. By the afternoon of the third day, eight men who had been hired a couple of days earlier, had already quit or been fired. Tom began to doubt the wisdom of hiring on and dreaded the fourth day when he was scheduled to be assigned to a diving crew.

Halfway through the afternoon shift, and without warning, a whistle began to blow. Men were shouting. Something drastic seemed to have occurred. Tom looked over the side of his platform, and saw great bubbles of air rising to the surface of the river. One of the foremen was yelling for the topside crew to keep the compressor going and directing others to get below and lend a hand. Tom stood looking on, confused as to exactly what was happening, but witnessing a disaster in progress.

Just below the water line, Tom could see a rupture in the caisson, which had protected the men from the pressure of the river depths. A few of the men had scrambled out of the caisson and were now lying prostrate on the platform. Two of the men were convulsing violently, their bodies jerking involuntarily.

"They got bent for sure," one of Tom's work mates said, leaning over the ropes next to Tom and observing the scene below. Some other men emerged from the ruptured caisson, and those who were able, quickly cleared the platform, gaining the relative safety of the ladders running from the base of the bridge abutment to the upper support platform where Tom stood. As the first of these men reached Tom's level, a foreman grabbed the wild-eyed man.

"What happened down there?"

"I dunno. We just lost air. I thought we'd never get up."
He was disoriented and nearly incoherent.

"Who else is missing?"

Tom could see the man was in shock and unable to reason. Looking back down toward the diving platform, Tom saw one of the men, who was having a seizure, struggling to get to his feet. He had no equilibrium and stumbled about on the platform. Suddenly, the stricken man flopped over the side into the river and disappeared into the dark water. Shouts rose again from the men on the upper tier, who were also watching the scene below. Without thinking, Tom immediately jumped off the support platform, landing in the river alongside the diving platform. The cold water momentarily took his breath away, but as soon as he surfaced, he took a great gulp of air and dove again below the surface.

The murky water afforded no view of the man, and after groping about blindly for a few moments, Tom came up again for more air. Then, taking a deep breath, he submerged again and by feel, descended the cables toward the river bottom, clinging tightly against the current of the river. About fifteen feet down, he brushed against something that moved. Tom reached out and felt an arm, which he grasped tightly and pulled toward him. The man was entangled in the cables, but changing his grip, Tom was able to grab the man by his belt and begin struggling up the cable, pulling with one hand toward the surface and dragging the limp body with him. He needed desperately to take a breath of air, and just when he thought he couldn't live another moment without breathing, he broke the surface.

Three men who had descended to the lower platform reached out for Tom, calling to him to swim toward the platform. Tom pushed the now unconscious man ahead of him, toward the waiting hands, but he lacked the strength to pull himself up. The men pulled the injured worker aboard as Tom struggled to tread water. Flailing about in the current, the exhausted Irishman passed out and the light slowly disappeared before his eyes.

———— ❧ ————

The next several minutes were lost to Tom, but as he gradually regained consciousness, he saw he was ashore, lying beneath the main bridge abutment, and heard the foreman talking to him.

"Ah, you're coming around, lad."

"Is he all right?" Tom asked.

"Tony? Yeah, thanks to you, young man, he's alive, but he and Sean got bit by the bends. They're both on the way to the hospital."

"What happened?" Tom asked.

"Don't worry about it, lad. It's over now. You just rest for a while."

"The other men?" Tom asked, grabbing the foreman's shirt.

"We lost two good men, lad, and two more have the bends. But, if it hadn't been for you, we'd have lost Tony, too. It's a good day's work, lad. Just take it easy."

As Tom leaned back against the stone pillar, someone handed him a tin cup full of hot coffee. It warmed both his hands and his insides.

By the end of his shift, Tom was back to feeling normal, and as he rode the trolley to his evening job, he had time to contemplate the day's events. More concerned than ever about the safety of going down in the caisson, Tom found himself unsure about the job he'd taken and the merits of taking such risks, even for five dollars a day.

After his four-hour shift, spent cleaning trolleys, Tom

decided to stop for a drink. On the street between St. Timothy's and Clancy's Pub, he crossed paths with Father O'Leary.

"Which direction you headed, lad?" O'Leary asked. Tired and as yet unsettled as to what he was going to do about going back down in the caisson, Tom was caught somewhat off guard by the smiling prelate.

"Well, Father, I thought I might grab a pint and head home early this evening."

"You all right, lad? You look a bit shaky."

"It's been an interesting day, Father."

"Mr. Callahan, what say we amble down to the rectory? I've got a bottle of malt liquor and you look like you could do with a stout drink."

Too tired to protest, Tom followed after Father O'Leary. Once they were inside O'Leary's living quarters, he offered Tom a seat, which the weary Irishman gratefully accepted, along with the glass of beer the father handed him.

"There you go, lad. Maybe we can carry on the palaver I mentioned the other night. But first, you just lay back there and rest for a few moments. I'll attend to another matter and be back shortly."

Tom drained his glass, then leaned back in his chair. He closed his eyes, and the image of the workman falling into the water played again through his mind. Father O'Leary found him asleep when he returned, and, laying a blanket over the young Irishman, the kindly priest picked up the empty glass that had slipped from Tom's hand and set it on the sideboard.

⁓

Waking to the aroma of sausage cooking, Tom opened his eyes, unsure for a few moments where he was.

"Back from the dead, I see," Father O'Leary said.

Tom tossed back the blanket and got stiffly to his feet. Cramped from sleeping all night in the chair, he stretched and yawned.

"Never seen an Irishman go out like a light from just one glass of malt liquor," O'Leary taunted.

"What time is it?" Tom asked, suddenly anxious.

"Just after seven," O'Leary replied.

Tom shook his head and shrugged his shoulders. Then, taking a deep breath and holding it momentarily, he said, "Well, there goes one good job. But, on second thought, maybe it's all for the best. Smells good, Father. Taking in boarders, are you?"

"The occasional meal, lad, when justified. Here, sit at the end and I'll show you a good old fashioned Irish breakfast, bangers and all." O'Leary piled Tom's plate high with sausage, fried potatoes, and scrambled eggs and filled their cups with steaming hot coffee.

"Now *that's* a breakfast," Tom declared as Father O'Leary filled his own plate and sat down across the table.

"By the time we have breakfast together, most call me 'P. J.' Patrick James, as me mother said in the old country."

"Umm," Tom mumbled, his mouth full of potatoes. "Suppose I stick to 'Father' P. J., just so's I know my place," Tom grinned, wiping his mouth with the back of his hand.

"Well and good, lad. Well and good. So, what's this job you think you just lost?"

"A job working on a bridge repair crew, Father. I signed on three days ago, and since then I've had misgivings. I saw two men killed yesterday, and even before that several good men have quit or been laid off. It was my turn to go under the water today. I guess the foreman will think I'm a bit afraid when I don't show."

"Are you, Tom?"

Tom looked up, filling his mouth again with sausage. "Might be, Father. I never got the chance to find out, what with the accident and all yesterday."

O'Leary pushed his plate aside and refilled both their coffee cups. Placing his elbows on the table and holding the coffee mug in between his cupped hands, he said, "I read something about that in the morning papers. Were you involved?"

"Ummm," Tom mumbled, working his way through the eggs.

"Aye," O'Leary said, his eyes brightening. "You'd be the 'Tom' the story said pulled the other Irishman out of the river. If your job's gone, lad, and you've got some time on your hands, maybe it's time for the conversation I spoke about."

"I've still got work, Father, both morning and evening, but it'll never pay enough to get me to . . ." Tom paused, not sure how much of his inner thoughts to reveal.

"She's somewhere else, is she?" O'Leary asked, smiling.

Tom grinned in spite of himself. "Ya got this uncanny knack, Father, of looking into a man's soul."

"That's me business, Tom, and I been at it for over forty years now. I've helped many a young lad set himself straight once he arrived here in the States, and some, as I mentioned the other night, I lost along the way."

It was Tom's turn to counsel. "You can't save 'em all, Father. Some of us are just dead set on our own path."

"I know you're right, lad, but like I said, that's my job. And my joy, I might add. You'd be surprised how alike people are once you get inside 'em and get 'em to open up. Now tell me about this lass and how you come to be so set on finding her."

"Ever heard of Utah, Father?"

81

Two hours later, Father "P. J." O'Leary knew everything worth knowing about Thomas Matthew Callahan and had found himself liking the boy. O'Leary's warning counsel about Utah didn't surprise Tom. He had already heard stories about the wild doings among the Mormons—that they were a group of religious zealots that had adopted the Old Testament practice of plural marriage. One of the other boarders where Tom lived had told some particularly lurid tales about old Mormon men taking young wives, and Tom had been worried about Katrina. But to be fair, Father O'Leary said that it was his understanding that Mormon church leaders had for the last several years, officially decried the practice of plural marriage. The priest explained that there had been a national debate on the matter, and that Utah had thus far been denied statehood over the issue.

Tom's determination, however, had convinced O'Leary that the lad intended to make it to Utah, and so Father P. J., also a determined Irishman, advised Tom that the easiest way to go west would be on the railroad. And if one couldn't afford passage, then riding the rails as a paid employee was the next best thing. He offered to introduce Tom to a parishioner who worked for the New York, Baltimore, & Ohio Railroad. Mr. Donohue, Father O'Leary advised, was a fair man, and would likely do what he could to help Tom get on in some capacity.

By three o'clock that afternoon, cap in hand once again, Tom Callahan had been hired as an apprentice oilier for the New York, Baltimore, & Ohio Railroad. The company was headquartered across the New York harbor in Bayonne, New Jersey, where Tom was to be provided living quarters near the switchyard, to facilitate his availability.

Convinced now of Father O'Leary's concern, and grateful to him for his help, Tom expressed appreciation to the kindly priest. As they said good-bye, Father O'Leary handed Tom a letter of introduction addressed to Sister Mary Theophane, the head nursing sister and chief administrator of Holy Cross Hospital in Salt Lake City. Father O'Leary explained that he and Sister Theophane had known each other in Ireland and had come to the United States at about the same time, many years before. He thought she might be of some assistance to Tom in Salt Lake City and wished to be remembered to her if Tom succeeded in getting to Utah.

Following a quick visit to the Stanicich Construction Company to pick up his three days' wages, grudgingly authorized by the crew foreman, in consideration of Tom's heroic action, Tom found himself later that same day in small, but clean quarters, a half-mile from the railroad switchyard in Bayonne.

In America for three months, with not quite six months left on his promise to find Katrina Hansen, Thomas Callahan had moved exactly seventeen miles west from his point of entry in New York City. One thousand, nine hundred and eighty-three miles remained.

6

26 *June 1895*

Dear Nana,

What a wonderful place Salt Lake City is, Nana. To the west is barren desert, but the mountains surround the valley and when Poppa took us on a buggy ride up into Cottonwood Canyon, it reminded me of our country cottage and the beautiful hills of Norway. You would like it too, Nana. It is not like Horten, and we are far from the sea, but it is so beautiful.

Next month the city holds a Pioneer Day celebration to remember those who first came. It has been forty-eight years since they arrived. I laugh when I tell some of my friends at school that we have churches in Norway that are over one thousand years old.

People are here from all over Europe,

but mostly from the British Isles. I will like it here, Nana.

Yeg elske deg,

Trina

P.S. Anders is not so happy, because Poppa wants him to become more active in the Church affairs. Anders has not embraced the gospel fully as yet, but you know Anders well. He is a good man and has a good heart. He will see the truth of it when the Lord determines it is right. He is a great support to me and a wonderful older brother.

In Salt Lake City for nearly two months, Lars Hansen had purchased a house six blocks south and four blocks east of Temple Square. A city of 75,000 people, Salt Lake had, in nearly fifty years, become an important economic hub and the literal crossroads of western America. When, in 1869, the transcontinental railroad had linked up and the rail line had been extended into Ogden, Utah, just twenty-five miles north of Salt Lake City, the nation had not only completed its union, but Utah had been linked to the rest of the nation.

With Denver on the eastern slopes and Salt Lake City framing the western edge, the Rocky Mountains stretched for over four hundred miles east to west between the two cities. Many cities and towns had been established in the beautiful valleys and high meadows that were nestled in the Rockies, and during the intervening five decades since the

earliest pioneers had blazed trails through the high mountain passes, easier routes had been found, roads had been
built, and the trek to Utah no longer presented a hazardous
undertaking. Still in all, it hadn't come easy.

It wasn't until the Hansens arrived in Utah and learned
the full story of the settlement of the Valley, that they
became aware of the magnitude of the exodus, unparalleled
in history, that had brought the early Mormon pioneers
west. In the course of their learning about Joseph Smith and
the restoration of the gospel, Lars Hansen and his family
had understood the importance of young Joseph's spiritual
message, but remained ignorant of the political repercus-
sions of the westward movement, and how the settlement
of Utah related to American history. As much as the gospel
had encompassed their lives, the founding of Salt Lake City
was not part of their heritage, other than viewing it as a
refuge that provided them the liberty to practice their religion.

By 1895, many Mormon families were into their third
generation of residency in Utah. In some respects, Salt Lake
City was still a frontier town, absent many of the centuries-
old edifices which were present in Oslo and central
European communities that Lars had visited on business
trips. The Hansens quickly discovered that the mostly
Mormon community had brought culture and education
with them as they packed their wagons and handcarts and
established what they referred to as, "The Lord's house in
the mountains."

The existence of a university, opera performances,
ballet, symphony concerts, and many smaller public performances of plays and musicals convinced Lars and Jenny
Hansen that their family had found their place. The closeness of community spirit was enhanced by the shared

spiritual goals, something that, following their conversion, had eluded them in Norway. Within several weeks, Lars felt he was home, and was enjoying the added advantage of a large LDS Scandinavian population that had welcomed him and his family. Even the age-old divisions between the Danish, Swedish, and Norwegian peoples over which King or Queen should rule were absent. The people had melded into a solidified block of Scandinavians—and Mormons.

Following the arrival of his woodworking equipment, Hansen's furniture making business was an instant success. Lars found a wealth of craftsmen among those who were already living in Utah, many of whom were eager to staff his factory. There was an ongoing demand for business and residential furnishings, and so, renting a large warehouse facility near Sugarhouse for his production line, Lars launched into business with a fervor. Within three months, he had his factory producing cabinets and furniture that he sold at a brisk pace, out of a small, retail store on South Main Street.

The two younger Hansen children, Sofie and Hilda, were enrolled in school, while Anders went into the furniture business with his father. Katrina, whom Lars and Jenny agreed needed to marry as soon as possible, found her way to the university located in Salt Lake City and began to take courses toward becoming a teacher. Completely unaware of her father's communication with Harold Stromberg, Katrina thought frequently of Tom Callahan and whether he would keep his promise and one day show up on her doorstep.

In quick order, the Hansens had moved smoothly into life in turn-of-the-century Utah. The talk of imminent statehood infused the community with energy and excitement. At long last, it was beginning to appear that the Mormons had accomplished their purpose in their escape to the West: the Lord's kingdom had been saved from destruction. And Utah would soon have the added advantage of joining the rest of America in its growth and expansion.

That the Hansens were not part of the pioneer heritage of Utah proved no deterrence. By 1895, fewer than twenty percent of Utah residents were descendants of those who had come by wagon train and handcart. Such was the success of Church missionary efforts throughout America and especially in the British Isles and Scandinavia, that the burgeoning population of Salt Lake City had become a cosmopolitan gathering of Saints. Then, too, attracted by favorable living conditions, employment opportunities, and the strategic location of Salt Lake City, many nonLatter-day Saints had begun settling in Utah. The once tiny, exclusively Mormon settlement was growing up and statehood would be a crowning achievement.

In those final evenings on the ship and during their brief stay on Ellis Island, Tom and Katrina had not had the time or the forethought to formulate any communication lines, and so, day by day, all she could do was hope that he would carry through with his promise to come for her. Still, in the recesses of her heart, she had begun to wonder if, indeed, it had just been a "shipboard romance," such as she had read about in a certain dime novel. As the months passed, Katrina thought more and more about the reality of how far it was from New York to Salt Lake City, and the memory of Tom faded. She developed a growing suspicion that Tom Callahan had more important things to worry about than her. Survival for one thing. Living alone in a new land, without such support and structure as that provided by her father, it would be difficult for anyone to make their way. And then there was her father's attitude about the Irishman—an attitude that had gone unspoken since they

89

had left Chicago, but which she knew her father kept firmly in place. A poverty-stricken, Catholic, Irish ruffian would never be an acceptable suitor for Lars Hansen's daughter. Thomas Callahan would amount to nothing, her father had declared, and it would take a miracle to persuade him otherwise.

But at night, as she lay her head on the pillow and closed her eyes, she would revisit in her mind that he had the deepest blue eyes, and a smile that had made her heart pound on those few evenings they spent together, so long ago, on the deck of the *Antioch*.

"*Katie, me darlin'*," he had called her. "*Katie, me darlin'*."

The evening that Harold Stromberg presented himself for the first time at the Hansen household provided one of the most humiliating experiences in Katrina's young life. Out for the day with new friends from school, Katrina returned home to find her family seated in the parlor and her father anxiously awaiting her arrival.

"Katrina," he exclaimed as she entered the foyer. "We are so glad you are home. Come, see who has returned."

Katrina's first glimpse of Harold Stromberg filled her with joy and surprise. The special attention Elder Stromberg had paid to her in Oslo had not escaped Katrina's attention, but she had also admired his ability to keep his feelings under control. In spite of whatever he may have felt toward her, Elder Stromberg had behaved with perfect decorum. In fact, his restraint was such that during the religious discussions, which Elder Stromberg and his companion conducted in the Hansen's parlor in Oslo, Katrina had felt somewhat ignored by him. But when her mother explained how these young American missionaries were not permitted to

90

associate with young women, Katrina formed the opinion that Elder Stromberg was a man of character and dedication. She had been fond of him, and seeing him now, on his return from Norway, was truly a joy.

Noting his daughter's obvious delight, Lars Hansen mistook her feelings for those of a young girl pleased to have a suitor call, and Mr. Hansen's intention—to bring this young couple together as quickly as possible—seemed well within his grasp.

"Katrina, sit and join us. Elder . . ." Lars paused and smiled at his continued use of the missionary term, which Stromberg had advised was no longer necessary, "I mean, Harold, has been home for a few days and has come to express his pleasure at our safe arrival and to see if he can be of any assistance in our settling into Utah."

Seated on the divan next to her mother, Katrina smiled at Harold. Her two younger sisters sat on the floor at Stromberg's feet. Anders, out since early afternoon, had not yet become aware of Elder Stromberg's visit.

"Sister Hansen, it is indeed a pleasure to see you again," Harold opened.

"Thank you, Elder Stromberg. I'm so glad you could come to visit. What will you do now that you are home?"

"I plan to enjoy the summer while it lasts, and then re-enter the university. I'll study the law and work in my father's law office downtown."

"How exciting," Katrina exclaimed.

Lars Hansen, whether from his impatience at waiting for Katrina to arrive home, or from his long standing thoughts concerning the matter and his discussions with his wife about Katrina's need to marry, then made a social blunder on that fine summer evening in the parlor of his home in Salt Lake City—one that deeply offended and embarrassed his daughter. Mr. Hansen announced to all present, that Mr. Harold Stromberg had asked permission to formally call on Miss Katrina Hansen, and that he, as father, had given his permission.

Without considering the effect it would have on Katrina, or on Harold, Mr. Hansen stated his opinion that Katrina would do well to pay strict attention to Mr. Stromberg's merits, and offered too his advice that her prospects for a happy life would be enhanced if she were to find Mr. Stromberg a suitable candidate for a husband. It was his considered opinion as her father, that such a marriage would be highly beneficial to both parties.

Katrina's look of complete surprise and shock, her plaintive cry of "Poppa," and her departure from the room in tears, only served to convince Mr. Hansen of her happiness.

Even Mrs. Hansen, who would later come to acknowledge this moment as the point at which Katrina had formed her independence from her father, was shocked at the statement delivered by her husband. Barely twenty minutes after Mr. Harold Stromberg entered their home, and less than ten minutes after Katrina had sat to welcome him, her husband had succeeded in pushing Harold Stromberg into a corner and completely humiliating his daughter.

As for Harold, he was also flabbergasted by Mr. Hansen's blunt declarations. That he was to be accepted as a suitor did not surprise him, for he had visited privately with Lars Hansen several days earlier to speak of his interest in Katrina. He was astounded, though, by the tactless way Lars Hansen had gone about the fatherly formalities of accepting the first suitor to call upon his eldest daughter. While Elder Stromberg was, in all respects, an excellent candidate for young Katrina's hand, within twenty minutes of his arrival, the course of what might have been true love had been thwarted by her thoughtless father. Moreover, Lars had succeeded in reinforcing Katrina's determination to escape her father's heavy-handed guidance. Katrina was being forced to declare her independence.

Thomas Matthew Callahan, still struggling to make his way west, continued to work each and every day, unaware that in spite of his determination to do otherwise, Lars Hansen had opened the door a crack for the young Irishman, when he had meant, instead, to slam it shut for all time.

18 July 1895

Dear Nana,

I am so humiliated tonight Nana. Poppa has done the most unbearable thing. The young man who taught us the gospel in Oslo has returned to Utah and came to visit us tonight. Without a word to me, Poppa announced to all that he thought it would be a good idea if I seriously considered Mr. Stromberg as a suitable marriage candidate. Momma was mortified, and even poor Harold, (that's his name Nana) was shocked. I ran from the room in tears.

Oh Nana, what can I do. If Poppa insists, I . . .

Please guide me Nana. Help me to understand Poppa. I know he only wants *what's good for me, but I felt like I was being sold on the block.*

Jeg elske deg,

Katrina

The one member of the Hansen household who was not happy with their new life in Utah, was Anders Hansen. Unsure of his feelings from the beginning of their investigation of the Church, Andy went along with the family decision, first to keep peace at home, but also because his father had been dogmatic about the decision, not allowing any room for discussion. As long as the family was in Norway, it hadn't really been a problem because the small branch that they attended only had eleven members, and they came together only on Sundays. Since coming to Utah, however, religious activity was more pervasive. That brought Anders face to face with decisions he needed to make.

The first sign of overt rebellion came as a result of Ander's refusal to be ordained to a priesthood office. Baptized with the family in Norway, his early ordination to the Aaronic Priesthood came as a matter of course, even though he was already seventeen at the time. Since learning of the responsibilities that accrued to a Melchizedek Priesthood holder, and having developed a respect for, if not a belief in, the office which Harold Stromberg had explained to him, Andy refused his father's demand that he become an elder.

Coming home late, the same evening that Harold Stromberg had visited, and finding Katrina distraught over the evening's developments was the final straw for Andy. He declared to himself that his father would play no more of a

94

role in his life than was absolutely necessary as they worked together each day. Sitting on the edge of her bed in tears when Andy knocked, Katrina buried her head in his shoulder when he entered the room and sobbed her story to her closest friend. The disparity between Katrina's absolute commitment to the Church and her unshakable testimony of the message Elder Stromberg had delivered in Norway, and Andy's less-enthusiastic reception of that same message had done nothing to dispel the close-knit bond they shared as brother and sister, friend, and confidant. This evening was no exception.

"He's gotten even more controlling since we came to Utah, Klinka, and it's only going to get worse," Andy vented. "I've a good mind to move out and take an apartment of my own, that is if I was sure he wouldn't fire me just to bring me under his economic control again."

Katrina winced at the thought. "Please, Anders," she sobbed, holding on to him in her confusion, "please don't leave the house. You're the only one I can talk to."

"I know, Klinka," he replied, using the nickname he had assigned her when she was only four years old. "We've got to face this together. Have you spoken to Mama?"

"No, but she didn't approve of his behavior either. I could tell," Katrina responded.

"Do you like Harold?" he asked.

Katrina sat upright, wiping her eyes with a tissue. "Ya, I do, Anders, but . . ."

"But you don't think you can love him?"

"I just don't know, Anders. Really, it's just too soon to know my feelings. I don't know how I feel."

"Maybe you should give him a chance, in spite of Poppa's meddling. I like him," Andy volunteered. "He's always been very nice to us. I think he's smart, his family is secure here in Salt Lake City, and well, you know he's always taken a liking to you."

Katrina smiled thinly. "I know. But I'm so embarrassed. It's like Poppa put me on the selling block."

"Ya," Andy replied, "but I'm sure Harold would understand. He has parents too, you know," Andy laughed, making Katrina smile.

"Anders," she said, hugging him tightly, "I love you so much. You always know how to make me laugh. I'd like to see Harold again, but there's still . . ." she hesitated, not sure what to say.

"There's still Tom Callahan," Andy finished for her.

Katrina stood, going to her dresser and looking at herself in the mirror, wiping away the remaining tears. "I don't know if there *is* a Tom Callahan, Anders," she answered.

"Ya. Maybe not. Let me see if I can speak with Harold and explain how you feel about Poppa's actions. I know he'd like to see you, and he doesn't want you to feel like a package, either." Andy stood and moved behind Katrina, both reflected in the mirror as he placed his hands on her shoulders. "Harold or Tom," he smiled over her shoulder, "I should be so lucky to have a woman like you feel that way about me. They are lucky men, ya, so they are."

Katrina raised her hand to her shoulder and covered Andy's hand. "She's waiting for you, Anders, and I'm going to see that you find her," she laughed again.

"Hurry, please, Klinka, I'm sick of living in this house, and it's time I moved on."

"Not too soon, Anders, please, not too soon," Katrina pleaded.

Bayonne proved slightly less crowded and confusing than New York City, and Tom quickly settled in to his routine, actually enjoying his new job as apprentice oilier on an engine crew. His crew leader, a German engineer whose job was to maintain six steam engines, took a liking to young Callahan and made Tom his assistant.

Teaching Tom the ins and outs of the heating and ventilating system in the large repair facility, Heinrich was pleased to see that Tom took quickly to mechanical things and within several weeks was able to keep the warehouse and repair shop equipment running. The job, however, kept Tom in the roundhouse at the switching yard, and he could see that while the job was interesting, paid fairly well, and offered good working conditions, it would take him no farther west. In light of his living expenses, six months was not enough time to save enough money to buy a ticket to Utah, even at the better rate of pay.

Heinrich Hostetter, the lead engineer, learned all of this from Tom over their first two months together, and so it was no surprise to Heinrich when Tom volunteered for the winter rail crew when the company posted the job.

The organization of a winter rail crew was a company

maintenance strategy that had been in effect for two years. Forming a crew of about twenty, and outfitting two rail-cars—one for new rail storage, and one for crew quarters—the plan called for the two cars to move with regularly scheduled trains heading between Bayonne, New Jersey, and Omaha, Nebraska, placing the work cars on sidings in each successive region as rail repair was accomplished. Rather than outfit crews from each area of the region, the one crew, specialized in their job, followed the major rail lines and accomplished repairs along the way. Most New York, Baltimore, & Ohio employees did not volunteer because it took them on the road for months at a time and in the case of the more difficult winter run, they would leave in late September, be gone through the holidays, and not return until approximately February, after making the run to Omaha, then south to Kansas City and, finally, back east to Bayonne. Family men abhorred the assignment, and so the company tried where possible to take all volunteers. Tom saw it as his chance to move west at the railroad's expense, as Father O'Leary had suggested. So even though Heinrich had been easy to work for and helpful, nothing he said to Tom could deter the young Irishman from signing on for the winter run.

The third week in September, five months and four jobs after Tom's arrival in America, the repair crew pulled out of the Bayonne switching yard. The twenty men settling into their claimed bunks in the crew car began grousing almost immediately about the quality of the food, which was pre-pared by a cook who operated a kitchen at one end of the car, alongside the small room occupied by the road foreman, Mr. Sutherland.

A few days before Tom's departure, he took the oppor-tunity to return to lower Manhattan to pay a visit to Father

O'Leary. A priest who was considerably younger than Father O'Leary, whom Tom hadn't previously met, answered the rectory door, and Tom introduced himself, asking to see Father O'Leary.

"Mr. Callahan, did you know Father O'Leary well?" the priest asked.

"Not well, Father, we only had a brief acquaintance," Tom responded, aware that the priest spoke in the past tense.

"Father O'Leary has passed on, my son," he said, crossing himself. "He had a heart attack about six weeks ago."

"Oh, I see," Tom mumbled. "I'm sorry to hear it, Father. Did he have any family?"

"None. Father O'Leary has been alone for quite some years now. His family," the priest said, with a sweeping gesture of his arm, "were the people in this neighborhood."

"Aye," Tom said. "When you visit with him, Father, you can tell him that one of his sons will say a rosary for him."

"I understand, my son," the priest said, smiling at Tom. "Can I offer you a cup of tea before you leave?"

"No, thank you, Father, but you could put this in the orphans' box if you would, please, in Father O'Leary's name," Tom said, handing the priest a five dollar bill.

"Thank you, my son. God's blessings on you."

"Thank you, Father, I'll be needing 'em. Good day to you."

"And to you, my son."

———

During his return trip across the river to New Jersey, Tom thought back on the two occasions when he had been with Father O'Leary. It hadn't been a long association, as he'd told the other priest, but very significant, to Tom's way of thinking. "*Six months will tell the tale, lad,*" Tom recalled O'Leary warning him about the path he was on. *Well, Father, I've used up two of 'em, and the future looks better than it did. I thank you for that,* Tom thought.

<hr>

The arrival of September didn't provide any relief from the summer heat in Salt Lake, and Katrina, used to the early advent of winter in Norway, found it enjoyable to be able to continue the outdoor activities associated with pleasant weather. True to his word, Andy met with Harold Stromberg, and as he later explained to Katrina, found that Harold was almost as shocked by Mr. Hansen's behavior as Katrina had been. Andy arranged a meeting for the two, unknown to Lars Hansen, and to her pleasure, Katrina found herself liking the newly returned missionary.

<hr>

"Klinka, please hurry. We're going to miss the train," Andy called out as he passed her room, bounding down the stairs, and causing Mr. Hansen to look up from his newspaper.

"Going out, Anders?" Lars asked.

"Ya, Poppa. Klinka and I are going to Saltair to swim," Andy replied.

"I wish that girl would become serious for once and see young Harold again," Lars said, exasperation in his voice.

"You know Klinka, Poppa. Headstrong, just like—" Seeing his father's stern look, Anders thought better of his comment.

"The Poppa has a responsibility to see his daughters are properly watched over, Anders, and married into a fine family. You'd do well to learn that before you think about becoming a father yourself."

"Ya, Poppa," Andy answered, waiting impatiently for Katrina to come down the stairs.

"Ready, Anders," Katrina said, walking toward her father and giving him a kiss on top of his balding head, and then rubbing it into his bare spot, a habit Mr. Hansen tolerated as a show of affection from his daughter.

"See you watch your sister, Anders," Lars warned, "and don't let any of the rowdies get you in trouble. I've been reading about the growing troubles at this Saltair. It might not be safe to go out there, if someone doesn't put a stop to it."

"It's fine, Poppa," Anders said. "The papers exaggerate everything. Besides, some of Klinka's friends will be there too," he continued, winking at Katrina from behind her father's back.

Closing the front door, Andy took Katrina by the arm as they headed off down the street toward the trolley stop. *"Klinka's friends will be there too,"* Katrina mimicked. "You should have said, 'one special friend,' right, Anders?"

"Don't be giving me a hard time, little sister. We just might see someone else at Saltair, mightn't we?" he teased.

"Is Harold . . ."

"He just might be," Andy laughed as the trolley arrived.

"This would be so much easier if you'd just tell Poppa you're seeing Harold. He'd turn the house upside down to help you if he knew."

"Please, Anders, I don't want Poppa to know, at least until I know how I feel. I like Harold, of course, but I still want to keep this between us. Harold agrees to that, why can't you?"

"I have agreed, in case you didn't notice, little sister. I'm here, aren't I?"

Katrina smiled, tugging at his arm as they sat side by side on the trolley seat. "Ya, you're here, Anders, but so will Martha Young be." Andy remained silent in the face of Katrina's teasing him about Martha.

After leaving the trolley and entering the Union Pacific Rail depot, Andy left Katrina by herself while he went to buy tickets for the excursion train to Saltair. The station was crowded with Saturday revelers, and trains ran every fifteen minutes to accommodate the crowds.

Saltair had become the most enjoyable attraction in the Salt Lake Valley, for young and old. Situated on the southern shore of the Great Salt Lake, a large Moorish style building, with onion-domed towers, housed an enormous dance pavilion, rides, and bathing facilities for swimmers, and weekend visitors now often numbered in the thousands.

The first time Katrina and Andy had gone to Saltair, she had been amazed by the thousands jammed into the dance pavilion. In that crowd, she was also astonished when Harold Stromberg suddenly appeared. Andy's knowing smile made it evident to Katrina that Harold's arrival was no coincidence. Still, she had thanked Andy on the train ride home for his efforts in arranging the meeting. Today, she had done the same thing for Andy, by inviting Martha Young to meet them at Saltair.

When Andy returned with the tickets, he was accompanied by Harold, but this time, Katrina was not surprised.

"Good morning, Katrina," Harold said, removing his hat.

"Good morning, Harold," she smiled.

Each weekend now, for four weeks, Andy and Katrina had gone off together to a prearranged meeting where

Harold had joined them for the day's outing. Katrina's feelings for Harold were beginning to concern her. Everything Andy had said that night, after Poppa had humiliated her was true. Harold was smart, he came from a well-respected family, and his education toward becoming a lawyer was just getting under way at the university. He supported himself by working afternoons in his father's law firm, and his future seemed secure. He treated Katrina with the utmost respect and courtesy, and he had even agreed, although he was reluctant to deceive Mr. Hansen, to meet with Katrina in secret until she determined to tell her father that she was seeing Harold.

Harold Stromberg was everything a girl could hope for, something that was confirmed by the way other young women looked to him in the places he and Katrina went. Some of the local girls were resentful of the new immigrant girl, who seemed to have the inside track on the eligible Harold. Katrina knew he could shift his attentions to any of a dozen girls, yet he seemed content to wait until she found her way, or decided how her feelings were developing.

Given Katrina's beauty and the feelings he had for her, Harold was willing to be patient. He sensed also that if he pushed her for a commitment, she'd run. As for Katrina, herself, she still didn't know whether she'd run *toward*, or *away*, from Harold Stromberg.

"What's it to be today, Katrina? Rides, swimming, or just sunning outside?" Harold asked, smiling.

"Oh, yes! All of that," Katrina answered, laughing, "and dancing tonight, please."

"The young lady's got an iron constitution," Harold said to Andy.

"And an iron fist when she's mad," her brother quipped.

103

"C'mon, let's get a seat on the train, or we'll have to stand all the way."

⊰⊱

The last train back from Saltair ran at midnight, but Lars Hansen had strictly instructed Andy that he was to have his sister in the house before midnight, so they took the ten forty-five train back to the station, Harold accompanying them and parting company as Katrina and Andy prepared to board the trolley toward their home. Harold politely kissed Katrina's hand, the first gesture of affection he had made toward her. It was sufficient to make her blush and get a little light-headed. She recognized the boldness of his growing interest, and it both thrilled and concerned her.

"Katrina," he said, "I hope your day was as enjoyable as mine, and I'd like to think we could have many more together. Would you consider coming to Church with my family tomorrow and having dinner with us afterward?"

"Thank you, Harold, but I'd better not. I should help my mother with the dinner for our family. Some other time, perhaps."

Harold smiled and released her hand. "I hope so, Katrina. *God kvell*," he said in Norwegian.

"*Tusan tak*, Harold," she replied.

As the trolley rolled east on South Temple, Andy stared at Katrina until she responded. "What?" she asked.

"He may not wait until next year, you know."

"Next year?" she said, feigning ignorance of his intent.

"Ya, next year, when your promise to wait for Tom is over."

"Oh, Anders, I don't know what to do. I like Harold, really I do. But I still think of Tom. You like Tom, too, you know you do."

"Ya, I like Tom Callahan, but we may never see him again."

Katrina was silent, looking out the open air trolley window as they passed Temple Square and admiring the magnificent six-spired temple, gleaming white with the newness of its completion just two years before. She thought of how much she desired to be married in the temple, something Harold offered, but that Tom . . . "I know, Anders," she said, plaintively. "But he did ask, and I did promise. I must wait."

"Ya, I suppose you must."

Katrina turned back to look at Andy, taking his arm again and leaning her head on his shoulder. "God has given me such a wonderful brother, Anders. Thank you for understanding."

"It's *Harold's* understanding that should concern you, Klinka."

"Ya," she replied, looking again out the window.

21 September, 1895

Dear Nana,

Today we spent the day at Saltair, the bathing place I told you about. Anders and I met Harold Stromberg and Martha Young for the day. Anders thinks Martha Young is wonderful, but just between you and me, Nana, she is not for him.

As for me, well, Harold is really a good man. He is considerate and patient, and has not made me feel embarrassed over the time Poppa announced him as the suitable candidate. The truth is, Nana, he is in every way a suitable candidate, and offers much more than the life I think Thomas could, but still, Nana, you understand, I know. In my heart, I still think of Thomas. Perhaps it's just a dream, since I haven't seen him and we can't write, but, still, I promised to wait.

What if he comes, Nana, and I don't feel the same? What if I come to love Harold and Thomas has come all this way because I promised to wait? What if Thomas doesn't come, Nana?

Jeg elske deg.

Trina

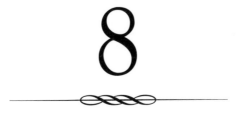

By early November, the New York, Baltimore, & Ohio rail repair crew had worked its way to Omaha, making faster time than anticipated. Tom thoroughly enjoyed the trip, seeing parts of America that he had only read about or seen in magazine pictures. The only negative aspect of the trip was the assistant crew leader, a disagreeable Englishman named Max Tooney, who had taken a dislike to Tom and made it his mission to make life miserable for the young Irishman. Still, the crew all worked hard when rail repair was in progress, so Tom ignored the intentional taunting about Irish "Paddy's" and "hooligans," and chalked it up to what he privately considered a bloody, ignorant "Brit." Only when Tom's name had appeared on the galley roster short of his normal rotation had he complained, and on that occasion, he was told by Tooney he could take it or leave it. The crew could do without him, anyway, Tooney had said.

Tom swallowed his pride on that occasion and accepted the additional galley assignment, aided by the knowledge that the cook liked him and thanked him for being one of the crew who didn't complain about the cooking.

As the crew started the southerly run from Omaha to Kansas City, snow began to fall and soon a full-fledged prairie blizzard encompassed the train. Finding the narrow passageway between two hills drifted-in with snow, the train came to a stop while crew were assigned to clear the track ahead. As shovels flew, and the rails began to be cleared, Tooney sent Tom up the hill to a nearby grove of trees to obtain additional firewood for the potbellied stove in the crew quarters. He did so on the pretense that they might be snowed in farther up the track and have to remain overnight on the prairie, where no wood could be obtained.

In a stand of dead trees, located several hundred yards uphill from the train, Tom swung his ax in the snowstorm, felling several smaller trees, allowing the physical exertion to dispel his anger as well as keep him warm. There was plenty of firewood on board in the coal tender behind the engine, and Tom felt Tooney had once again used his authority to push him into an unnecessary, extra assignment. Not until Tom heard the engine make steam did he realize that Tooney intended to leave him on the prairie, somewhere between Nebraska and Missouri.

Dropping his ax and shouting for them not to leave him, Tom began bounding his way through the waist deep snowdrifts, down the hill to where the train was slowly gathering steam and beginning to make slow headway uphill, against the newly cleared track.

Stumbling every few feet, Tom realized that if he didn't reach the last railcar before it crested the top and began to pick up speed down the far side, he'd likely freeze to death. His clothing was soaked with perspiration and melting snow, and he was gasping for breath. Nearing the railroad right-of-way, Tom was blocked by the bank of snow the crew had piled up as they cleared the tracks. Stumbling and slipping, he fought to clamber over the top, then sliding down the other side, he sprawled headlong in the snow next to the tracks, just as the last car crawled by. He scrambled to his feet and began running behind the train, down the middle of the newly cleared tracks. The blowing snow blinded him, and he strained to catch hold of the ladder on the back of the flatcar used to transport extra rails, which was the last car on the train. Finally, just before his strength gave out entirely and the last railcar rolled over the top of the grade, he was able to grab the railing on the rear steps, and with a strength summoned from desperation, he pulled himself up onto the bed of the car and lay there, gasping for breath and shaking with rage, as the train gathered speed and rolled down the far side of the hill.

Exhausted, he lay there for a minute, until he began to lose the feeling in his face and hands and feet. The wind kicked up by the speed of the train made it even colder, and his wet clothing began to freeze.

Tom knew he was in a desperate situation. He needed to traverse the flatbed railcar to reach the crew compartment, one car ahead.

Crouching and moving unsteadily on top of the snow-slick stack of rails, he made his way forward, lurching from side to side as the train rocked on. When he reached the front of the flatcar, Tom paused to gather his strength, and then leaped across the gap above the swaying couplings, to the back of the crew car, where he fell through the door, face down on the wooden floor and unconscious.

Several minutes later, he became aware that his hands were being rubbed and someone was trying to pour hot coffee down his throat. He was wrapped in a blanket and two or three of the men supported him as he sat on a stool next to the potbellied stove.

"What happened, Tom?" the foreman said. "We thought everyone was on board."

Tooney was standing behind Mr. Sutherland, and Tom glared at him until Tooney looked away. Tom's face was so cold he couldn't speak, so he said nothing, but sat quietly, content for the moment to soak up some heat from the stove and let the hot coffee do its work.

The men gradually drifted away to their bunks and other interests, leaving Tom to warm up and regain his strength. After a while, the cook brought him some soup, and he eventually felt strong enough to stand and walk about.

Tooney was lying on one of the top bunks, looking at a magazine when Tom approached him. The rage that had filled Tom when he realized he was being deliberately left behind, suddenly roared up, and he grabbed Tooney by his shirt and dragged him off the bunk to the floor. Placing his knee on the struggling man's chest, Tom struck him a vicious blow in the face and would have hit him again, except that he was restrained by several of the crew.

Sutherland came immediately forward. "Here, Tom!" he shouted. "What's the matter with you?" he said, glancing back momentarily at Tooney who was sitting on the floor, holding his face and shaking his head.

"He sent me out there to chop wood, and he *knew* I wasn't back," Tom charged.

Sutherland looked again at Tooney, who was now regaining his feet, and then back at Tom.

"Tom, I'm sure it was an oversight, lad, but we can't have trouble on the crew. We're only half through this trip, and from the looks of this storm, we'll have trouble just getting to Kansas City."

Tooney pulled on Sutherland's shoulder, spinning him around, so they stood face to face. "You know the company rules, Henry. No fighting. Callahan's temper has done him in this time. I demand you fire him."

110

"You *demand?*" Sutherland challenged.

"Or I'll take it to the regional director in Kansas City."

Sutherland's shoulders slumped, and he turned around to look at Tom. After a moment, he said, "He's right, lad. I'm sorry, but my hands are tied. When we get to Kansas City, draw your pay, and I'll see what I can do to help you find a job before we have to leave." Sutherland turned, looking angrily at Tooney. "It's a long trip east, Max. Who ya gonna' bully on the way back?" he said, pushing past Tooney.

"Well, Callahan, it seems you Irish riffraff never learn, do you?" Tooney sneered.

"Aye, it would seem so, Mr. Tooney," Tom said, smiling finally and looking around at the crew members who had watched the scene play out. "But then, . . ." he said, surprising Tooney with a short, hard jab to his mouth, once again sending Tooney to the floor of the crew car, "we wouldn't be expecting any deeper understanding from a bloody Brit, now would we?" He stood over the downed Englishman, rubbing his knuckles and continuing to smile, enjoying the laughter that erupted in the car. Down at the end of the car, Mr. Sutherland smiled and turned away.

Food, a couple of cups of hot coffee, and the passage of three hours eventually calmed Tom down, and as he lay in his bunk, Kansas City looming over the horizon, he collected his thoughts. All in all, Tooney's actions had saved Tom the problem of explaining to Mr. Sutherland that he intended to leave the crew in Kansas City, the farthest point west on this trip. The repair crew intended to travel back by a slightly more southern route, continuing their repairs into the early spring and reaching Bayonne by the first of March.

111

Being fired didn't set well with Tom, but it had at least eased his concern about being responsible for leaving the crew short-handed for the return trip.

⸺⸺

Kansas City, Missouri, a rail head for many years for cattle drives coming up from Texas and other ranching areas south, presented itself to Tom as a genuine piece of the American West. Boasting trolleys and some other modern conveniences, such as he'd seen in New York, it still had an air about it of untamed wildness, perhaps the result of its location in the middle of a prairie, broken only by the mighty Missouri River, which flowed sluggishly past on its way east toward the Mississippi.

After Tom drew his pay, Sutherland introduced him to the resident Well's Fargo agent and commended him as a hard worker. The man told Tom to come back in the morning and he'd see what might be found in their freight operation. Tom thanked Sutherland, who left to go back to the train crew, while Tom sought a place to obtain a bath and some new clothes, including a heavy winter coat, suitable, the salesman told him, for surviving the harsh winters found on the plains.

By evening, Tom felt better and had not given any additional thought to the altercation with Tooney, until he saw him later that night in the saloon. Ignoring Tooney, Tom remained at the bar, content to drink by himself. After a while, Tooney left the saloon in the company of three other men with whom he'd been drinking at a table near the piano. Tom finished his drink, left two bits for the barmaid, who had given him advice on where to find a cheap hotel for the evening, and left the saloon.

As he worked his way along the street, Tom saw two

112

men emerge from an alleyway between two buildings, and fall in silently behind him. As he came to the next alley, a third man stepped out into his path, and Tom immediately recognized the game, so often used in his own youth, as he and his mates set out to trap some poor unsuspecting soul.

With an evening's drinks in him, Tom knew his head was not as clear as the situation demanded, but he also knew he would need to act quickly if he was going to survive the attack. The men closed in on him, forcing him toward the alley the single man had occupied moments earlier.

"Evening, Paddy," one said. "The limey tells us ya got a few bucks back pay on ya. Now ya wouldn't want to go around not sharing, would ya?" he sneered.

One of the men shoved Tom's shoulder, intent on intimidating him into giving up his money. But Tom, always wont to take the initiative, smiled at the three and reached for his wallet. The man in the center grinned, a look of easy victory crossing his face. When the man glanced momentarily down at Tom's wallet, Tom swung at him, but either the drinks had slowed him down or the fellow had quicker reflexes than Tom figured. Whatever the case, the punch missed, causing Tom to lose his balance and his assailants were immediately upon him. They knocked him to the ground, and all three began to kick him. Tom grunted with pain as the blows from their boots connected with his ribs and kidneys.

Tom knew that unless he gained some control of his situation, he stood in danger of not only losing his money but receiving a severe beating and perhaps being killed. He grabbed the foot of one of the men, pulling it toward him and jerking him off balance. As the man fell, Tom quickly got to his feet, and ducking under a punch from one of the other men, landed a heavy blow to the side of the head of the larger assailant. As the man staggered from the blow, Tom bolted forward, driving a shoulder into the man's chest and knocking him backward into the wall of one of the buildings. He pinned the man against the wall, ripped two blows to his assailant's midsection, and had the satisfaction of hearing the man wheeze in pain. One of the other men spun Tom around, and landed a stinging blow high on the Irishman's head. Tom came back with an elbow to the front of the man's neck, then kneed him in the groin.

Coming off the wall, the largest assailant moved toward Tom, who turned sideways, raised his leg, and drove his boot into the man's chest. The man flew backward, landing hard and sprawling across a pile of lumber. He screamed with pain, momentarily arched his back then lay still, moaning in agony.

Tom's blood was up, and he turned, fists raised, to face the two men who remained standing. But the fight had gone out of them, and they backed away. The man lying on the ground continued to moan, without trying to rise, and one of his partners bent over him and then gasped. The fallen man was impaled on a large metal spike.

Seeing his way free to run, Tom quickly snatched up his wallet from the ground and darted out of the alley into the street, as the two men behind him began shouting.

"Catch him! Get him! He's murdered Ike! Murder! Murder!" They continued to shout as Tom turned into another alley, emerged on the far street and ran hard back to the railroad yard. There, he found an empty box car and scrambled painfully into it. Crawling to a dark corner, he sat there panting and trembling, nursing his battered ribs and gritting his teeth against the cold. He pulled his new winter coat up around his ears and listened for any sound of a search. Lying there in the dark, afraid and hurting, Tom reflected bitterly on what had happened to him. He thought of Father O'Leary, and remembered his story about the young Irish lad who'd been executed in New York for the same kind of offense.

Sometime after midnight, Tom was aroused from his fitful sleep by the sound of men shouting and calling to one another. Shifting his position, Tom braced himself to be discovered. Just at that moment, however, one of the policemen called to the other that coffee had arrived and they went off in another direction. A few minutes later, the railcar lurched, and the train began moving slowly. After a time, it moved onto a trestle crossing the great Missouri River and picked up speed.

Tom remained huddled in the corner of the boxcar, dozing fitfully, enduring the cold, and struggling to find some relief for the ache in his side. Finally, after a miserable night, it began to get light. He noted with satisfaction that the sun was coming up behind the train. *West*, Tom thought as he watched the sunlight break over the horizon. *I'm still headed west.*

By sun reckoning, it was well beyond noon when the train began to slow, and Tom saw a sign that said *Salina, Kansas*, roll past. His stomach confirmed the lateness in the day. It had been many hours since he had eaten.

About a half-mile past the town sign, the train slowed even more, then creaked and banged to a stop. Tom got stiffly to his feet and stood in the doorway of the boxcar. Shading his eyes from the sun's glare off snow-covered prairie, he looked out over a vast, treeless landscape that flattened out to immense proportions and stretched away into the distance beyond the rail yard and the town. Ahead, up the track, he could see the train had begun taking on water. It poured from a wooden tank through a metal boom into the locomotive tender car, and seeing the heavy stream reminded Tom of how thirsty he was.

He could hear men shouting in the distance, but seeing no one nearby, Tom climbed painfully from the boxcar and began walking gingerly up the tracks toward the water tank. He was startled and stumbled slightly when a switchman suddenly emerged from between two cars, but recovering quickly, Tom instinctively flashed the smile that he had learned to use to put people off their guard. Even though his coat was somewhat rumpled from a fitful night and a half day spent sitting and lying on the floor of the railcar, it was quickly evident to the switchman that Tom was no bum. His clothes still displayed their sheen and newness.

"Any chance for a drink of water up ahead?" Tom nodded toward the water tank.

"Sure thing," the switchman said, looking around to see where Tom had come from. Aware of his curiosity, Tom continued to smile and rapidly formulated an explanation.

"Where are we?" he asked, looking around.

"Salina, Kansas. How'd you get here?"

Tom laughed, holding his bruised ribs as he bent over with the pain. "Just out for an evening stroll last night, and three, shall we say *gentlemen*, sought to relieve me of my meager funds. The first thing I knew, I woke up in one of the railcars," he said, jerking his thumb back toward the direction he'd come.

"Well, I'd better call the sheriff and see if we can't get you some help."

"Nah, no need, but I appreciate the offer. Just a drink will do. And maybe something to eat. Where's this train headed anyway?"

116

"Straight across to Denver," the man replied.

"Denver? Is that west of here?"

The switchman snorted. "Straight west," he pointed.

"Aye," Tom smiled broadly, "if I could possibly purchase something to eat," he said, pulling a small wad of bills out of his coat pocket, "and something to drink, I'll just hop back into my private railcar and be on my way, no trouble to anyone."

"I don't know," the switchman said, shaking his head. "We're supposed to keep people off the freight cars."

"I understand," Tom replied. "Would five dollars be enough for a small bite to eat?" he said, fingering the bills and looking up at the switchman.

The man looked at the bills in Tom's hand. "I suppose, just this once," he answered, looking furtively around the rail yard. "But you'd have to get back in the car quickly."

"Done," Tom said. "Why don't you bring me something to eat? I'll get a quick drink of water, and then I'll cease being a bother to you, sir."

Twenty miles further west, with several pieces of greasy chicken digesting in his stomach and the growling quieted for the time being, Tom attempted once again, as dusk overtook the train, to get a few hours of sleep. The switchman's lunch had been cold and had resulted in a bad case of indigestion, but Tom was grateful to have obtained something to eat, and through his conspiracy with the switchman, to have also escaped any real hassle while passing through Salina. The cold, which had abated slightly from the intense temperatures of the previous evening, was made somewhat more bearable by the straw bundles the switchman had offered Tom, lingering just long enough during their delivery to indicate that the additional service was worth at least another fiver. The fact that the switchman

117

had never asked how it happened that Tom got mugged, dumped on the train, and yet still had money in his pocket, had not escaped Tom's notice. Still, he felt reasonably assured that the rail worker would take his newfound ten dollars, not say a word to anyone, including his wife, and be grateful for his good fortune.

As for Tom's fortune, sleep came no easier the second night, and the first light of dawn, viewed once again through the open door of a drafty railcar hooked into the westward moving train, found him fitfully turning on his bed of straw. He was thoroughly miserable: he was cold, his ribs were sore, and he was hungry again.

The rolling landscape of the American Midwest had given way during the night to more broken ground. And now, as daylight continued to gather, Tom stood shivering in the open doorway of the boxcar, arms folded, holding his coat pulled tightly around him, and staring out at the passing scene. Tall clumps of sagebrush poked through the snowdrifts in the arroyos alongside the railroad right-of-way. As the sun finally rose behind Tom, the train finished pulling up a long grade and crested a rise, and the young Irishman was startled by his first glimpse of the Rocky Mountains.

Stretching from north to south, the mountains lay in a long, unbroken line clear across the western horizon. Though fronted by a gently rising landscape of foothills, the enormous mountains appeared to jut up suddenly out of the great plains. They were still a long way off, but the clear air gave the mountains the appearance that they were much closer than they were. Their rugged tops were bathed in sunlight, and looking at their majestic snowy heights, Tom was filled with the same sense of awe he had felt while standing alongside Katrina and first seeing the great swells of the Atlantic Ocean from the deck of the *Antioch*.

A full knowledge of the true vastness of America was beyond his understanding at present, but Tom knew one thing from the maps he had studied while on the winter rail crew: the only thing that stood between him and Katrina Hansen—between him and this unknown land of Utah— had just risen suddenly out of the ground. And as the train rolled on, his mind slowly grasped the reality that while only one geographical obstacle remained, it appeared more and more formidable, the closer he got.

Tom was surprised to discover that even though Denver was farther west, it was larger than Kansas City. Of course, his knowledge of Kansas City, he smiled to himself, consisted of running through back alleys and retracing his steps to the rail yard.

Entering Denver, Tom found himself in different circumstances than when he had arrived in New York. He had some money, although not enough he felt, to simply purchase transportation for the remaining five hundred miles to Salt Lake City and arrive there with ample funds to allow him to obtain accommodations and to find Katrina without seeming to be a destitute immigrant. Denver would have to do for a short time. He would need some employment, and he could use the time to allow his injuries to heal before continuing his trip. Since it was only the second week in November, Tom felt he still had ample time to reach Salt Lake well ahead of the New Year. Had she waited as promised? That was the question that was beginning to nag at Tom, although he pushed it aside whenever it came to the fore. He'd come too far to turn back now.

After renting a room in a small boarding house, Tom inquired as to the whereabouts of a doctor and during his first visit, was not surprised to be told that he had two broken ribs. His breathing had become labored the second day of his confinement in the empty railcar, and he had considered the possibility that he might develop pneumonia if he didn't find comfortable and warm accommodations soon. The boarding house answered that need.

When she discovered Tom's injuries, Mrs. Hortense, the Mexican lady who ran the boarding house, immediately took control, and, much to his chagrin, plied him with soup and homemade bread. For the next few days, she saw to it that he remained in bed and had his meals served there. It was the most comforting three days Tom had enjoyed in many months, and lacking any immediate worry about finances, he allowed himself to relish the pampering.

By the end of the first week, he was up and around the house, and had taken to sitting on the upstairs outside balcony, much to Mrs. Hortense's protest because of the cold. The mountains to the west continued to provide a panoramic view that enthralled Tom, and he sat watching them for hours, reading the Denver papers to get the flavor of the community and to learn more about this new land into which he had driven headlong.

Memories of Ireland were distant, but, occasionally, Tom found himself wondering how his family was doing and if the course he had taken would indeed lead to prosperity. Father O'Leary's advice remained with Tom, as well as the name of the Sister who ran the hospital in Salt Lake City. O'Leary had made him promise that when he arrived in Utah, he would immediately find Holy Cross Hospital and present the letter of introduction the priest had given him. That letter, along with the copy of the Book of Mormon and a few extra clothes Tom had been carrying in a cheap bag, had been abandoned in the alley in Kansas City. Tom remembered the name: Sister Mary Theophane. But that was for later. For now, it was time to heal and gather himself for the last leg of his journey.

The time spent in Denver would have been a completely restful time, except for the scene that frequently played through his mind of the altercation in the alley in Kansas City, and the shouts of "murder!" that rang out as he fled. That a man had died bothered him terribly, and though he knew he had acted in self-defense, he couldn't erase the memory of what had happened. Besides that, he worried constantly about being pursued by the authorities and overtaken. He vowed, therefore, to spend no longer than necessary—a few weeks at most—in Denver, before pushing on across the Rockies.

He was drawn once again to the rail yards, and by the end of his second week in Denver, Tom had gotten a job working in the livestock pens, loading sheep and cattle onto freight cars. At the request of his foreman, Tom made two runs with cattle up to Cheyenne, assuring that they were watered en route. Another run, down to Roswell, New Mexico, provided another view of America and a first glimpse at Indians living on a reservation. In his travels, Tom had seen some squalor by that time, but he was appalled at the conditions in which the Indians lived.

In mid-December, the foreman advised Tom that four hundred head of cattle were being transported to Ogden, Utah, over the Christmas holidays. The foreman told Tom he was sorry, but as the new man, Tom was being assigned the run. His reaction to Tom's smile was one of bewilderment.

Two delays in the arrival of the cattle set the trip back, but finally, on December 26, the day after Christmas, Tom and another man got under way with four hundred thirty-two head of cattle, only to be halted in Fort Laramie where reports of a track blockage across the Wyoming flats prevented them from going on.

Finally, on December 30th, they reloaded the cattle, arriving in Ogden on New Year's day, 1896. After they had delivered the consignment of cattle, received the signed documents, and were prepared to board the return run to Denver, Tom told his partner farewell, explaining that he was staying in Utah. He took a room in a cheap hotel and spent the next two days having his clothes cleaned, removing the cattle stench, and wallowing in the nervous excitement of knowing that he was now only forty miles from the woman who had compelled him to come more than halfway across America.

9

───────⬳⬳⬳───────

At seven in the morning, January 4, 1896, the Union Pacific Railroad station in Salt Lake City was packed with people as Tom stepped off the train from Ogden. Purchasing his fare, he had smiled. He had traveled over two thousand miles by rail from Bayonne, New Jersey, and this was the first time he had bought a ticket. He had worked as a laborer on a rail repair crew, been a hobo, and then a cattle tender. It struck him as remarkable that he had ridden as a paying passenger for only the last forty miles. Yet, he had succeeded in reaching Salt Lake City.

Outside the station, a number of people crowded into a horse-drawn trolley car. But Tom fell in with the dozens of people who were walking toward what appeared to be the main part of town. As they walked, the crowd grew to larger proportions, and Tom wondered what all the excitement was about. The streets were filled with trolleys, buggies, men on horseback, and people on foot. A brass band was playing, and enterprising young men circulated in the crowd, selling small American flags and pieces of fruit. Down the center of Main Street, wider than most city streets Tom had seen, a line of power poles separated the two trolley tracks that ran north and south. Remembering New York, Kansas City, and

Denver, Tom was struck by the orderly design of the streets and the uniformly square blocks that had been laid out.

The atmosphere was one of revelry, and the cold didn't seem to bother people. What seemed to be a kind of town square was surrounded by a wall. Inside the square, a huge, six-spired cathedral rose above any other building in the area, and on the south side of the cathedral, facing Tom, an enormous American flag hung draped from the upper tier of the building.

Tom stared up at the flag, slowly backing away from the wall to obtain a better view, and stepping backward into the street. Suddenly he was grabbed and jerked back onto the foot path and nearly pulled off his feet in the process, as a horse and buggy passed, the horse nervous in the crowd and its driver struggling to bring it under control.

"I'm sorry, sir, I thought the horse was possibly going to trample you."

Tom looked around to assess the situation, realizing how foolish his gawking had been. "My fault. Thanks for the help. It wouldn't do to come all this way and be killed in the street my first morning here, now would it?"

The square-shouldered young man who had grabbed him, smiled and nodded. "It would be unfortunate, to say the least," he laughed.

"So," Tom asked, looking around, "what's the occasion today? Some kind of celebration obviously."

"Utah's about to become one of the states of the union. Today, we've joined the United States of America. We're waiting for word that President Grover Cleveland has signed the legislation approving our entry."

"I see. A good day to arrive then, I suppose," Tom laughed. "My name's Tom Callahan, sir, and you are?"

"David McKay. D.O., to my friends," he said, pronouncing it "Dee Oh."

"Are you from here, D.O.?"

"Actually from a small farming community up north, but I attend the university here."

"Well, D.O., please allow me to express my appreciation for saving my life," Tom grinned. "It means a lot to me."

David laughed out loud and offered his hand. "If you've just arrived, where are you staying, Mr. Callahan? Have you got a place yet?"

"No. But perhaps you could give me some directions. I'm looking for Holy Cross Hospital. Do you know it?"

"Oh, yes. You're on the right road. It's ten blocks east on South Temple. That's the street we're on now. Can't miss it," he pointed.

A horse bolted upright, rearing on his hind legs as the sound of two shotgun blasts echoed through the street. People began to cheer and shout from about a half-block down Main Street. "I guess that's it," David said. "Looks like we're now part of the great Union." He patted Tom on the back, joining in the enthusiasm overtaking the crowd. "Welcome to Salt Lake, to Utah, and to the United States of America, Tom. I'm off to meet with some friends, but here," he said, taking a pencil from his pocket, and writing on a small card. "If things don't work out at the hospital, and you find you haven't a place to stay the night, here's my address. It's only an impoverished student's room, but don't hesitate to come if you need a place to lay your head, and even if you don't. Maybe after you settle in we can get together for dinner some evening. You can tell me a bit about the Emerald Isle and I'll answer your Utah questions."

"That obvious, is it?" Tom exclaimed.

"Kind of a hard accent to hide, Tom, but music to my ears. My people came from Scotland originally."

"My thanks to you again, D.O. I'll head up toward the hospital if I can get through this crowd. Congratulations to you and to Utah."

David waved and crossed the street, heading south on Main while Tom crossed the intersection and headed east to find Holy Cross Hospital.

<hr />

One block south, on the corner of First South and Main, a three minute walk from where Tom and young David O. McKay were talking, Katrina Hansen and Harold Stromberg had been mingling with the crowd, waiting for the news of statehood to arrive. In contrast to the fun-loving nature of the people around them, Harold seemed unusually sober. Katrina had noticed his mood, but neither of them had mentioned it.

"We're in," Harold shouted at the sound of the shotgun blasts. He grabbed Katrina, lifted her off the ground and swung her around in circles as the crowd added to the celebration, now at its peak throughout the length of Main Street, from South Temple to First South.

"Katrina Hansen," Harold said, putting her down and looking at her intently, a smile fixed across his face. "This is a momentous day. My father's law firm will be pleased, our citizens will be pleased, and it's a time for new beginnings. Now the Prophet will be able to listen to the Lord again and follow His counsel.

"What do you mean, Harold?" Katrina asked.

"Oh, just the political necessities. You know, the Manifesto. Nothing to worry about. The Church knows what it's doing, and now that we've been granted statehood, the Prophet will see the right thing to do. But let's talk about us."

"Us?" she asked.

"Yes, us. For nearly six months we have been seeing each other, Katrina, and on this first day of our new statehood, I want you to know how I feel about you. I want to ask you, Katrina, to consider becoming my wife."

The suddenness and the business-like way Harold had declared his proposal left Katrina startled, in spite of the fact that for months she had known how Harold felt and that he was just being patient. It came as no surprise, other than his timing and his direct approach. He waited silently as she considered his question.

"Harold," she stammered, "I'm honored, but today is so hectic, and this is all so sudden."

"Katrina, you know how I feel. I know you do."

She nodded slightly, acknowledging his comments. "Please try to be patient just a bit longer, Harold. I, . . . I will pray about it, Harold. I know it's right to do so."

It was Harold's turn to nod. "Yes, it is. Katrina, try to find your feelings for me. I know I can make you happy."

The crowd began to move as one toward the telegraph office, wanting to read the message that had been received, and Katrina found herself pleased to not have to deal with the question as they were swept along. Harold did not broach the subject again until later that evening, as he took Katrina home.

"I do not think it unfair to request your considered response, Katrina, over the next week. I think we know each other well enough for that."

"I agree, Harold. I'm truly sorry that I don't know my own mind, but so much has happened with leaving my country, my new schooling, and—"

"I know," Harold responded. "Just think about it, please."

"I will, Harold. I promise."

January 4, 1896

Dear Nana,

Oh, I am in trouble now, Nana. If I ever needed your advice, I need it now. Harold has asked me to marry him. I like him, perhaps I even love him, and I can see what a good husband he would be, but oh, Nana, I don't know what to do!

Jeg elske deg,

Trina

Walking east on South Temple, Tom easily spied Holy Cross Hospital. Approaching the large complex, with new wings under construction, Tom was a little intimidated. He walked along the west side of the main building, then stood for several minutes across the street on First South, looking at the imposing gothic structure and admiring the large number of trees and well-kept grounds. There was an extensive rose garden, pruned back for the winter, exactly as his mother had done to her rose bushes.

Twenty-eight years after Brigham Young and the first pioneers had settled in, two Catholic nursing sisters from the Order of the Sisters of the Holy Cross arrived in the Salt Lake Valley. In October of 1875, they opened their small hospital, a twelve-bed facility located west of the present site. Several years later, in a foresighted move, they instituted a health insurance program for the local miners. For the payment of one dollar a week, while in good health, Holy Cross Hospital would provide in return, full hospital and medical care during any subsequent illness or injury. Sister M. Holy Cross, a Welsh woman, was assisted by Sister M. Bartholomew, the two of them comprising the original nursing staff. Over the following years, other nursing sisters arrived to join the growing cadre of caring nurses, and local young women were trained specifically as nurses, without being required to take holy orders.

Tom walked up the front steps and through the large, double doors, stepping into the vestibule. He continued through a second set of doors and entered a large foyer, fully twelve feet across. On the right side, the door to a small chapel was open, and Tom noticed several people seated in the pews, some on their knees in prayer. A nursing sister walked by, smiling at Tom as she paused to address him.

"May I be of assistance, sir?"

Tom removed his cap, and flashed his disarming smile. "Yes, thank you. I am seeking a Sister Mary Theo . . . Uh, Sister Mary . . ."

The sister laughed politely. "You must mean Sister Mary Theophane," she said, pronouncing it *Theo-fane*. "Please wait here a moment, and I'll see if I can find her."

Tom stood in the hallway, able to see in both east and west directions down the long corridors which made up the first floor of the hospital facility. Several minutes passed, and Tom walked to a small bench situated against the north wall of the entryway. The foyer and hallways were carpeted and the waiting area in which he was seated was beautifully appointed with fine furnishings. Everything was neat and clean.

He continued to sit nervously as his message was delivered to Sister Mary. Two nursing sisters walked by, their crisply starched habits rustling as they walked, and smiling at him in passing. After several minutes, a Sister dressed in a black habit approached from the east end of the hall, smiling brightly as she neared Tom's seat. He rose, turning his cap in his hands as she stopped directly in front of him.

"Good morning, I'm Sister Mary Theophane," she said. "How may I help, my son?"

Sister Mary Theophane, the person Father O'Leary had suggested Tom seek once he arrived in Utah, was a tall and handsome woman. Her manner was direct and she seemed genuinely friendly. Tom was put immediately at ease as he began to explain his purpose in calling on her.

In 1854, fifteen-year-old Moira Molloy had left Waterford, Ireland, joining in Cork with two dozen prospective postulants, and several priests, newly ordained from the seminary. All were intent on a new life in America, in service to their Lord. Among the young priests, straight out of All Hallows Seminary in Dublin, was one Father Patrick James O'Leary, from County Kerry, with whom Sister Mary Theophane would serve for the following twenty years.

The Sisters of Holy Cross, in Notre Dame, Indiana, trained Moira Molloy to be a nursing sister. Adopting the name of Sister Mary Theophane, Moira quickly lost herself in the work of nursing and care-giving, and from that point, never looked back. She had found her life's work.

Father P. J. O'Leary was assigned to a nearby parish. An early illness, requiring hospitalization, placed him in the care of Sister Mary, and that became the basis of a forty-year friendship between the two Catholic ministrants—one a nurse and the other a priest.

Sister Mary served from 1862 until 1865 with several sisters from the congregation at Mound City Hospital, Cairo, Illinois, caring for soldiers wounded during the Civil War.

Her completion of that task left her with vivid memories of the horrors of war and an excellent knowledge of emergency nursing care.

When, in 1875, the request went out from Bishop Lawrence Scanlan of the Church of Saint Mary Magdalene in Salt Lake City, for several sisters to establish a hospital, Sister Mary Theophane was not long in following Sister M. Holy Cross to the assignment. By the time Tom arrived in Utah, Sister Mary had been a nursing sister for over forty years, eighteen of them at Holy Cross Hospital in Salt Lake City, and she was serving as chief administrator of the facility—probably the finest in Salt Lake City.

"Good morning, Sister. I'm Thomas Callahan. I believe we have a mutual friend in New York, and when he learned I was coming to Utah, he asked me to look you up. Father P. J. O'Leary."

A bright smile lit up Sister Mary's face. She turned, looking behind her, and took Tom's arm. "Let's have a seat in the parlor," she said, walking toward a large, well appointed room just off the vestibule, opposite the chapel. She motioned for Tom to be seated on one of the couches, and she took the seat opposite, in an overstuffed chair.

"Ah, Father O'Leary. Now did he tell you how long an association we have?" she said, intentionally slipping a bit of her Irish brogue into the speech.

"He said you came over from Ireland together some years ago," Tom replied. Sister Mary was an impressive woman, with intelligent, piercing eyes. She was dressed in full habit, and small wisps of graying hair escaped the closeness of her headdress. Tom guessed she was in her late fifties, but her skin was remarkably wrinkle free, except right around her eyes, where there were some crinkly laugh lines.

"Some years ago, indeed," she laughed. "And how is the dear Father?"

Tom's face stiffened, and he lowered his eyes. Without him saying anything, Sister Mary knew the answer to her question. She bowed her head slightly and crossed herself, then raised her eyes and asked, "How long has the dear Father been at rest?"

"He died shortly before I left New York, Sister. It was a heart attack, in September, I believe."

"Such a kind-hearted man he was, Mr. Callahan, but I'm certain if you knew him, you'd be aware of that." Her face brightened again, and she resumed her smile. "What assistance can I provide to you, Mr. Callahan?"

"Well, Sister, I'm planning to locate here in Salt Lake, and I was hoping that you could direct me to a good boarding house, and perhaps give me an idea about employment in the area."

Sister Mary thought for a moment, then leaned forward. "Mr. Callahan, do you know anything of building maintenance, especially heating systems?"

"I do, Sister," he nodded.

Sister Mary began to stand, and Tom rose as well, his cap still clutched in his hands.

"Well, then, Thomas . . . May I call you Thomas? Let me show you around the hospital. Perhaps we can help each other," she offered.

Later that evening, Tom sat alone in one corner of the hospital cafeteria, finishing his meal. He could scarcely believe his good fortune. A bed in a room in the basement of the building had been made up with fresh sheets and blankets provided by Sister Mary. And he had employment.

He ate slowly, considering his next move. Sister Mary had named him maintenance man at the hospital, and he not only had a place to stay, but meals were included in his wages, and Sister Jude, in charge of the kitchen, had instantly taken him under her wing. All in all, it had been a profitable first day in Salt Lake City.

While Sister Mary presented a kind and considerate demeanor throughout Tom's indoctrination, his stroll with her through the hospital facilities made it evident that she was in tight control of every aspect of the hospital's operation. She imposed particularly stringent rules for the management of the nursing sisters. Tom had taken note of the requirements for the staff that were posted on the nurses' bulletin board. The rules left little room for personal interpretation. The posting read:

VALUES AND PRIORITIES

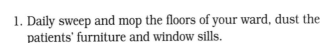

1. Daily sweep and mop the floors of your ward, dust the patients' furniture and window sills.

2. Maintain an even temperature in your ward by bringing in a scuttle of coal for the day's business.

3. Light is important to observe the patients' condition. Therefore, each day fill kerosene lamps, clean chimneys, and trim wicks. Wash the windows once a week.

4. The nurse's notes are important in aiding the physician's work. Make your pens carefully, you may whittle nibs to your individual taste.

5. Each nurse on day duty will report every day at 7 A.M. and leave at 8 P.M. except on the Sabbath on which day you will be off from 12 noon to 2 P.M.

6. Graduate nurses in good standing with the director of
   nurses will be given an evening off each week for
   courting purposes or two evenings a week if you
   regularly go to church.

7. Each nurse should lay aside from each pay day a
   goodly sum of her earnings for her benefits during her
   declining years so that she will not become a burden.
   For example, if you earn $30 a month, you should set
   aside $15.

8. Any nurse who smokes, uses liquor in any form, gets
   her hair done at a beauty shop or frequents dance
   halls will give the director of nurses good reason to
   suspect her worth, intentions, and integrity.

9. The nurse who performs her labors and serves her
   patients and doctors faithfully and without fault for a
   period of five years will be given an increase by the
   hospital administration of five cents a day providing
   there are no hospital debts that are outstanding.

Reading the list, Tom was grateful he had not the incli-
nation to become a nurse and felt somewhat sorry for those
who had. Now that he had met with Sister Mary, it was first
things first, he thought. And, following procurement of a
job and lodging, there was only one thing remaining.
Katrina Hansen. For the first time in some months, life
looked good.

For the first ten days at Holy Cross, each evening after
work, Tom either walked down the hill toward the Temple
Square or took the trolley that ran along First South toward
town, intent on finding out as much as he could about the
community and hoping to find a lead on where the Hansens
might have located. It would not have been difficult to find
the Hansens in Salt Lake City, but Tom had not confided
his plans in anyone. He wanted to go about that part of his
quest in his own way.

One other thought had privately crossed his mind

during the first days at Holy Cross. Almost a year had gone by since Katrina had agreed to wait for him. Tom actually found himself fearing that since she was only sixteen, it might have been a romantic whimsy that brought her to such a hasty agreement. Had she waited? Would she even remember who he was? Was there someone else who had noticed the blossoming beauty within the young girl?

The thought even crossed his mind that maybe the Hansens had not even made it to Utah. Katrina had said that they had relatives in Chicago, but Tom had not thought to stop there. But if they had not come all the way to Utah, then what? Back to New York?

Many of the homes he passed along South Temple or First South were reminiscent of the estates owned by the landed gentry in Ireland. The more successful folk, it seemed, made their residences in that area, which made his walk past their homes pleasant enough, but also brought to mind the gap between himself and Katrina Hansen's family. Where did they live, he thought, and what kind of home would Mr. Hansen have obtained? Certainly more than Tom could offer Katrina, which at the moment, he mused, was next to nothing. He tried to imagine how it would sound to invite a wife to join him in the custodian's quarters of Holy Cross Hospital. It was unthinkable, and the thought depressed him.

While sitting in a café one evening, during his second week in Salt Lake City, Tom picked up a discarded copy of the *Deseret News* and saw in it an advertisement for Hansen's Fine Furniture. "Lars Hansen, Proprietor," it said. Walking just five blocks south on Main Street, Tom located the store front, now closed for the day. Smiling to himself, he looked briefly through the front window at the furniture displayed on the floor, and determined to come back

135

Saturday during daylight hours and discreetly determine if this was the same Hansen family. He had little doubt that it was, but the idea of just walking up to Katrina after all that time, when he wasn't certain how she felt or what might have happened to her, was not going to be easy. Though he was excited to see her and had in fact thought of little else for many months, in a way he dreaded doing so.

Within one hour the following Saturday, Tom had spied Andy Hansen entering and leaving the store. His first glimpse of Katrina had left him trembling as he watched her from across the street. She followed the European tradition of sweeping the walkways and store frontage, maintaining a tidy area around the approaches to the furniture store. Tom's courage failed him, and he decided not to approach her without preparation.

Tom watched for several hours, and as noon approached, Andy left the store and walked north toward the heart of town. At an intersection, he stepped close to Andy and growled, "Yer money or yer life, lad."

Andy spun around, taking a moment to recognize who had accosted him. "Tom Callahan," he cried, embracing Tom and pounding him on the back. "How did you get here? Where did you come from?" The questions rolled off Andy's tongue as fast as Tom could listen and faster than he could answer.

"If you'll buy me a bit of lunch, I'll spin the tale for ya, Mr. Hansen," Tom teased.

"Certainly, Tom. It's so good to see you again."

Seated in the dining area of the Knutsford House, an imposing eight-story hotel situated on the corner of Third South and State Street, Tom waited patiently as Andy continued to tell of their relocation to Salt Lake and ask questions about Tom's trip west. Tom was careful to omit the

Kansas City incident, but otherwise gave Andy a fairly accurate rendition of the previous eight months.

The primary subject of Tom's interest had not come up as yet, but as Andy's questions diminished, Tom grew silent, waiting to hear. Finally he asked directly.

"Katrina?" he said, softly.

"What?" Andy said.

Tom just looked at him silently waiting for Andy to respond.

"Oh, Katrina. Of course. She's attending university, studying to be a teacher. She's been kept really busy."

"And how might I meet this busy person?" Tom asked, beginning to perceive some reluctance on Andy's part.

Andy shook his head. "She can hardly find time to see me, Tom, and I live in the same house with her."

Tom held Andy's eyes, not speaking, waiting for Andy to cease his evasive answers.

"What's wrong, Andy?"

Andy shook his head, then wiped his mouth with his napkin and set it aside. "She's been seeing someone, Tom."

"Is she seriously involved?"

"Well, I . . . I don't know if even she knows," he replied. "I know Poppa wants her to be serious about him."

"Who is he?"

"His name is Harold Stromberg. He's the missionary who taught our family in Norway, and since he returned home, he has been courting Katrina."

Tom recalled Katrina mentioning Stromberg during their discussions on the boat. "Does she love him, Andy?"

Andy shook his head, unsure how to respond. "I don't know, Tom. Truly, I don't."

"I've got to see her, Andy."

"Tom, I can't . . . they have, well, they have . . . plans."

137

"Plans? Look, Andy," Tom said, reaching across the table and holding Andy's forearm, "I've come a long way and have thought about her for the entire time. If she tells me she's found someone else, I'll not interfere, but I must see her. You have to understand that."

Andy nodded. Then after a few moments of silence, he said softly, "I'll do it, Tom. I owe you that much. Meet me Tuesday evening down at Temple Square, and I'll arrange to have Katrina there. They have concerts in the Tabernacle on Tuesdays, and I'll try to get her to go with me."

"Andy, don't tell her I'm here yet, please. Let me just meet her and speak with her for a few minutes. Can you bring her without this Stromberg fellow coming too?"

"Yes, I can. We often do things together. Tuesday, Tom, about six-thirty on Temple Square."

"Thanks, Andy."

"I don't know if it's good thing for either of you, Tom."

"Aye. Let's just see what happens, Andy."

The sound of the boiler kicking on, in the room immediately adjacent to his small living quarters, brought Tom to his senses abruptly, interrupting the dream he'd been having of the old days in Ireland. For the two weeks, ever since he'd moved into Holy Cross, his sleep had been frequently interrupted by the noisy heating system—but decreasingly so as he got used to it. He figured that, eventually, it would become part of the surrounding noise and he'd be able to sleep right through it.

His thoughts before drifting off had been of the impending meeting with Katrina. However, his subconscious took him back to a more peaceful, less unsure time during his

138

early youth in Ireland—a time before his youthful rambunctiousness had brought him so much trouble.

The light tap on his door would probably not have awakened him had he not already been alert. Quickly standing up, he threw on his trousers, and opened the door. Sister Mary stood there, a sheepish smile on her face.

"Please excuse the lateness of the hour, Mr. Callahan. But might I have a word with you?"

Curious about what she might want, Tom stepped aside and nodded for her to enter. "What time is it, Sister?" he asked, fumbling to light the lamp.

Again she smiled, somewhat embarrassed. "Just past two o'clock, Mr. Callahan. I am truly sorry to bother you, but I have a favor to ask."

Sensing her sincerity, Tom offered her the one chair in the room and then sat down on the edge of his bed. "If I can be of service, Sister," he offered, stifling a yawn.

"First, Mr. Callahan, I must swear you to secrecy. Now I know that must sound intriguing and cause more curiosity than it deserves, however, if you will agree to keep private the mission we are about tonight, I would be ever so grateful."

Tom's nodded his agreement, and waited for Sister Mary to explain.

"Good," she said, standing once again. "I'll meet you in the carriage house behind the hospital in twenty minutes. Kindly hitch up the mare to the buggy. Oh, and dress warmly, Mr. Callahan. It's very cold out tonight. We are likely to be outside for the better part of two hours."

"Sister?" he entreated.

She smiled even more broadly, pausing in the doorway only to say, "I'll explain on the way, Mr. Callahan. Please hurry. We must be finished before dawn." Then in a swoosh of her habit, she was gone. Tom had lingered in his doorway, and part way down the hall, Sister Mary stopped and turned around. "We *will* have to do something about that old boiler, won't we?" she laughed. "Or else we'll have to change the job specifications for our maintenance man to include 'hard of hearing.'"

Tom gave a small wave of acknowledgment, then sat back down on his bed to pull on his socks and lace up his boots. Fifteen minutes later, he was standing outside the rear entrance to the hospital, stomping his feet to get the blood circulating and cupping his hands in front of his mouth to blow warm breath into them. He had already hitched up the mare to the buggy and was waiting for further instructions. Snow covered the ground, and there was a clear, winter night sky overhead.

Sister Mary appeared, carrying a small wooden crate full of groceries. She motioned for Tom to come and help lift several other similar containers from inside the back entrance of the hospital. Together, Tom and Sister Mary quickly loaded a dozen crates into the buggy and then Tom helped her mount the seat before jumping up alongside her. Sister Mary busied herself tucking a large woolen blanket around her legs and unfolding another one for Tom. Wrapping his legs with the blanket, he untied the reins and looked to Sister Mary for instructions. She pointed straight ahead, and they were off into the night, the mare moving smartly, blowing plumes of steam from her nostrils into the cold night air.

Tom's quizzical look elicited another grin from Sister Mary who said only, "West on South Temple, Mr. Callahan. Down toward town and out past the railroad depot, please."

Tom clicked his tongue at the single horse, and the mare settled in to a brisk pace, seemingly glad to have the opportunity to move, now that she had been forced to leave her warm stable. They started down the hill toward town and rode for several blocks without speaking. Tom sensed that Sister Mary would speak when she was ready.

By the time the buggy reached Temple Square, devoid of any sign of life at this hour of the morning, the horse was breathing regularly and the sled runners under the buggy were sliding smoothly across the hard packed layer of snow that blanketed the valley.

"Do you know much about the residents of Salt Lake, Mr. Callahan?" Sister Mary asked.

Tom thought for a minute before responding. "Not really, Sister. Father O'Leary told me a bit about the Mormons' unusual practice of multiple marriage, but he said they were also an honest, hard-working lot. I presume now, that he got that information from you," Tom said, glancing at her.

Sister Mary smiled again, and nodded. "We did correspond over the years. He was right, of course. The people of Salt Lake are as diverse a group as you'll ever find, Mr. Callahan. The great majority of them, like us," she smiled, "are immigrants from Europe. The Mormon missionary program has expanded their numbers greatly over the years since they arrived here. It's been nearly fifty years, Mr. Callahan, since the first settlers entered the valley." The horse continued her gentle plod toward the western edge of downtown Salt Lake, past homes lying dark and quiet.

"They had it hard at first, as do most newcomers to an unsettled area. You and I," she explained, interjecting— "I came out in '77, right after Sister Holy Cross founded the hospital—have it much easier, I can assure you. One has to admire the faith and tenacity it took to follow their leaders and leave behind the comfort of solid homes, businesses, and families. But then, it was hard, too, for some of the 'Gentiles,'" she said, emphasizing the word. "That's what the Mormons call non-Mormons, Mr. Callahan. When the Gentiles came, they felt like 'outsiders,' but eventually, as their numbers grew, it became increasingly apparent that the Mormons were not to have this valley to themselves. After some bitter struggles, especially over the past twenty years as politics have played an increasingly larger part in the affairs of the community, an accommodation of sorts has been reached. Admission to the Union is a kind of culmination for Mormon and Gentile alike—it's something both sides have wanted for a long time."

Tom continued to listen, content to drive the buggy as he learned a bit of history. "And the Church, Sister?" he asked. "If the Mormons settled this valley, how did the Catholic Church come to be here?"

"We go where there is need, Mr. Callahan," she smiled, watching him. "And Bishop Scanlan, assigned here from California, is a most dedicated servant of our Lord." Tom nodded quietly. "Head north on the next street, Mr. Callahan," she instructed as they approached yet another intersection. "The third house on the right. Just stop for a moment and we'll leave one of these parcels."

Tom pulled back gently on the reins, hopped down, and came around to assist Sister Mary as she climbed down from the seat. "This one, Mr. Callahan," she said, indicating one of the wooden crates, which Tom took from the back of the buggy. "In case you're wondering, it's food we're delivering about tonight."

Tom grunted, following her up the walk, trudging through the snow that had drifted into several piles a couple of feet deep around the house. "Right here will do nicely, Mr. Callahan, thank you very much."

They quickly resumed their seats on the buggy and headed farther up the street, stopping where Sister Mary indicated and dropping off the boxes. After a number of additional stops, their last parcel was gone. "Back to a warm bed, Mr. Callahan," she laughed, as Tom started the mare toward South Temple and the gentle climb back toward the hospital.

"Remember now, Mr. Callahan. This night's work is just between us."

"Then these families would be some of our Catholic neighbors, Sister?" he queried.

She turned to look at him, her eyes sparkling in the crisp early morning starlight. "I'd not be knowing, Mr. Callahan."

"Sister?" Tom said, a quizzical expression on his face.

She smiled broadly again, pulling the blanket around her and tucking it in behind her knees. "We do God's work, Mr. Callahan, wherever it is needed."

Tom continued to drive the buggy east, again past Temple Square and up the hill toward the hospital. "Sister, I'm a bit confused. With the Church . . ."

"Mr. Callahan," she interrupted, "we have, as I indicated earlier, reached an accommodation of sorts in this valley. You'll come to understand that, and to appreciate the need for each of us to do what we can. Continually, we have new immigrants, and our population grows constantly. God's work knows no boundaries. In answer to my prayers, God has never asked me where the people attend church, and I am pleased to serve Him where and how I can.

"Let me tell you something, Mr. Callahan. God sent you to us for a purpose. I knew that the moment you entered Holy Cross Hospital. I don't know why, and I can see, neither do you. But in good time, Mr. Callahan, He will reveal himself unto you. Until then, we are pleased to have your services."

Tom drove silently for a few minutes, his thoughts flitting back to Katrina's comment about the Lord's purposes for him, and how she would not be concerned about his welfare. "And if that direction leads toward the Mormon way, Sister?" he asked, turning to see her face in the moonlight.

"As I said, Mr. Callahan, they are good people."

Tom pulled up to the entrance of the hospital and assisted Sister Mary down from the seat. "As are you, Sister. Thank you for allowing me to assist," Tom said.

She reached for and held his hand momentarily as she parted. "It is an elderly Mormon gentleman who provides us the food, Mr. Callahan," she smiled. "And he doesn't ask who receives it. We all work together for the common good. Twice a week we shall make these distributions, God willing."

"Count on me, Sister. It will be my pleasure to help."

"Thank you, Mr. Callahan. And God's blessings to you," she said, leaving Tom to unhitch and stable the horse and to contemplate the evening's work.

Ye knew when ye sent me here, didn't ye, Father O'Leary? Aye, that ye did.

10

Tom saw Katrina and Andy before either of them spotted him. Standing off to the side of the temple building, Tom allowed them to pass before stepping out onto the foot path. He followed at a distance and watched as several groups of people greeted the couple. A number of young men in particular made certain to say hello to her, and Tom saw that Katrina had apparently become popular. He noted that she carried herself confidently, and it suddenly became very apparent to him that there was a broad social gap between him and the vivacious young woman. It occurred to him how little he had to offer her, and he briefly considered turning around and leaving.

Though she was clearly the same young woman he had known, standing now only a few feet from Katrina, Tom experienced a strange sensation that he didn't know her, that she bore little resemblance to the woman whose image he had entertained in his mind for nearly a year. And now that she was within reach, he hesitated, not certain how to proceed. Still, he had worked hard to achieve this moment, and the Irish in him gave him the determination to see it through. He hurried to catch Anders and Katrina, and as the couple approached the entrance to the Tabernacle, he closed to a few feet, and spoke softly.

"Katie?"

At the sound of her name, she turned. A look of astonishment turned to pleasure as she recognized Tom. She had imagined for so long what it might be like if he ever came. She had pictured herself running into his arms, but now she didn't know how to react. She just stood there, looking into his face with amazement and clinging to her brother's arm. Then tears began to well up in her eyes, and she didn't trust herself to speak, even if she had known what to say.

Tom moved closer, smiled at her, and reached without looking away from Katrina to shake Andy's hand. For several moments Tom and Katrina stood looking at one another, while Andy stood by, nervously shifting his weight from one foot to the other.

"'Tis a vision of loveliness I see this evening," Tom finally said, trying to grin but not succeeding very well.

Katrina recognized the first words Tom ever spoke to her, standing together on the deck of the *Antioch* that first morning at sea. But she still stood speechless, trying to gather her senses and continuing to cling tightly to Andy's arm.

"May we have a few moments, Andy?" Tom finally asked, shifting his gaze to Anders. "I'd like to walk with Katie for a while."

Andy looked at Katrina. She let go of her brother's arm and somewhat tentatively took hold of Tom's.

"I'll meet you here after the concert, Klinka," Andy said.

The couple walked to the north, toward the gated exit from Temple Square, and then turned west on North Temple as they left the temple grounds. They walked without speaking for a minute or two, following the outer

146

perimeter of Temple Square and mingling with those headed for the concert.

"You look well, Thomas," Katrina finally said.

"As do you, Katie. Utah seems to have been well suited for your new home. Andy tells me you are attending the university, training to be a teacher."

"Yes," she smiled. "I really enjoy my studies. How about you, Thomas? What have you been up to this past year?"

Tom laughed—a hearty laugh that answered Katrina's question almost without words.

"Finding your way to Utah, I guess," she said, embarrassed. "And when did you arrive?"

"I got to Salt Lake the day of statehood," he replied. "I was in Ogden for a day or two before that, finishing up some work."

"You've been here that long?" she asked.

Not knowing quite how to defend himself, Tom didn't answer immediately. Then he said, "I've been busy getting settled. I didn't know for a while whether or not you were actually living here."

Katrina scarcely heard Tom's reply. Her mind had gone back to statehood day and Harold's proposal of marriage. She'd been in constant turmoil since then. Now her worst fear and her strongest desire had come face to face. Tom had, indeed, come. But he had arrived too late. Just three days earlier, while on a horse-drawn sleigh ride with Harold, he had asked Katrina if she had given his proposal due consideration. She had made him almost deliriously happy by simply saying, "Yes, Harold. I will marry you." Now, she was firmly caught between both of them. A promise to one, and a promise to the other. The realization of what she had done brought a sudden feeling of embarrassment, that bordered on panic. She didn't know what to say, and they walked in silence for a while longer.

"Have you found a place to stay and work?"

"Aye. I live and work at Holy Cross Hospital, up on Tenth East. It's a good situation for me. Sister Mary Theophane, who hired me, is a wonderful person and a good friend."

Katrina nodded as they continued to walk around the square, cutting through the center a couple of times and reversing their path. After nearly an hour and a half of conversation about Utah, Salt Lake City, and other pleasantries, Tom led Katrina to a bench north of the temple, where they sat together for a few moments without speaking.

Tom broke the silence. "I've not forgotten you, Katie. Not for a moment this past year. But Anders has told me that someone else has entered your life."

Katrina looked down at her feet, uncertain how to answer. Not wanting to hurt Tom, and not entirely certain of her own feelings, she had no reply.

"It's not my intent to cause you worry, Katie, or to interfere in your life if indeed you've found someone else. But I know from your face when I first spoke to you tonight, that you were glad to see me. Surprised, but glad. Do we have the time to finish what we started on the boat? Do we have the time to see what fate has in store for us, Katie?"

"Oh, Thomas, I'm so confused. I waited and prayed for you to come for so long, and then I didn't know if you would. I just didn't know what to do. Poppa wanted me to . . . , well, he hoped I would find someone and get married, but I was angered by his insistence. I suppose Anders has told you about Mr. Stromberg?" she asked.

"Some," Tom said.

"He really is a nice man, Thomas," she offered, biting her lip as she realized that a litany of Harold Stromberg's good traits were of no interest to Tom.

Tom remained quiet for several minutes. "Will I not have the chance to see you, then, Katie?"

"Thomas, Harold has asked me to marry him. In fact, he's asked several times over the past few months."

"And what was your answer, Katie?"

"Oh, Thomas," she whimpered, the tears now overflowing her eyes. "I . . . , I've given him my answer. I told him I would marry him." Rushing her words to finish her explanation, she continued, "I didn't know if you would come, Thomas, and Christmas came and the year was up, and . . ."

Tom stood abruptly, leaving Katrina seated, tears now freely flowing down her cheeks. "I do understand, Katie. Perhaps it's best I go. I didn't come to Utah to disrupt your life. If you have found someone else, maybe we should each get on with our lives."

"Thomas, do you see this temple behind us? You just asked me if we had time to see what fate had in store for us. I want to know what the Lord has in store for me, Thomas. I told you on the boat that I was concerned about my religion too, and . . ."

"I understand, Katie, I truly do." He didn't intend it, but he sounded curt. A hollow ache in his chest threatened to bring on tears of his own, and he wanted to leave.

People were beginning to exit the Tabernacle, and as Anders came out of the building, he spotted Tom and Katrina and began walking toward them. Not wishing to put on a happy front and afraid he would not be able to mask his emotions, Tom said, "I'll say good-bye now, Katie. Andy is coming."

Tom turned to leave, waving briefly to Andy and

heading quickly for the north entrance to Temple Square. By the time Andy reached Katrina, Tom was just rounding the gate post. He looked back briefly before disappearing behind the wall.

Without speaking to Andy, Katrina jumped to her feet and ran to the gate.

"Thomas, please, wait. Thomas!" Clearing the gate, she turned east in the direction Tom had gone. He stopped and turned to face her.

"Oh, Thomas, I do care for you. Truly I do, and I am so sorry for the trouble I have caused. When you suddenly appeared tonight, it was as if all my concerns had surfaced at once. Can you understand?"

He reached out to touch her hair and looked into her eyes. He was smiling sadly. "Katie, the Lord has a purpose for us all, Catholic and Mormon, and we must follow our hearts in whatever direction He leads us. I'm sure He knows your heart, too. I told you I didn't attend Church, but I never said I didn't believe in Him. Sister Mary has . . . Look, Katie, I'd best say good-bye now," he whispered, feeling his eyes beginning to water.

"Oh, Thomas, I'm so sorry. Please understand."

"I do, Katie, and I'll never forget you, or your loveliness," he said, gently stroking her cheek with the back of his hand. "God's blessings on ye, Katie, me darlin'."

21 *January 1896*

Dear Nana,

My heart is pounding so hard tonight, Nana, that I can scarcely breath. He's come. Thomas has come to Utah. I knew the moment I saw him again that I love

150

*him. I love him, Nana. I love him with all
my heart, but I have agreed to marry
Harold. Oh, please help me, Nana.
Jeg elske deg,*

Katrina

On St. Patrick's day, March seventeenth, Sister Mary and a couple of the nursing sisters surprised Tom by decorating his room in the basement of the hospital. Coming back that afternoon from an errand Sister Mary had contrived to get him out of the hospital, he went to his room to pick up some tools and found various green and gold decorations covering the walls. The picture of the river Shannon flowing gently through County Limerick's countryside stopped Tom dead in his tracks, and he stood staring at it.

The light tap on his door broke his thought, and he quickly wiped the tears from his cheeks before opening the door.

"Happy St. Paddy's day, Thomas Matthew Callahan," Sister Mary exclaimed. Sister Mary immediately sensed something was wrong, and she stifled her enthusiasm as she tried to discern Tom's mood. Stepping into the room, she closed the door behind her.

"Thomas, what is it? What's wrong?"

"Aw, 'tis nothin', Sister," he said, turning away and moving a few things on his make-shift dresser. "Just a bit of homesickness, I guess."

Sister Mary took the single chair, placed it against the door, and took a seat.

"Mr. Callahan, I've noticed lately, and so have several

of the nursing sisters, that you've been rather quiet—not your usual self. Is it something you'd care to talk about?"

"Sister, you've got more to worry about than the foolish whims of yer maintenance man."

"Is that what you think you are, Thomas? Our *maintenance* man?"

He turned to look at her and saw she was smiling in a kindly way at him. "Thomas, I have always been proud of Holy Cross Hospital, and taking nothing from the good people at the other hospitals in Salt Lake, I think we give the best care in Utah to our patients. But I want to tell you, Thomas, that since you've come to live and work with us, Holy Cross has taken on a new air. You've brought us a feeling of joy, of enthusiasm, aye, even of humor. And that's not an easy thing to do in a hospital, where people are often dying.

"Please, sit down for a moment," she said, motioning to his bed. Tom complied. "All the nursing sisters, Sister Jude, Sister Josephine, Sister Thomasina, . . . I could go on and on. All of them, Thomas, at one time or another, over the past two months, have taken occasion to express to me how they feel about you and the wonderful contribution you are making to Holy Cross. It's a rare thing you have, and you are loved here. Don't you feel that, Thomas?"

Sister Mary sat silently, waiting for his response. Finally, Tom raised his eyes and saw in her face the love and concern she had just expressed. Aside from his mother, no one had ever said such a thing to him, and Sister Mary's words, coming as they did at this low point in his life, touched his sentimental Irish heart in a particularly tender way.

"Sister Mary," he mumbled, "I don't know what to say." But say something, he did. He poured out the whole story: The pain he had felt when leaving Ireland; meeting Katrina on board ship; the struggle he had made to find his way to Utah; and the crushing disappointment he had experienced when Katrina told him she was already engaged to be married. He lamented the fates that had made Katrina a Mormon and Tom a Catholic, blaming Katrina's domineering father for driving her into a marriage she did not want.

Sister Mary had known much of the story. During their midnight charitable forays, Tom had said enough for her to know more about him than he suspected. What he hadn't disclosed, she had surmised.

"In all fairness to her, Sister, she didn't know if I'd ever make it to Utah, and her father pushed her toward this other fellow," Tom said, dropping his face into his hands.

"And today, of all days, St. Paddy's day, I see the notice of her wedding in the paper. In two weeks she'll . . ." Tom lowered his head again, while Sister Mary sat with her hands folded in her lap, quietly assessing the situation.

After a time, she said, "Thomas, whom do you love?"

He raised his head. "I don't understand."

"As we sit here, at this moment, of all the people in the world, whom do you love?"

Tom thought for a few moments, his hands clasped together, the fingers rubbing each other in a massaging motion. "My family?"

"Will you ever see them again?"

"I don't know."

"What if you don't?" she said. "Will you still love them?"

"Well, I guess so. Yeah, of course I will," he stated, more emphatically.

"Do you love *me*, Thomas?" She was looking at him earnestly, a kindly smile lighting up her face.

"You're a *sister*, Sister," he laughed.

Her smile dissolved into a serious expression. "Yes, Thomas, I am a nursing sister. But do you love me?"

"I guess I do. In a different sort of way. You've been very kind to me."

"Thank you, Thomas. I appreciate that. And I'm glad you love me, Mr. Thomas Matthew Callahan, because I must tell you, as we sit here in the quiet of your room, that I most certainly love you."

He looked at her again, unsure how to respond. "Thomas," she went on, "there are many kinds of love, and our Lord and Savior loved everyone—even those who nailed him to the cross. He *loved* them, Thomas, and he asked his Father to forgive them, even as they brutalized him. His love wasn't based on the actions of others toward him. It was unconditional.

"I know the loss of love is very painful, Thomas. But love is only lost, if you let it go. Do you really love this girl? Can you keep loving her, Thomas?"

"What do you mean, Sister?"

"I mean that if you keep loving her and the memory of her, especially the things she inspired in you, then you needn't lose her love, even if she becomes someone else's wife. You can love the wonderful things you found in her, and, privately in your heart, you can treasure them."

"But, Sister, I wanted to *marry* her," he said.

"I know, Thomas," she said, softly and compassionately. "And that may not happen, but if you become bitter, if you let your disappointment destroy the love you feel for her, then both *your* happiness, and possibly *hers*, if she knows how you feel, will be affected. Can you understand that? Let her be happy, Thomas. Love her enough to let her be happy."

154

Tom nodded, though he wasn't certain he fully understood what Sister Mary had told him.

"We'll talk more about this later, Thomas. I know how important it is to you. But for now," she stood, removing the chair and placing it against the wall, "several of the sisters have prepared a cake and punch treat for dear ole' St. Paddy. They're quite excited that we now have our own resident 'Paddy'—that's you, Thomas—" she laughed. "They're hoping you will join us. Will you?"

"Aye, Sister," he said, standing and running his fingers through his hair, managing to affect a sad smile. "Aye, that I will." Hesitating, he then said, "I *do* love you, Sister Mary. Thank you for caring." He looked down, embarrassed to say the words, but strongly feeling the emotion.

"Thomas, as I'm sure Father O'Leary, bless his soul, told you, that's the business we're in, and fortunately, our joy. Now let's go try some of that cake."

11

Magnus Stromberg Jr. was born in Salt Lake City in the summer of 1848, the first year after his father, Magnus Stromberg, arrived with one of the earliest companies of pioneer settlers. Raised in the harsh and difficult early years of valley settlement, Magnus Jr. learned the hard lessons of life, but under the tutelage of his father, he became a staunch member of the Church and an outspoken supporter of the Prophet and of the Brethren.

Young Magnus was encouraged by his father and several prominent Church leaders to develop his considerable, God-given intellectual abilities, and by 1872, Magnus had returned to Salt Lake City from Yale University with a prestigious law degree. Joining a prosperous law firm in Salt Lake City, Magnus married Harriet Cumberland, the senior partner's daughter, early in 1873, and practiced law for the next eight years, becoming a partner after just three years. Harold Stromberg, their first child, was born in December, 1873, and when the boy was only six, his father responded to a call to serve a mission to Wales. His willingness to set aside his growing law practice and his young family, though such a sacrifice was not thought unusual in the Mormon community, was evidence of his commitment to the Church and loyalty to the Brethren.

Over the years, Cumberland, Stottle, & Stromberg became one of Salt Lake City's premier law firms, representing banking interests in Utah, as well as affiliate financial interests on the east and west coasts. When the elder Cumberland died, and his original partner, Frederick Stottle, became disaffected with the Church, Magnus Stromberg bought out Stottle's shares, and by 1886, Stromberg, together with his new partner, Jacob Thorensen, represented clients from throughout the western United States. Along the way, Magnus Stromberg Jr. had become a highly respected and influential member of the community, while continuing to be a devoted member of the Church.

Harold Stromberg's return in 1895 from his mission to Scandinavia and his enrollment at the University of Utah, was all part of his father's plan to see the continuation of the law firm of Stromberg, Thorensen, & Stromberg. Harold's pending marriage to Katrina Hansen would provide the young man just the kind of responsibilities his father felt Harold would need to ensure his professional and spiritual growth.

Magnus Stromberg's lasting desire, however, was that the Church follow the will of the Lord in the matter of plural marriage. He had understood the political expediency of the issuing of the Manifesto, but with statehood now securely in hand, he had no doubt the Prophet would reinstate "the principle" as a matter of official or unofficial Church policy and practice. The will of the Lord could now be carried out by His people.

That assurance, and a strong desire to help the process along, was the reason behind the meeting Magnus Stromberg had arranged for early one morning in March,

1896. With statehood now an accomplished fact and General Conference scheduled to begin the following week, Magnus was certain that President Wilford Woodruff would reinstate the Principle and all would be right again in Zion.

"Good morning, Sister Adams. I believe I have an appointment this morning with President Cannon," Stromberg said, entering President George Q. Cannon's home, which was situated two blocks west of Temple Square.

"And a good morning to you, Brother Stromberg. The President is just meeting with one of the Brethren. I'm sure he'll be right with you. Please, have a seat."

"Thank you," he said.

George Q. Cannon served as First Counselor to President Wilford Woodruff in the First Presidency of the Church, the senior ruling body that, together with the Quorum of the Twelve Apostles, determined the policies of The Church of Jesus Christ of Latter-day Saints. In earlier years, President Cannon had been a fugitive from justice and was briefly imprisoned for practicing plural marriage in violation of federal laws forbidding it.

The Church's practice of polygamy isolated the Church and angered many in the United States, but none more than those congressmen and senators who opposed Utah's quest for statehood. Along with the institution of slavery, polygamy was popularly referred to by the enemies of the Church as one of the "twin relics of barbarism." The Church was also viewed nationally with suspicion for what was perceived as the exercise of inordinate influence in the affairs of Utah government.

In Magnus Stromberg's mind, the Manifesto, in which President Woodruff declared the end of the practice of polygamy, was but a capitulation to mobocrats, notwithstanding their congressional titles. Now that statehood had been achieved, he felt that error could be rectified. And the sooner the better, Stromberg thought. The Church had endured enough government intervention. It was time for the will of the Lord to be upheld.

"Good morning, Brother Stromberg," President Cannon said, wrapping a huge embrace around his old friend. A large man, whose silver hair curled around the edges of his gentle face, President Cannon was beloved by his people and by those of his household. A publisher by trade, Cannon had founded in 1866 a retail bookstore and publishing house that did business under the name George Q. Cannon & Sons.

"And what brings you to my humble home this beautiful morning, Magnus?" Cannon smiled.

"Just a friendly visit, President, and one long overdue, I'm afraid. I haven't taken the opportunity to shake your hand since statehood became a reality. I'm most appreciative of the role you played in our success."

"It was a long time coming, Magnus. A very long time," Cannon said, motioning for Stromberg to take a seat.

"And how is Frank progressing toward becoming our United States Senator, President?" Stromberg asked, aware that President Cannon's son, Frank, was a prime prospect for appointment.

Cannon smiled broadly. "It seems the state legislature thinks he's the man."

"Good. Very good. Anything that my law firm can do to assist, President, you know we're only too glad to help."

"Thank you, Magnus," Cannon offered. "That's reassuring. And your son, Harold, is about to be married, so I hear."

"Indeed he is. To a lovely girl from a new family. The Hansens from Norway. A family he baptized, I might add."

160

"Fine thing, Magnus. Wonderful news. So," he said, "what can I do for you this morning on the eve of our first general conference since statehood?"

Stromberg smiled a wide, happy smile. "We're in, President. After all the bickering, infighting, and opposition from all quarters, even the Gentiles agreed with us that it was time for statehood. How does the President see it?" Stromberg queried, referring to President Woodruff.

"He's very pleased, Magnus. He believes that now the people can get on with their lives, turn their hearts toward the Lord and go on about His work."

"Exactly," Magnus Stromberg stated, rising and crossing to the window of Cannon's front room office. "I couldn't have said it better myself. That's a wonderful piece of news, President."

Turning to look at Cannon, Stromberg said, "So, we might expect some formal announcement from President Woodruff on the matter in conference?"

"Announcement?" Cannon said.

"Perhaps not an announcement, but some . . . clarification maybe," Stromberg offered. "I can imagine that you, of all people will be most relieved. Your steadfastness in keeping the Principle has been an inspiration to us all. I am heartily pleased that you will now profit from its reinstatement. It will be a blessing for your family, George."

Cannon rose and came to stand alongside Stromberg at the window. They were about the same height and they stood now, eye to eye. "I don't follow, Brother Stromberg. What reinstatement?"

"Well, . . . the President . . . the Manifesto. I mean, I've supposed there will be some kind of declaration of the Church's intent, but perhaps only an informal understanding is to be given."

161

President Cannon looked away then moved back to his desk. Taking his seat, he leaned back in his chair and folded his hands comfortably on his ample stomach. Stromberg followed him from the window and stood in front of the desk.

"President?" Stromberg asked, leaning forward and seeking confirmation of his assessment.

President Cannon leaned forward. "I mean no offense, Brother Stromberg, but you are mistaken. President Woodruff intends to do nothing more than what the Lord has already given him to understand. There is to be no modification of the principles stated in the Manifesto."

Stromberg was stunned. Embarrassed by the reprimand and confused by President Cannon's refusal to acknowledge what needed to be done, Stromberg was for the moment speechless.

"Magnus," Cannon said, rising and coming around to the front of his desk to stand next to the attorney, "we *are* following the will of the Lord. He has spoken and President Woodruff has declared the direction the Church *must* take. There is to be no announcement to the contrary."

"And the rest of us—those families who have already left for Mexico and exile?"

Cannon smiled. "They're not in exile, Magnus. They've formed another branch of the Church and are furthering the process of expansion that Brother Brigham initiated so long ago. They are fully in accord with the Manifesto and intend to remain so."

"But I thought . . ." Stromberg began.

President Cannon assumed a serious expression, stepped forward, and placed his hands on Stromberg's shoulders. Looking tenderly into his friend's eyes, he said, "President Woodruff has been shown what would have befallen the

Church had we not ceased the practice, and the *Lord* is the author of that revelation."

Stromberg was not convinced. "Perhaps I need to see the President and discuss the matter. It seems so clear what has happened. The way has been opened to put things right. We needn't let the government dictate how we live our religion."

Cannon's eyes grew stern and his voice firm. "There is no need to steady the ark, Magnus. It is in good hands."

Stromberg turned and headed for the door, pausing in the opening just long enough to smile back at his longtime friend and say, "Let us not part in anger, President. I have only the best feelings for you. And, please, give my regards to young Frank. I hope his senatorial bid goes well."

"Thank you, Magnus. And a good day to you."

25 April 1896

Dear Nana,

I never imagined getting married without you here. Today I will marry Harold Stromberg and will leave Poppa's house. I am very frightened, Nana, but excited too. Harold's father, Magnus Stromberg, seems a nice man, and has kindly welcomed me into his family. Our two families had a formal dinner at the Stromberg home on Wednesday. Mother and Father Stromberg, (that's what they want me to call them, Nana) gave me a lovely china set for a wedding present. Harold has

163

obtained a nice house not too far from Poppa's.

It is only four-thirty in the morning, Nana, and the household is fast asleep. In six hours, at ten-thirty on this Saturday morning, I will enter the Lord's temple and receive my endowments, and when I leave, I will be Mrs. Harold Cumberland Stromberg. Harold is a good man, Nana, and I know he will care for me. I will do all I can to make him a good wife.

Be with me, Nana. Yeg elske deg,

Trina

P.S. I do love Harold, and I know he loves me.

As the horse trudged slowly up South Temple Street, Tom let her have her head. The clear, springtime night sky was blanketed with stars, made more bright by the absence of the moon. It was dark, but the mare had no trouble finding her way. She had become as used to these early morning deliveries of food as Tom had.

"Seven families will eat better tomorrow, Sister," Tom said.

"They will, indeed. And how are you eating, Thomas?"

"Sister?" he asked.

Sister Mary Theophane remained quiet, waiting for Tom to answer her query.

"I'm eating fine, Sister. And I'm feeling fine."

She raised her eyebrows, and looked at him a moment longer, exercising the skill that enabled her to entice a person to talk freely without her having to probe for information.

Tom raised his hands in his defense, holding on to the reins in the process. "Really, Sister."

"And food for the soul, Thomas?"

"Ah, c'mon, Sister. I'm doin' the best I can."

"I know you are, Thomas. But have you given any further thought to what we discussed on St. Patrick's Day?"

Leaning forward with his elbows resting on his knees, Tom clicked his tongue at the mare and slapped the reins, urging her up the hill. "I'd rather not love someone, Sister Mary, who doesn't love me."

"That's an understandable feeling," she said. "But, Thomas, if we were all able—"

"Sister, someone's walking up ahead," Tom interrupted, as the horse continued to plod along. In the early morning mist, Tom could make out what looked like a man and a child walking at a brisk pace in the shadow of the trees on the side of the road. As the buggy pulled even, they turned, the man taking care to keep the young boy away from the road and out of the path of the horse.

"May we be of some assistance, sir," Sister Mary offered.

"Thank you, Ma'am," the man responded, "but we're not far from where we're going."

Tom thought there was something familiar about the man. "D.O.?"

The man approached the buggy, smiling as he recognized Tom. "Mr. Callahan? A most unusual time and place to meet, I'd say."

"Can we help you, D.O.?"

"Well, this young lad here came to roust me out of bed.

165

His uncle is ill. I'm just going to see if I can be of some assistance."

Sister Mary looked at Tom. "I'm sorry, Sister. D.O., this is Sister Mary Theophane from Holy Cross Hospital. Sister, this is David McKay, a friend I met on the day I arrived in Salt Lake."

D.O. removed his hat. "My pleasure to meet you, Sister."

"Mr. McKay, if we wouldn't be intruding, lift the young lad up and we'll give you a ride to your friend's home."

"Thank you, Sister, that would be most kind. He lives about four blocks up the hill, and half block down Eighth East."

Lifting the boy up and climbing aboard himself, D.O. sat down on the backseat of the surrey. "Have you settled in well, Tom?" he asked.

"Well," Tom laughed, "Sister Mary was just asking me the same thing, in a different way. I guess I could say I'm comfortable. I've been worse," he laughed again.

"We'll have to get together for that dinner I spoke of."

"I'd like that, D.O. South on Eighth East, you said?"

"Yes. About halfway down the block, on the right side."

Tom reined in the mare in front of the only house on the street showing any lights. "Hurry, Brother McKay," the young lad said as he hopped down from the surrey. "Uncle Robert's bad sick."

"Let's go see what we can do," D.O. offered, taking the young boy's hand, stopping only to thank Sister Mary and Tom for the ride.

Sister Mary spoke up. "Mr. McKay, might I be of some assistance, please? I *am* a trained nurse."

D.O. paused for a moment, then said, "That would be very helpful, Sister." He stepped back to the buggy and offered his hand as she descended from the seat. Sister Mary looked briefly at Tom, who waved her on. "I'll just stay here with the mare, Sister. You go ahead with D.O."

Inside the house, a young woman in her late twenties sat by the bedside of a man who was perspiring and writhing in pain. The young woman had been wiping the man's face with a wet cloth, but she stood when D.O. appeared. The man on the bed looked to be in agony. He raised one hand in greeting but said nothing as he continued to roll from side to side, groaning as he did so. The young woman gave D.O. a questioning look as she glanced quickly back and forth between McKay and Sister Mary.

"Sister Thurston," D.O. said, "this is Sister Mary from Holy Cross Hospital. She was kind enough to pick us up and give us a ride. She's a nurse at the hospital and asked if she could help. Sister Mary, these are the Thurstons, Robert and Alice." D.O. bent over Robert to see if he could determine what was wrong with his friend.

Alice Thurston's face was pinched with worry, and she said to D.O., "He's been like this since bedtime last night. He's got a fever too. I haven't known what to do."

Sister Mary stepped to the other side of the bed and leaned over Robert. "May I?" she asked as she put her hand to his forehead then reached for his wrist to take his pulse. Her professional demeanor was evident.

"What seems to be the complaint, Mr. Thurston?" she asked.

Robert Thurston tried to rise, his desire to be courteous outweighing his discomfort. Sister Mary smiled, and gently pressed his shoulder down against the bed. "Perhaps it would be best if you remained at rest, Mr. Thurston. Where is the pain?" she asked.

"In his lower abdomen," his wife responded for him. "He's been sick to his stomach almost all night too."

167

Sister Mary looked at his midsection, covered by the bed clothes. "May I?" she asked again, placing her hand lightly on the blanket. Robert nodded, gritting his teeth.

Sister Mary turned back the covers, allowing Robert a modicum of privacy as she did so. Pressing gently on his lower abdomen, she watched his face as she released the pressure. He grimaced and groaned out loud.

"Ummm," she murmured, glancing over at D.O. Tom had come into the house and was standing in the doorway to the bedroom, watching the situation develop. "He needs a doctor to confirm, Mr. McKay, but I believe Mr. Thurston has appendicitis and should immediately be taken to a hospital. We are very close to Holy Cross, and I know Doctor Benedict, a fine surgeon, is remaining overnight to observe a very ill patient. He is an excellent doctor, and has performed other appendectomies."

D.O. turned to look at Alice Thurston, whose concern had increased as she listened to Sister Mary's diagnosis. Alice looked to D.O. for direction.

"Holy Cross will be excellent, Sister. May I have a few moments with Brother Thurston? And then, Tom," he said, turning toward the door, "perhaps you could help me get Robert into the buggy."

Sister Mary rose from the bedside and exited the room, motioning Tom to come with her and closing the door behind them. D.O. and Alice remained in the room with Robert.

Tom was curious at the delay. "Sister?"

"I believe Mr. McKay is going to give a priesthood blessing to his friend. I don't think it will take long," she smiled.

"A priesthood blessing? Is D.O. a priest?"

"Not as you understand it, Thomas, but as I told you,

I've been here nearly twenty years. I'll explain later. Let's get a few blankets and have the buggy ready."

"Right, Sister."

Later, as dawn began to lighten the hallway through the hospital windows, D.O. and Tom were sitting with Alice Thurston outside the surgery as Doctor Benedict walked toward them, a tired smile fixed on his face. "He'll be fine now, Mrs. Thurston. He just needs a few days to rest, and he'll be fine."

"May I see him, Doctor, please?" she asked.

"Of course. He's still sleeping, but you may go in and sit with him if you wish."

Sister Mary took Alice by the arm, and together they entered the room where Robert Thurston was recovering from his overnight surgery.

"D.O., I know just where we need to go," Tom offered. McKay glanced at the young lad sleeping on one of the benches in the corridor. "He'll be fine," Tom said. "The sisters will watch out for him, won't you, Sister," he said, as Sister Josephine walked by and smiled her assurance.

Down the hallway and down one flight of stairs, D.O. found himself escorted into the large kitchen of Holy Cross Hospital.

"If you think Robert got good care upstairs, D.O., you'll be amazed at what Sister Jude performs regularly down here," he laughed. "Ready for a bite of breakfast?"

Sitting together in one corner of the kitchen, Tom and David finished eating their breakfast but sat for a while longer to talk.

Tom said that he couldn't understand the Mormons' reluctance to drink a good, hot cup of coffee.

"It's what gets me going in the morning," Tom explained.

"Yep," D.O. nodded, "and many others, too."

Changing the subject, D.O. said, "You mentioned in the buggy earlier that, 'you've been worse,' I believe were your words. Things not going well for you in Salt Lake?"

Tom took another sip of his coffee. "It's not Salt Lake that's the problem, D.O. It's fine living here. I've just had some personal concerns."

"An affair of the heart, I take it," D.O. said, smiling knowingly.

"Maybe you *are* a priest, after all," Tom joked.

"Excuse me?"

"Sister Mary said you were going to give a blessing of some sort to Mr. Thurston. Now I find you also deal in treating personal problems. Maybe you really *are* a priest," Tom grinned.

D.O. tilted his head back and began to laugh loudly. The sound echoed in the hospital kitchen, and he quickly stifled it, glancing over at Sister Jude and her helper who had looked up from their work. "You could say that, Tom," he said quietly, "but it will take some time to explain it to you. I'd love to have the opportunity, but for now, how can I help?"

"Seems to me you've already done a night's work, D.O. And you're still looking for more?"

"It's not that. I just want you to know I'm available if I can ever do anything for you."

"I appreciate that, D.O.," Tom replied. "But what happened is no longer of any consequence. In fact, it's a dead issue. The young lady in question was married to someone else in your beautiful temple a couple of weeks ago, and according to the paper, she left on a trip to Yellowstone Park for her honeymoon."

"I see," D.O. said. "And you say this young lady was someone you knew before?"

"You haven't had much sleep, D.O. Are you sure you're up to hearing a long story?"

"They're the best kind," he smiled.

———

A couple of hours later, as they made their way back up the hill from walking Alice Thurston and her young nephew home, D.O. McKay knew considerably more about Thomas Callahan, and young Tom understood, or at least had heard, David's explanation about temple sealing and eternal marriage.

"So her concern," Tom said, "if I understood you right, may have been more for finding an eternal companion than it was for which man to choose?"

"Perhaps some of each, but I can't truly say, Tom. Without even knowing the young woman, if she is a Mormon, I know she would have been concerned about your differing religions."

"Seems to me there's more to this, D.O., than simply my not being a Mormon, and I suppose I'm angry over coming so far for my dream when she never even really gave me a chance to make my case. If it was just a matter of a difference in our religions, why wasn't she willing to wait until I could learn something about it? She gave me a copy of your Book of Mormon, and I've read about the brothers in the early chapters."

"That's good, Tom. I don't know what to tell you. Perhaps she just wasn't the one. You said Sister Mary told you the Lord had a purpose in sending you here. Do you believe that?"

"I don't know, D.O. I haven't seen it so far."

"Well, perhaps He has yet to reveal it to you, Tom, but be patient. The Lord seldom seems to work according to our timetable. Well, I'd better be heading home now. It's been a long night, and I've got classes this morning. Can we carry on this conversation at some later date?"

"Aye. Thanks, D.O. I'm glad we had the opportunity to meet again."

"Me, too, Tom. Take care, now," he said, turning to walk toward his house.

"I will, D.O. And don't worry," Tom called after him, "I'll look in on your friend, Thurston."

"Thanks. I think Sister Thurston will probably move in if the doctor lets her," D.O. offered, as he waved good-bye.

12

In the summer months, Friday night was a popular dance night at Saltair. At the urging of Sister Mary, Tom had agreed that getting involved in a social life would be the best way to get over Katrina. "Besides," Sister Mary had said, "who knows? You might even meet a nice Catholic girl."

Tom knew Sister Mary meant well, but he had no interest in meeting any kind of girl just then. Though he seldom went very long without thinking about Katrina and about what might have been, he knew in his head that to continue pining over her was useless. But he couldn't get his heart to let go.

The dance pavilion was packed. Literally thousands of people had crammed into each nook and cranny, and the orchestra was pumping out the latest tunes. Tom made it through "Sweet Rosie O'Grady" once again, with only a brief flit of memory about the night Katie sang it on the *Antioch*.

When he went to the bar to order drinks, it amused Tom that the majority ordered lemonade or one of the new carbonated drinks. He too, ordered only soft drinks, which made him wonder if people thought he was a Mormon.

Beer was sold at Saltair, but Tom didn't partake. That

decision had been made on the train from Kansas City to Denver, as Tom lay shivering in the cold night air, wondering if, when he arrived in Denver, he would be arrested and hanged for the murder of a man whose name he didn't even know. Father O'Leary's warning was constantly in his mind during that lonely ride, and Tom had surprised even himself when he decided that from that moment forward he would consume no more alcohol. The memory of his father's abusive treatment of his mother, the image that had been fixed in his mind of a faceless young man strapped into an electric chair, and the recognition of his own loss of control after drinking, had solidified that decision.

Tom *had* killed a man. That much was certain. But what he hoped was that if he were arrested, he could somehow convince the authorities that he had acted in self-defense.

On that lonely train ride across the prairie, Tom had bargained with God—asking Him to help him escape arrest and promising in return never to drink again.

The most surprising thing to Tom about his commitment was the way he adhered to it. Not even Sister Mary was aware of his promise, and there was no one who could berate Tom for failing to live up to his private bargain with God. Yet he had, from the day he made the pledge, honored it strictly. For an Irishman to give up his pints was quite a thing, and it was an evidence of how fearful Tom was of being apprehended and charged with murder, to say nothing of how seriously he took the promise he had made to God.

⸺

Had Tom been there with someone he cared about, he might have found the resort at Saltair a remarkably romantic place. The gigantic onion-domed structure sat on the southern shore of the Great Salt Lake. The huge dance floor was constructed of polished wood and the pavilion opened to the west, affording an unobstructed, open-air view of the lake, Antelope Island, and the glorious sunsets beyond.

But Tom found it difficult to generate much enthusiasm. There was lively music and a big crowd, and as the evening progressed, several young girls cast the same coy look at Tom that he knew so well from his cavorting days in Ireland. The fact that he didn't have a beer in his hand, he guessed, rendered him "safe" to the mostly Mormon girls in the hall. He danced with a few and chatted superficially, but his heart wasn't in it. At least not yet.

Tom didn't see Katrina immediately, as she stood against a crowd of people, looking at him and smiling uncertainly. When he finally became aware of her, it was her eyes that he noticed first. Her hair, which she had pulled up on top of her head, gave her an older, more sophisticated appearance.

When she saw that he had finally focused on her, Katrina didn't know what to say. They stood there for a moment, looking at each other, before Katrina said, "Good evening, Thomas."

"Good evening," he responded, then added awkwardly, "You've changed your appearance, uh . . . Mrs. Stromberg."

"Oh, my hair," she laughed, touching her head with her finger tips. "It's not quite so long."

"But just as beautiful."

Not knowing how to follow up the compliment, Tom abruptly downed the rest of his drink and set the empty glass on the counter. He looked again at Katrina, but she lowered her eyes.

"Well," he said, "I was just about to catch the next train. If you'll excuse me . . ."

"Thomas, it is nice to—"

"Katrina, I've been looking for you," Harold announced as he shouldered his way through the crowd. She turned to greet her husband, who had his eyes fastened on Tom.

"Harold, this is Thomas Callahan. We met on the ship coming from Europe," Katrina offered.

Harold glanced quickly at Katrina, and back again at Tom. Taking a firm hold of Katrina's arm, Harold lectured, "There are too many people here for you to go wandering off alone, Katrina."

Tom offered his hand, but Harold ignored the gesture, while continuing to glare at the handsome Irishman.

"It was nice to meet you, Harold. Katrina, all the best to you. Good evening," he said, turning his back on them and stepping away.

Tom was surprised when Harold grabbed him by the shoulder and jerked him back around. Tom's eyes went to Katrina, rather than Harold.

"The next time you speak to her, you'll address her as 'Mrs. Stromberg.' Is that understood?" Harold spat out. "In fact," he added, "you'd best avoid either of us, Mr. Callahan. I've heard all about you from Mr. Hansen, and neither Katrina nor I wish to have any further contact with you."

"Aye," Tom said, turning once again to leave.

Harold's second jerk on Tom's shoulder brought fire to the Irishman's eyes, and he was able to restrain himself only because of Katrina's presence. "Do you understand, Mr. Callahan? There's no place here for your kind."

"And what kind would that be?" Tom asked, smiling disarmingly and thereby confusing Harold.

"Irish riffraff. Peasants," Harold prodded.

"Aye," Tom said, continuing to smile. "It was nice to see you again, Katrina," he said, looking into her eyes, then turning once again to go.

176

Harold's final mistake was pursuing Tom a third time and trying once more to spin him around. "I told you not to call her *Katrina*. Are you entirely stupid?"

"Aye," Tom replied, landing a short, hard punch to Harold's mouth, knocking the man off his feet onto his back on the dance floor. Some of the women who had been watching screamed and turned away, and others in the crowd fell back into a small circle, in the center of which Harold lay sprawled, his lips bloodied. Katrina went quickly to Harold, bending to help him up and glaring at Tom as she struggled to lift her husband.

"I'm sorry, Katrina," Tom offered. "He didn't give me much choice."

"Callahan," Harold said, spitting blood, "I'll have the law on you for this."

"Have a go, Stromberg," Tom said, gesturing with his arm at the large crowd that had watched what had gone on. "There are plenty of witnesses to your, shall we say, *provocation*. But if your Poppa's so important, maybe he can protect his little lad. That's what *your* kind needs, isn't it?" Tom looked again at Katrina. Her face was white and she was trembling, and Tom suddenly felt great pity for her. He had frightened her, he could see.

"I truly am sorry, Katrina. Please excuse me," he said, before making his way through the crowd.

"You've not heard the last of this, Callahan," Harold shouted after him.

"Harold, let's just go. Quietly, please," Katrina pleaded.

"Taking his side, are you?" Harold threatened.

"Harold, please," Katrina voiced, embarrassed beyond words to have been the center of such a public spectacle.

Tom boarded the train back to Salt Lake, his blood up and trying to calm his anger. Back in his room, the sound of

177

the boiler, long since accepted as part of the ambient noise in his quarters, kept him awake for hours until the dawn.

The next morning, in the kitchen, hunched over a plate of scrambled eggs and bacon prepared by Sister Jude for her favorite customer, Tom sat silently eating as Sister Mary greeted him on her early morning inspection of the hospital.

"Have a good evening, Thomas?"

He looked up and smiled thinly at her. "Not so you'd notice, Sister. But I've had worse."

29 May 1896

Dear Nana,

I saw Thomas this evening at Saltair. I love him!
God help me, Nana, I love him.
Jeg elske deg,

Trina

"Top of the mornin' to ya, Mr. Thurston," Tom said as he entered the hospital room.

A bright smile lit up Robert Thurston's face. "Good morning, Mr. Callahan."

"Just on me way to some morning chores down this wing, and thought I'd pop in to say hello. How are you feeling?"

"Like a team of six horses drove over me, but better than a couple of days ago," he laughed. "But if it hadn't been for

178

you and Brother McKay, I'm told it could have been much worse. And, of course, Sister Mary."

"Aye, Sister Mary would be due all the praise, Mr. Thurston. I just drove the buggy, and maybe one of the six horses," he grinned.

Thurston laughed and nodded appreciatively. "Have a seat, please. Brother McKay seems to think quite highly of you, Mr. Callahan."

"Really? I've never given him any cause. But what say we dispense with the 'Mister' and you call me Tom? And I'll call you Robert, or is it Bob?"

"Robert's fine. How long have you been in Salt Lake, Tom?"

"Only about six months, I think. And not much longer than that in America. I suppose you're from here?"

"Guilty. I was born here."

Tom judged Robert to be in his late twenties or early thirties. "A member of what they call the 'pioneer families,'" Tom joked.

"You could say so, I guess. My grandfather came out with one of the handcart companies."

"That seems to be the badge of honor you need to be a member of the establishment here."

Robert turned his gaze out the window momentarily. "I guess it might seem that way to someone new, but," he said, looking back toward Tom, "anyone is welcome in the 'establishment,' Tom. I'd be glad to show you how," he smiled again.

"Careful now, Robert, you're in a Catholic hospital at the moment, and we're likely to convert *you* 'piece by piece,'" he teased, pointing toward Robert's incision.

Thurston laughed out loud, wincing and holding his abdomen. "That's a novel approach to missionary work."

179

"Aye, but then there's no going back."

"I see your point, Tom. Well taken, I might add. So what do you do here at the hospital?"

"General maintenance. Plus everything else Sister Mary can think up."

"Does that usually include a four A.M. house call?"

"Oh, that. Nay. Sister Mary and I were just attending to one of her hobbies."

Robert's eyebrow went up slightly. "So Brother McKay has told me. Seems he knows more than he's supposed to."

"Well, Sister Mary's got her heart in the right place, that she does. And where do you work, Robert?"

"Zions Bank. I've been with them since I went to the university. About eight years."

"I see. Do you enjoy it?"

"I do, indeed. And you?"

"Well, these are fine folk here at Holy Cross, but I haven't decided what to do yet. Just kind of following what comes at the moment," Tom said, reflecting to himself how his answer was as surprising to him now, as it had been that day on the *Antioch* when Anders Hansen had asked him what he was going to do in New York. "Something'll turn up. I'd kind of like to have a look at this university everyone's talking about."

"You want to go to college?" Robert asked.

"Don't know. Might look into it. I'd thought about Trinity College in Dublin once, but then . . . ," he hesitated. "But now Sister Mary seems to think it's a good idea, and my work schedule here would permit it, she said."

"That's great, Tom. You know, we have apprentice opportunities at the bank for bright, young lads," he smiled. "That's how I got in," he added, with a wink.

"Well," Tom said, standing up, "best be on about me chores. Do you play chess, Robert?"

Thurston's eyes brightened. "I certainly do. And you?"

"I'll drop around after dinner this evening, Robert," Tom smiled, "and see if I can't take advantage of a sick man."

"With the care I'm getting here, Tom, that won't be much of an advantage," Robert laughed.

"I'll be telling Sister Mary you're pleased with the service, then," Tom said, leaving. "See ya this evening."

"Right. I'll look forward to it, Tom."

"That could be quite expensive, Mr. Stromberg," the private detective said.

"Look, I said I want the work done quietly, and quickly. You'll be paid."

"Oh, I have no doubt of that, Mr. Stromberg. Where did you say he came from?"

"Ireland, man. I said, Ireland. But I have little idea how he got here. Just that he worked for a while for the railroad getting here. Can you find out what I need?"

"We have a nationwide service, Mr. Stromberg. The Pinkerton Agency is the premier detective agency in these United States."

Their Salt Lake City office located on the third floor, above a bank, the Pinkerton agency was a branch of the investigative firm that had been well known since its inception during the Civil War. At forty years of age, Ken McGuire was the senior resident agent in Salt Lake City in the summer of 1896. He was a broad man, prematurely bald, with a ruddy complexion and a square jaw. He wore a handle-bar mustache that was well-waxed and that he frequently reached up to smooth under his nose.

181

"Good. That's what I've heard. And don't rely on the standard mail service. Use the telegraph. I want results fast. Anything you can find, McGuire. And make it confidential. I want you to report directly to me with each piece of information you find."

"That I'll do, Mr. Stromberg. Will your father's firm be the client in this case? We'll need a small retainer, if that's, . . ."

"It's *my* firm as well, McGuire, and this is *my* case. I've drawn a check for you. One thousand dollars should be enough to initiate your investigation."

"Certainly, sir. I didn't mean to imply . . . That will be quite adequate, Mr. Stromberg."

"And there'll be a generous bonus for the man who turns up, what uh, . . ."

"*Incriminating evidence*, I believe is the term you're searching for, Mr. Stromberg."

"Right. Enough to bring this troublemaker what he deserves."

"I understand, Mr. Stromberg. I'll be in touch."

"Excellent," Harold replied. "I'll be hearing from you, then."

"You can count on it, Mr. Stromberg."

<hr />

Leaving the Pinkerton office, Harold Stromberg headed back to the law office of Stromberg, Thornton, & Stromberg, so renamed by his father in anticipation of Harold's joining the firm following the completion of his law studies.

That Magnus Stromberg had already added his son's name to the masthead, before the young man even had his law degree, provided the members of the local legal fraternity another reason to amuse themselves at the expense of Magnus Stromberg. There were many in town who thought him to be a pompous twit, and who resented him for his general arrogance—specifically for the way he flaunted his friendships with members of the Mormon hierarchy, particularly President George Q. Cannon. Young Harold hadn't much helped his father's image by prematurely taking on the air of being a lawyer—an affectation that all his peers and many of the real attorneys in town found especially galling.

"Ah, Harold, I've been hoping you'd return. I've just received a very interesting telegram this morning," Magnus Stromberg said.

"From whom, Father?"

"From an old contact in Mexico. A client, actually. Don Sebastian Cardenas. I represented him once, years ago, on a land transaction with the United States government. I thought he might be in a position to help us, and it turns out he is. Come into my office, and I'll tell you about it."

Whatever else Magnus enjoyed, he liked elegance. His law office was richly appointed. It was a showplace of fine furnishings, original paintings, and art objects, and he never tired of showing it off. Magnus took a seat in his expansive leather chair and pointed Harold to one of the arm chairs arranged in front of the ornate, highly polished wood desk.

After the two men were seated comfortably, Magnus continued. "The case involved a dispute Don Sebastian got into with the United States government over the family's original Spanish land grant. The property lay inside the Republic of Texas. You'll recall, Harold, that Texas enjoyed a brief period as an independent nation. Once Texas became a state, in '45, the government refused to recognize his claim. They just confiscated his 200,000 acres. It's a long story, but I was able to help him eventually obtain a settlement of several million dollars. As you might imagine, he's been most grateful ever since."

Harold had never been told the whole of that story, but it was easy for him to imagine the fee his father must have realized for handling the case. In part, it was the potential for that kind of income that attracted Harold to the practice of law.

"I telegraphed Cardenas several weeks ago to inquire about land that might be available in Mexico. Now he's telegraphed, favorably, I might add, to indicate that he's located something he feels is suitable, and I need you to go down there and meet with him."

Harold brightened. "Are we ready, Father? You're convinced there's no chance of bringing President Woodruff to an understanding?"

"He's counseled by fools, Harold. I don't know why I couldn't see it earlier. He means well, of course, but he's been misled by those who don't understand the Lord's will, and who have only political gain in mind. *Senator* Frank Cannon and his father in particular."

"What is it you want me to do, Father?" Harold asked.

"I want you to go down to Mazatlán and meet with Don Sebastian. Look over this tract he assures me is prime land, near the ocean, with excellent farming potential. I want you to take Fred Bowen with you. He's old, but no one knows soils and farming better than he does. Have him look at the land and evaluate it.

"Listen to him, Harold. Don't let your youth or your intelligence get in the way. There're many types of intelligence, and you need to learn to distinguish which is which and how to use each to your advantage. Do you understand, Harold?"

"I believe so, Father. But I've actually got something going at the moment," he said, thinking about the detective. "When would you need me to go?"

Magnus studied the calendar on his desk. "I need to go to Denver for a few days first. Then we could, . . . about three weeks, I believe. I think you'd better plan to be gone about six weeks."

"That's fine, Father. And Katrina?"

"Don't confide in her yet, Harold. We need to keep this within the family, so to speak, at least until our plans are finalized. We'll watch out for her while you're gone."

"Excellent, Father. It looks like we're actually going to make the move, doesn't it?"

"I just wish I'd seen the light earlier, Harold. We've wasted over two years waiting for Church leaders to act, all the time thinking . . . Well, recriminations serve no purpose. Our course is set. Let's just get on with the Lord's will. He will bless our venture if we remember His counsel to Brother Joseph."

"How many do you think will join us, Father?"

The elder Stromberg rose, moving to the window of his office and looking west, across the lake, toward the mountains, the Salt Flats, and the desert that stretched endlessly toward California.

"About forty initially. And about two hundred, once we make improvements and can provide housing."

He turned from the window and hooked his thumbs in the pockets of his vest. Looking at his father, Harold thought again what a distinguished figure he made. Handsome, gray-haired, and wearing an expensive suit of clothing, he resembled in every way a successful and prosperous barrister. Beyond that, he held strong religious views and had commanded the respect of many Church members.

"We won't have to endure the hardships our family did on the trek to this valley, Harold, but I expect living conditions in Mexico won't be much different than what they found here, at least until we get established."

Magnus stepped back to his desk and stood in front of his chair, looking across the polished desk top at Harold. "Now, about your trip. It will serve no purpose to advertise what we have planned. After you get to San Francisco on the train, book your passage down to Mazatlán under some other name. When I return from Denver, I'll have arranged bank drafts that will demonstrate our good faith to Don Sebastian. I think it best to keep our transaction out of the view of our friends at Zions Bank, at least for now."

"I understand, Father. I'll be discreet."

Harold hesitated, then said, "Father, are you certain of our plans?" showing for the first time any hesitancy on his part.

"It is the *Lord's* plan, Harold. And there are many anxious to join us in implementing it." Leaning forward, Magnus made a fist, and gesturing with it, he said, "We can be a beacon light in this matter. But, Harold, be strong. I need your strength and your youth."

"I'm with you, Father," Harold said.

"Excellent, Harold, because when you arrive in Mexico, I'll have one other task for you, and it may prove difficult. It will require all your faith."

"Can you tell me more about it, Father?"

"Harold, I must ask you to trust me on this."

"Always, Father."

"Wonderful. Go home now and see to your bride. Mother is expecting you both to meet us for dinner at seven."

"Good," Harold smiled. "One more generation of pioneers then, eh, Father?"

"For your sons, Harold," he said, taking Harold's hand in both of his. "For your sons."

⊶⊷

Harold stepped through the entry way to his home and hung his hat on the vestibule coat rack. "Katrina!" he called.

As she came into view, Harold wrapped her in his arms. "And how have you spent your day?" he asked.

"I had a wonderful day, Harold. I took the trolley up to the university and spoke with one of the administrators about my program."

"Your program?" he asked.

"You know. Like I told you. My teaching program."

"Katrina, we've much more important things afoot now, and I'll need your support. Besides, I don't want my wife working outside our home. It wouldn't look right. You know how I feel about that. Your influence will be most needed at home, with our children."

"But, Harold, I think—"

"Let's get ready, shall we? We're supposed to meet Mother and Father at the Alta Club for dinner at seven."

"Harold, I'd like to talk about this, please," she said.

"Katrina, our world will shortly take on new dimensions. You'll be counted among the new pioneers of the Church and you'll be much too busy for any foolishness at the university."

"What do you mean, *pioneers*, Harold?"

He kissed her on the cheek and turned her toward the stairs. "Get ready, Katrina. And wear the new dress I bought you last week. Mother will love it."

"Harold, I—"

"I'll be in my den until you're ready. I've some work to do."

187

13

"But, Mr. Stromberg, no charges were ever brought. It was clearly a case of self-defense. Witnesses who had been in the saloon that night told the police in Kansas City that they heard this Tooney fellow contract with three goons to jump Callahan. There wasn't even a warrant sworn out for his arrest. It's all right there in the report."

Harold Stromberg sat glaring at the papers in the file that Detective McGuire had presented him. The agency was good. It had taken just over a week to produce the report, but what they had found wasn't what Harold Stromberg had planned on. Still . . .

"Mr. McGuire, are the Salt Lake City police aware of this case?"

"Why would they be? It *isn't* a case. No charges were filed and no warrant was ever issued," McGuire pointed out again.

"So, Mr. McGuire, since, as you say, charges were never brought, there's no reason to involve the local police. Agreed?"

"Clearly," McGuire said, somewhat exasperated by Stromberg's struggle to get the facts into his head.

"Right. Then here's what I want you to do." For ten

minutes, Harold described to Ken McGuire how he wanted the situation handled, with McGuire interrupting on several occasions to protest.

Finally, Harold overcame McGuire's resistance by saying, "Look, McGuire. This lout has been making unwarranted advances toward my wife. I want him out of town. I'm not asking you to perpetrate a fraud. You don't even have to lie. Simply tell him you know what happened in Kansas City, and that as an officer of the court you have a duty to inform the local police. Tell him . . . tell him, oh, I don't know what! Tell him there's always a chance of some mistake in these things, and that in fairness to him, you'll give him, say, forty-eight hours to consider his actions, before you go to the authorities. Would that be so hard to do?"

"I don't know, Mr. Stromberg. It seems we'd be pushing this Callahan fellow into a corner."

"That's where he belongs, McGuire. Be sensible. In a few days I have to leave town on business, and I'll be gone for several weeks. Would you want someone like that menacing *your* wife if you weren't there to take care of the matter?"

"Well, actually, I'm not married, so—"

"Confound it, man! That's beside the point!" Harold shouted.

Then, adopting a softer tone, Harold said, "Look. Maybe there's a way for us to do a little more business. I would like the premises of my home watched while I'm gone, just to be sure that this Irish scum doesn't disturb my wife during my absence. Can your firm handle that extra business?" Harold asked, holding out the carrot, in the form of a roll of money he had taken out of his pocket.

Certain now of the kind of man he was dealing with in

190

Stromberg, the detective said, "I'm certain we can, Mr. Stromberg." Then, eyeing the money, he asked, "Now, exactly what is it you want me to tell Callahan?"

Harold Stromberg went over it again, McGuire nodding as he rationalized in his mind how he could skirt the edge of ethical misconduct and satisfy his well-heeled customer, without interfering too drastically with the rights of an insignificant Irishman named Tom Callahan.

"Then we are in agreement?" Harold asked.

"That we are, Mr. Stromberg."

"Good. When can you approach Callahan?"

"This afternoon, if I can locate him."

"Good. Very good."

———

"Tom, a man named McGuire is asking for you upstairs in the main parlor."

Tom looked out from underneath the cluster of wires and control panels he was helping to install in the basement of Holy Cross Hospital. The project was proving more difficult than any one could have imagined. But Sister Mary was determined to have an electric call bell installed in each room of the hospital, and Tom had been assigned to help the electrician who had contracted to do the work.

"Did he say what he wants?" Tom asked.

"Nope, just asked if he could see you."

"Thanks, Hernando, I'll be right up," Tom said to the gardener.

Five minutes later, Tom walked down the hallway in the east wing and into the main reception area. A solidly built man holding a brown derby in his hands and wearing a brown business suit and boots with silver toe tips was standing there.

A thin leather satchel lay on the couch next to him, and he was studying one of the framed paintings on the wall.

"Mr. McGuire?" Tom asked.

"I am. Are you Thomas Callahan?"

"Aye. How can I help?"

"Is there somewhere we can speak privately, Mr. Callahan?"

McGuire wasn't wearing a uniform, but Tom tensed up, on guard because of McGuire's official behavior.

"Sure. But what's it about?"

"I have a matter of business we need to discuss. Where can we talk?"

Tom led McGuire down the hall to a small room normally used as a family waiting area. It was vacant, and as they stepped in, McGuire closed the door.

"What's this all about?" Tom asked again.

Moving to take a seat on one of the chairs in the room, McGuire said, "Sit down, Mr. Callahan."

As they sat, McGuire began.

"Mr. Callahan, I'm with the Pinkerton Detective Agency, and I've learned of an incident involving you that took place in Kansas City, last November twenty-second."

Tom's heart leaped, and he suddenly felt woozy. His first impulse was to jump and run, but he somehow managed to stay seated. McGuire noted with satisfaction the look of alarm on the young Irishman's face and was instantly certain he could accomplish what he had come to do.

McGuire continued. "I've been made aware of what happened there and your part in it. A man named Skomolski—Isaac Skomolski—was killed in a fight that night, and there is reason to believe you are the one responsible for his death."

Even though he half expected that was what McGuire

was going to say, the words jolted Tom. He eyed McGuire, quickly evaluating what kind of a chance he would have against the muscular detective if it came to a fight. Tom's throat was dry, and when he spoke, his voice nearly failed him.

"How do you know about it? Are you a policeman?"

McGuire pressed his advantage. "No, Pinkerton's is a private investigative agency. But I *am* an officer of the court, and I have an obligation to report such things to the police when they come to my attention."

"Then, why have you come to me? What do you want?"

"I think I can help you, Callahan."

That was the first hopeful thing McGuire had said, and Tom was immediately curious, though he remained cautious.

"What are you saying?"

"I've been retained by a party who I'm not at liberty to identify. My client has an interest in having you get out of town, and I'm here to see that, one way or another, that happens. You *will* be gone, Mr. Callahan. Count on it."

Tom's mind was racing. "It's Stromberg, isn't it?" he stated.

"That's for me to know and you to guess, Callahan. I'll only say that my client is a real hard case, and he's got the goods on you.

"Now here's what I'm willing to do. I'll wait forty-eight hours before I go to the police and tell them what I know. Between now and then, you decide what you're going to do. If it were me, though, I wouldn't have to think about it."

"What's your stake in it, McGuire? Why not just turn me in?" Tom asked.

"Let's just say . . . it looks to me like the wrong pig's getting stuck."

Leaving the hospital a few minutes later, McGuire felt as though it had been a good afternoon's work. His was a grungy business, but every once in a while, a chance came along to do something fun. He'd lifted some money off that pompous Stromberg and been able, without saying so directly, to let the kid know who had fingered him. He'd earned his money. Callahan would get out of town, and maybe the kid would get a chance to get even one day. Stromberg, coward that he was, might yet get what he deserved. *Yes, sir,* McGuire congratulated himself, *all and all, it hadn't been a bad afternoon's work.*

Just before one A.M., Tom completed the note to Sister Mary, having had great difficulty in expressing his shame over leaving in the middle of the night. A second note, for D.O. McKay, and a short third note for Anders Hansen, were enclosed with Sister Mary's, and she was asked to see that they were delivered to each man.

The early morning train west, departing at six-fifteen from the station in Salt Lake, would allow Tom to be long gone before someone came to his room to determine why he wasn't available for work. In the note, Tom asked Sister Mary to contribute his final pay to the children's surgery fund.

Climbing the stairs from the basement, his small valise in his hand, Tom moved quietly through the halls toward the side entrance to the first floor, east wing. As he hurried through the reception area, toward the main entrance, a noise from the chapel startled him, and he suddenly found

194

himself face to face with Father Lawrence Scanlan, Archbishop of the Salt Lake Diocese.

Noticing the valise in Tom's hand, Scanlan looked up at Tom. "Coming or going, my son?" he asked softly.

"Going, Father."

"Well, so am I, lad. I have a buggy outside. May I offer you a lift to your destination?"

"It's just down the hill, Father. To the train station."

"Right on the way. Come along, and we can introduce ourselves in the buggy."

Tom hesitated, but then followed Father Scanlan outside. He laid his piece of luggage in the rear of the buggy and climbed up to the passenger seat. "I believe I know who *you* are, Father Scanlan."

"Do you now?" Scanlan said as he lightly tapped the whip on the horse's back. "Then you have the advantage, although I believe Sister Mary spoke of you some time ago. If I'm right, you'd be young Mr. Callahan, late of Ireland," he laughed. "And I haven't been able to hear such a pleasant accent in many years now. But tell me, Tom, if I may call you Tom, I was under the impression that you were quite happy at Holy Cross and we would be able to depend on your services for a while. Has something happened to change all that?" the Bishop asked, looking directly at Tom.

"Ah, Father, it's not an easy story."

"They never are, my son. But God has a listening ear, and He's asked me to be patient each time I sit in for Him. So, what part of Ireland do you come from, Tom?"

"County Tipperary, Father."

Scanlan eyed Tom and smiled. "What parish?"

"Pallas Grean."

"You don't say! Neighbors, we are, young Tom. I hail from Ballytarna, just down the road. In that neck of the woods, maybe we're even relatives. What was your mother's maiden name?"

"Ryan, Father. Margaret Ryan."

"Not Margaret Ryan, daughter of Matthew Ryan and Margaret Donohue, per chance?"

Tom was surprised. "Aye, Father. One and the same."

Scanlan laughed. "Well, bless my soul! Your mother is my cousin, Tom, and that makes us first cousins, once removed. Blood relatives, can you believe it, lad! All the way from Ireland to run into your cousin in the wilds of Utah. The Irish are popping up everywhere, Tom. Just everywhere," he laughed heartily.

Born September 23, 1843, to Patrick and Catherine Ryan Scanlan, Lawrence Scanlan, as oldest son, followed an accepted tradition and attended All Hallows Seminary in Dublin, becoming an alumnus nearly fifteen years after Father P. J. O'Leary had followed the same course.

Father Scanlan's career, however, had been somewhat different than O'Leary's. Taking a clipper ship around the Horn in 1868, Father Scanlan landed in San Francisco, and was immediately assigned to a small mining town in Nevada, eventually moving to Petaluma, California, as parish priest. His assignment to Utah came in 1873, to preside over about 800 Catholics in the region, then the largest territorial Catholic diocese in the United States.

Recognizing the need for medical care for indigent miners, Father Scanlan petitioned the Church to establish a hospital and, in 1875, the Sisters of the Holy Cross complied. Holy Cross Hospital was born shortly thereafter, and Father Scanlan continued to preside as bishop over the Salt Lake diocese.

Part of that history was briefly related while the horse

slowly made her way down South Temple, toward the train station.

"But back to your story, Tom. Is there some way I can be of assistance? Anything I can do to encourage you to stay? After all," he smiled, "I'd not be gaining and losing a relative in the same day, or night, if I had a choice."

Tom laughed nervously as the buggy approached Temple Square and the center of Salt Lake City. "Father, it's an honor to be related to you, and certainly Sister Mary has been the soul of kindness since my arrival, but I just think it best I move on. For all concerned."

"Is the law chasing you, my son?" he asked directly, surprising Tom with his insight.

"Father," Tom said, looking down at the buggy floorboard. "I had some bit of trouble on the way out to Utah, and it does seem to have caught up with me."

Scanlan reined the horse over to the side of the road, stopping at the corner of West Temple and South Temple. He tied the reins to the brake handle and then looking directly at Tom, he said, "If you're intent on leaving, son, would you like to make your confession?"

Tom was embarrassed and stumbled his speech. "It's been some time, Father."

"I understand."

Silence ensued as they sat together, in the shadow of the recently dedicated Mormon temple, with the time approaching one-thirty in the morning. Tom thought how often he had been here at this very spot, and how often it had been just as late, or later, as he and Sister Mary delivered food to needy families throughout the poorer sections of town.

"Father," Tom said, his voice soft and contrite. "Will you hear my confession?"

"Certainly, my son," Bishop Scanlan said as he reached inside his coat for his vestments.

Later, much later, his story of the fight in Kansas City purged and his sorrow over the loss of Katrina expressed, Tom wiped the tears from his eyes as Father Scanlan refolded his vestments. Then the bishop spoke in a directive rather than a compassionate voice.

"Tom, although we are the minority religion in Utah, I am not without some influence. I could perhaps render some assistance, if I had some time."

"Father, I think it's best I go and avoid any further conflict. The Church should not have to bear the embarrassment of having their maintenance man arrested for murder. Plus, I'm scared, Father. Ever since I heard that story from Father O'Leary, of the young Irish lad who was executed in New York, I've worried the same thing could happen to me."

Scanlan nodded. "I'll extract one promise from you, son. That you write to Sister Mary when you locate and let her know where you are. It will be in the form of a private, privileged communication, and I will have her advise me. We need to have someplace to write to you, in case we can turn something up to exonerate you. Because it was self-defense, you shouldn't have to run from it for the rest of your life."

"I will, Father. You have my word."

"That's good enough for me. And your money, my son. Are you able to provide for yourself?"

"I have sufficient, Father. The room and board at the hospital has enabled me to save most of my salary."

"Excellent," he said, gently tapping the horse again and beginning the short ride remaining to the train station. Arriving there, Scanlan halted the buggy and Tom jumped down, retrieving his valise and standing on the footpath just below Father Scanlan.

"Thank you, Father. I'm very sorry for my hasty departure. I only hope it doesn't cause Sister Mary too much disruption. And thank you, Father, for your care and concern."

"Tom," he said, offering his hand, "it's been a true pleasure meeting one of my long lost cousins. Remember your promise, lad. And one more thing. May I ask your permission to discuss this with Sister Mary? Not, of course, the nature of your transgression, but the cause of your departure and to enlist her help in finding a way to overcome this problem."

Tom spoke without hesitation. "Aye, Father. I'd trust Sister Mary with my life," he said, smiling as they both realized how literally that was true. "Good night to you, Father," Tom added, doffing his cap.

"And God's blessings go with you, my son," Bishop Scanlan replied.

14

Without either of them realizing it, Harold and Tom departed San Francisco within hours of each other, on successive tides, their respective ships turning in opposite directions once out beyond the broad harbor entrance. The train trip from Salt Lake had occurred two days earlier for Tom, and, once Harold learned from Detective McGuire of Tom's departure, he obtained the bank drafts from his father, booked his own trip, and bid Katrina farewell.

Tom had two days in San Francisco before his ship departed, and as fortune would have it, he attended a Mormon Tabernacle Choir performance in the city, part of a concert tour the choir had undertaken to the West Coast. Having never heard the choir in Salt Lake City, he sat in the audience, enjoying the music and thinking how odd it was to hear them on his last night in America, so far away from Salt Lake City.

In the only letter Tom had exchanged with his mother, while he was living at Holy Cross Hospital, she had informed him that his Uncle John had written and was still living in Alaska, in the town of Anvil, on the Bering Sea, near St. Michael's. For Tom, those were just names, but they conjured up a vision of wild animals, treacherous waters, and endless snow fields. With no particular destination in mind, Anvil seemed as good as any other and as far away from police problems as he was going to get, short of sailing to the orient. Thinking about the possibility, he even became excited to hook up with his Uncle John, his mother's brother, and his only known relative, aside from the newly discovered Father Scanlan, outside of Ireland.

The steamship *Pacific Challenger* out of San Francisco, made excellent time, stopping for three days in Seattle, and, once clear of the Strait of Juan de Fuca, making a straight run for Dutch Harbor, on the west end of the Aleutian Islands. During his stopover in Seattle, Tom sent a telegraph to Sister Mary, advising that he was bound for Alaska, but no response was received by the time the *Pacific Challenger* put back out to sea.

Balmy weather accompanied the ship during most of her run across the northern Pacific Ocean, the ship remaining well south of the Gulf of Alaska. Tom spent much of his time reading the ship's library books about Alaska. In Seattle, he had also purchased a copy of a newly published novel *The Red Badge of Courage*. He was fascinated by the story and intrigued how the author, Stephen Crane, who was only two or three years older than Tom, and who had been born long after the American Civil War, knew so much about it.

Two-thirds of the way across the Gulf of Alaska, their luck ran out. A violent southwester rose out of the calm, and within four hours, the *Pacific Challenger* was fighting for her life. Unable to make headway in the port beam sea, the captain had no choice but to turn tail and ride with the storm in a northeasterly direction.

For seventy-two hours the storm raged, finally giving way to fair weather as the sun broke over the horizon on the third day. Damage to the ship was not extensive, but after taking a sighting to determine position, the captain decided to continue northeast and lay over at Kodiak, Alaska, for repairs.

Tom weathered the storm well enough, and in fact earned praise from the first mate for showing up in the galley, well into the second day of the storm, looking for something to eat. Most of the other passengers did not set foot outside their berths until the ship had entered the calm waters of Kodiak harbor.

On the other hand, Harold Stromberg enjoyed a relatively easy journey down the coast of California and past the Baja Peninsula, turning into the mouth of that cavernous inlet, and making land on the mainland of Mexico at Mazatlán, a community of fishermen and, to the interior, cattle ranchers.

Left behind in Salt Lake City, was Katrina Hansen Stromberg, who became aware within two weeks of Harold's departure that she was pregnant. She also learned from Anders that Tom had gone to Alaska. Neither piece of news was entirely welcome, though she felt guilty for feeling so. With Harold gone for several weeks, Katrina turned increasingly to her letters to Nana for solace and was grateful for Anders, who could almost read her mind and was always there to understand and comfort her.

By 1896, Alaska had been a United States territory for nearly thirty years. In 1867, when Secretary of State Henry Seward agreed to pay the Russians some twenty-three million dollars for Alaska, he was subjected to one of the more vitriolic treatments the press had ever afforded a United States public servant. Dubbed, "Seward's Folly," the purchase of Alaska was thought to be a monumental mistake, one that benefited the United States only by providing an increased population of polar bears and Eskimos. The nation wondered what use they would ever make of a perpetual "ice box."

Evidence of the long-time Russian occupation abounded on Kodiak Island, and the original government house was still standing when Tom arrived in 1896. In the Russian cemetery in Kodiak, the decaying wooden tombstones, filled with Russian names Tom could not pronounce, painted a bleak picture of early settlement life in this far flung colony of Mother Russia.

In one plot, the tombstones told a specially poignant story of the hardships endured by the people who dared to settle there. Reading the inscriptions on the markers filled Tom with both sorrow and a feeling of awe. He was able to imagine how those courageous people had suffered in that isolated place and harsh climate.

In one set of graves, Alexander Potemkin lay side by side with his wife and three children. The inscriptions gave ample information for Tom to piece the story together. Anna was born 22 April 1768, and died the next day. Nicholi was born 30 May 1769, but lived only six days. The third child, a daughter named Katrina, was born 17 December 1770 and lived only eight days, dying on Christmas. Tom stood for many minutes looking at Katrina's grave marker, marveling at her name, and trying to imagine the pain the parents must have felt as they buried their infant children.

Alexander Potemkin's wife, Sophie, died in 1771, a

young woman, just twenty-six years old. Potemkin followed her eight months later. He was only thirty-four.

Looking at those old grave markers and trying to imagine how it had been for these people, Tom found it easy to believe that after burying her three babies, and dying herself within a week of the last child, that Sophie Potemkin likely succumbed to a broken heart, rather than some illness.

Such stories were also told by the grave markers Tom had seen in the cemetery in Salt Lake. The cost of pioneering new lands was always high, and thinking of such things always put Tom in a mind of home and Ireland, where the terrain had been claimed and the land settled for generations and where, in spite of poverty, relative safety and civilized comforts were readily available.

For ten days the *Pacific Challenger* remained in Kodiak, giving Tom the opportunity to travel inland with a small hunting party from the ship and to observe firsthand, the taking of a giant Kodiak bear. Never in his life had Tom seen a creature so big. When spotted, the majestic animal had simply tried to make its way peacefully to safety, but once shot in the hind quarters, it had turned and raised to its full height, nearly eight feet, as measured following the fusillade of shots from the inexperienced and frightened hunters who finally brought it down.

Out to sea, the *Pacific Challenger* once again made good time on the run down the Alaska Peninsula, cutting through the chain of islands at Dutch Harbor and running north by northeast for St. Michael's. Tom arrived the last week of July and immediately took local transport by water to Anvil, across a large inlet. Miraculously, within four hours of arriving in Anvil, Tom had located his uncle who had just returned from a trip inland.

"By all the saints 'tis good to see ya, Tom. You're a strapping, lad, that ye are. Tell me, lad, how's that passel o' young'uns?"

"All were well when I left, Uncle John. Of course, that's been over a year now. Ma's letter back in May said they were still doing fine."

"And how's your father treating m'sister?"

Tom lowered his head. "About the same, I'd be guessin', Uncle John."

"Aye. 'Tis sad. But knock off the 'uncle' bit," he said, taking the edge off the conversation. "We're in the wilds of Alaska now, lad. Partners we be, not kin. Least not so we need to show the world."

"Aye," Tom replied.

"So, what brings ye two-thirds of the way around the world, Tom? Surely not a visit with yer uncle."

"Just a series of events, Uncle . . . I mean, John. Your letter said it was a bright place, full of promise, and I thought I'd see for myself."

"It's a bright place now, Tom, but come winter, well, you came at the right time, lad. We're off in a few days. If you'd been much later, I'd have been gone."

"Off? To where?"

"Up the mighty Yukon river, lad. Inland, hundreds of miles. I was up there a few years ago and met a man named Carmack. George Washington Carmack. Rough sort of fellow, with a Scotsman named Henderson for a partner. He had a couple of Indian or Eskimo relatives, and they were mining."

"You're going into the mines?" Tom asked, incredulous.

John laughed and slapped his knee. "Not 'into the mines,' lad, but *mining*, sure enough. *Panning*, to be more exact. We're after gold, Tom. The gold of a man's dreams."

"In Alaska?"

"In Canada, actually. Well inland, past the Alaska territory. In a place called Dawson. Just a wee campsite, actually. Carmack's found some color, and he wrote me last month to come on over and have a go at it. So, what do ye say, Tom? Ready for a bit more travel?"

"On the river?"

"Aye, lad, and we've got to get moving. The river will freeze up late September or October and then nobody travels in Alaska, 'cept by the dogs."

"The dogs?"

"Sled dogs, Tom. Aye," John laughed again, a full throated uproarious laughter that reverberated through the small cabin where Tom had located his uncle. "I've got a right 'nuff *cheechako* on me hands."

"A chee . . . what?"

"A greenhorn, lad. Somebody who don't know nothin' about Alaska. Somebody who'd die in thirty minutes outside during the winter without someone what's gonna protect him."

"Well, I've been traveling for the better part of six weeks, John," Tom said with a grin. "I suppose another couple of weeks won't kill me."

"Just might, Tom. 'Tis a hard land you choose to visit to see your old uncle," John laughed. "Just might kill ya."

"This chee . . . cheechak . . . , or whatever, intends to stay alive, Uncle John, unless you'd rather write Ma and tell her what you did with her son."

John's face grew serious for a moment, and then he smiled at Tom. "Good to have ya, lad. A man needs a partner in this here land, and kin's the best kind of partner a man can have. Put your hand on it, lad. Partners we be, and partners we stay. Fifty-fifty, come gold or come mud. What say ye?"

"I say I'm hungry, John. Any food in this land you're boasting about?"

"Down to the saloon, lad," John said, standing up and grabbing his mackinaw. "Where all good Irishmen should be to celebrate their good fortune, or maybe the thought of it."

"John, what's 'color'?"

"What?"

"You said Carmack found some 'color.'"

John laughed again. "C'mon, lad. A few pints of the brew, and you'll know all about the color of gold."

Harold Stromberg's trip south took him to a much more hospitable climate. In 1519, leading an expedition of several ships from Spain, Hernan Cortez made landfall on the western shore of the Gulf of Mexico. His arrival marked the beginning of the conquest of the New World. Directed by King Ferdinand II to find gold, Cortez was determined to obey his sovereign. Finding a harsh, inhospitable land, difficult to traverse, he broke his company into several parties with instructions to seek out and conquer the natives, plundering whatever they might find that would be of worth to His Majesty.

By 1536, under another king, Cortez had extended his exploration and discovered the Baja Peninsula. He sent out separate parties to explore the surrounding land, and to Captain Garcia Cardenas fell the task of marching north and west toward the mythical Seven Cities of Cibolo, or cities of gold. On the western coast of central Mexico, a natural harbor was encountered. Captain Cardenas figured that from this harbor, where he would establish a port, his ships could easily load the gold and return to Spain laden with the treasures that were certain to bring honors to his family name. Surrounded by marshy terrain, the land abounded with deer, which the local natives called *mazat*, and in 1540, Mazatlán, which did not actually become a city until the early nineteenth century, was entered onto explorers' maps. Over the next three centuries, Mazatlán became a haven for pirates, ships flying foreign flags, and a headquarters for the Catholic missionaries who accompanied the conquistadors, as eager to capture the souls of the local natives and bring them unto Christ as the soldiers were to subject them to their individual desires and royal greed.

By the time Harold Stromberg arrived there in the late nineteenth century, Mazatlán had experienced three hundred and fifty years of European influence, and Don Sebastian Cardenas, a direct descendent of Captain Cardenas, was well established as the Patron of Mazatlán. Closely allied with Porfiro Diaz, President of Mexico, Don Sebastian's holdings were vast.

His residence in Mazatlán rested on a high promontory, overlooking the large harbor. It was a site easily defended from sea assault by the guns of a single outpost situated on the rocky point at the entrance to the harbor.

As his ship entered the harbor, Harold Stromberg was met by Don Sebastian's oldest son and several *caballeros* who rowed out to the ship. Speaking excellent English, Miguel Antonio Cardenas greeted Harold with a flair that surprised the Utah native and which immediately established his status in the community. Those with Miguel saw that *Señor* Stromberg was a man who Don Sebastian held in high esteem, and who was to be treated with great deference and respect, a role Harold quickly and easily assumed.

Don Sebastian spoke English surprisingly well. He

explained to Harold that the house in which they currently resided was his town home. His hacienda, he said, was located about eight miles north. Twelve miles beyond there, farther up the coast, was the land Don Sebastian had described to Harold's father, consisting of about eighteen thousand acres, some marsh land, but mostly excellent farming land with ample vegetation for cattle. Miguel, the Don said, would escort *Señor* Stromberg to the site as soon as he had sufficiently rested from his arduous journey, a two- or three-day process during which he would be well cared for.

After being shown to his room, Harold unpacked some of his clothing, then stood on the balcony, admiring the view of both the harbor and the town of Mazatlán. In the center of town, the spires of a magnificent cathedral rose above the red tile roofs of the buildings surrounding it, its bells pealing pleasantly, calling the faithful to evening worship.

Below, in the quadrant, several riders made a dramatic entrance, their horses' hoofs clattering on the floor of the cobblestone paved courtyard. Servants rushed to attend to the horses, controlling the spirited animals as the riders dismounted. Harold's eyes were riveted to one of them. She wore a black, tailored riding skirt, a white, long-sleeved silk blouse, and polished, black leather boots, and her eyes were shaded by a flat-brimmed Spanish riding hat with dangling tassels. Dismounting skillfully and with an air of authority, she handed the reins of her excited stallion to one of the grooms. Stepping away from the horse, she loosened the wooden slide on the cord under her chin, allowing her hat to fall from her head to the back of her neck. Then, removing a comb and shaking out her long, black hair, she turned toward the house. Before disappearing from the courtyard, she glanced up at the balcony, catching Harold's eye, smiling slightly and nodding to acknowledge his presence. Then she was gone.

As the courtyard cleared, Harold remained for a time on the balcony, feeling as though he had been granted the privilege of observing the royal party. He returned to his room, where he slept, lying on his bed, until he was roused by a light tapping on his door.

"*Señor* Stromberg?" an accented male voice called through the door.

Startled from his unplanned sleep, Harold stirred slowly. "Yes, yes."

"*Señor*, dinner will be served in thirty minutes, *por favor*."

"Yes, of course. I'll be there," Harold responded groggily.

The servants were waiting with cool lemonade as Harold descended the spiral staircase and found Miguel Antonio on the verandah. As was the case from his room, the view was magnificent, encompassing the entire harbor and the colorful boats of the fishing fleet anchored there. They were quickly joined by Don Sebastian, who greeted Harold as Magnus had advised him to expect, with the most cordial of Mexican greetings. "*Mi Casa, Su Casa*," Don Sebastian declared.

The courtesy of saying "my house is your house," in the Spanish tradition, meant exactly that. Full privileges of the house were afforded, and the guest was treated as family by the servants, made to feel completely at home. His father's advice had proved correct, and the custom was exactly to Harold's liking. He would revel in the courtesies being extended him.

"Don Sebastian, I brought some documents from my father," Harold said, handing a sealed packet to his host.

"*Gracias, Señor*," Don Sebastian responded. "And how is your father?"

"Quite well, sir, thank you. He sends his regards and asks that you take no insult from his not having come in person."

"Ah, *de nada, Señor*. It is nothing. We are most honored to have his eldest son with whom to conduct our business. Surely you will wish to see the land we have proposed to your father, but first we must show you some of the hospitality of Mexico and of our beautiful Mazatlán. Do you ride, *Señor?*"

Harold smiled. "*Sí*, Don Sebastian. My father taught me to ride as a young boy."

"Ah, *bueno*. Then tomorrow, perhaps you and Miguel can ride some of the countryside, and you will learn a bit about our land and our people."

"I would like that, Don Sebastian. If that would be acceptable to you, Miguel," Harold said, looking toward the younger man.

"My pleasure, Harold. It is my hope that we become good friends, as we shall be neighbors shortly."

Harold's eye caught a flurry of activity as several servants moved toward the staircase and *Señor* Cardenas and Miguel turned toward the inner room. Harold watched as the young woman he had seen earlier gracefully descended the staircase. Her eyes locked for a moment with Harold's, and then she turned her attention to her father, smiling at him as she came forward.

Harold hadn't thought she could look more beautiful than she had appeared in riding costume earlier, but her presentation this evening was stunning. She wore a simple, yet elegant, full length, powder blue, empire-waist dress of satin material, accented only by a pearl necklace and matching single pearl earrings. Her dark hair, now removed from the plaiting she had worn earlier, hung in a dramatic single coil, cascading over one shoulder.

"*Señor* Harold Stromberg, allow me to present my daughter, Teresa Maria Cardenas. Teresa, this is my old friend Magnus Stromberg's eldest son, Harold."

Teresa performed a slight curtsy and nodded her head as she offered a smile to Harold. "*El gusto es mio, Señor,*" she said softly. Switching to English, she continued her greeting. "It is a pleasure to welcome you to my father's house, Mr. Stromberg. It is our hope you will find everything acceptable. I am at your service, *Señor,* to make your stay as pleasant as possible."

Harold stood quietly, enjoying her beauty and marveling at the grace with which she assumed the role of hostess in her father's house. Don Sebastian spoke to break the brief silent interlude.

"My wife has been dead for some years now, Harold, and Teresa has graciously accepted the responsibility to serve as the woman of the house. We pay great respect to the hostess," he laughed, "and I'm certain you will find that Teresa will spare no effort to assure you are welcomed with proper Spanish civility," he said, wrapping his arm proudly around his daughter.

"Don Sebastian, that I may be deserving of such hospitality is my foremost desire, and, through a growing friendship with your son," he said, looking at Miguel, "to solidify the relationship you have formed with my father. And, of course, your lovely daughter," he added, taking care to smile directly at Teresa and receiving in return a pleasant smile from the beautiful young woman. "Thank you most humbly for this warm and gracious welcome."

Don Sebastian smiled broadly, nodding toward his son and looking back toward Harold. "Well said, young man.

213

Your father has been a great friend to us and rendered us a valuable service. It will be an honor to have the Stromberg family as our neighbors in Mazatlán. To your health, *Señor*," the Don said, raising his glass. "And rest assured, Harold," he added, "your father has long ago explained to me your religious beliefs with regard to alcohol. I assure you that you will have them honored while in my household. Now," he gestured toward the dining room, "if you would be so kind as to escort my daughter to the table, *Señor* Stromberg, we will commence with dinner."

Teresa moved toward Harold, waiting for him to initiate their movement toward the dining room. Realizing that all were waiting for him, as the lady's escort, Harold stepped off lightly. A waiting servant assisted with her chair, the one at her father's left. Harold, at the unspoken direction of another servant, was seated on his right, directly across from Teresa.

At the conclusion of dinner, the four removed to the drawing room, a spacious, leather appointed room filled with books of all origin, many in English, as during the next several days, Harold would come to discover. Pleasant conversation consumed the evening until shortly before eleven, when Teresa excused herself. Her father and brother stood, bringing Harold to his feet also as she prepared to leave.

Before exiting the room, she glanced at Harold, then turned to Miguel. "Perhaps, Miguel, *Señor* Stromberg would like to join us for an early morning ride."

Miguel looked at Harold for his consent.

"It would be my pleasure, *Señorita* Cardenas."

"Excellent," she said. "Shall we say six o'clock?"

Harold nodded. "I will look forward to it. Until then," he replied, enjoying the dramatics of the situation and bowing slightly as she exited the room.

"Well," announced Don Sebastian, "I think it's time an old man also took his leave. One thing, Harold," he added. "Your father included this envelope in the packet of documents he provided. I believe it is for your eyes." He handed Harold a sealed envelope that had his name boldly written on the outside.

"Thank you, *Señor* Cardenas. If you'll excuse me, I think I would also like to go to bed. It's been a long day, and six o'clock will come early. Thank you for providing such a warm welcome."

"*De nada, Señor* Stromberg . . . , uh, Harold. We are glad to have your presence. Miguel," the Don said, looking toward his son, "you will see to the household, *sí?*"

"*Sí*, Father. Good-night."

After the older man had taken his leave, and before he left to secure the house, Miguel asked, "Do you have ample riding gear, Harold, boots and all?"

"Yes, thank you, Miguel. My father described the pleasures I might enjoy here, and I came prepared."

"Excellent. Until tomorrow then. I bid you good-night."

"Good-night, Miguel," Harold said, "and thank you."

⚬⚬⚬

Back in his room, Harold removed his shoes and loosened his tie, then sat on the bed to open the letter from his father. *Strange*, Harold thought, *that Father didn't simply give me the note before I left, or advise me to open it en route on the ship.* He slit the envelope and unfolded the pages.

Dear Harold,

By now you will have been warmly welcomed by Don Sebastian. No one knows how to make a guest feel more at home than the Spanish nobility. You will no doubt be curious why I

215

didn't instruct you as to the contents of this note before you left home. That will become apparent quickly.

Harold, this new and bold venture upon which the Strombergs and many of those who will follow us will enter is a dramatic step. After a great deal of soul searching, I have come to the conclusion that the so-called Manifesto wrongly precludes faithful followers from living the Principle that the Prophet Joseph taught and died for. Whatever the reason (I see it as political), the Church has taken a wrong turn that will lead to its ruination. It is clear, the President is being counseled by fools, and I would not be true to the understanding I have been given if I failed to act. I know there are many who share this vision of things and who will look to us for an example.

As we have discussed, the establishment of our new colony will once again allow us to re-institute the true Church and the principles we should follow.

You know that for several years now, my other families have been secreted throughout Utah, and that your dear mother is the only one with whom I have been allowed to openly reside. But my love for my other wives and children has not diminished. I sense that you know and understand these things.

Young Katrina will make a fine addition to our family, and we are pleased to have her in our household. However, to establish a firm and lasting relationship with the Cardenas family, Don Sebastian and I have agreed to cement the family ties by arranging for the marriage of my eldest son to his daughter, Teresa, during your visit to Mexico. If you see the wisdom in this arrangement, you, my son, will commence the colony in Mexico as the husband of Teresa Maria Cardenas. By the time you receive this note, she will have been apprised of the arrangement, and, as is customary in their society, she will have been prepared to enter into the marriage, in accordance with the wishes of her father.

While this will no doubt come as a surprise to you, so quickly arranged and all, and so soon after your marriage to Katrina, it will also establish you as the heir apparent to the Stromberg line and the person with whom Don Sebastian will be most anxious to reach agreement.

Be assured, my son, that the Lord is pleased with our actions. Because it is only our desire to follow His will, we shall be blessed.

One final note: Do not under any circumstances advise Señor Cardenas or any of his household of your recent marriage to Katrina. We must move carefully so as not to offend Mexican or Catholic sensibilities. Proceed with due caution, and may your trip and mission to establish our colony be blessed with success.

Lovingly, Your father

P.S. I offer my deepest regrets that I will not be able to attend your wedding. Follow the established Catholic tradition, Harold, as would be proper and acceptable for a guest, and we shall arrange for the ultimate proper ordinance as quickly as possible.

In the west wing of the house, a light tap on Teresa's door brought her small voice. "Come in."

Don Sebastian entered his daughter's bedroom, where she had changed into her night clothes and robe.

"Well, my daughter. It is not so bad a proposition, is it?"

Teresa smiled at her father. She had been brushing her long, dark hair in the light of the kerosene lamp on her dresser, but she laid aside her brush to address her father.

"He has not the blood of our Spanish ancestors flowing through his veins, Father, but he seems a most respectable young man."

"Well said, my daughter. And as to your appreciation of him, personally?"

"He is not unattractive, Father. I understand our interests and will of course obey your wishes."

Don Sebastian moved close to his daughter, kissed her lightly on the forehead, and stepped back toward the door. Turning to admire her reflection in the mirror, he said lovingly, "You look so like your beautiful mother when she was at your age. Harold Stromberg is a most fortunate young man."

Teresa Maria Cardenas would be a major player in the amalgamation of two powerful families. She knew she had no choice but to follow her father's wishes and had in her heart hoped this Harold Stromberg would be someone she could love. Her assessment was that she could readily marry the handsome, young *Yanqui* who proposed to establish a new colony in Mexico. She would demonstrate her obedience to her father's wishes and at the same time produce heirs to two dynasties. To do otherwise would be unthinkable and unbecoming the obedient daughter of Don Sebastian Cardenas. Besides, she was confident of her ability to retain in her relationship with her American husband the same kind of independence she had always enjoyed under the hand of her father. She had no fears.

In Salt Lake, Katrina Stromberg filled her days with reading, sewing clothes for the expected baby, and watching for mail from Harold. Only one letter had come since his departure, and that had been posted in San Francisco the day his ship left for Mexico.

Katrina's mother, Jenny Hansen, was only marginally helpful in assisting Katrina to accept Harold's absence and to help her to deal with the discomforting early stages of her pregnancy. Her mother's counsel, understandable in the face of her own marriage, was simple: "You're married now, Katrina. Think to your husband and plan for your family. All will be well."

Living alone in the house Harold had rented was lonely, but Katrina frequently invited her younger sisters to stay with her, and on those occasions, Katrina reverted to her childhood and filled all their time together with fun and laughter.

Only in the quiet of the lonely nights did Katrina pour her heart out to Nana about the yearnings in her heart and the feelings she had that sometimes bordered on misery. Afraid of putting her eternal promises in jeopardy, she resisted the temptation to reflect on what she thought of as her "passing fancy," for that is what she had taken to calling Tom's journey through her life. She tried instead to dwell more on her forthcoming motherhood than on either Tom or Harold.

Another thing was that Katrina never felt entirely comfortable in her in-laws' home. Though she was treated in a kindly manner, Father Stromberg had become increasingly outspoken with regard to his feelings about what he saw as the Prophet's "lack of vision." Katrina frequently felt a dark spirit in her husband's parents' home, and although she was unaware of the full purpose of Harold's trip to Mexico, she had a feeling of foreboding that she found impossible to shake. She knew Father Stromberg's constant criticism of the Prophet was not right.

15

Nearly fifteen hundred miles up the Yukon River lay the small community of Ft. Yukon. Situated at the confluence of the Yukon and the Porcupine rivers, the settlement had been in existence since early Russian control of the territory, and had been an Athapascan Indian campground before that. A one day layover allowed Tom and John the opportunity to stretch their legs and buy some prospecting gear. Gold panning, or placer mining as it was technically called, didn't actually require much in the way of hardware, and in fact many a miner got by with nothing more than the traditional pan and a rock hammer. Rumors of higher equipment costs in Dawson, most likely started by the merchants in Ft. Yukon who wanted the business, convinced John that they should outfit before they arrived.

Since it was early in August, there were no immediate concerns about their ability to reach Dawson before freeze-up, and the late summer weather was pleasant enough, even though Ft. Yukon was positioned precisely on the Arctic Circle. For most of the trip, Tom had lazed about on the deck of the sternwheeler, watching spectacular scenery roll before him, mixed with endless miles of flat tundra, which was nearly as mind numbing as the prairie had been, west of Kansas City.

How long ago that all seemed. It was almost inconceivable to Tom that he had experienced so many changes in just over one year, and melancholy frequently overtook him. John's promptings for the lad to join him in "a few pints," nearly persuaded him on a number of occasions to abandon his determination regarding alcohol. The fact that John drank nearly as heavily as Tom's father had caused Tom some concern, but John's drunkenness produced a jovial, rather than a combative personality.

The trip provided Tom ample opportunity to reflect on all that had happened to him since his hasty departure from Tipperary. The walk through Ireland, the ocean voyage to America, and everything since then, seemed as though it were a dream—especially the part of his memory dominated by the innocent face of a blonde, Norwegian young woman. When he allowed himself to think about it, the fact that she should be married to another man filled Tom with a feeling of despair. Because they were so painful, when thoughts of Katrina intruded, he made an almost desperate effort to drive them out of his mind. One thing he frequently thought of was that because he had thrown a punch at some mayor's son-in-law in Ireland, he was now caught in the wilds of Alaska. He recalled as well the stories he had heard in Ireland of Irish and English alike being hauled before the courts and banished to the penal colony in Australia, merely for stealing a loaf of bread. At least he still had his freedom.

Before leaving Anvil, John explained to Tom that since transport out was impossible during winter, they would be in Dawson, or nearby, for the remainder of the year and well into '97. Tom's letter to Sister Mary, posted before they left Anvil, had been nearly as hard to write as the note he'd written the night he so quickly departed Salt Lake City. He left out the part about the law being after him, rationalizing that Father Scanlan had probably covered enough of that to ease Sister Mary's concerns. Tom's main purpose in writing the letter was to assure her that his departure had nothing to do with dissatisfaction over his job at Holy Cross or the treatment he had received there. Indicating "General Delivery, Dawson City," as his forwarding address through the year, Tom felt he'd honored his commitment to Father Scanlan to keep his friends advised of his location.

Several hundred miles further up the Yukon lay Dawson City and an unknown future for Tom. Spending a year with Uncle John would be tolerable, he figured, and as he'd explained in a letter to his mother, posted at the same time as the one to Sister Mary, it would be good to spend time with her brother. Tom knew the news that he had located Uncle John would please his mother and that she would feel her son was in good hands.

As the riverboat approached Dawson, Tom thought someone had made a mistake in calling it a "city." New York was a city. Dublin was a city. And even Salt Lake was a city. But the ramshackle cluster of wooden structures off the port bow of the riverboat would by no standard Tom knew qualify the place to be called a city. Within two hours of arriving on 19 August 1896, John Ryan had located Carmack, a grizzled, nearly toothless man with an almost skeletal physique, who had just arrived from his claim. John and Tom listened in astonishment as Carmack, his words whistling through his missing front teeth, breathlessly described his amazing gold strike of two days earlier. In town to file his claim, Carmack was heading immediately back to Fortymile, an even smaller cluster of shacks up the Klondike River, and from there to his claim. Ryan was welcome to join him, Carmack said, but he'd better file for a claim first, if he wanted to participate in the "find of the century," as he called it.

Of course, Carmack added, within the first few hours, most of the claims on Rabbit Creek, where he'd made his find, had been taken and miners were already en route to join in the bonanza. There were, Carmack suggested, small tributaries of Rabbit Creek, itself only a slightly larger tributary of the Klondike, and even though the various other feeder streams probably wouldn't be as rich as his claim on Rabbit, Carmack told John Ryan and his nephew that they most likely could scratch thousands of dollars from the sand and gravel laying in the stream beds.

And so it was that Tom Callahan, approaching his twenty-first birthday, and his uncle, John Ryan, these nine years out of Ireland, filed two claims on a small creek in the upper reaches of Yukon Territory, Canada. Each claim entitled them to five hundred feet on either side of the creek. Their two adjacent claims gave the Irish kinsmen one thousand feet of creek frontage to prospect. Not much was expected by either man, although John, having prospected for several years along tributaries of the Yukon, was aware that the color and concentration of Carmack's gold was of extremely high quality. Tom, totally ignorant of anything having to do with prospecting, simply followed along with what John said and got caught up in the gold fever rampaging through Dawson and Fortymile, both of which had been emptied of miners racing for their share of the golden dream.

Arriving at the site, Tom and John quickly staked their claims, which they named *Emerald One* and *Emerald Two*. From Tom's point of view, the location seemed fine, but John's assessment left him dour. The claims immediately above and below Carmack's had, indeed, been taken by early arrivals. The small creek which held Carmack's *Discovery* claim, was surrounded by *One Above*, *One Below*, and *Two Below*, traditional names attached to the claims surrounding significant gold finds. *Discovery* and *One Below* belonged to Carmack as the original filer, who, by tradition, was entitled to two personal claims. *One Above* and *Two Below* went to his two Indian brothers-in-law.

As miners arrived in growing numbers during the closing days of August and early in September, the traditional names of the creeks were quickly changed. Rabbit Creek became Bonanza Creek, in honor of the find, and an adjacent creek, Thron-diuck, was tagged Klondike, a name by which the entire region would come to be called. Within a year, the Klondike gold strike would make the world's headlines, and tens of thousands would scurry and scramble for their piece of Nirvana.

However, the most surprising development to the local miners, who raced to stake claims close to *Discovery* and *One Below*, would not be known to any of the parties involved until much later that year. It was the small, previously unnamed tributary, which flowed into Rabbit Creek, that eventually came to be called El Dorado. And the richest and most profitable claims, from which came wealth that exceeded even the wildest dreams of the most optimistic miners, were those in the side stream claims, the ones taken up by those who originally thought they were too late. It was in the sands and gravels of the El Dorado—the secondary stream to which Carmack directed John and Tom—that the gods of fortune had distributed their greatest concentrations of wealth.

Tom Callahan and John Ryan, uncle and nephew, by stroke of fate or fortune—or as Tom had told Katrina Hansen nearly a year earlier on the deck of the *Antioch*, intervention of the Lord—were sitting smack dab in the middle of the richest gold strike in history and would amass their fortunes before the rest of the world even knew of the find. But a backbreaking fall, winter, and spring would ensue before that occurred and they would be able to achieve their manifold destiny.

❦

Katrina sat patiently in the foyer inside the main entrance to Holy Cross Hospital, watching as people bustled up and down the corridor. Finally, a woman dressed in nun's habit approached and smiled at her.

"I'm Sister Mary Theophane. May I be of some assistance?"

Katrina stood, nervous and hesitant about how to proceed. "Sister, I would like to talk with you privately, if possible."

Escorting Katrina to a small room, off the main women's wing, Sister Mary offered Katrina a seat and then sat down facing her, "Now, how may I help, dear?"

"Sister, I don't really know how to begin . . . I . . ."

Sister Mary reached for her hand, smiling at her, and studying her fresh, young face. "Are you with child, my dear?" she asked, gently.

Katrina began to blush, surprised by the inquiry. "Why, yes, yes, I am, Sister."

Still holding Katrina's hand, Sister Mary sought to reassure her. "You needn't be afraid," she said. "We'll do all we can to see you through your pregnancy, and we'll help you find a suitable home for your child, if that is your wish."

Confused for a moment by Sister Mary's offer, Katrina suddenly understood and had to stifle a laugh.

"Sister, I think I've misled you. I'm married and carrying my husband's child. I don't need, uh, I mean, I'm not . . . ,"

It was Sister Mary's turn to blush. With an embarrassed look on her face, and holding her hand over her mouth, she at first didn't know what to say. But after a moment she began to laugh and shake her head. "Oh, dear," she said. "I'm afraid I've put my foot in it. I do hope you can forgive me. How may I help you?"

The misunderstanding served to lessen Katrina's nervousness. She was surprised to find this tall woman in a nun's habit could laugh at herself, and she relaxed somewhat.

"Sister," Katrina began again, "I hope I'm not acting improperly, but I've come to inquire about a Mr. Callahan. I believe he was in your employ not long ago."

"Indeed he was," Sister Mary responded. "Oh, yes, and you must be young Katrina Hansen, or uh, Stommen, is it?"

"Stromberg, Sister. Katrina Stromberg."

"Yes, indeed. And what about Mr. Callahan, Mrs. Stromberg?"

"Well, Sister, it's about a document I discovered a few days ago. My husband has gone to Mexico on business, and I was searching for writing paper in our desk drawer when I discovered this file," she said, taking a large envelope from her purse. "It is a detective agency report on Mr. Callahan."

Sister Mary remained silent, but was listening intently,

keenly interested in what the young woman might have to say.

"Sister, I have been led to believe, by my husband, that Mr. Callahan murdered someone and is being sought by the authorities in Kansas City. Mr. Stromberg also told me that, out of consideration for Mr. Callahan, he had informed Thom . . . Mr. Callahan that he was about to be apprehended and suggested he leave Salt Lake."

Katrina hesitated, embarrassed to admit she had caught her husband in a lie. "What Mr. Stromberg failed to . . ." Katrina hesitated again, but then pressed on, determined to see the matter through.

"Sister," she said resolutely, "what my husband didn't tell me was that Mr. Callahan had never been charged with that crime—that it was known he had acted in self-defense and that he had never been wanted by the police."

That much said, Katrina began to cry, and searched her purse for a handkerchief. Then, wiping her eyes, she continued, "My brother tells me Thomas has gone to Alaska, but wherever he is, he thinks he is wanted for murder. Sister, it isn't right, and I came hoping you have some way to contact him and let him know he doesn't need to keep running."

Sister Mary again reached for Katrina's hand. "I'm certain this was hard for you, my child. Rest assured, I have known of young Thomas's innocence for some time. But thank you for having the courage to come forth. I assure you that I will notify Mr. Callahan that he is not being pursued by the authorities."

"Thank you, Sister," Katrina said, standing up. Before leaving she said, "Would you communicate one more thing to him for me?"

"Yes, my child?"

"Please tell Mr. Callahan that I'm sorry for the insult my husband has paid him and for the disruption in his life."

"Thank you, Mrs. Stromberg. Thomas will be pleased to know of your concern. Good day to you. Please call on me if I can be of any further assistance."

———

There would be some scrub brush and marshy lands to contend with, but all in all, Harold Stromberg felt the land Don Sebastian had offered his father would prove excellent. Mr. Bowen who had accompanied Harold, concurred that the land was quite suitable for farming and that grazing for cattle was excellent.

Harold had spent three days in Mazatlán and then another two at the Cardenas hacienda north on the coast before undertaking actual inspection of the proposed site. He had not felt the time wasted, however, for he had spent most of it, accompanied by Miguel Antonio, in the company of the lovely Teresa Maria. The courtship, now that the couple had openly acknowledged their engagement, proved most satisfactory to each party. Their mutual admiration was evident to everyone, and Don Sebastian had reported the same in a telegram to Magnus Stromberg, Harold's father.

That is not to say Harold's conscience didn't plague him. Even though the second marriage had his father's tacit approval and fit in under the guidelines of the Order he was prepared to follow, he couldn't help reflecting on the impact such an arrangement was going to have on Katrina or how he would actually break the news to each of his wives about the other. His feelings became more acute when his father advised him by telegram that Katrina was pregnant. He knew also, that his original marriage would have to be kept secret for some time after the colony was established in Mexico, if they were to avoid inflaming Teresa's family and prevent coming into conflict with Mexican customs and Catholic propriety. How that would all work out, Harold preferred to leave in the hands of his father and Don Sebastian, but for the present, Harold was quite content to work toward his marriage to this exceptionally beautiful and aristocratic woman.

Teresa Maria Cardenas, though born in Mazatlán, Mexico, was of direct Spanish descent and, according to custom, had spent much of her youth in Spain, undertaking her education under the tutelage of family and professional associates of Don Sebastian. Well versed in Spanish, French, and English, Teresa actually knew more about world politics and the practical economics of farming and ranching than Harold, for Don Sebastian had not been inclined to allow his only daughter to function as a mere household decoration, as was the case with so many of his peers throughout Mexico. He had provided her with a most thorough education and was enormously proud of her.

As for Miguel Antonio, Don Sebastian was depending upon his only son, who was an able rancher, to carry on the family name and legacy. The marriage of his daughter into this American family would, at least down Teresa's line, dilute the purity of their Spanish pedigree, so carefully protected since Captain Cardenas had explored the area over three and a half centuries ago. Many Cardenas offspring existed throughout the territory, but none with proven or acknowledged family lineage records, other than those from marriages that had been sanctioned and blessed by the Catholic Archbishop of Mexico.

Unknown to either Miguel or Teresa, Don Sebastian had conferred with Mexican President Diaz, and the two

230

men had reached an understanding regarding the political benefit of establishing marital ties between the Cardenas line and a prominent *Yanqui* family, such as the Strombergs. Seeds of revolution continued to plague the Mexican government, and President Diaz, ever mindful of retaining power, felt that an American colony situated deep in Mexico, might one day provide leverage to compel U.S. military support should it ever be required to put down a full-scale insurrection. The sacrifice of Teresa Cardenas's noble heritage was a small cost to pay for such insurance.

Harold now understood that his father and Don Sebastian had arranged this marriage some time ago and that he had been the only one unaware. Teresa had long since prepared her trousseau, and the marriage bans had been officially posted several weeks before Harold's arrival. The customary three-year engagement, typical in Spanish families, had been waived on the basis of Don Sebastian's declaration that the marriage had actually been arranged several years before. Given his status, Don Sebastian's public explanation that it had been in the interest of both families to keep the agreement confidential was entirely acceptable.

Only on one occasion had Harold been bold enough to broach the subject with Teresa and to ask directly if she were in agreement with their fathers' arrangement of the marriage.

"Harold, I can think of no greater honor than to be the instrument in the merging of our two great families, and as for myself," she said, lowering her eyes and glancing at Miguel Antonio, discreetly positioned on his horse off to one side, "I couldn't be more pleased, if my father had allowed me complete choice in the matter."

Harold was flattered by Teresa's response. The idea of

being married to this darkly beautiful and exotic woman sat increasingly well with him. Whatever reservations he might have initially entertained were quickly being swallowed up in the adventure of spending time, galloping side by side on spirited horses, across her father's vast holdings. For increasingly long periods of time, he was able to quite comfortably put Katrina out of his mind and attend to the business at hand.

So, in the third week in August, 1896, nearly six weeks after Harold Stromberg's arrival in Mexico, with not so much as a single kiss having been exchanged between them, Harold Cumberland Stromberg and Teresa Maria Vasquez Cardenas were married in all the pomp and glory of a Catholic ceremony in the magnificent cathedral in Mazatlán, Mexico, the ceremony performed by the Archbishop of Mexico, himself, Father Hernando Portolo.

The guest list included Mexican President Porfiro Diaz, with whom Don Sebastian had labored long and hard to assure that the Cardenas name was retained among the inner circle. Diaz held some residual animosity toward the United States over the events of the Mexican-American War of 1845, and the loss of the territory of Texas to the United States. So he might have opposed Don Sebastian's plan to sell off part of his Spanish land grant territory to the gringos from the north, but Diaz recalled that the several other American colonies, located just south of the United States border, had been largely assimilated into Mexican culture by the second generation. The presence of this colony might also serve to help strengthen the local economy and raise the standard of living of the Mexican people in the area. Besides, the land purchased by the Strombergs was deep enough into Mexico so as to ease Diaz's mind on the potential problems. And, finally, the thought of using the colony as justification for requesting U. S. military support to forestall potential rebellion capped his decision.

By the middle of September, Harold and Teresa had returned from their honeymoon. They had taken a two-day cruise down the Pacific coast on a sailing ship to a quaint little village, where for a week, the proprietors of the inn waited on their every need. On the ninth of September, Harold again bid a new bride adieu, and sailed, together with Mr. Bowen, back to San Francisco. From there, they took the train to Salt Lake City, where Harold made a detailed report to his father. Offering his heartiest congratulations to Harold on his marriage to Teresa and expressing full satisfaction over the success of his son's trip, the elder Stromberg announced that it only remained to arrange for the relocation of about sixty families who had expressed their desire to join the Stromberg colony in Mexico.

As had been the case with Katrina, two weeks after Harold's departure, and just a month after the ceremony, Teresa Maria proudly informed her father that she was with child and that in late spring, the first Cardenas-Stromberg heir would appear. Don Sebastian was overjoyed.

———

Father Lawrence Scanlan's heart was heavy as he took his morning walk, the hint of fall hanging in the air over the Salt Lake valley. Scanlan had developed a reputation among the Mormon population of Salt Lake City of being even-handed in his approach to the question of polygamy. Not that he condoned such marriages, for as preceptor of the Catholic Church in Utah, Father Scanlan had often condemned the practice of plural marriage to his parishioners.

But, in his dealings in the public forum and with the leaders of the Mormon church, he had maintained a quiet, respectful demeanor, intended to soothe, rather than inflame the anti-Mormon fervor that had raged over polygamy in the non-Mormon population of the Valley prior to the Manifesto.

The issuance of the Manifesto by President Woodruff had been hailed by Bishop Scanlan as a great step forward and one that God approved. On that point, both Catholic and Mormon leadership were in agreement.

His meeting, however, with George Q. Cannon the previous evening had been most disconcerting. President Cannon had, of course, been as cordial as ever and had received Bishop Scanlan into his home with perfect civility. However, the news that Bishop Scanlan had brought to President Cannon was not so pleasant.

In an attempt to discover more about the *Yanqui* family moving from Salt Lake City to Mexico, Bishop Hernando Portolo, Archbishop of the Mexican Diocese, had written to Bishop Scanlan to inquire about the Stromberg family. In his discourse, Bishop Portolo had informed Bishop Scanlan that he was scheduled to perform the marriage ceremony for Don Sebastian Cardenas's only daughter, Teresa, to one Harold Stromberg of Salt Lake City. Any information that Father Scanlan could provide on the family would be most helpful.

Father Scanlan was not acquainted with Harold Stromberg, and in fact knew little of the man's standing in the Mormon Church. Sister Mary had told Father Scanlan about Katrina Stromberg's visit and the fact that Harold had acted vindictively toward their Irish friend. And Father Scanlan *was* acquainted with Magnus Stromberg, as he was with most of the prominent businessmen in Salt Lake. He had the impression that the elder Stromberg was highly regarded by the leaders of the Mormon Church. His going

234

to President Cannon was, then, a matter of professional courtesy. If Harold Stromberg intended to take a second wife, it was in violation of the Manifesto. And since it probably involved some duplicity *and* a Catholic woman, both churches had an interest in the matter.

President Cannon had received the news of the impending marriage without comment except to say he would look into the matter, but Father Scanlan left their meeting with the distinct impression that the Mormon leader had been saddened by the news of the pending plural marriage in the Stromberg family.

Now, as Scanlan approached Holy Cross Hospital on his morning walk, he, too, was saddened by the turn of events, for Sister Mary had been most complimentary of the young Stromberg woman and her desire to ensure that justice was done in the case of Thomas Callahan.

The final piece that concerned Bishop Scanlan, and over which he was now most perplexed, was the telegram from the western region headquarters of the Catholic Church, in San Francisco. "It is with regret," it had announced, "that we inform you of the unexpected death of Archbishop Hernando Portolo in Mexico City." His successor was not named in the telegram.

As Father Scanlan relayed all this to Sister Mary, it became readily apparent that he actually had no one to whom he could reply regarding Bishop Portolo's request for information on the Stromberg family. If he wrote directly to Don Sebastian, he would be interfering in family affairs and, of course, no individual had as yet come to him for advice or counsel.

The issue for the Catholic Church, at least for the present, had died with Bishop Portolo, who, if the dates indicated in his original letter were correct, had already performed the marriage ceremony. Delivering the news to Sister Mary, Father Scanlan suggested they keep the information to themselves and let the Mormon leadership handle it as they saw fit. Accordingly, in her next letter to Thomas Callahan, a follow-up to her letter several weeks earlier, neither of which would be received by Tom until the Yukon was passable in the spring, she made no mention of either Katrina Stromberg's husband's duplicitous behavior, or of the action Father Scanlan was certain President George Q. Cannon would take concerning Harold Stromberg's Church membership.

Father Scanlan's observations of President Cannon proved quite correct. Following Church policy in the matter, Harold's bishop and stake president were advised of the situation and asked to look into it. When questioned about his having entered into a second marriage in violation of the Manifesto, Harold confessed his action but argued his right to do so. In a Church court convened to try him for his membership, Harold was excommunicated, for the practice of plural marriage, contrary to the order of the Church.

In private meetings, President Cannon conferred also with Harold's father, Magnus Stromberg, a long-standing member of the Church, who was well respected in the community.

Magnus Stromberg's reluctance to accept Church counsel left little doubt as to his stance concerning the matter. Because the elder Stromberg had not entered into another plural marriage since the Manifesto, even though he maintained four wives and their families who lived in various locations throughout Utah, there was still no charge that could be laid against him.

Where he found himself in difficulty was his refusal to sustain the President of the Church and the declared word

236

of the Lord on the continuing practice of plural marriage. When pressed for his views, he finally revealed the full measure of his apostasy and left the meeting with President Cannon in a pique of anger, more determined than ever to bolt the Church and move himself, his families, and others who were supportive of his position to Mexico. The excommunication of young Harold, which followed quickly, for entering into an illegal plural marriage, was the final blow.

Magnus arranged for immediate departure of those families who sought to join the colony. With the number reduced to thirty-seven from the original sixty families, Harold was instructed by his father to make all necessary preparations to depart at the earliest opportunity.

Katrina was not advised specifically *why*, only that Harold had been excommunicated. She was led to understand by her husband and father-in-law that it had to do only with the Stromberg's determination to establish a Mormon colony in Mexico, contrary to the wishes of Church leaders. Magnus Stromberg told her that other colonies had experienced similar problems and that she should not worry. He assured her Harold would be quickly reinstated as soon as the colony came to be a permanent fixture and the Church leaders saw the merit in the relocation.

Katrina's father provided a different sort of counsel.

"This is not good, Katrina. You should stay here in Salt Lake until the issue is settled by the Church," he advised.

"Poppa, he is my husband. I must go with him. You have told me many times that the wife must obey the husband and follow his lead," she replied.

"Ya, but he is now out of the Church, Katrina."

"I know, but Father Stromberg told me not to worry. All will be made right, soon."

"Ya, well, he must know. He is longtime a member."

And so, against her father's wishes, Katrina sailed with Harold and something over a hundred others, some of them former members of the Church, as they left San Francisco for Mexico. Having been assured by both Harold and Magnus that all would shortly be well, Katrina was nevertheless alarmed as they neared the Mexican coast and their destination. Harold chose a moment when she was repacking their luggage just prior to their arrival, to talk to her.

"Katrina, for a while, it will be best if you pretend that you are my sister, and not my wife."

"What!" she exclaimed.

"It's only for a short time, Katrina. It's just that the land purchase is complicated, and I have many dealings with *Señor* Cardenas to complete. I will need to stay with them in their hacienda for some weeks, and it would be better if they did not know that I was married. I've arranged for you to stay with the Olsens until I can arrange for our house to be built."

"Harold, I don't want to stay with the Olsens. I want to be with you."

"I understand, dear," he said, taking her face in his hands. "Just be patient for a while, Katrina. I have our best interests at heart. Remember, if you'd not learned of the true nature of that Callahan lout, you might now be married to a murderer."

Katrina remained silent, though hearing such a blatant evidence of Harold's duplicity made her almost physically ill. He *knew* Thomas was not guilty of murder, and to hear him lie so callously was chilling.

When the ship entered the harbor at Mazatlán, and Miguel Antonio came out to meet Harold, Katrina was introduced as Harold's sister. Miguel insisted that, as a family member, she accompany them to the hacienda, but

Harold deferred, stating that she was needed to assist with the young Olsen children until the colony was able to construct permanent housing. Katrina's departure with the others left Harold little doubt that she was unhappy. His promise that he would see her in a few days did little to placate her anger or her resentment. But looking forward to his reunion with Teresa, Harold had little patience with Katrina's petulance and was frankly relieved to be away from her for a few days. He gave instructions to three of the men in the company, whom he had hired, to begin building a house for Katrina, and then, giving her a kiss on the forehead, left with Miguel.

16

The Mormon colonists arrived in early November and were greeted with many acts of generosity and hospitality by the Mexicans living in and around Mazatlán. Merchants, anxious to fill the orders for lumber, grain, and sundry supplies necessary to outfit a new community, were more than eager to welcome the newcomers, even though the colonists were not Catholic.

Harold was once again warmly greeted by Don Sebastian, but it was his welcome from Teresa that impressed Harold, assuring him of her affection for him and the degree to which she had missed him since his departure nearly eight weeks earlier. They had been married only four weeks when he had returned to Salt Lake City, and Teresa's request to accompany him had been difficult to deny, but eventually, with the support of Don Sebastian, Harold had convinced her to remain in Mazatlán and arrange for their future life together. How well she had accomplished that task was to quickly become a thorn in Harold's side.

As they retired to their bed on Harold's first night back in Mazatlán, Teresa had snuggled close to him and confided in him her joy that she had conceived and was bearing their first child. The news hit Harold like a thunderbolt, and he was relieved it was dark in the bedchamber, so that he did not have to explain the look of panic that came over his face. Lying there in the dark, he was able to make a reasonable expression of happiness at the news, but in reality, it was a complication he wasn't certain how to deal with. He was now the uneasy custodian of two wives, both pregnant, and each unaware of the other.

———◦◦◦———

The next morning, as he woke, Harold found Teresa up and already dressed in riding gear. She came and sat on the side of the bed, and with her hand, tenderly brushed back the tousled hair that she had come to recognize as Harold's morning trademark.

"I have a surprise for you this morning," she said.

"Just being with you each day is a surprise," Harold replied.

"Ah, then this will be extra special. I've laid out your riding clothes, and Manuel is preparing our horses."

"Where are we going?" he asked, rising, giving her a soft kiss, and heading for the bathroom.

Teresa followed, helping him to lather his face and watching in the mirror as he began stropping his razor on the leather. "I told you, it's a surprise," she teased.

"As you wish." He placed his hands on her shoulders and turned her toward the door. "I'll meet you downstairs for breakfast," he said, trying to have his morning bathroom ritual in private.

"The lord of the castle's wish, is my command," she laughed. "Twenty minutes, then breakfast and off into the countryside," she said as she left the room.

Cantering over the hilly terrain, Harold watched with pride as Teresa maintained her position ahead of his mount, riding as well as any man Harold knew, leading the way toward the surprise she had continued to tease him about through breakfast. His love for this woman had quickly become all consuming and he wondered how she would react when it came time to explain the marriage practices he and his father believed in. He did love Katrina, he thought to himself, but Teresa brought another dimension of excitement to his life and would be able to provide the social status in the community, which his father had determined to retain as the family left three generations of history behind in Utah. Marriage into the Cardenas line assured a continuation of that respect.

After about a thirty-minute ride, Teresa reined in her horse, looking back as Harold joined her on a small knoll that overlooked a lush, grass-filled valley. Below them, a small stream ran west toward the ocean, which was now in magnificent view from the position at which Teresa had chosen to stop. A large frame and stucco building was under construction off to their right, slightly higher up the knoll, and workmen were busily moving around the site. In front of Harold and Teresa, perhaps three miles farther on, but blocked from their view by the low, rolling hills, was the town site for Harold's new community, where the residents were also busy, building their new homes. The boundary of the land that Magnus Stromberg had purchased from Don Sebastian was just over the rise, marked by a small copse of Mesquite trees.

"You do give a body a workout when riding," Harold exclaimed, catching his breath.

"I love to ride. Father took me riding before I could sit a saddle. My equestrian instructor in Spain told me I should have entered competition, were I not returning to Mexico," she proudly exclaimed. Discovering this side of Teresa had initially startled Harold, for during their brief courtship, she had displayed no sense of accomplishment or outward pride, other than that engendered by her breeding. But soon after their marriage, it was as if Teresa wanted her new husband to know of her abilities and accomplishments, so that he might enjoy a greater sense of her worth.

"Is someone building here?" he asked.

"My father," she said, smiling.

"What will it be, another country home?"

"Yes."

Harold was puzzled and rose in his stirrups to look back over his horse in the direction they had come. "But the hacienda is only about five miles away. Why would he need another home so near our colony?" he asked, retaking his seat and looking at Teresa.

"For his daughter," she replied.

"His daughter?" Harold repeated, not fully comprehending.

"It is *our* home, Harold. The start of our hacienda," she explained, reaching across the space between their horses to lay her hand on his arm. "It is father's wedding present to us. In addition to the eighteen thousand acres your father purchased, Father has given us another fifteen hundred acres and eight hundred head of Longhorn cattle to start our herd."

Harold sat speechless in his saddle for several moments, watching the workmen scurrying about the building, now taking shape in his mind as a residence. "I had thought that we would live in your father's home for a while," he murmured.

"Father thought it best we have our own home, and that perhaps your father would stay with us, when he arrives, at least until he builds his own home. The homes your people are building are quite small. Only beginning homes actually. And when Miguel told me about your sister, I thought she should also move in with us, until her husband arrives and they can complete their home.

"Oh, Harold, it is magnificent," she beamed. "We will have our own home for our child to be born in. Let me show you what Father has done," she exclaimed, spurring her horse and leaving Harold alone on the crest of the knoll. He watched as she rode up the slope, dismounted in front of the house, and handed her reins to one of the workmen. Looking back once at Harold and waving excitedly, she entered the house.

From his vantage point, he could tell the home was exceptionally well situated to view the ocean and surrounding valley, yet close enough to the new Mormon community to enable Harold to be accessible to his people. Teresa had reasoned, that as the patron of his fledgling group, Harold should immediately command the respect due such a position by the establishment of a stately residence, located somewhat apart from the others.

Were it not for the presence of Katrina, Harold would have immediately agreed. As it was, the noose was closing around Harold's throat more quickly than he had planned, and the time was rapidly approaching when he would have to face the dilemma of how to introduce his wives to each other.

On a morning when Harold and Miguel rode into Mazatlán to order additional building materials for New Hope, the name the colonists had begun calling their settlement, Teresa set out with a buggy in the opposite direction for the colony. Harold had been silent on the subject of his sister coming to live in their new home, but had suggested that perhaps her assistance was still needed by the Olsens. Teresa rode past the house construction, spending a few minutes to observe changes since her last visit. Within three weeks, the foreman had said, the main part of the house would be livable and they would be able to move in. Certainly well before Christmas, he had promised.

Twice since Harold's return, Teresa had viewed the budding colony from a distance, but had not gone into the town, content to remain on horseback with Harold on the hillside overlooking New Hope. Twice Harold had gone alone to visit his sister, but had remained overnight only once, although he had held daytime meetings with the settlers of the colony on a more frequent basis.

Riding slowly into the area and guiding her horse and buggy around depressions in the rough road, Teresa was greeted with smiles and waves from those working on the new homes. One heavy-set woman preparing food for the workers, paused to wipe her hands on her apron, shading her eyes from the glare of the sun, and inviting Teresa to "light down and sit a spell."

"Thank you. It is becoming hot this morning," Teresa said as she wrapped the reins around the brake handle and stepped down from the buggy.

"Well, we've been at it since before sunup, but it's nearly

time for lunch for the crew, bless their hearts. How does a nice cup of lemonade sound?" she asked.

"Wonderful. You've made a lot of progress," Teresa commented, looking around the yard. "Do you think you'll be in your house before Christmas?"

"That's the plan, 'cept it'll only be a one-room cabin. That is 'til my husband gets 'em all built. Then he'll start on making each one a bit larger, as time and money permit."

"I see," Teresa said, perplexed. "How many cabins is your husband building? Is he helping another family?"

"We're all helping each other," the lady said, beginning to exercise caution. "Did you come to see someone in particular?"

"Yes," Teresa said, brightening. "I'd hoped to find Katrina Stromberg, Harold's sister."

"Harold's *sister?*" the lady asked, also confused. "Oh, yes, his sister," the lady repeated, covering her confusion. "Well, she'd be down to the large barn where all the children are. She's kind of looking after the kids."

"Excellent," Teresa responded, finishing her drink. "Well, I'd best be off. Thank you for the refreshment. It's just what I needed."

"Glad to help. Come again when you can."

"Thank you," Teresa replied, climbing back into the buggy. Slapping the reins softly, she nudged the horse along, picking her way through the budding community toward the large barn that had already been built and which was in use as a storage facility for building materials. She stopped outside, climbed down again, and hobbled the horse before entering the building.

Several men were removing lumber, and at the far end of the structure, Teresa could see about a dozen children arranged in a semicircle, seated around a young woman.

247

Teresa approached quietly, without disturbing the lesson and listened as the young woman read to the small gathering of youngsters.

Katrina looked up, and noticing Teresa, offered a smile. After a few minutes, she came to the end of the story and closed the book.

"Now," she said, standing, "who's ready for some fresh air and sunshine?"

All the hands went up together and Katrina laughed at the children. "Jenny, will you take charge please, and see that the younger children are allowed to have a turn on the swings?"

"Yes, Sister Stromberg," Jenny replied, starting outside.

Katrina walked over to where Teresa stood, both women smiling as the children quickly ran outside, leaving the barn empty except for the two of them.

"Good morning," Katrina said.

"Yes. And good morning to you. I'm Teresa, and you must be Katrina Stromberg, Harold's sister."

Katrina bristled slightly at the use of the term "sister" in reference to her relationship to Harold. "Yes, I am. Can I show you something or be of some help?"

"Well, I was hoping that you might have time to come for a short ride with me this morning. There's something I'd like to show you."

"Oh?" Katrina queried.

"It's not far, really. Just about a twenty-minute drive. Will the children be all right?"

Katrina looked toward the large barn door where the children had exited. "Sister Olsen will be back shortly. Eight of the twelve are hers," Katrina laughed. "I guess they'll be all right." Katrina looked carefully at Teresa, admiring her Latin features, olive skin, and black hair, not certain what the Spanish woman had to do with her. She seemed friendly enough, but who was she?

"I'm not sure I know who you are. Did you say *Teresa* was your name?"

Teresa laughed out loud. "That Harold. It's just like a man, isn't it? I'm Teresa Stromberg. Harold's wife."

Teresa watched as Katrina's face dissolved from an inquisitive smile to a look of unbelief, her eyes growing wide, then rolling back slightly in her head as she collapsed on the floor.

Quickly, Teresa moved to a water pail near where the children had been sitting, and removing a kerchief from her sleeve, dipped it in the water and returned to gently wipe Katrina's brow. As Katrina opened her eyes, she found herself lying on the sawdust covered floor, her head in Teresa's lap, and the dark stranger continuing to mop her forehead with the damp cloth.

"I'm terribly sorry," Teresa said. "I must have startled you."

Katrina didn't speak, attempting to gain some sense of this event and the woman who had introduced herself as Harold's wife. Sitting up slowly, Katrina placed her hand to her head, pushing back the strands of hair that had fallen over her eyes. "Please excuse me," she offered. "The heat perhaps. I'm not used to the temperatures."

Teresa laughed. "You'll have to get used to it. It's November now. Wait until next July and August."

Katrina smiled weakly, and tried to stand. "I guess the heat," she paused, "the baby and all, was just too much."

"Baby?" Teresa brightened. "Are you with child?"

"Uh, yes, I am."

"How wonderful. So am I. Does Harold know of your

249

child yet? Is your husband with the colony or perhaps coming later?"

"Well, I'm not sure if, uh . . ."

"Oh, I have forgotten my manners," Teresa said. "Too many questions. Let's just go for a short ride and see if we can't get some breeze flowing over you. That will help your circulation."

"Yes, perhaps it will," Katrina responded.

As they climbed into the buggy, Katrina sat quietly as Teresa urged the horse to retrace the path she had taken into town, directing him toward the far hillside and the short ride toward the new home under construction.

By the time the buggy reached the edge of town, it had all become too clear to Katrina—the other families who were with the group, some with multiple wives from before the Manifesto, Harold's excommunication, his request that she introduce herself as his sister—all of it suddenly made sense. But the realization brought with it a wave of nausea. Raising her hand to Teresa, signaling her to stop the buggy, Katrina leaned over the side of the wagon and retched. Several moments passed while Teresa worked to still the horse and Katrina took deep breaths, trying to regain both her dignity and her faculties, determined not to let this woman receive any further advantage through her own childish behavior.

"Are you all right, Katrina?" Teresa asked.

"Yes, thank you. I'll be fine. Let's press on."

"Good. You'll be excited, I hope. I want to show you the house Harold and I are building for our home. We'll want you to come live with us, of course, until your own home is finished and your husband is . . ."

"I'm not married," Katrina said flatly, allowing herself for a moment to actually believe the statement.

They rode along quietly for a few moments. The only sounds were those of the horse wheezing slightly and its hooves thudding in the soft dirt of the road, as it picked its way up the rising hillside, beyond which lay the new Stromberg house, now nearing completion.

"Well, then," Teresa finally said, "we'll just have to see that you are well taken care of during your pregnancy." She reached over and took Katrina's hand as they drove. "I would like to be your friend, Katrina. Will you allow me to help? With my baby coming too, we'll go through this together."

Katrina looked over at this woman who had so recently entered her life, just as Teresa turned to look at her. Their eyes met, and Teresa smiled warmly. She reached again for Katrina's hand, and continuing to look into her eyes, asked, "Friends?"

Katrina allowed a wry smile to play at the corners of her mouth, and she shook her head in disbelief. What she was hearing didn't seem possible. In the space of a few minutes, she had discovered her husband to be a bigamist, and now his other wife, who too was pregnant, was offering to be her friend. She didn't know whether to laugh or cry or what to say. And she had no idea how this would work out, or if it would.

Her mind flashed to Harold's behavior—the dirty business of leading Thomas into believing he was wanted for murder; his perfidy in secretly getting married on his initial trip to Mexico; his request that Katrina represent herself as his sister, instead of his wife. She wondered if he had ever told her the truth—about *anything!* And he must have lied in similar ways to this woman sitting beside her, who apparently didn't have the slightest suspicion that Harold might have another wife.

The small joy she would derive from watching Harold squirm as he returned to find the two of them together had not yet crossed Katrina's mind, as it would later in the day. But for the moment, she found it hard not to accept and even to like this woman who had only just met her, and who, within moments, had accepted Katrina as a sister—an unmarried and pregnant one at that. Teresa's immediate offer had been, "How can I help?" Harold Stromberg had two wives, one of whom knew of the situation, one of whom thought of the other as Harold's sister, and both of whom were going to have his baby. An eventful day, all in all.

⸺⸺

Seeing Katrina and Teresa sitting calmly together on the verandah of the hacienda, filled Harold with consternation. He could see that they were engaged in amiable conversation, but as he closed the distance from the doorway to their table, overlooking the quadrangle inside the hacienda compound, his mind was racing. What they might have discovered about each other flashed through his mind, and he searched desperately for something he might say or do. Clearly, he had been caught, or was in danger of it.

"Harold," Teresa said pleasantly, looking up from her chair to greet him. "Look what a surprise I have for you!"

"I . . . , I . . . , I see," he stammered.

"Well, aren't you going to give your wife a kiss, and one for your sister as well?" Teresa asked.

"Ah, yes, of course," he mumbled, bending to kiss Teresa on the cheek and then stepping over to Katrina to kiss the top of her head as she remained seated in her chair, silently watching and trying to understand how the man she thought she had loved could be guilty of so much deceit.

"I told you that Katrina should stay with us. It was good

that Mrs. Olsen no longer needed her assistance, don't you think?" Teresa asked.

"Yes, ah, yes, of course," Harold repeated, taking a chair from the wall and placing it between the two women, assuming his seat. "And how did this all come about?" he asked, beginning to regain some control of his thoughts.

"I went to New Hope and found Katrina. We've had a lovely day. I showed her the new house, and she's agreed to live with us until . . ." Teresa also hesitated, unsure how to phrase her thoughts—". . . until the baby comes. She needs family to look after her, Harold, and we can both look after each other. Won't that be wonderful?"

"Yes, of course."

Throughout the evening, Harold stumbled his way through introductions and most discussions. Don Sebastian returned from a trip down the coast to check on his holdings, and introducing Katrina as his sister, created in Harold an acute sense of embarrassment. He avoided looking at Katrina, but it was painful to imagine the loathing she must be feeling for him. Dinner was the longest ordeal of Harold's life as Don Sebastian, Miguel, and Teresa all extended themselves to get to know this new person in Harold's family, who was often at a loss to answer their questions about her and Harold's early lives.

But Katrina stood the test well. She retained her composure and carried off the pretense that she was Harold's sister very well. If Harold had not been worrying so much about how he was going to explain himself to her, he would have been proud of his young wife for her pluck.

As the evening ended, Teresa and Harold walked Katrina toward her bedroom, pausing for Teresa to give Katrina a quick hug and a kiss. "I'm so happy to have a new sister. I always wanted someone besides Miguel, since I grew up as the only girl on the hacienda. We'll be great friends, I just know it."

Halfway to their room, Harold excused himself and walked back toward Katrina's room, tapping lightly on the door. Katrina opened the door, stepping back inside as Harold entered and carefully closed the door. He stood silent, facing Katrina as she glared at him, her eyes blazing and her manner defying him to condone his actions. Katrina spoke first.

"And when did you plan to tell me of this charade, Harold, *after* the children were born?" she demanded.

Harold started to answer but ceased as Katrina held her hand in front of her face, palm facing Harold and fingers spread apart, turning her head so as not to hear his answer. "Not a word," she demanded through clenched teeth. As she continued to speak, it was clear to Harold that she had taken the day to make some sense out of her discovery and to decide on her course of action.

"I have honored my agreement to perform as if I were your *sister*, Harold," the words coming in staccato, "and I will continue to do so as long as it is necessary. But, you will not see me alone again until this charade has ended and you have made your choice. Is that clear?" she demanded.

Harold nodded his head slowly, his eyes on the carpet in front of her feet.

"I understand it all now, Harold—your excommunication, the family's decision to move to Mexico. I have no understanding, however, of what thought you took for our vows in the temple—my Church membership, my feelings, or those of our coming child. This is *not* the way of the Lord, Harold, and I will have no part of it."

Harold interrupted her. "Katrina, the Lord is pleased . . ."

"*No*, Harold," she spat out. "The Lord is *not* pleased and

254

neither am I. I will write my father and request his assistance in this matter. Whether I will stay or not is uncertain. Until that decision is reached, I will not dishonor you in front of your . . . " she hesitated briefly, waiting until Harold raised his head to meet her eyes, " . . . your new family," she said, lowering her head a moment before resuming her stare directly at Harold—"as you have dishonored *our* family, Harold."

She waited silently as Harold stood quiet, unable or unwilling to respond. "I think you should leave now," she said.

"Katrina, I . . ."

"*Good night*, Harold!"

"Good night, Katrina. I am truly sorry it had to take place this way."

"Harold," she said, folding her arms across her chest and continuing to stare directly at him, her five-foot-six frame as intimidating as she could make it, "I am truly sorry it had to take place *at all*."

17

By early December, the Strombergs' new home was completed, and Harold, Teresa, and Katrina had moved in. Teresa had noticed, but had not made mention of her observation, that Katrina took pains to avoid Harold. The two women, on the other hand, formed a firm friendship, riding through the countryside at every opportunity, with Teresa teaching Katrina about horses and Spanish saddles. By the end of December their occasional rides were accomplished in the buggy Teresa had originally used to bring Katrina into the hacienda. In her seventh month, Katrina's pregnancy no longer permitted horseback riding.

A week before Christmas, Magnus Stromberg arrived with the second contingent of colonists, bringing the total in New Hope to just over three hundred people from about eighty-five families. The residents of New Hope kept to themselves a good deal, but they did patronize local artisans, shopkeepers, and businesses in Mazatlán, a situation that enhanced the local economy, just as President Diaz had anticipated.

If the local residents knew anything of the practice of polygamy among Mormons of an earlier day, nothing was made of it now. There had been some notice taken of the inordinately large number of women and children as compared to men. However, nothing had been said and no challenge to the colony's practices had been issued.

When Magnus arrived, accompanied by his wife, he stayed for a few days with Don Sebastian. In a frank discussion, Magnus explained to *Señor* Cardenas that he did indeed have three other wives with their children, and they were also being relocated to New Hope. They had been members of his household for many years, and he wanted to live out his life in Mexico without fear or pressure from church or government sources. Don Sebastian, while voicing his religious disagreement over the issue, nevertheless was a compassionate man and most understanding of Stromberg's desires.

Moving in temporarily with Harold, Teresa, and Katrina, Magnus brought his first wife into the household as well, arranging temporary accommodations for his three other families in New Hope, in housing that Harold had prepared prior to his father's arrival.

Christmas might have been a joyous occasion for all, except for the tension that Teresa noted between Katrina and her father, Magnus Stromberg. There was no evidence of affection, and, given the relationship that Teresa had with her own father, it seemed odd to her that Magnus never embraced his daughter or even paid much attention to her. Teresa came to the conclusion that *Señor* Stromberg disapproved so of Katrina's unmarried status and her pregnancy that he couldn't bring himself to forgive her.

Determined to ease young Katrina's burden, Teresa tried all the harder to build the friendship the two young women had formed, and Katrina responded warmly, confiding her feelings, as much as she could, to the gracious and loving Spanish woman.

The most startling discovery Teresa made regarding Katrina's strange behavior, came quite by accident. By the second week in February, Magnus and his wife had already moved into their unfinished home in New Hope. Accompanied by Miguel, on horseback, Teresa returned home unexpectedly one afternoon from a buggy ride to her father's house. As they entered the house, they heard angry voices upstairs, coming from Katrina's quarters. Not wishing to interfere in a brother and sister quarrel, they actually smiled at each other for a few moments, recognizing the argument as similar to those they'd had in earlier years. Miguel excused himself, saying he'd return the next day to talk to Harold about their cattle buying trip. Teresa slowly mounted the stairs, intent on reaching her own room without further embarrassing Harold and Katrina.

Perceiving, however, that Katrina was near tears, Teresa moved quietly toward the sound of the quarrel, waiting for an opportune moment when she might intervene and try to calm things down. It was evident that Harold and Katrina were arguing over Katrina's baby, confirmation to Teresa that the Strombergs were continuing to struggle with the idea of Katrina's condition.

"I refuse to agree to that, Harold," Katrina screamed.

"But there's no other way, Katrina. The baby's name will still be Stromberg," he said.

"As well it should be, Harold, it's *your* baby," she cried.

Teresa paused at the door, her hand on the door knob, stunned by the accusation she had just heard. She turned, retracing her steps to her bedroom and closed the door behind her, totally confused by the revelation. *Harold's* baby? His *sister*? Unsure how to deal with the issue, Teresa retrieved a woolen shawl to ward off the evening chill and went back downstairs, quietly leaving the house and

259

walking to the stable. Roderigo had unhitched her horse and was grooming him following her ride with Miguel.

"Roderigo, prepare the buggy, please. I'll be going out again."

"*Sí, Señora,*" he replied.

Pushing the horse, Teresa overtook Miguel about two miles from her father's house, and explained that she felt she didn't want to intrude on Harold's argument with Katrina, and so she had decided to return to the Cardenases' hacienda to spend the night. She'd return home in the morning, she said. Miguel laughed, calling her a coward for avoiding domestic issues in her own household.

Instructing one of the Cardenases' household staff to ride over to her home and advise Harold that she would not be home until the morning, she went up to her old bedroom where she remained all evening and through the night.

Teresa's stay at her father's hacienda stretched into four days, with Harold appearing the first morning for a scheduled trip with Miguel to buy cattle. They would be gone about ten days according to Miguel, and in the brief meeting Teresa had with Harold, he discerned nothing out of the ordinary, and Teresa did not divulge her newfound knowledge.

Late on the evening of the fourth day, one of the servants from Harold's home awoke the Cardenases' household with news that Miss Stromberg was having her baby. Teresa was awakened by the disturbance downstairs and descended the stairs to discover what was happening. Calling for the midwife to get ready and instructing Manuel to rig the buggy, Teresa raced back upstairs and got dressed.

When Teresa and Carmen, the midwife, arrived at Teresa's home, Katrina was in deep labor.

"She's nearly six weeks early," Teresa told Carmen.

"*Sí, Señora*. We will do what we can," Carmen said and went to work examining Katrina. Within moments she had identified that the baby was coming breech and told Teresa. The development was withheld from Katrina, who was experiencing painful contractions and unsure of how to proceed. Both women tried to calm Katrina down, Teresa sitting by her side with a damp cloth, and Carmen waiting at the foot of the bed, preparing to help deliver the child.

Hours later, as light filtered through the drapes drawn over the window, signaling the arrival of dawn, Katrina slept soundly, the ordeal having exhausted her strength. Carmen had gone away with the stillborn son, and Teresa remained, fitfully dozing in a chair at the bedside. A small groan from Katrina awoke Teresa, who moved closer to the bed, reaching out to stroke Katrina's pale face.

Katrina opened her eyes and reached for Teresa's hand. "The baby?" she asked, her eyes now wide in anticipation.

Teresa held Katrina's hand and sat without speaking, not knowing how to deliver the news. Looking into Katrina's tired face, now filled with anxiety, Teresa felt a great wave of affection for this woman she had accepted as a sister. Choking with emotion, Teresa couldn't speak, but her tears said it all. Katrina also began to cry, and the two women sat for awhile, holding hands and sharing the grief.

Teresa's mind reeled also with another concept—the relief brought about by knowing that the baby's death provided a partial solution to the problem of its incestuous conception, something that had weighed almost constantly on her mind for the past four days.

"Katrina, perhaps," Teresa tried to say, " . . . perhaps it is for the best," she said.

"What?" Katrina asked, confused at such a statement. "Why?"

"Your brother's child, I mean. Perhaps God took the matter into his own hands."

"What do you mean?" Katrina asked.

"Katrina," Teresa pleaded, ". . . I overheard the argument you had with Harold. Your brother's child, Katrina, . . . perhaps it's for the best."

Understanding slowly dawned on Katrina. Not yet having come to terms with the loss of her baby, and weak with fatigue and sorrow, she had now to wrestle with this new accusation. Her mind raced: *Somehow, Teresa has discovered the baby is Harold's, and since she has the impression he is my brother, of course she would assume . . .*

"He's not my brother, Teresa. He's . . . , he's my *husband.*"

Now it was Teresa's turn to sit stunned. She stared in disbelief at Katrina for several long moments, then stood up from the bed, and moved to the window. Throwing open the heavy drapes and allowing the blinding light to diffuse the darkness of the room, Teresa asked incredulously, "*Your* husband?"

"Yes, Teresa," Katrina said weakly, "He's deceived us both."

For long moments Teresa stood looking out the window as Katrina lay silently on the bed, her breathing coming in shallow drafts, her eyes closed as exhaustion took its toll. Finally, Teresa turned and walked back toward the bed. Watching Katrina sleep, she whispered softly, "Our husband . . . *Our* husband."

<hr />

Before Harold returned from his trip inland, Katrina had recovered quite well physically, although the emotional toll had yet to fully register. The two women had shared much during the intervening days between the death of Katrina's son and his father's return.

Some deep concerns were broached and the merits and demerits of plural marriage were thoroughly explored during their discussions. In the end, Teresa understood that Katrina had not known of Harold's deception until her arrival in Mexico, and in fact, until the moment Teresa had introduced herself, Katrina thought that Harold's reason for presenting her as his sister had been his concerns over the establishment of the colony and the need for him to be gone so frequently. Teresa saw no need to inform Katrina that most of Harold's absences had been to stay with her in her father's hacienda, north of Mazatlán.

That both women were religiously opposed to plural marriage created a bond of sorts, beyond that which had been established as a result of the simple fact that they liked each other. Katrina, though several years younger than Teresa, and not of the nobility, was nevertheless a woman of growing intellect and charming disposition. Teresa found herself constantly in awe of Katrina's ability to accept people and conditions with a positive outlook. Katrina's early acceptance and even friendship toward Teresa had proved that no hostility existed. Teresa wasn't certain, had she been the first wife, that she could have accepted Katrina in the same way.

The final decision reached by both women, was that Harold was not to know of their knowledge, at least until after the birth of Teresa's baby. Teresa's move into the guest room, explained to Harold as having been suggested by the midwife to assure the rest necessary during her final weeks, was supported by the tragedy that had befallen Katrina and Harold's first baby.

So, as Harold arrived home toward the end of the

second week of his trip, the conditions that greeted him were depressing. Katrina had lost her baby, Teresa had moved into isolation to protect her final weeks of pregnancy, and Harold found himself virtually alone in the house, as both women kept to themselves and shared their thoughts only with each other. All in all, it was not the situation Harold had contemplated when he thought of the establishment of New Hope and the reinstitution of the Principle, at least not as his father had explained it.

18

⎯⎯⎯⎯⎯⎯⎯⎯⎯⎯⎯⎯⎯⎯⎯⎯

The winter beauty of Alaska was spectacular, and Tom almost immediately fell in love with the country. Although they were actually in Canada, most of the miners still referred to the area of the Yukon River and its tributaries as part of Alaska. The cold air provided wonderful visibility, and on a clear day, standing on the ridge above their claim, Tom could literally see for well over a hundred miles.

He had seen beautiful mountain country while traveling through the Rockies the previous winter, but one evening in Alaska, he saw a spectacular phenomenon, such as he had never experienced. As the calendar advanced, it had grown dark earlier each evening, and then one night in late October, long after Tom had gone to sleep, he was awakened by a strange light shining through the wall of their tent. Thinking someone was searching their camp for gold, he pulled on his boots and jumper and carefully lifted the tent flap to peer outside. The air was bitterly cold, and the hair in his nostrils crackled, but the sight he beheld was the most fascinating he had ever seen. The thought even crossed his mind that perhaps the world was coming to an end; for the sky was ablaze with a kaleidoscope of vivid, constantly changing, colored lights. The effect was truly amazing, and awestruck by the vision before him, Tom watched the sky for some moments before thinking to alert John.

Stepping back into the tent to wake John, he urged him to get out of bed and view the magnificent display. But taking one glimpse through the open flap, John simply rolled over and pulled his bedroll up around his ears, mumbling, "It's just the northern lights, lad—'God's paintboard,' they call it. Go back to sleep."

Seeing no concern on the part of his uncle, Tom went back outside, no longer frightened that some catastrophic event was in progress. He spent the next several hours enjoying his first encounter with the aurora borealis, or "northern lights," the luminescent nighttime display that can be observed north of the Arctic Circle in the winter months. For centuries, mankind had been startled and amazed by the natural phenomena and enthralled by its beauty. Many times throughout the winter, Tom found the show exciting enough to brave the cold and lose a few hours sleep to watch its cascading shadows.

Tom learned that at that northern position, ice and snow were almost permanent fixtures. Even in late April, winter retained a fast grip on the land, and, according to the sourdoughs, most of whom still took pleasure in ribbing the young Irishman about his *cheechako* status, "old man winter kin throw a blanket 'round you quicker'n a grizzly kin get mad and rip your heart out."

Through the fall and winter months, it was apparent that the tributaries on which Tom and his uncle had established their claims, were producing exceptionally fine gold and in quantities in excess of those being panned by Carmack and his brothers-in-law down on Bonanza Creek. Over a hundred miners had finally found their life's dream, and through the winter of 1896–1897, they sat around the campfire at night, figuring how they were going to spend it. Many of the old-timers had been digging and scratching in the dirt and stream beds for nearly thirty years, ever since the United States purchased Alaska from Russia, eking out a sparse living off the land while they searched for gold. Ever gold.

The previous October, in a celebration quite rare, since most miners worked through all daylight hours, and as much also as they could by lamplight in the dark, the small cluster of men around *Emerald One* and *Emerald Two* had gathered to usher Tom through his twenty-first birthday.

"Rich before he's dry behind the ears," said one of the old-timers. "Reckon we oughta be sure he stays wet behind them ears, don'tcha reckon?" he threatened. Whether or not they actually would have thrown Tom in the creek in the middle of a Canadian winter, he didn't know, but Tom was grateful for the intervention of his uncle.

The surprising thing to Tom, apart from the difficulty he had in accepting their good fortune, was the fact that the miners seemed unconcerned about theft by their neighbors.

"Oh, the thieves'll come, all right," John had said. "But it won't be 'til next spring, after word gets out. Then we'll see 'em, all kinds, whooping it up, snatching claims and the like. Then we'll all have to guard our gold like it was," he laughed, "like'n it was *gold*."

The first hint of spring came as the runoff from the watershed caused their small tributary to swell considerably, disrupting the placer operations they had constructed on the banks of the stream. Working knee-deep in water so cold it threatened to freeze their legs, the men continually dredged up gravel and sand, working it in their pans, ever alert for the "color" that was gold.

267

On one particularly bright day, their gold dust stashed all around the campsite in leather packets, tin cans, and any other container that could be used to hold the precious grains, John announced he was heading in to Fortymile.

"It's time for a wallop, I reckon," he declared.

"A what?" Tom asked.

"A long drunk, my young nephew. And since you don't imbibe anymore, you can keep pulling that there yellow stuff out of the river, so's I can pay for the drink I intend to consume."

"Aye, I'll stay," Tom responded, no argument forthcoming.

Two days after John and two of the other miners left for Fortymile, a great northwester blew in, leaving eighteen inches of freshly fallen snow on the campsite. It only took about a day and a half to walk to Fortymile, so Tom had no concerns that John had not reached his destination, but he knew his uncle would be unable to return quickly. That much snow around their claim site, at a low elevation, was certain to mean that the pass through which the miners traveled to Fortymile would be heavily snowed in. Tom didn't expect John to return for several more days, until after the snow had melted enough to let him walk the trail.

Five days later, the two miners who had gone with John made their way into Tom and John's claim. No horses were available to the miners for lack of feed through the winter, and the two men were on foot, lugging a blanket rigged between two poles. Each miner was struggling to lift one side of the contraption. Instantly, Tom knew something was wrong. He waded out of the stream and walked toward the approaching pair.

Setting their burden down on the ground, one of the men said, "Tom, we got bad news for ya, lad."

Tom could see it was a body wrapped in the blanket, completely covered except for the boots sticking out at one end—boots Tom recognized as belonging to John.

"John got into a fight the first night in town, with that German fellow from down on Bonanza Creek. He didn't pick the fight, Tom, it just kind of got started. Anyways, John said he didn't reckon he'd stick around to waste a good drunk, so's he took about a dozen bottles in his pack, and started back for here, thinking, I s'pose, he'd get liquored up here at camp."

"What happened?" Tom asked.

"Reckon the storm caught him, Tom. He were near drunk when he left Fortymile, and we found him yesti'day afternoon when we was comin' back, froze solid 'longside the trail."

Tom knelt down by the body and unwrapped the blanket from around the head. Bits and pieces of ice dropped away from the covering. John's mustache was coated with frost and his hair was frozen in place. But his face was peaceful as he lay on the jerry-rigged stretcher.

"Reckon we could get that preacher fella, up to *Six Above*, to come down and say a few words, Tom, if'n you'd like."

Tom just nodded. Then, without waiting, he got a shovel from the tent and moved to a spot up the hill from the stream. There, he attempted to dig, but was unable to make much of a dent in the frozen ground. One of the other miners brought a pick to help Tom dig his uncle's grave, while his partner started up the creek for *Six Above* to bring the preacher down.

For the next three days, Tom moped around the camp, going about the ritual of daily work, missing John more than he would have thought, and glancing frequently up the hill at the pile of rocks he'd arranged on the mound of Uncle John's grave.

On the third day after John's burial, one of the old-timers, who'd known John in Anvil, stopped by the camp. He'd heard about his friend's death, and he told Tom about some of the adventures the two had shared. After a bit, the old fellow fell silent. Then he said, "What do ya plan to do, young fella?"

Without waiting for an answer, he went on, "This summer, son, hordes and hordes of folk are gonna come plunderin' down this valley, searchin' for their dreams. I seen it in Californy when I were but fifteen. It won't be a pretty sight, that it won't," he said. "I've started takin' my stash out, bit by bit, into Fortymile. And after breakup, I'll hit for Dawson. Reckon at my age, I got enough to last the rest o' my life."

Tom sat quietly, listening to the older man ramble. After some moments, he gestured to the jumble of containers stacked around the inside of the tent, and asked, "How much do you think we got here?"

The grizzled old man glanced around at the stash. Then, shaking his head, he squinted at Tom and said, "Dunno, lad. Cept'n you take it into Dawson and get it assayed, you ain't sure. But from what I done took down already, I'd say you got into the millions."

Tom stared at the old man. "*Millions?*" he asked.

There were two topics Tom and his uncle had never discussed—one was the dollar value of their pannings, and the other was the tattered picture of a young woman Tom kept pinned to the sloping wall of his tent, above his bedroll. For some reason, Tom had never attached a monetary value to the gold they were accumulating. The dust had become so commonplace, and there was so much of it, it had lost its ability to excite him. There was nothing about it that resembled wealth; it didn't even sparkle very much. So its value had ceased to be a consideration. It was gold. And Tom knew they were rich. *How* rich, didn't matter.

The picture of Katrina had been another matter entirely.

Over the winter, Tom had spent hours, hunched over the stream, performing the repetitive task of sluicing his pan. The work was mundane and mindless, and his thoughts went frequently to Katrina.

It was curious, that as much as he thought about her, Tom never spoke to John about Katrina, even though John had come into the tent on a number of occasions to find John looking at her picture. John's silence was the product of either not wishing to interfere in Tom's personal life, or disinterest. Either way, Tom had let the subject lay dormant, apart from his own continuing remorse over losing Katrina to another man. But as for that, Tom always thought of her as Katrina *Hansen*. Katrina *Stromberg* wasn't part of the fantasy.

But, the old man's comment about millions had raised the unspoken question of value, startling Tom. "*Millions!*" Tom said again.

"Reckon that'd be 'bout right. That's what I figger I've got, and it weren't as much as you and your uncle got piled up. I'll be glad to help you load it out, lad. I'm leaving any-way, come breakup. I'll be headin' in to Fortymile to get a couple of horses to haul it all out. We could do it together. What say? I know you're still a young man, but you reckon you got enough?" he said, looking around the tent again.

Tom stood, lifted the tent flap and stepped outside into the fading light of day. The sun had disappeared behind the western mountain, which shaded their campsite from the sunset throughout the winter months. The old man

271

followed him out, tossed the remains of his coffee into the stream, and stood next to Tom in the twilight. After a few moments, Tom turned to look at the older man.

"Reckon I've got enough," Tom said.

———— ✺✺✺ ————

Teresa drove the buggy hard, trying to reach her home as quickly as she could. In her eighth month of pregnancy, she had become bulky and awkward. The lean, athletic body she had always enjoyed was temporarily gone, and she sat uncomfortably on the buggy seat as it bounced and rocked along.

She had been surprised by how angry her father had become. Don Sebastian was not a man given to fits of temper or open displays of frustration, but the news Miguel brought from the village had transformed him into an enraged man. Displaying a degree of anger she had never seen in him, he had made violent threats toward those who had deceived him.

Even now, almost an hour later, his words continued to ring in her ears.

"They will not live on my land and continue this barbaric practice. They have deceived me!" he shouted, pacing back and forth in the study. "Miguel, who told you these things?" he demanded of his son.

"Father, Señor Rameriez in the village told me himself. His oldest daughter was taken in marriage by one of the colonists—a man with two wives already," Miguel repeated.

"No! We will not tolerate this!" Don Sebastian declared, slamming his fist down onto the desk.

"They are organizing the men to retrieve her. They ride with anger, Father."

Recognizing the potential for disaster, a degree of

272

caution began to overtake the older man. In his youth, he had been involved in a prolonged family feud and had seen enough of violence. He wished now to spare his people the kind of ugliness he had seen and the sorrow that always came from such conflict.

"We must not have a blood bath, Miguel. You must ride with them and bring order to this vengeance."

"*Sí*, Father. I will do what I can, but the men are very angry."

Before leaving hurriedly for her home, Teresa had seen Miguel organizing their father's *caballeros* and had heard the hooves of the horses as her brother and the men from the hacienda rode out, intent on joining the mob from the village. Whether to calm or to inflame, she knew not, for what she had seen in her brother's eyes frightened her.

Teresa knew what Don Sebastian did not: the woman taken in marriage had been fancied by Miguel, and he had been bested by the *Yanqui*—a *married Yanqui*.

"Miguel, please be rational. You must not do this thing," she had pleaded.

"Go home, Teresa. Stay in your house and tell Harold also to stay away from the colony. You must not be involved in this."

"But I am. *We* are, Miguel. I am married to one of them, and now, Juanita is married to one of them as well."

"So you are. So you *both* are," he said, mounting his horse. "If Harold is to stay alive, see that he stays home with you," he ordered, spurring his horse and leading the men at a gallop, out through the gates of the hacienda and toward the nearby Mexican village.

The memory of the encounter with her brother and father still fresh in her mind, Teresa stopped the buggy in front of the house and was met by one of the stable hands, who helped her down from the buggy. "*Señor* Harold?" she queried.

"*No es aquí,*" he replied.

"Then where is he?" she asked, racing up the front steps of the house.

"*Señor* Stromberg is in the colony," he pointed, indicating New Hope.

"No!" Teresa cried. "Katrina," she shouted, running to the bottom of the stairs, her swollen belly the unwieldy companion of a woman in haste. "Katrina!"

Appearing at the top of the stairs, Katrina moved quickly down the steps.

"What is it?" she said.

"We've got to get to the village. To warn the people and Harold."

"Warn them of what?" Katrina asked.

"The villagers are organizing. They're very angry, Katrina. One of the local girls has been taken in marriage by one of your colonists—one who already has two wives. A mob, with Miguel and some of father's men, is riding toward the village. We must warn them."

"Let me get a coat. Are you sure you should go?" Katrina asked, concerned for Teresa's pregnancy.

"We must. Hurry, Katrina, hurry!"

The two women rode in silence, the horse laboring to keep pace with the demands Teresa placed on him after the earlier gallop from her father's house. Reaching the outskirts of New Hope, they could see the colonists, some of them toiling in the fields, others working on partially constructed houses, and a group loading a wagon with lumber that was being stored in the large barn where Teresa had first met Katrina. The horse raced down the slope toward the village, the buggy careening along behind and both women

274

hanging on over the bumpy, rutted cart path. Pulling her horse to a stop in front of the barn, Katrina stood up in the buggy, looking about wildly for Harold. He had seen the buggy coming and now came running from where he had been overseeing the construction of a house.

"What's happened?" he asked.

"Harold," Teresa blurted out, "some of the villagers are coming to rescue the village girl one of your settlers married."

"*Rescue?* She's not being held captive."

"Harold," Teresa said, "this cannot continue. The local people are angry. To live out your family lives in peace as your father promised my father is one thing, but to continue this terrible practice—the people will not tolerate it."

"It is none of their business," Harold stated flatly.

Teresa was quiet for a moment, holding Harold's stare. "Harold, if my father knew of *our* arrangement," she said, pausing to look at Katrina and back again to Harold, "he would kill you himself, if Miguel did not do it first. You have deceived us all—not only my father, but me and Katrina as well. This must stop, Harold. Here and now!"

Harold's face reflected his shock at the knowledge that both Katrina and Teresa knew of his duplicity. A group of men had gathered behind him and were watching the scene unfold. Harold turned to them.

"We've got trouble," Harold said. "Teresa says a mob is coming and they want Brother Williams's wife returned."

One of the men nodded knowingly. "Didn't think it was a good idea—a local girl, I mean," he said. "Better get the women and children into the barn," he suggested.

"Right, and round up the men. And Frank," Harold said, glancing up at Teresa and Katrina for a moment, "better have them bring their guns."

"Come, climb down, Teresa. You and Katrina can stay in the barn with the women. We can't risk the baby."

"Harold, you've got to get away from here," Teresa pleaded again.

"No, I've got to stay. These are my people. And Father will be here in a few minutes. C'mon, let me help you down. Katrina, give her a hand," Harold commanded.

"No!" Teresa shouted, striking out at Harold with the buggy whip. "I can stop them," she said, urging her horse forward. Katrina held on, looking to the rear as Harold stood helplessly, watching them drive away.

"Teresa!" he hollered after them. "Stay here."

Teresa turned the buggy around at the far end of the compound and raced back past where the men were busy herding the women and children into the barn. Harold stepped out in an attempt to head the horse and stop the buggy, but Teresa steered wide of him and went on by.

Pulling out of the colony and beginning the climb back up the rutted road, Teresa and Katrina saw the first of the Mexican riders come into view on the crest of the hill. They paused to assess the scene below and wait for Teresa to drive the buggy up to them.

As she jerked her horse to a stop in front of the first riders, another group, this one led by Miguel, galloped up in a swirl of dust. He spurred his horse through the cluster of horsemen, over to the buggy.

"Teresa," I told you to stay in your home," he said. "This is no place for you or Katrina."

"Miguel, you cannot do this. They are armed and will defend themselves."

Standing in his stirrups and looking around to the group of about thirty men on horseback, he shouted, "Do you hear that, compadres? She says they are prepared to defend themselves. Are we ready also?" He was answered by a chorus of angry determination, shouted by the massed men.

Miguel sat back down on his saddle and leaned over to speak to the man riding next to him, who immediately dismounted and approached Teresa's horse.

"Remain here, dear sister, and do not interfere," he said. "We want no more of these blasphemous marriages, and it is time to tell them so. They have deceived Don Sebastian," Miguel exhorted, his voice rising, so the men could hear his comments.

Spurring his horse, Miguel led the column of riders down the hillside toward the cluster of New Hope men who had been standing near the barn but who now scrambled for cover behind their wagons and buildings. The young Mexican man who had dismounted, remained behind, holding the bridle of Teresa's horse to prevent her from leaving. The two women watched as the riders neared the community, the first shot ringing out loudly as one of the Mormon settlers, frightened by the approaching mob, fired at the horsemen. A volley of shots was fired immediately by both groups and several of the men on horseback fell from their mounts, the rest quickly riding for cover behind the homes and partially completed buildings.

The man restraining Teresa's horse had his attention focused on the skirmish below, and Teresa suddenly lashed out with her whip, striking him across his face and causing the horse to rear. The man lost his hold on the bridle, and Teresa quickly drove the buggy past him, heading back down the hill toward the exchange of gunfire going on below. Katrina held on with both hands as the buggy gyrated wildly over the uneven ground.

As they neared the bottom of the hill, one of the rear wheels of the buggy rolled over a rock that sent the buggy

277

careening wildly sidewise before overturning and catapulting both women off the seat and into a small, brush-filled gully. The horse raced on, dragging the wildly bouncing vehicle after it.

Katrina hit the ground hard, stunned by the impact and her breath knocked out of her. Dazed and struggling to breathe, she rolled around in agony on the hot, rocky ground, afraid for a few panic-filled moments she was not going to be able to catch her breath. Then, recovering slightly, she began to look about frantically for Teresa.

She saw her lying a few feet away, sprawled in an awkward position, with blood running from her scalp, down over her face. Katrina crawled painfully to Teresa's side, and cradling the bleeding woman's head in her lap, she began to rock back and forth, crying uncontrollably.

Hurting and shaken, Katrina didn't know what to do. The sound of gunfire continued to ring out, and she feared for a time they might be hit by stray bullets. They were lying, however, in the bottom of a little gully, which afforded some shelter, but Teresa obviously needed help.

How long they remained there, listening to the sound of the gun battle, Katrina did not know. She lost consciousness and slept through the rest of the afternoon, finally reviving as evening approached and Teresa began groaning. Random gunfire could still be heard from the direction of the village, although from their position in the gully, Katrina could not see the buildings or any of the actual fighting.

Darkness slowly enveloped their sanctuary and Katrina could tell that Teresa was in pain. She groaned more loudly and almost continuously. Regaining consciousness, Teresa struggled to speak and finally said in a weak voice, "The baby comes."

"Oh, please, no!" Katrina cried. "We must have help," she said, looking around.

"No time," Teresa said.

Through the night, the only light was the distant glow of the fires that were consuming the village. In the darkness of the ravine, Katrina worked to help Teresa deliver her baby, praying constantly as she did so. Ever since she discovered Harold's duplicity, she had neglected her prayers, feeling somehow unworthy to ask for help, but her supplications to Father in Heaven this night were born of fear and desperation, and she plead for help and for Teresa to survive her ordeal. In spite of the desperate situation she and Teresa were in, Katrina was somewhat comforted and knew what to do.

By the time it began to get light, Katrina knew that the baby boy she had wrapped in his mother's torn petticoat, if he survived, would never know the loving and caring mother who had given him life—a woman Katrina had come to love in spite of their duplicate roles in Harold Stromberg's life. During the brief period they had been allowed to share knowledge of their respective positions, Teresa and Katrina, while not in agreement with the practice, nevertheless had come to understand how two women could love each other and, indeed, the man also to whom they were jointly married.

Teresa's breathing grew more shallow during the predawn hours, and finally, as it began to grow light, the exhausted woman surrendered her spirit. But before succumbing to her injuries and the strain of childbirth, Teresa Cardenas Stromberg whispered a request and received a promise from Katrina.

Coming out of hiding after sunrise, two men from the Mormon colony found Katrina and Teresa's baby in the gully. The mob of angry villagers was gone, their bloody work done.

"Sister Stromberg?" one of the men asked, climbing out of the wagon bed where he had been riding and approaching the scene.

"Yes," Katrina answered. "I have a baby here, too," she said.

"You'd better come with us, Sister Stromberg. We must get away from this place before the Mexicans come back."

"Where's Harold?" she asked.

Ignoring the question, the man took the baby from Katrina and handed it to the wife of the driver of the wagon. Then he helped Katrina to her feet. "We can't leave Teresa," she said.

The man looked at Teresa, lying crumpled and silent in the brush. "She's with God now, Sister Stromberg. We can't help her."

Moving quickly, he helped Katrina into the back of his wagon then scrambled in himself as the wagon moved ahead. He took the baby from the woman on the seat of the buckboard and handed it back to Katrina, who sat numbly, holding the crying baby and staring to the rear, watching as the site where Teresa's broken body lay, receded into the distance. In a few minutes the wagon moved over the hill and out of site of the grisly scene.

"Harold?" she asked again.

"I'm sorry, Sister Stromberg, Harold's dead. And so is his father. Eight of our men are dead, and two sisters."

Without a word, Katrina faced backward, jolting along

in the wagon bed, too numb and exhausted to cry, watching the smoke from the ruins of New Hope rising through the early morning mist. As the wagon slowly creaked its way north, away from the massacre in and around the village, Katrina dozed, and the baby slept too, oblivious to the carnage that had surrounded his entrance into the world.

The sight of a small group of Mexican horsemen riding toward the wagon late that afternoon, filled their hearts with dread. Surrounding the wagon, the riders roughly dragged the two Mormon men to the ground and at gun point took them off into the scrub brush.

One of the riders spurred his horse toward the back of the wagon where Katrina sat, holding the baby tightly against her chest, her head lowered in fear. The man sat his horse in silence, looking down into the wagon, waiting until Katrina finally looked up at him. With the sun behind him, she saw him in silhouette and his face was only a shadow under his sombrero. Without sound or apparent compassion, he gestured for her to get out of the wagon. Holding the baby and climbing down, she looked up fearfully at the man and saw the stern and angry face of Miguel Antonio Cardenas.

19

Excitement filled the air in Dawson City as miners prepared for breakup when the ice would free, opening the way for riverboats to arrive. Since the last week in May, Tom and the old codger who had helped him haul his gold out had lingered about, talking with those in town about who had the most gold or whose claim had produced the most in the shortest time. Tom kept quiet about his findings, but it didn't take long for the word to get around that his take was among the largest, valued at well over two million dollars. Those whose claims had been located near *Emerald One* and *Emerald Two*, knew that since Tom and John had been partners in both claims, Tom had doubled his earnings by also bringing out his uncle's share.

All told, nearly forty million dollars in gold was stashed in various places around the wharf in Dawson, waiting for the ice to break up and make it possible to float the Yukon down to St. Michael's on the Bering Sea. From there, the men would board a steamship to Seattle or San Francisco.

It had taken Tom and the old fellow, supported by three pack mules, three weeks and four trips to haul out their stashes, along with the few personal possessions they wanted to take with them. They left their tents and most of their other gear right where it had been used. Tom's claim document and that of John Ryan, duly probated in Tom's name, both of which had been filed timely and legally, were in his pocket, and several of the old timers told him that if he played his cards right, he could sell them in Seattle for double what he had in gold. The fever would be that high, they speculated.

A lottery had been started on the exact date and time breakup would occur. A light rope had been stretched across the river between two jagged peaks of ice. When the river began to flow again, the ice would move and the rope would snap. That would determine the exact moment of breakup. Nearly two hundred thousand dollars in gold dust was wagered on that single event. Tom missed by two days and seventeen hours and lost ten ounces of gold dust. The winner added another $120,000 to his take.

The most depressing aspect of the time spent in Dawson City was the fact that the city had no food. As miners continued to pour into the ramshackeled town, food was not to be had for any price, and much of the population was in danger of literally starving to death. As the food shortage grew more acute, the darkest joke around town was that when the riverboat finally did arrive, they'd find the richest dead men in the world.

On the next to last day of May, eight days after official breakup, the first paddle wheeler arrived, having wintered at Ft. Yukon, and bringing with it fresh vegetables, meat, and other provisions. Unknown to the riverboat crew, waiting for their arrival on the docks in Dawson City, if the hodge-podge of ice-broken pilings could rightfully be called a *dock*, was a motley collection of nearly seventy, fabulously wealthy miners, some even millionaires. Young and old, they were waiting to transfer their newly acquired fortunes to the deck of the first vessel to arrive. From their appearance, after a winter spent panning for gold, living off the land, and following several weeks of meager rations in Dawson City, a New York banker might have had the gracious impulse to flip any of the ragged and disheveled men a dime and feel he'd done his good deed for the day. However, by the time the ocean steamer transported these bedraggled-looking men to Seattle, those same bankers would claw their way through solid rock to accept the deposit of the first fruits of the largest gold strike in American history, and would stand in line to wine and dine even the raunchiest-looking miner, even before his bath.

The riverboat unloaded its cargo and passengers and turned around within hours, heading downriver and spreading the news of the strike at every stop along the way. A second riverboat docked in Dawson City two days later, and the remaining miners boarded, heading west and then south with their fortunes and urging the captain to make all haste.

By the middle of June, both riverboats had traversed the two thousand miles of the Yukon River, arriving at its mouth on the Bering Sea, where two oceangoing steamships lay anchored offshore near St. Michael's.

The two riverboats, anxious to turn around for Dawson, quickly took on passengers and cargo, and within hours were on their way back north. Included in that cargo were two sacks of mail, and in one of them was Sister Mary's letters to Tom, in which she had joyfully informed him that he was not being sought by the authorities in Kansas City and that there was no murder charge pending against him.

During the course of Tom's journey down the Yukon, one thought continually occupied his mind. Possessed of what he was assured was a fortune, he was unable to take any comfort in his riches. What worried him most was that he was still a fugitive. Until and if his name was cleared, he would always be looking over his shoulder and constantly on the run. He gradually came to the conclusion that he would use part of his wealth to hire an attorney and that he would return to Kansas City in an attempt to establish his innocence. Just how such a thing could be accomplished, he didn't know, and what might happen to him should he fail, filled him with fear. But he reached the conclusion that the way to start would be to consult a lawyer as soon as he got to Seattle.

Obtaining accommodations on the southbound vessel, Tom waited impatiently as the oceangoing steamship completed unloading its cargo and took the tide out into the mouth of the channel, turning Southwest as she made her way into the Bering Sea, bound for Seattle.

In late July, 1897, the steamship *Portland,* with sixty-eight millionaires or near-millionaires on board, steamed into United States waters and threaded its way through the islands of Puget Sound, bound for the port of Seattle. One enterprising newspaper reporter had taken the initiative to hire a boat to intercept the steamship prior to its arrival at the port. His news headline, A *Ton of Gold Aboard,* flashed around the world in hours, and the great Alaskan gold rush was on. Several years would pass before the world would come to realize that the men on board the *Portland* had already claimed well over seventy percent of the gold that would ever come out of the Klondike find.

Within days, thousands of almost desperately anxious men and some hardy women, crowded the docks in Seattle, seeking passage to Alaska on anything that would sail. Within weeks, the numbers milling about the waterfront would swell to over one hundred thousand.

Arriving in Seattle, Tom went ashore to make his

banking arrangements, and received all the courtesies that might have been paid to the largest landholders in Ireland. It was quickly confirmed for him that in America, the possession of wealth was the single largest factor in determining how one was treated by the upper classes. It was evident that ancestry, accent, or in fact physical attire, were all secondary considerations in acquiring social acceptance. In Tom's case, it was *gold* that opened all the doors he would not have been able to pry open in any other way.

As he sat in the richly appointed foyer of the First Western Bank, his crates of gold at his feet and still wearing his miner's clothes, he was uncomfortable and felt out of place. An officious looking man, dressed in a suit, approached him, and Tom stood, respectfully removing his cap and holding it in front of him. He smiled nervously as the man addressed him.

"Mr. Callahan?"

"Aye, sir," Tom replied.

"Allow me, Mr. Callahan," the man said, gesturing to several of the bank's younger employees to carry the crates.

Not wishing to give offense, but intent on safeguarding his stash, Tom stood protectively over the crates, until the smiling banker succeeded in assuring him that all would be well. "We'll just weigh and measure your gold, Mr. Callahan. I can guarantee you that everything will be satisfactory," he smiled again. "Please, sir, step this way into my office."

Turning to a young woman seated behind a nearby desk, the banker's tone changed. "You there, girl, bring some coffee into my office for Mr. Callahan," he demanded. Then turning again to Tom, he said politely, "Right this way, sir."

Once in the office, Tom took a chair as offered but declined a cigar. "The First Western Bank will be pleased if you consider our complete facilities at your disposal, Mr. Callahan."

"Much obliged," Tom replied.

The young woman entered, carrying a tray loaded with an ornate silver urn, two empty cups, and a sugar bowl. She poured the cups full and nervously served one to the bank official and one to Tom. As she reached to place the cup on the desk in front of Tom, she accidentally sloshed a small amount out of the cup, onto the shoulder of Tom's jacket.

Instantly angry, the banker quickly stepped to Tom's side, using his handkerchief to wipe the spill from the jacket.

"You stupid, stupid girl," he shouted. She stepped backward, holding her hand over her mouth, and began to apologize. Her boss continued to berate her, calling her a clumsy oaf and ordering her out of his office.

Before she could leave, Tom rose to his feet and said to the banker, "Hold on a minute."

Turning to the girl, Tom smiled kindly and said, "You'll have to excuse him, Miss. He doesn't know how it is you speak to a lady."

She glanced at her employer and then back at Tom. "It was my fault. I'm sorry, sir," she said.

"Not to worry, lass," Tom said. "This jacket's seen much worse the past year," he laughed.

Turning to the banker, Tom looked at him for some few seconds, then turned back and asked the young woman, "Would there be another bank close at hand?"

Again, she looked toward her employer before responding. But Tom continued without reference to the surprised banker.

"Another bank?" he asked again, smiling.

"Uh, yes, sir. The Bank of Seattle is on the corner, just down the street."

"Would you mind goin' to the Bank of Seattle and askin' them to send a couple of men to assist me with my crates?" Tom asked.

"But, sir," she hesitated, looking again toward her employer.

"Don't be concerned over your job, lass," Tom smiled. "How much does this bank pay you?"

"Uh, well, uh, six dollars a week, sir."

"Aye. 'Tis an important task I'm askin' of ye, lass. 'Tis worth fifty dollars to me to have you notify the Bank of Seattle that I have a deposit to make, and," he added, reaching for her hand and walking her toward the door, "I'll be happy to put in a good word for you with the bank manager there."

"Sir, I must protest," the banker said as he stepped toward the pair.

Tom turned his attention back to the banker. "Aye, and so you should. Would you have your men bring my crates to the front door of your bank?" Tom said to the man.

"But Mr. Callahan, we can reach an accord. She's just a foolish girl. Surely you don't, . . ."

"Aye, but I do, sir," Tom replied, exiting the office and striding toward the bank entrance, with the banker trailing behind and continuing to protest.

Within two hours, Tom had deposited his gold in the Bank of Seattle, helped the young woman find new employment, and also obtained directions to a men's clothier. Emerging an hour or so later, Tom was attired in what the proprietor assured him was the latest in fashionable dress for the successful man, and he was carrying a valise packed with additional new clothing.

Tom was beginning to understand what it means when people say "money talks." It was evident to him that, at least on the surface, there was only one difference between the classes: money.

Over the next couple of days, Tom found a lawyer and presented his case of self-defense in the Kansas City incident. Through an exchange of telegrams with an attorney in Kansas City, the lawyer was able to determine that the police inquiry into the death of one Isaac Skomolski had found that his was a "death by misadventure" and that the case had been closed right after the inquest was held.

Until that word was received, Tom spent a very nervous two nights, fully anticipating a return to Kansas City to answer a charge of murder. When the attorney informed him what he had learned, Tom sat before him, stunned, scarcely daring to believe what he was hearing. Wanting to make sure he understood what he had been told, he asked, "Are ye tellin' me, sir, that I've no need to run anymore?"

"That's correct, Mr. Callahan. The sad thing is that there was no need to run at all—not then and not now. You're a free man," the lawyer assured him, "and a mighty rich one too, from all accounts. Where will you go, sir?"

Tom stood and walked to the window of the attorney's office. Looking out across Puget Sound to the distant tree-covered islands, he said, "San Francisco, I guess, then back to Ireland, maybe."

"I see. May I be so bold as to offer some advice?" the elderly lawyer said, coming to stand beside Tom.

Tom turned to face the older man. "You've brought me nothin' but good news so far," Tom said. "What else would you have to tell me?"

"When you get to San Francisco, see a man named Simonsen—Gary Simonsen. He is a very astute business-man who brokers proven mining claims. When news of the *Portland* reached San Francisco, Simonsen sent me a communiqué asking for referrals. His immediate interest is in available sites in Alaska, and his services could prove invaluable to you, if you wish to dispose of your claim."

"You trust this, uh, Simonsen, you said?"

"Totally."

"Fine," Tom replied, shaking hands. "Thank you for your help."

"It was my pleasure, Mr. Callahan. May God go with you, sir."

A broad smile crossed Tom's face. "I believe He already has, sir. Indeed, He already has."

The morning the steamer left for San Francisco, Tom wired Sister Mary to advise he had returned from Alaska and to inform her that he wished to establish a fund for Holy Cross Hospital. He told her he was heading for San Francisco, intent on staying at the Grand Union Hotel where she could contact him the following week. He made no mention of his thought to return to Ireland.

Upon his arrival at the Grand Union Hotel in San Francisco, Tom found a telegram from Anders Hansen waiting.

Sister Mary advised your arrival. Need your help to find Katrina. Arriving San Francisco twenty-eighth. Please wait. Anders.

The term "find Katrina" puzzled Tom, and the time available for speculation before Andy's arrival only added to his concern. Finally, two days before Anders's arrival, Tom

291

followed the advice of the Seattle lawyer and sought the offices of one Gary Simonsen.

Simonsen was all that the lawyer had said. In short order, Tom was offered a staggering sum of money for *Emerald One* and *Emerald Two*, his two claims in the Yukon, near Rabbit Creek. After verifying that Tom had deposited exactly two million, three hundred thousand, seven hundred and eighty-three dollars in the Seattle bank, from only eight months of work, Mr. Simonsen offered Tom two million dollars on the spot for his two claims.

"Two million?" Tom said, hesitantly. "For *two* claims on the richest stream in Alaska? How many other claims have you bought so far, Mr. Simonsen?"

Simonsen looked Tom over, smiled broadly and stuck out his hand. "Three million, then, Mr. Callahan, cash in the bank tomorrow, and we're done. More than double your take last winter," he laughed, "and with far less effort."

Tom grasped his hand and smiled. "Good doing business with you, Mr. Simonsen."

Simonsen grabbed his hat and cane, and took Tom's arm. "C'mon, lad. You're going to get the best steak in this town, and, if you're willing to reconsider your plans to return to Ireland, I propose to give you a free lesson in how to turn your five million dollars, plus a couple 'o hundred thousand in change," he laughed, "into some *real* money. Interested?"

"You're calling the shots, Mr. Simonsen. Lead on."

"'Buck,' lad. Everybody calls me 'Buck.'"

———

Returning to his hotel late that evening, Tom was greeted by Anders, who was waiting nervously in the lobby.

Overshadowing the joy of their reunion, was the news Anders brought.

That Katrina had relocated in Mexico was astonishing news to Tom, and the disaster in Mazatlán added to the puzzle. He had never imagined such a thing, and the possibility that she was missing, and perhaps dead, was almost more than he could bear. It had never occurred to him that Katrina was anywhere, other than safe in Salt Lake City, and he was stunned by the news.

Anders told Tom that he had telegraphed Don Sebastian Cardenas, the man from whom Magnus Stromberg had arranged the purchase of the land, requesting additional information, but no answer had been received. One of the colonists had made it out of Mexico, and a sketchy report of the destruction of New Hope had been published in some newspapers. But that was all Anders had been able to learn. It was his plan to leave immediately for Mazatlán to find Katrina and bring her out of Mexico, if in fact, she was alive and could be found. He hoped Tom would go with him.

Lars Hansen had put up a reward for information leading to his daughter's safe return, but he had advised Anders against going to Mexico to search for her. The political climate was too dangerous, he said, and he didn't want to lose Anders also. Anders explained to Tom that he had told his father he must go. Someone must. But Anders had not told his father of the telegram he'd sent to Tom Callahan and of his plans to meet the Irishman in San Francisco.

After a night's sleep and further consideration, Tom explained to Anders that he had some reservations about making the trip.

"It's simple, Andy. She told me once she could no longer

293

see me. I don't want to interfere in her life again. If she and Stromberg are still alive, then they have no need of me."

"But what if Harold isn't? What if the rumors are true, and he's dead?" Anders pleaded.

"Andy, I'm committed to goin' with you and doin' what we can. But I just want you to know that if they're still alive and well, I'll need to back out and disappear. I've no right to be pursuin' Mrs. Stromberg. D'ya understand, Andy?"

"I do, Tom. We'll proceed cautiously. When can we leave?"

"I looked into that when I got up this morning. We can board a freighter tomorrow afternoon and be there in a couple of days."

"Good. Now, how about we obtain some supplies and maybe a map of Mazatlán, if we can find one? I think we've got a task on our hands, Tom."

"It's more than a task, Andy. It could well be Katrina's life."

For six weeks, Katrina lived and cared for Teresa's baby in the shelter of a small hut she had been provided, many miles from the ruined colony at New Hope. The tiny structure, located at the top of a steep sandy beach on the ocean, was really more of a bower, open on two sides, constructed of poles with a thatched roof. It afforded only the barest shelter from the heavy rain storms that often developed during the afternoons, but it did provide shade for Katrina and the baby during the heat of the day.

She lived in isolation. No word on the fate of the colonists was available to her, and except for a few rudimentary Spanish words she had learned from Teresa, the only way she could communicate with the two or three local Mexicans she had seen, was by sign language. Winter was, she presumed, not far away, and although she knew it would not bring the snow of Utah or Norway, she worried about how the baby would cope with colder temperatures.

She depended for food and water on a Mexican family that was living several hundred yards down the beach. The man, a surly, toothless fellow, brought fish from his catch and provided a daily gourd of warm, foul-tasting drinking water to Katrina, a task that she could see he resented, but one which she assumed Miguel required of him.

Miguel had returned only once, since depositing Katrina on the beach. That visit provided the goat, now staked nearby, which was furnishing the milk that was sustaining the baby. During his brief visit, Miguel had taken no interest in the infant, and Katrina had not told him that the baby was Teresa's.

Why Miguel had not killed her, and whether or not such a fate had befallen the other occupants of the wagon in which she had been riding, she didn't know. Miguel had been very angry and had not conversed, other than to tell her to remain here and to inform her she would be fed. If she attempted to leave, he had warned, she would die. He then rode away, returning only once, the next morning, when he brought the goat.

For the first several days after her arrival on the beach, Katrina had moved about in a stupor. She ached all over from being thrown from the buggy into the ravine where Teresa had died, and her hands and wrists and face became sunburned and swollen. Barely able to care for herself, she had to force herself to look to the needs of Teresa's baby. She tore up her petticoats to use for diapers, washing them out in the surf when they became soiled, and struggled to learn how to milk the goat efficiently to provide milk for the infant. The heat, blowing sand, and an infestation of fleas that bit both her and the baby made life miserable.

After a time, Katrina settled into a routine that seemed to ensure that she and the baby would survive, but she became despondent, filled with loneliness and despair. She spent many days fantasizing that Harold would come to rescue her. Once she thought of Tom Callahan, and the idea that he might somehow come to carry her to safety, exploded in her mind and occupied her thoughts for several hours, filling her with a kind of euphoria that faded as time wore on.

During all this, Teresa's baby provided the only companionship for Katrina. At first, she resented his crying and the constant care he required, but in time, Katrina developed a growing affection for the infant boy and spent many hours talking to him in Norwegian and English, looking into his dark eyes, playing with him, and enjoying his developing personality. Without consciously deciding to do so, she began calling him "Sebastian," after his grandfather, Don Sebastian Cardenas—a name Katrina felt Teresa would approve.

One evening, toward the end of her second week on the beach, her routine having been established, Katrina sat on the seashore, listening to the surf wash onto the sand and watching the sun dip into the ocean. Due to the press of survival, the hopelessness of her plight had only periodically occupied her thoughts during the early days of her isolation. But as the light waned on this quiet evening, a deep, welling ache began way down in her chest, and she found herself suddenly sobbing. As she wept, she cried out in despair to the God in heaven, whom she felt had abandoned her. She had followed His counsel in every instance: she had joined the Church, married Harold instead of Tom because Harold had offered the hope of an eternal companionship, and she had come trustingly to Mexico. Now she had lost her baby and her husband and had been left to die in this God-forsaken place! A monstrous sense of the unfairness of it all washed over her, and she succumbed to a feeling of bitterness that threatened to overwhelm her.

For a space of time, she sat huddled, with her arms pulling her knees up against her chest, rocking back and forth, surrendering to despair and hopelessness. As she rocked, she alternately prayed to God and leveled angry accusations at Him.

As the moon rose in the night sky, Katrina's thoughts drifted again to Tom Callahan and the decision she had made to reject his courtship. Abject hopelessness overtook her as this final thought convinced her that nothing of worth remained for her in life. God, or as Tom had put it, fate, had taken all.

Finally, she stood and walked mindlessly toward the low-rolling surf. Drawn to the sea, she waded out and felt the warm waters rise about her. It seemed so easy. All she needed to do was go a little farther and then relax. In a moment it would be over, and she would be relieved of her suffering.

The sound of the crying child broke her spell, and she turned, looking back toward the shack and then out to sea again, toward the reflection of the moon on the water. Shaken from her stupor by the sound of human distress, she turned frantically toward shore. Standing in water, now up to her chest, with the swells lifting her feet off the bottom, she panicked. Her clothes hung heavy about her, and the current threatened to draw her farther out to sea. But, then, her fear was replaced by a feeling of defiance.

Looking up into the cloudless, moonlit sky, she raised

her arms, and with her hands balled into fists, cried out, "I have done *everything* You asked and was obedient to thy servants, Lord. I stand helpless before you, *but I will not quit!* You *will* see me through this!" Without waiting for an answer, she thrashed and eventually waded her way toward shore, fighting her way heavily out of the surf and back up the steep beach to the shelter and toward the wailing baby.

Through the rest of a sleepless night, dozens of thoughts crowding her mind, Katrina felt, rather than saw, the dawn breaking behind the shelter. As she had lain there in the darkness, it had come to her. God *had* answered her prayers. He had called out to her, and the child, more helpless than she, was the voice He used. As hopeless as her situation appeared, Katrina determined on that morning, barely two weeks since the savage attack on the village, that she *would* survive and that though God would help her, it would be by strengthening her. No one else would come to save her, she would have to save herself. God's help, she came to understand, would be forthcoming in the form of her perseverance, her independence, and her fortitude. The dominance of the two men who had controlled her life to this point now gone, she would have to call upon the woman within to emerge.

Through the following several weeks, Katrina struggled to survive and to provide sustenance for herself and the baby. Still overcome at times by fear and depression, Katrina nevertheless continued to exist, day to day, on the edge of the Mexican jungle. To survive and to save the baby had become the focal point of her existence.

———— ∞ ————

Tom posted two letters the following morning before checking out of his hotel. One, to Sister Mary, contained a copy of his will, executed the day before Andy arrived and leaving everything to the Sisters of Holy Cross, to be used in caring for children in need. The other letter, written after Andy arrived in San Francisco, was an instructional letter to the Bank of Ireland. It contained a draft drawn on Wells Fargo Bank in San Francisco. The letter contained an order for the Irish bank to provide monthly payments to Mrs. Margaret Callahan of County Tipperary until further notice.

Andy had brought Tom a couple of letters, given to him by Sister Mary on the day he left Salt Lake City, including a forwarded note from Tom's mother advising that his father had passed away some months earlier. She had sold the shop and was living off the proceeds. Two of his younger brothers had left home, but one had returned following their father's death. Tom's bank draft assured them of a comfortable living for the indefinite future.

Except for the sense of urgency to discover what had happened to Katrina, Tom and Anders's ocean trip down the coast of California and around the Baja Peninsula was peaceful and uneventful. Tom took the opportunity to reflect on the past year. Running away from Kansas City, then Salt Lake City, escaping the law, no money or prospects—all of it seemed eons ago. Receiving news of his exoneration while in Seattle had taken some time to work its way into Tom's everyday thought process, but now he actually felt as though his fugitive status had been lifted, and that feeling changed his outlook on life.

Tom had purposely not told Andy about his good fortune in Alaska. The only person he had confided in, via his letter, was Sister Mary and even then, only that he'd had good fortune in Alaska, but not *how* good. His mother and family taken care of, Tom felt the Lord had truly stood by his side and as Katrina had said, he would have no worry for his future with such a companion.

During the voyage to Mazatlán, Andy told Tom about some of the developments at Holy Cross Hospital and why he had decided to leave his father's household and accept employment with Sister Mary. It was long overdue, he said. Even Lars Hansen had come to accept the move, Andy said.

By the evening of the third day, the ship rounded the southern tip of the Baja Peninsula and began crossing the gulf to Mazatlán. The offshore islands presented a beautiful picture as Tom stood by the railing, observing the ship's approach to the narrow gap between two towering rock formations, behind which lay the natural harbor that Captain Cardenas had discovered nearly four hundred years earlier.

Watching landfall from the deck of a ship, Tom thought, was becoming his routine. He had seen such views in New York harbor with its majestic Statue of Liberty, in Seattle, in Alaska on the western edge of North America, and of course, in the wide entrance to the harbor at San Francisco. Though he found that he had fairly good "sea legs" and didn't mind being on the water, Tom could not envision a life at sea for himself. He much preferred having land beneath his feet.

Taking a carriage into the center of Mazatlàn, Tom and Anders arrived in the town square, a center dominated by a large Catholic cathedral, the likes of which Tom had seen in several places in Ireland. The hotel did not match the accommodations of the Grand Union in San Francisco, but then neither had the tent in which he had spent most of the past year in the Klondike.

Inquiries to the local police provided no more information than the fact that the remaining Mormon colonists had left by wagon and on foot for the north of Mexico. Reports were that they had arrived at an old, established Mormon colony just south of the United States border. Andy did the questioning while Tom remained quietly to the side.

A guide was located, and on the morning of their third day in Mexico, they procured horses and rode out to the remains of New Hope. There they saw the charred rubble that had been the barn and several houses. The houses that had not been torched had been torn down for their lumber and other materials. All that remained as evidence that people had once lived there was the rutted road in and out of the place and the hard-packed, bare ground in front of the burnt or dismanteled dwellings. Off to the east, in a small grove of trees, the villagers had buried those settlers who had died during the skirmish on the evening of the raid.

The graves were not marked, but the guide told them that at least two women were buried in the grove. Tom stood over the grave sites under the trees, wondering if Katrina lay beneath his feet. The thought of her being dead created a great hollowness in him, though he would hardly allow himself to believe such a beautiful young woman was actually gone, her promising future ended in disaster in Mexico. Unwilling to contemplate such a fate for Katrina, he turned and headed back toward the deserted community.

"We've got to go see Don Sebastian," Andy commented on the ride back to Mazatlàn.

"You said he didn't reply to your inquiry," Tom said.

"That's right. But we're here now. Maybe he'll see us."

Two more days spent in town provided some information on the whereabouts and habits of Don Sebastian. His routine, it was said, included Saturday evening worship at the cathedral. The following Saturday, Tom and Andy sat in the town square surrounding the cathedral and watched the residents come and go, in and out of the church. Don Sebastian's carriage was easy to spot, and as the distinguished gentleman was helped from his seat by a servant, Andy rose to intercept him. The servant, more a bodyguard, moved between the two as Andy approached.

"*Señor* Cardenas, my name is Anders Hansen, and I seek your assistance in locating my sister, Katrina Stromberg. May I please speak with you for a moment?"

Don Sebastian paused, then continued walking, grunting something in Spanish to the guard, who waved Anders off.

"Please, *Señor*. I would like to know if she is alive," Andy said to the old man who shuffled away, toward the steps of the cathedral. Tom stood close behind, but said nothing as Andy pleaded.

Don Sebastian hesitated, then turned to Andy, observing Tom's presence as well. "Mr. Hansen, I do not know if your sister is alive, but I do know that *my* daughter is dead—as I am dead. I can be of no assistance to you. Please, allow me to grieve in private."

Andy was embarrassed to have troubled the man, seemingly old beyond his years and the suffering which he had borne evident in his manner. "I am truly sorry, *Señor*, for your grief. Please excuse the intrusion."

Tom and Andy stepped back, retreating to the bench they had been sitting on and resumed their seats, unsure how to proceed next.

"Did you see the sorrow in his eyes?" Andy asked.

"He looks like a man in deep grief," Tom replied. "It may have been that more people suffered than just the Mormon colony."

Thirty minutes passed while they sat, discussing their

inability to proceed without some sort of lead. Then, looking up, they saw Don Sebastian's body guard approaching.

"*Señor* Cardenas instructed me to advise you that his son, Miguel Antonio, is in residence at the small hotel at the end of the plaza," he pointed. "He may be of some assistance."

"Thank you," Andy said. "And, please, thank Don Sebastian."

"*Sí, Señor. Buenos noches.*"

They watched the carriage drive off, catching a final view of *Señor* Cardenas through the carriage window as it turned the corner. He was slumped in his seat, his chin lowered onto his chest, and he didn't acknowledge those who stood and bowed their heads respectfully as the carriage passed.

"A man of honor, I think," Tom said.

"And respected by the people of the city, by all appearances," Andy added, watching as the carriage disappeared around a corner. Looking at Tom, Andy nodded in the direction of the hotel, a question in his eyes.

Tom agreed. "Aye, let's go see if Miguel is there. We've got to find someone who knows something, Andy," he said, rising from the bench.

In the lobby of the hotel, they asked directions to *Señor* Miguel Antonio Cardenas's room.

"*Señor* Cardenas is in the cantina across the street," the desk clerk said in broken English.

"Thank you," Andy replied.

Seated alone outside the cantina, at a small table in a courtyard lighted by colorful lanterns, was a man drinking beer from a bottle. Music and some laughter came from the open door, but the man paid no attention. A cluster of empty bottles was scattered about him on the table where he sat.

303

Approaching the man, Tom followed his hunch. "Miguel?" he asked, and the man looked up.

"*Sí*. Miguel. What is it you want?" he said in slurred English.

"A word with you, if possible," Tom said, pulling up a chair and sitting down. Andy remained off to one side and watched.

"We have come looking for the sister of my friend," he said, motioning toward Andy. "Her name is Katrina Stromberg."

Tom could see the man bristle at the mention of the Stromberg name. "Can you help us, please?"

"I don't know anything. Be on your way."

Tom looked down at the table and back up into the man's eyes. "We've come a long ways, and anything you might know would help," he said.

"What makes you think I know anything?"

"Your father sent us to you, *Señor*. He seemed to think you might be able to help us."

At the mention of his father, Miguel looked directly at Tom. "You have spoken with Don Sebastian?"

"Briefly. At the cathedral."

"Is he . . . he is well?"

Tom held the man's eyes, reading the family trauma that had somehow separated father and son. "No. He is not well."

Miguel lowered his head, maintaining silence between them for moments while Tom allowed him time to contemplate. Finally, Miguel looked up at Tom and spoke. "I have not been home since the night of the raid. I was responsible for . . ." he hesitated, staring off into the distant night. Looking back at Tom, he continued, "About twenty-five miles north, on the beach, at a place called Point Lobos.

304

You may find her there. You can go by sea. Just tell anyone in the harbor you want to go to Point Lobos."

"And her husband?"

"Her *husband?*" Miguel queried, confused.

"Harold Stromberg," Tom said.

Miguel's face registered his shock as he realized that Teresa and Katrina had also been part of the deadly game. "He is dead," Miguel said flatly.

Tom maintained his composure at the surprising news of Harold's death, and standing to leave, he said, "Thank you, Mr. Cardenas." Miguel didn't acknowledge his thanks, but sat, head drooping, continuing to stare down at the table. Before turning to walk away, Tom said, "Miguel, your father needs his son," but receiving no answer, he joined Andy, and the two men walked through the town square, back toward the hotel.

"Any luck?" Andy asked.

"She's apparently about twenty-five miles from here."

"He knew where she was?" Andy asked, excited.

"Yes."

"Wonderful. When can we go?"

"In the morning," Tom said, continuing to walk.

"Tom?" Andy asked, seeing his concern.

"Tragic family, Andy. He didn't know that Harold was Katrina's husband. I wonder what happened here."

"Maybe Katrina knows."

"Maybe. Let's get some sleep and see about a boat in the morning," Tom said. "Oh, and Andy. Harold Stromberg is dead."

"Then Katrina is alone out there."

"Until we find her," Tom said.

20

Working inland of the offshore islands, the wind-powered fishing boat took several hours to navigate the twenty-five miles to Point Lobos, tacking to take advantage of the shifting winds.

About noon, the forward crewman pointed as they rounded a spit of land that thrusted abruptly out from the steady, even coast line they had been following. "Point Lobos," he said. A small cluster of huts, thatched palm leaf roofs, and naked children signaled the appearance of the fishing village the skipper had told Tom and Andy about. They pulled the boat in until it grounded itself against the smooth, sandy bottom, and one of the crewmen jumped out and held it fast. Tom and Andy also jumped over the side and waded through the warm surf to shore, then walked with wet pants across the broad beach toward the village.

The skipper, who spoke both English and Spanish, accompanied them to translate. He asked the first man they met as they approached the village about reports of a gringo woman living in the area. Without speaking, the villager pointed south on the beach, and returned to mending his nets. The three men walked farther along the beach, keeping to the hard wet sand where the surf had washed up.

They encountered villagers also walking the coast line, gathering driftwood and scavenging the beach. After a walk of several hundred yards, they came to two small huts but found them both abandoned. Though they were clearly deserted, Andy glanced anxiously into each of them, only to announce, "No one here."

They came at last to a place where several Mexican women were foraging in the brush, inland from the beach, and a group of small children was running and playing in the area. Two of the women each had a baby strapped to her back as they gathered firewood. Andy walked toward the women, signaling the fishing boat skipper to accompany him to translate. As he neared, the women stopped gathering to watch his approach, shielding their eyes from the glare of the sun off the water at Andy's back. As Andy drew near, one of the women took a hesitant step or two toward him. She was dirty and her hair was matted on her head, in desperate need of combing.

Tom watched as Andy spoke with her through the interpreter and then began the walk back toward the beach.

"Any news?" Tom asked.

"She left. A week ago," Andy replied.

"Where to?"

"They don't know."

<hr>

As dark descended on the fifth day of her trek, Katrina worked at starting her nightly fire, which she desperately wanted, knowing it would comfort her and the baby through the dark hours. Obtaining the matches had been the final detail in her plan to quit the beach and strike out overland for New Hope and, eventually, Don Sebastian's hacienda. She had stolen them from the Mexican who came twice a week with a donkey and cart to Point Lobos to purchase fish for his inland village. Stealing the matches from his cart had filled Katrina with fear, but she knew she would have no chance in the jungle without the ability to start a fire.

Now, only four matches remained, and she had not yet recognized any landmarks, although she felt certain she must be nearing familiar ground. Her plan to go to the hacienda had seemed the right thing to do, although she was not at all certain how Don Sebastian might receive her. She found herself banking on his responding favorably to Teresa's baby.

After surviving nearly three months in the shack on the beach, the decision to leave had not come easily. But no further sign of Miguel Cardenas during that time had convinced her that she was indeed on her own, and an indefinite contest for survival on the beach seemed fruitless.

But it was the baby who, once again, had made the decision for her. Sebastian had survived—something that several times hadn't seemed possible—but he hadn't gained much weight, and his stool was constantly loose. A steady diet of goat's milk seemed to be inadequate to properly nourish him. Then, too, Katrina constantly reflected on her promise to Teresa.

For part of the time, Katrina actually had labored under the belief that she would keep the child—would raise him as her own. In her prayers, she had bartered with the Lord, arguing that Sebastian was little enough compensation for all she had lost and all she had endured. But even as she prayed, she knew it wasn't right. Besides, she had promised Teresa to deliver the baby to Don Sebastian, and her conscience wouldn't allow her to do less. His dark hair and dark skin served as a constant reminder that the baby was

Teresa's child—and Don Sebastian's grandchild. Only his blue eyes linked him to his father.

But it was a dream that convinced her of what she must do. She saw Don Sebastian standing before her, smiling and holding out his arms to her—either for her or for the child, she could not decide which.

It took her nearly two weeks to hoard enough food to begin. She saved some fish by drying it and obtained a few ears of corn from the villagers. During that time she experimented leading the goat on a tether. At first it had been balky and resisted, but by working with it each day, she was finally able to coax it along.

Then, early one morning, she tied her few provisions into a bundle, and strapping Sebastian to her back in the native fashion, she led the goat away from the beach and headed inland into the jungle.

Miguel had brought her to the beach, riding behind him on his horse, where she had struggled for several hours to hold on and manage the baby without dropping him. Miguel had pushed the horse hard, and Katrina arrived exhausted, chafed, and unspeakably sore from bouncing painfully on the hard leather skirt of Miguel's Spanish saddle. Now, she was trying to retrace that route, but at a much slower pace. She knew that it might take her several days to cover the same ground Miguel had ridden in one long day.

Now into her return trek five days, she still had not come to the familiar land around New Hope. Traveling with the baby strapped to her back, sleeping wherever darkness caught her, and leading the goat by a tether, she felt she must have made less than five miles a day. Finding enough drinking water was her greatest concern, but she had been successful in locating several small streams, and at every opportunity she filled the two gourds she carried in her small bundle. Still, the infant suffered from the journey, and her own strength was failing her. How many more days she could travel in such a condition she didn't know, and it began to frighten her, but she knew there was no turning back. She felt that if she could reach New Hope, shelter and the well the settlers had dug would provide some respite. From there it was only about twelve miles to Don Sebastian's hacienda.

Tom and Andy arrived back in Mazatlàn tired and discouraged. The villagers had provided little information other than to say that the *Yanqui* woman and the baby had gone inland a week earlier. The fishing boat skipper suggested they obtain horses and a guide and make the trip by land, following the inland trail from Mazatlán back toward the fishing village at Point Lobos. By doing so, they might intercept Katrina along the way. He was skeptical about her chances of surviving alone in the jungle, but Tom and Andy felt it was their only hope.

After a night's rest, they procured some horses and a pack mule, outfitted for a week on the trail, and with the assistance of a local guide, rode north toward New Hope, where they camped the first evening. The next morning they started out again, advising their guide to lead them from New Hope to Point Lobos via the jungle. The man's English was only basic, but conversation was possible.

They had been riding for several hours and had stopped at about midday to give their horses a blow in the intense heat of the jungle, when a rider overtook them from behind. Listening to him speak excitedly in Spanish to their guide,

Anders and Tom knew that he brought important news. In broken English, the guide translated the rider's message.

"The woman is found, *Señors*."

"Found?"

"*Sí*. She is with Don Sebastian Cardenas."

Tom and Anders looked at each other and smiled broadly, filled with relief.

"She made it," Tom said.

"She's alive!" Andy shouted.

"Aye. How far to Don Sebastian's?" Tom asked the guide.

The guide looked up at the sun momentarily and replied, "by dark, *Señor*."

Tom motioned toward the rear. "Lead on, Pancho."

"*Sí, Señor*," he smiled, reversing course and following the rider whom Don Sebastian had sent to find the two men.

<hr/>

A short time after dark, the lights of Don Sebastian's hacienda appeared on the horizon and the four riders urged their weary mounts into the same cobblestone-paved court-yard where Harold Stromberg had first seen Teresa as she dismounted from her early morning ride.

Servants took charge of the horses and Tom and Andy were led into the main house where they were met by Don Sebastian, who, unlike the first time they had seen him, had a bright smile on his face.

"Your sister is well, *Señor*," he said to Andy. "She is sleeping now."

"And the baby?" Andy asked.

"Also well. The doctor is in attendance, and he has

assured me they will be fine. They are both exhausted, but otherwise uninjured," he continued, still smiling.

"Thank you, *Señor*, for sending a man to find us," Andy said.

"*De nada, Señor*. Now, you shall bathe and rest. Tomorrow your sister will be awake and you can talk. Let me show you to your rooms. If you please, *Señor*," he said to Tom as they ascended the stairs.

Some time later, after having bathed and eaten food brought to his room, Tom stood by the window, looking out into the night. The house had quieted, and he thought about what he ought to do. His first thought was to leave a note for Andy and depart early in the morning. But as the night wore on, and sleep eluded him, in spite of how tired he was, the thought of seeing Katrina again took hold. Katrina was no longer married.

"*Señora* Stromberg is asking to see you, Don Sebastian," the servant said, in Spanish.

The old man was sitting on the verandah, taking the morning air, sipping his coffee, and watching the swallows flit in and out of the eaves of the hacienda. His days had been filled with emptiness since the men from the small village near New Hope had brought Teresa's body home for burial. Since that fateful morning, he had not seen or spoken to his son, Miguel, but reports had reached his ears that Miguel had been in on the raid against New Hope and that after several weeks of absence, had taken up residence at a hotel in Mazatlàn. The Don, fearing the truth, had not tried to see Miguel nor sent messengers to him.

When, nearly three months after the massacre at New Hope, his servants had informed him that the young *Yanqui* woman had arrived at his hacienda, weak from hunger and dehydrated, bringing with her a malnourished infant, he had quickly responded. Providing immediate care for Katrina and the baby, the Don had also sent his riders into Mazatlàn to inform the two *Yanqui* men who had been seeking her. When Don Sebastian learned the two had left on a search and rescue mission into the interior, he had sent his *caballeros* in several directions hoping to find them and call them back. That is how Tom and Anders happened to be overtaken on the jungle trail and brought to the hacienda.

"Is she well this morning?" the Don asked.

"She is awake, *Señor*, but weak."

"And her brother?"

"The *Yanquis* are also awake, *Señor*."

"*Sí*. I will go to her. Inform the men and bring them to her room also."

"*Sí, Señor*," the servant replied.

As Don Sebastian entered Katrina's room, she looked up at him, a weak smile crossing her face.

"My child, you are looking better this morning."

"The baby?" Katrina asked.

"Ah. He is also well," he responded, motioning for a servant who stepped from the room and quickly returned with the infant, placing him alongside Katrina in the bed. Katrina pulled the baby close and peeked into the soft blanket wrapped around the tiny bundle.

"You both will need some care and nourishment, but in due time, you will both be well again," Don Sebastian assured Katrina.

"But there is another surprise for you this morning," he smiled, turning toward the door.

Katrina followed his gaze to find Andy standing in the doorway. Smiling broadly and stifling a cry, he quickly stepped to the side of the bed and leaned over to embrace his sister.

"Anders, how? Oh, thank God, Anders!" she cried, holding him tightly and beginning to weep.

After a time, Anders stood up from the bed, taking Katrina's hand in both of his and looking lovingly into her tired and sunburned face as she wiped at her tears with the sheet.

"You have a brave sister, *Señor* Hansen," Don Sebastian said. "She must have walked through the jungle for many days to reach my home."

Andy continued to hold Katrina's hand, glancing at the infant and back again at Katrina. "You need some time to regain your strength, Katrina, and then we'll take you home."

"Home," she said softly, smiling through her tears.

"Someone has come with me to help find you, Klinka," Andy said.

Katrina looked into Andy's eyes, waiting for him to continue. Then a movement over his shoulder caught her eye, and she raised up slightly from her pillow to look toward the doorway. There, Tom stood quietly just inside the room, watching as Katrina recognized him and burst again into tears. Astonished to discover him there, Katrina was suddenly filled with a sense of the love and concern being concentrated in her by these kindly men, and overwhelmed by her emotions, she surrendered to uncontrolled sobbing.

Not knowing exactly how to comfort her or what to say to her, the three men stood awkwardly by. Finally, the Don said, "Perhaps we should leave this young woman and her child so they may rest. It will be some time before they are back to normal strength."

The three men turned to leave, but before they could do so, Katrina shook her head and struggled to speak.

"*Señor*," she finally managed to say to Don Sebastian. "*Por favor*," she said, patting the edge of her bed.

Don Sebastian came forward and stood at her bedside, waiting for her to regain her composure.

After a time, she drew a deep breath and said, "Don Sebastian, I am so grateful for your assistance, and I want to tell you how sad I am over the loss of your daughter."

Katrina's voice broke again, but after a moment, she was able to say, "Teresa was very kind to me, *Señor*, and I loved her like a sister."

Don Sebastian nodded his head, standing by the bed and saying nothing, tears welling up in his eyes as well.

Katrina went on. "There was something that she made me promise . . . just before she died," she said, dissolving again into tears. After a time, she cleared her throat, and reaching for Don Sebastian's hand, said, "She made me promise . . . that I would deliver your grandson into your care."

The old man, who had continued to smile at Katrina as she spoke, turned his head now to look at the infant. Katrina pulled back the blanket wrapped around the sleeping, three-month-old infant, a smile on her face, mixed with the tears glistening on her cheeks.

"Can you not see the "Cardenases' features?" she asked, smiling. Katrina continued to look into his eyes—eyes that were moving back and forth between the infant and Katrina. After what seemed like minutes, a look of understanding came across his face.

"But I assumed . . . the baby was someone else's . . . perhaps from the village . . . "

"Don Sebastian, he is *Teresa's* son. *Your* grandson. I was

316

present at his birth and for some short hours, Teresa knew her son and knew that he would be in good care with his grandfather. The boy needs you, Don Sebastian. He needs to learn his heritage—the *Cardenas* heritage," she said, lifting her chin slightly, in one of the proud mannerisms she had learned from Teresa.

Don Sebastian reached out his hand to lightly touch Katrina's cheek as she lay on the bed before him. She laid her head back on the pillow, turning to look at the infant and gently stroking the child's hair. Don Sebastian placed one hand on Katrina's head, his other on the child, and after a moment, said emotionally, "*Gracias,* my child. Thank you. Thank you for your love, and for caring for my . . . grandson," his voice breaking. "I know Teresa Maria loved you, too, child."

Katrina smiled at the old man, whose tears were channeled from his eyes in the deep wrinkles of his weathered face.

Leaving Katrina to rest, the three men left the room, but only after Anders and Tom had promised to stay nearby and be available to talk later in the day.

⚬⚬⚬

That evening, Katrina felt well enough to get out of bed and get dressed. Don Sebastian ordered a small and private supper for her and· Anders and Tom, which they ate together in the dining room. Katrina was full of questions about home and how Tom and Anders had managed to get together, and how things had gone in Alaska, and about a hundred other things.

She briefly related the horrible happenings that had taken place during the attack on the colony. She was embarrassed to describe Harold's deceit, but spoke lovingly

317

of Teresa and the things they had endured together. She was too tired to talk at length about losing her baby, or Teresa's death, or all that had happened to her while struggling to survive on the beach at Point Lobos, but she promised to say more about those experiences at another time.

Listening to all of this, Tom offered on a couple of occasions to leave the room, but Katrina said she wanted him to know what had taken place, and in the end, it was Anders who excused himself, leaving Tom and Katrina together, seated across from each other at the dining table, in a room where the only light came from the candles burning in an elaborate candelabra.

After Anders left, Tom and Katrina sat for awhile in silence. When Katrina brought it up, they agreed that it was incredible that they would be seated together, in a hacienda in Mexico. Though it was much on Tom's mind that with Harold Stromberg now dead, Katrina was no longer married, he knew it would be completely wrong to discuss that situation. Still, he was having difficulty trying to ignore the possibilities that fate seemed to have reordered.

Katrina looked into Tom's eyes and said, "Thank you, Thomas, for coming with Anders to look for me. It seems you have been rescuing one or the other of us ever since we first met." She smiled and reached across the table and took Tom's hand, rubbing his knuckles with her thumb. Tom noticed but did not mention her rough and sunburned hands.

Looking now into that face, still reddened and puffy from her ordeal, Tom experienced a flood of sympathy for her. "Katie, m'darlin'" he blurted, "I told you before, you're a strong woman. I'm proud of what you've done, how you've survived."

Katrina laughed. "I don't feel so strong right now."

"Aye, but you'll soon be better."

318

They sat there, gazing at each other in the candlelight, and after a moment Tom spoke again, "There're so many things I want to say to you, but I know now isn't the time . . ."

Katrina smiled, tears welling again in her eyes. "I know," she said. Then wiping at her eyes with her fingers, she said, "I feel like a perfect fool, crying every time someone says anything nice to me."

Tom smiled at her. "What you need is rest, Katie. I guess we'll have plenty of time to talk, that is, if you don't mind listening to my Irish palaver."

"It was that Irish 'palaver' that first attracted me," Katrina said, smiling, "Do you remember the first words you said to me?" she asked.

"'Tis a vision of loveliness I see before me," Tom immediately said, " . . . but of course, I was referrin' to the sea," he teased.

Katrina smiled again—the same smile that had captured his heart, the first time he ever saw it, on the docks at Cork.

Standing, Tom continued to hold Katrina's hand across the table and raised her up. "I'll say good-night to you, now," he said, then added, "It seems you were right, Katie."

She looked at him quizzically.

"It seems both of our lives have been in the hands of the Lord, and he *has* watched over each of us."

Reverting to her Norwegian accent, Katrina smiled and said, "Ya, you're surely right, Mr. Callahan."

Tom laughed out loud, then said, "Rest, Katrina. We'll have plenty of time to talk when you are stronger. I'll be here. You have my word on it."

The first evening at sea, with occasional lights along the Baja Peninsula showing off to their right, some ten miles away, Tom came on deck to find Katrina in a pose etched in his memory. She was leaning against the railing, this time on the starboard side, so she could watch the lights glide by. Without speaking, he came alongside her and leaned forward, resting his elbows on the railing.

Three weeks of rest at Don Sebastian's hacienda had provided a refreshed and determined Katrina Hansen. The decision to return to her former name had come of her own accord, but Tom was quietly pleased with the decision.

They had talked a great deal during her period of convalescence in Mazatlàn, but no words of their future plans had as yet entered their conversations. Tom frequently almost ached to declare himself, but he knew it was proper to wait for Katrina, now a widow, to give the signal.

One thing Katrina *had* tearfully confided in Tom was the dread she experienced every time she thought about leaving little Sebastian in Mazatlán when it came time to sail back to the United States.

With regular feedings and constant care from not only Katrina but several of the women on Don Sebastian's household staff, he had quickly gained weight, and at nearly four months of age, was smiling and following people with his deep blue eyes. He seldom cried and was the focus of everyone's attention in the hacienda.

Caring for the infant during the weeks of deprivation and hardship in the small hut on the beach at Point Lobos, had provided for Katrina a bonding with the child. Though the little boy had been frequently ill and not easy to care for, his vulnerability and pain had touched Katrina's heart, and she had learned to love him as she nurtured and protected him. She felt now, something like the loss she had experienced when she lost her own baby, only in some ways this was more acute. This was a baby whom she had bathed and cuddled and prayed for. She had come to know his personality and to love his appearance. Then, too, his was the voice the Lord used to call out to her and to rescue her from her despair. By returning the child to Don Sebastian, in fulfillment of her promise to Teresa, Katrina felt as if she were parting with her own baby and the person who had provided her sole purpose for living during the difficult time at Point Lobos.

Her pain was somewhat balanced by the pleasure she took in seeing Don Sebastian returned to life again, but it was an ache and a loss she would not soon get over.

As the ship moved on, Katrina turned to Tom and lifting his arm, she nestled close to him, laying her face comfortably on his chest and continuing to watch the shoreline slowly edge past.

What thoughts she had, Tom could not know, but having Katrina again in his arms was the fulfillment of a thousand fantasies he had entertained ever since meeting her—especially those in Alaska where he had lain night after night in his bedroll, holding her picture in his hands and studying it until the paper had begun to separate from the emulsion of the photograph. Now she was, indeed, in his arms and he ached to make her his.

He finally found his voice. "Once before we stood like this, Katie. A long time ago, it seems. And you made a promise to me at that time. We've both come a long way since then, but you've never been far from my thoughts."

"Thomas, I haven't . . . "

"Shhh," he whispered. "You may need some time, Katie, for your wounds to completely heal. The hurtful memories I can't begin to imagine. But I want you to know one thing for certain, Katrina Hansen, I continue to love you with all my heart, and if you'll have me—when you're ready, of

321

course,—when that time comes, I want you for my wife, Katie, m'darlin'. We dock day after tomorrow in San Francisco then it's only a couple of days to Salt Lake by train. If you'll have me . . . "

Katrina put her fingers to his lips to silence his words, looking up into his eyes and thinking of the words she'd written about him in her journal, so long ago. How often she had confided to herself that she did indeed love this brash Irishman—this man who had come thousands of miles to rescue her from an unknown fate and now to claim her for a second time.

"Thomas, I can't change the past, and I *was* married to Harold. I knew nothing of his intent, though, and . . . "

"Katie, Harold is dead. The past is dead. Ahead of the bow of this ship lies the future. I want you to be part of my future, and I want to be part of yours. Can we not go forward into that future together, Katie? Will y'not let me enter your life?"

He gazed at her, a look of love and longing on his face—the one she had memorized so long ago. She placed her hand behind his head as she had once before on the *Antioch,* and pulled him down to kiss her, trembling with emotion as he held her in his arms.

"Thomas, if you will have me as your wife," she said, stepping slightly out of his embrace, but never wavering her eyes from his, "then I will gladly accept. I will try to be a good wife, Thomas, but I must extract one promise from you."

He stood quietly, scarcely able to believe the words he was hearing.

"My belief in my religion has not changed, Thomas. You must understand that. I will continue to practice that belief if, in light of my situation, the Church leaders will permit me. If you can give me that promise, Thomas, and also that our children will be allowed the same privilege, then I will be happy to become your wife."

"Aye, Katie," he said softly. "I've learned much about the Mormons from Sister Mary, and I know that those who went with you to Mexico meant well, but that they did not represent the Church. Anders has explained that. I give you my word, Katie. I will never interfere with your practice of your religion or that of our children, God willin'. But you also must know that I make no promises about becoming a Mormon, other than a willingness to listen and learn. I am Catholic, Katie. You know that. I intend to remain a Catholic. Is marriage acceptable under those terms?" Tom asked, his heart beating rapidly at the prospect of losing this woman a second time.

She kissed him again, and pressed her head against his chest. "It is, Thomas Callahan. It is."

◦◦◦

The wedding in San Francisco, with only Anders in attendance, had no pomp or ceremony and was performed by a justice of the peace at City Hall. The evening before the brief marriage service, Tom lay in his bed in the hotel, unable to sleep. Thoughts swirled constantly through his head and the myriad changes that had taken place in his life over the previous eighteen months ran together, presenting Tom with the confused thought that indeed fate, or as Katrina would say, the Lord, had surely taken a hand in his life.

Rich beyond his wildest expectations, his dream of marrying Katrina about to come to fruition, Tom could think of nothing left undone, whomever or whatever had been the instigator of these changes. Toward dawn, after sleeping

323

only in short snatches, Tom left the warmth of his bed and stood by the hotel window looking out over the slowly awakening city of San Francisco. He had learned during their trip back from Mexico that Katrina had some reservations about her brief marriage to Harold Stromberg, and that she was humiliated over how it must appear to Tom. Nothing had been directly addressed, but even the brief comment from Anders when he had told Tom that Katrina would need time to heal had made Tom think that Anders was perhaps against the marriage. However, Andy's second statement, that the marriage should take place as quickly as possible rather than have Katrina go back to Salt Lake and fall back under the nearly dictatorial influence of their father, had eased Tom's mind.

Less than five hours were left, by Tom's pocket watch, until their ten o'clock appointment with the magistrate. As of yet, Tom had not told Katrina about his Alaskan fortune, preferring to wait. Why, he didn't know. She had loved him once, or at least had deep feelings for him, he thought, when he was poor and without prospects, and he didn't want his newfound riches to influence her decision, one way or the other.

As the view of the San Francisco Bay became clearer with the growing light, Tom's thoughts once again drifted to the cause behind all the changes in his life. His mother, like Katrina, would be quite certain of the origin of his good fortune, and even though Tom wasn't openly religious, he had come to admit to himself that for whatever reason, God had smiled on him. His good fortune, in the form of the woman he loved being once again in his arms, and his golden discoveries in Alaska, had changed his life forever.

The prayer came slowly at first, Tom's knowledge of such things being limited to the rote prayers he had learned in school and church in Ireland. But, in a natural way, he was finally able to clothe his feelings and emotions in words, and by the time the sun had cleared the tops of the low range of mountains to the east of San Francisco, Tom had made an expression of thanks and had sincerely asked that he be allowed to understand what he must do to ensure the happiness of this lovely but emotionally wounded woman.

In Tom's second talk with the Lord, he expanded upon the promise he had made to God while lying in misery on the straw flooring in the boxcar between Kansas City and Denver. This time, Tom assured God that the riches he had been permitted to amass would be used to help those in need. Sister Mary Theophane's image continued to place itself in Tom's mind, and he knew the kindly Catholic sister would be the conduit through whom such charity would flow. As he stepped back into the room and began to draw his bath, Tom Callahan felt a peace within himself that had eluded him for the last several years of his life. Within hours he would take a wife—a woman his mother had not yet met, but a woman he felt certain his mother would approve.

In the afternoon, after the wedding, Anders left on the train to go back to Salt Lake City, while Tom and Katrina remained behind, planning to spend the next three days in San Francisco. On the following Friday, they also boarded the train to Salt Lake.

At Tom's request, Anders had reserved a suite at the Knutsford House, the same hotel in which Tom had taken lunch with Anders the first time they had met in Salt Lake, almost a year and a half earlier.

Not until during the train trip did Tom discuss his Alaskan fortune with Katrina. He enjoyed seeing her astonishment. But it pleased him more to know that she had married him for himself and that she had been willing to commit herself to what she had presumed was the same poor, ignorant Irishman her father had warned her about.

The second errand Anders performed, was to forewarn his parents, Lars and Jenny Hansen, that Katrina was married again, this time to the Irishman from the *Antioch*. Anders was still unaware of Tom's financial status, and so, when Lars Hansen asked how Tom expected to provide for Katrina, Anders had no answer.

The first meeting between Lars Hansen and young Tom Callahan after the couple's return to Salt Lake City, had no better effect than their first meeting at dinner on the *Antioch*. Katrina, sworn to secrecy about Tom's wealth, listened politely as her father abused Tom and, looking directly toward her, told her in no uncertain terms that she was not to come home looking for a handout when her new husband couldn't find work or feed her.

Katrina thanked her father for his concern, and kissed him on the head before retiring with Tom to their suite in the hotel. Tom's last sight of Lars, was as the man gathered his cane and briefcase, leaving Tom with the sarcastic epithet, "Try to make something of yourself, young man. It's the least you can do for my daughter."

Tom smiled politely, shook Mr. Hansen's hand, and ushered him to the front entryway of the Knutsford House.

The following morning, Katrina, her two younger sisters, and their mother, drove off in a carriage for a day's shopping and visiting, an outing prearranged to give Tom the day for business. Walking the several blocks from the hotel to Temple Square, Tom entered the lobby of Zions Bank and asked for Mr. Thurston. The young clerk asked if he had an appointment, which Tom confirmed. Shown to Thurston's office, Tom entered smiling as Robert rose from behind his desk, coming around to greet Tom and pump his hand vigorously.

"You're looking a lot better than the last time we met," Tom said.

"Good care at Holy Cross Hospital did the trick, I think," the banker laughed.

"So," he said, pulling up a chair for Tom to take a seat. Robert leaned back against the front of the desk, folded his arms across his chest, and smiled at Tom. "Thousands . . . , no, tens of thousands, are scrambling, clawing their way, and gambling their lives' savings to get to Alaska, and here you sit, with most of Alaska's gold already in the bank. Nice timing, Mr. Callahan."

"Then you received my telegram from San Francisco?"

"Indeed, I did. And the bank draft. That should keep you out of noisy hospital basements for some time, Tom."

Tom stood, walking to the window that looked out toward Temple Square. "Maybe it'll give me the opportunity to assure that the next occupant of that room doesn't have such a sleeping problem," he said, looking back at Robert and smiling.

"A bit of philanthropy, eh?"

"No. I don't see it that way, Robert. Maybe giving a bit of His own back to God. And more importantly, I don't want others to see it that way. In fact," he said, retaking his seat, "I don't want others to see it at all. Is that possible?"

"Certainly. Zions Bank can handle that chore as discreetly as you wish, Tom."

"I don't want Zions Bank to handle it, Robert."

Robert paused in the act of taking his seat behind the desk. He placed both hands flat on his desk and leaned over toward Tom.

"I don't understand."

Tom smiled broadly, and began to laugh. "Of course you don't. I'll explain. At least, partly explain. In San Francisco, before my trip to Mexico, I sold my Alaska claims to a man named Simonsen."

"Yes," Robert said, seating himself and picking up some papers from his desk. "I believe his name is on these documents he sent."

"He gave me two pieces of advice, which I later discussed, after my Mexican trip, with some other bankers in San Francisco. They tended to agree with Simonsen. Now I come to you for confirmation of their opinion."

Robert leaned back in his chair, waiting for Tom to reveal this new twist to his deposit of over five million dollars in Zions Bank. A deposit that had startled and, ultimately, pleased Robert Thurston, who had chuckled to himself that the young Irishman who had come to help him late one night when he was in excruciating pain with appendicitis, had hit it big in Alaska.

"No, I don't want Zions Bank to make the arrangements, I want Utah Trust Bank to do the job for me."

"Utah Trust Bank?" Robert said.

"Right."

"There is no Utah Trust Bank, Tom," Robert said.

"Not yet."

Robert's eyes grew larger. "But . . . there . . . will . . . be," Robert said, stretching out the words.

"There will be, if—" Tom said, pausing to allow the little 'if' word to expand in Robert's mind, " . . . if, I can find the right man to run it."

With that much said, Tom leaned back in his chair to allow Robert the time to grapple with what Tom had intended to be an idea and a job offer, all in one.

Understanding immediately what Tom was after, Robert shook his head and fought to control the smile that was smearing itself all over his face.

"So, Simonsen suggested opening a bank, did he?"

"He did. And he said gold wasn't the only metal to mine. He told me that Utah is apparently full of silver, zinc, and copper, and that the mining industry here is ready to erupt. His advice was to be a part of it. 'Find a good partner,' he said, 'and get into it quickly.' So, what do you say, Mr. Banker? I've got about four million I'm willing to put into a bank. Simonsen would like to be a partner with one-third interest and has two million to invest. That gives some young, enterprising man with banking experience a new venture with six million dollars in assets. Do you know of anyone who would be interested in such a proposition?" Tom smiled again.

"Why me?" Robert asked, becoming serious.

"Because D.O. McKay vouched for you, Robert, and I quickly came to trust his word. And because Sister Mary liked you, and she's a good judge of character as well."

Robert leaned back in his chair and laughed. "Can I discuss it with my wife?"

"Of course. I did with mine," Tom replied. "Tell you what," Tom said, rising from his chair. "I'll leave it with you over the weekend, and we'll have lunch on Monday, if that suits you. I want to see Sister Mary and make a few arrangements of my own. The plan would be, Robert, if you're interested of course, that I will arrange for a new home to be built and then Katrina and I are going to Europe for several months. Your job, if you agree to be part of the effort, would be to start up the bank while I'm gone and see about getting us into the mining business. You would have a

329

partnership interest, of course. Is that enough time to consider the proposition?"

"Yes, yes, Tom. Plenty of time. Tell me, Tom," Robert said, coming out from behind his desk to walk Tom to the door. "When last we met, I don't recall your having much knowledge about banking or business. How did you . . . ?"

"I still don't profess to be an expert, but my uncle had three books in Alaska. *Law*, *Mining Law*, and *Properties of the Earth's Minerals*. The nights were long and I read a lot, Robert," he laughed.

Robert nodded, shaking Tom's hand as he departed. "See you Monday, Tom. About eleven, if that's all right."

"That'll be fine, Robert. Good to see you again. By the way, how is D.O.?"

"David's been called on a mission, Tom. He's in Scotland."

"I see," Tom nodded. "Well, perhaps I can write to him. Good lad, D.O. He was very kind to me when I arrived."

"It seems circumstances have all been kind to you, Tom. I'm happy for you."

> *Aberdeen, Scotland*
> *10 October 1897*

Dear Thomas,

I was pleased to receive your letter, yet disheartened to learn of the difficult time your wife experienced in Mexico. I trust she is well and recovering from her ordeal through the love and comfort you have offered. Thank you for your kind note the evening you left for Alaska. I was sorry to have not seen you before your departure. Now that you are back in Salt Lake City, and I am in Scotland, it seems this friendship is destined to be conducted over the ocean for a while.

Tom, your questions go to the heart of the matter concerning God's relationship with the human race. Not wishing to offend your sensibilities, or insult you personally, for I know you to be a good man, I must nevertheless testify of what I know to be true.

How, you ask, could our early pioneers have withstood the terrible onslaught in Missouri, Illinois, and even in Utah, retaining their faith in a God who would allow such atrocities, while, under similar circumstances, the Mormon colonists in Mazatlàn fell into strife, internal discord, and loss of their unity? How, indeed?

Tom, the answer, is at the root of our Mormon religion. I believe with all my heart that the Lord speaks to man through but one voice at a time. We believe that voice to be the Prophet and President of the Church. When the early Saints followed Joseph Smith through the hellfire of public abuse, even to the murder of innocent people, they did so as a manifestation of their faith. It sustained them and unified them in their purpose.

The Mormon colonists in Mazatlàn, having once possessed such knowledge, but having ignored the Prophet's counsel in pursuit of what they believed to be the Lord's will, left behind that one guiding principle, which sustained the early Saints: Faith. Faith in the ability of the Prophet to reveal the Lord's will. Without that guiding light, their unity and direction were lost—and they became as sheep, lost in the wilderness.

I hope not to have offended you, Tom, for I value our friendship. However, I testify to you that as the Lord liveth, these things are true. Until such time as we meet again, I offer my most sincere wishes for your happiness and that of Sister Callahan.

Warmest regards,

Elder David O. McKay (D.O.)

331

21

In July, 1876, a strapping fourteen-year-old Ute Indian boy found a home with troopers of the U.S. Seventh Cavalry, stationed in the northwestern United States. Working primarily with the camp cook, he had also been taken in by the blacksmith at the fort and taught how to care for and repair leather gear for the troopers. Though his name was Walking Horse, the troopers soon began calling him "Stitch," because he repaired their saddles, boots, and bridles.

At Little Big Horn, during the time Colonel Custer's troop was being obliterated by Sitting Bull and the warriors of the Sioux nation, Stitch was away from the action, back at base camp, helping the cook with kitchen chores. Several days after the massacre, General Terry arrived with a relief column and Stitch rode away, one of the few members of the Seventh Cavalry fortunate not to have been under Custer's direct command that fateful day.

Eventually, Stitch made his way to Fort Douglas in Salt Lake City, where he enlisted in the army and was assigned to a local troop. There he was content to remain, working with military horses and gear for the next twenty years, never asking for, or receiving, reassignment.

When he mustered out of the army in 1896, Stitch opened a small leather repair shop in Salt Lake, continuing to live quietly and simply, going every day about his work.

On a day in late 1897, when Anders Hansen first entered his shop, Stitch and Andy began a friendship and an association that would last for many years, although neither party could have predicted so.

"I am told that you tool leather and personalize it. Is that correct?" Andy asked.

"I do. What is it you was lookin' for?"

"I need a large traveling trunk. One with a leather top or sidebar. I'd like the name 'Callahan' engraved into the leather. Can you do that?"

"I can. Stitch is my name. And your name?"

"Anders Hansen, Stitch. Just call me Andy."

"I will, Andy. I will. Put that name down in writin' so I can be sure it's right. Callahan, you say?"

"That's right, Stitch. C-a-l-l-a-h-a-n."

"I can do that. What kind of trunk you lookin' for, Andy?"

"Well, I thought maybe we could pick one out together, so you can be sure you can work on the leather. Have you got time to go with me to the shops in town to find a trunk?"

"Yes, sir. Let me just lock up here."

⸺

The large travel trunk Andy presented to Tom and Katrina for a wedding present was magnificent. Completely wrapped in tooled leather, the trunk had silver buckles on the straps, which provided double protection, in case the latches failed. Stitch had done an excellent job of personalizing the leather covering, and it made a handsome gift.

Preparations for Tom and Katrina's European trip involved, among other things, contracting to begin construction on a new home during their absence.

Tom originally had it in mind to build and furnish the home as a surprise for Katrina. But when he shared that idea with the Thurstons, Alice Thurston quickly convinced him of the folly in such a plan.

"Thomas, I don't mean to interfere, but I can't imagine anything more unsettling to a woman," she said.

"What do you mean?" Tom asked. "Just thinkin' about the look she'll get on her face when she walks in makes me grin."

"The look she'll get on her face will probably make you do something besides grin," Alice said. "Katrina will have some definite ideas about how she wants her house built and furnished. I suggest you involve her in the planning and find some other way to surprise her, Thomas."

Tom had taken Alice's advice and been glad of it. As it turned out, Katrina took a keen interest in every detail and had some excellent ideas about the floor plan and appearance, including things that would never have occurred to Tom or any other man he knew.

Amid squeals of delight from Katrina and a number of hugs and kisses, Tom informed her of his plan to build them a mansion. He put her in touch with the architect, an excellent man by the name of Forsey with the premier architectural firm in Salt Lake City—Frederic Albert Hale, Architects. Hale's firm had already designed several mansions located on "Brigham Street," and Forsey had some excellent ideas. He convinced the Callahans to let him draw up plans for a large, English Tudor style home.

Tom had already contracted with Lars Hansen to build a complete household of furniture, per his daughter's specifications. The surprised look on his father-in-law's face when Tom placed the order and said he would be paying cash in advance, was worth all Tom could imagine. Of course, Mr. Hansen eventually learned the source of Tom's newfound wealth and of his banking and mining interests, but Tom and Katrina enjoyed keeping him in the dark for a while and watching his consternation.

From the moment Tom confided in Katrina about the new house, she filled her hours with frenetic activity, coordinating plans with the relevant parties to ensure the home had her personal stamp on it. She became acquainted with the sales clerks at ZCMI, and the department store manager frequently arranged lunch to be provided for Mrs. Callahan during her long sessions with his drapery and linen personnel.

Her excitement was such that she wondered, half seriously, if they shouldn't postpone their European trip until construction was actually under way. Whatever excitement Tom imagined he would have seen in Katrina's eyes if he had actually pulled off such a surprise, was now available for him to see every day. She was completely absorbed by the project and took great delight in every little bit of progress.

The one thing Tom *did* surprise Katrina with was the lot he chose. Located on a branch of the stream that ran out of Red Butte Canyon, the heavily wooded site was situated on South Temple, immediately east of Holy Cross Hospital. It would, Forsey assured Mr. and Mrs. Callahan, lend itself very nicely to his design.

Tom's initial meeting with Father Scanlan and Sister Mary, after his return to Salt Lake also went very well. They welcomed him warmly, and Father Scanlan declared his pleasure in having a true-blue Irish relative as a member of his diocese. It was a surprise to both Father Scanlan and Sister Mary to learn just how successful Tom had been in Alaska. While he kept his banking plans confidential, his proposal to establish a permanent fund for the hospital thrilled Sister Mary, for whom obtaining adequate funding to operate the hospital was always a challenge.

" . . . and I propose that the fund be used primarily for children, to pay for their hospital and surgical care, Father, with Sister Mary serving as the gateway through which people may access the fund," Tom said, completing his presentation to the Catholic leaders.

"Thomas, this is a most generous contribution. Is there no way we can convince you to allow us to publicly acknowledge such a gracious gift?" Father Scanlan asked.

"Father, I prefer it this way, beggin' your permission, of course. It's selfish actually. If people knew I was the provider of such a fund, many others would come askin' for other contributions. Also . . . " Tom said, looking out the window in Father Scanlan's office, ". . . me mother used to say all the time, that 'man's charity to man should be known but to God.'" Turning to look at Father Scanlan and Sister Mary, both seated and watching him, he added, "But I suppose, that as God's servants on earth, you two don't count in that exclusion," he said, grinning happily at each of them.

"As you wish, my son," Father Scanlan said, rising. "Sister Mary will be in charge of the distribution of the funds, and she may call on me as she requires for assistance."

"Tom," Father Scanlan said, laying his hands on Tom's broad shoulders, "you are a most unusual man, with wisdom far beyond what one would expect, given your age. But if I might be permitted to exhibit a bit of pride, it is what I would *expect* of my cousin. I'm very proud of you, Tom. And

I'm most pleased with your exoneration from the troubles that have previously plagued you.

"Now, on another subject," he said, lowering his head and looking over the rims of his glasses, "if I could only persuade you to sanctify your marriage in the eyes . . . "

Tom raised his hand, his eyes pleading respectfully with Father Scanlan. "I'm sorry, Father, but I've given m'word to Katrina that I'll not be interferin' with her religion. I intend to keep that word. Not only will I not interfere, I'll support her, when and where I can. Please understand me, Father."

Father Lawrence Scanlan, Archbishop of the Salt Lake Diocese, simply nodded his head and walked with Tom toward the door to his office. Sister Mary followed and after the three stepped into the hallway of the rectory, she gave Tom a hug.

"If you tell anyone about that hug, Mr. Callahan, I'll not recall a moment of it," she winked. "But I want you to know how pleased I am for you. I knew God had a purpose in sending you to us, and you have begun to fulfill that purpose, Thomas. May God continue to bestow His good graces on you. You have a strong woman by your side now, and a God-given helpmeet for your future. See that you honor her, Thomas, and that you comport yourself as would be worthy of your newfound status in the community."

"Sister, you sound like my mother," Tom laughed.

"Aye, and you'll be obeying me too," she said, shaking her finger in front of her smile, "like you would her. I care for you a great deal, Thomas. We are about God's work here, and as I told you on one of our early morning deliveries, we care not by what name they call their religion. They are all God's children, so we do His work, no matter whom we serve. Also, Thomas, I admire your stand in support of Katrina's beliefs."

"Thank you, Sister," Tom said. "But since you mentioned our early morning deliveries," he added, "is there anything I can do to help with your . . ."

"No, Thomas," she smiled, shaking her head. "Those needs are taken care of, and the man currently involved needs the blessings of his service. If the time comes, I'll let you know."

"I'm sure you will, Sister. Well, I'm off to see what our new house will look like today. Katrina is having a wonderful time with her plannin' 'n schemes."

"Where will it be located, Thomas?"

"Close enough for you to have lunch with us occasionally, Sister. Just up South Temple from the hospital. Near the intersection at Thirteenth East."

"Excellent."

"A good day to you, Sister. Please call if you need anything, although we'll be leaving soon. I'll leave instructions with Mr. Thurston. You'll recall him—the emergency appendectomy we stumbled on early one morning with David McKay."

"Oh, yes. I remember him well. A fine man. I'll call on him if I need anything while you're gone, Thomas. Thank you," she said, taking his hand in hers.

Two weeks before his meeting with Father Scanlan and Sister Mary, Tom had been well pleased when Robert Thurston agreed to become the President and General Manager of the newly incorporated Utah Trust Bank. Surprisingly, he had only one question at the time.

"Why Utah Trust Bank, Tom?" he'd asked.

Tom laughed. "On the train from San Francisco, when I told Katrina of my intentions, she expressed doubt. 'What do you know of banking, Thomas?' she said, and I replied, 'Nothin'.' I asked her what she thought was the most important characteristic of a bank, and after some thought, she said, 'They'd have to trust you with their money. They'd need complete trust.' Wise counsel, I thought, and so I came up with the name, Utah Trust Bank. Together, we'll see if we can deserve the name, Robert."

"We will indeed, Tom. I like it. I like it a lot. So, when do you leave?"

"In just a month. We sail from New York three weeks after that. That should give us some time in New York. Katrina wants to see it, and I would like another look at the haunts I learned to know during my stay there. We should be back sometime in early May. I'll keep you advised by telegraph. I'll also give you a schedule so you can get in touch if you need to, but I have total faith in your judgment."

"Six months in Europe. Quite a trip. You should be able to see most of it in that time, at least the major cities," Robert said.

"I believe so. Think you'll have the bank up and running when I return?"

"If I don't, I'll be knocking on Zions' door, looking for my old job back," he laughed. "In all seriousness, I'm sure we'll be well along the way. I've already made some connections with prospective mining interests who wish to consider our proposals."

"And you're not even on salary yet," Tom reminded him.

"Right," he nodded. "I will be soon enough. I gave notice to Zions for the end of the month. About that, Tom, I wanted to express my appreciation at your allowing me to determine the appropriate salary level for the position."

Tom nodded, thoughtfully. "As I said, Robert, I trust

your judgment. I want your full attention to our venture, because as much as I *don't* know, I *do* know that without your guidance, we won't succeed."

"Thanks, Tom. How about a going away dinner at our home a few days before you leave? We'll invite Sister Mary and a few of your friends."

"We'd like that. Just let me know when, Robert."

The final four weeks flew by, and Katrina was certain that the house needed much more attention. With Tom's assurance that they could telegraph any major concerns, and that the architect had been instructed to cable with any important issues, she agreed to leave. The actual departure was difficult for Katrina and tears flowed freely as she hugged Andy at the train station. After her ordeal in Mexico, she had found comfort and security again in Salt Lake City, feeling toward the city as her home, forgetting completely that she had been in Mexico nearly as long as she had been in Utah.

Sister Mary came to the train station to see them off, as well, along with Katrina's mother and two younger sisters. Lars Hansen had not yet reached an accommodation with the idea of his daughter actually being married to a Catholic Irishman. He said his good-byes privately to Katrina, several days earlier, grudgingly admitting, as Katrina teased him, that the "Irish lout" was looking better all the time.

Two events during their closing days in Salt Lake made Katrina's future considerably more pleasant, and therefore, her departure somewhat easier. The first was a decision on the part of Church officials that Harold's duplicity in taking a second wife in Mexico was no cause to call Katrina's membership into question. It was clear that she had been victimized and was an innocent party. President George Q. Cannon had taken time to interview Katrina and had taken the sweet young woman to his heart.

President Cannon also met for a few minutes with Tom, impressing the young Irishman by his openness and tolerance. He told Tom that he admired and respected Father Scanlan and Sister Mary for their work, suggesting that he knew more about it than Tom would have suspected.

After the interviews were complete, the Mormon Apostle stood for a moment with the Callahans outside the door to his office, a hand resting affectionately on a shoulder of each one. He thanked them for coming to see him, then winking at Katrina, and squeezing Tom's shoulder, he said so Tom could hear, "See that you bring this young fellow into the true church at the earliest opportunity."

The second exciting event occurred during the final week of their preparations, when Katrina secretly arranged, so as not to be embarrassed if the venture failed, an audition with the director of the tabernacle choir. With Assistant Conductor, Horace Ensign, at the piano, Conductor Evan Stephens talked with Katrina for a while as Brother Ensign casually played a melodic sequence of notes on the keyboard. Brother Stephens answered Katrina's questions, and then politely asked her to sing the musical phrases that Brother Ensign had just played. Katrina was surprised, but she had subconsciously entertained the melody in her mind and was easily able to repeat it, with only a slight deviation.

Brother Stephens appeared to be delighted and asked if Katrina had come prepared with any of her own music. He listened attentively as she performed three of her own selections and two of his choosing. She apologized for the condition of her voice, admitting that she had practiced very little.

She had, Brother Stephens judged, "an outstanding lyric soprano voice" and told her that if she wished to do so, he would be pleased to have her join the choir upon her return from Europe. She beamed proudly as she delivered the wonderful news to Tom, but he brought her back down to earth by asking if the choir was likely to let her sing "Sweet Rosie O' Grady."

So, in late October, 1897, Thomas and Katrina Callahan boarded the transcontinental train in Salt Lake City, Utah, bound for New York City and from there, to Cork, Ireland, the first of many European sites they intended to visit on an extended honeymoon. Eighteen months, and many trials after they originally met, Thomas Callahan, rich beyond his wildest expectations, only twenty-two, and married to his first true love, and Katrina Hansen, not yet twenty, married, widowed, mother of a deceased child, and married again to the Irish larrikin her father had warned her about, were on their way back to where they had started, much wiser than when they had originally boarded the *Antioch* that spring morning in Ireland.

The *Ille de France*, a four-stack steamship, made slow headway as the New York harbor tugs retreated to their berths, their task accomplished. Under her own power, and at the direction of a harbor pilot, the ship cautiously made her way toward the open sea, her fog horn sounding as a warning to all shipping that the large, oceangoing vessel would not, in fact, could not, give quarter to any smaller craft foolish enough to invade her path.

For the first time as man and wife, Tom and Katrina stood at the bow railing, straining to gain a glimpse of the

Statue of Liberty, which was shrouded in an early morning mist that blanketed New York Harbor. Bound for Europe, the couple would enjoy two weeks of extended solitude at sea, the first such since their return from Mexico.

Katrina enjoyed their stay in New York City immensely. She and Tom took in all the latest shows, shopped extensively for trendy clothing, and enjoyed the food and luxuries that wealth can provide. Though the Hansens had not been fabulously wealthy, Katrina had been brought up to enjoy a certain level of creature comforts. Still, she was somewhat conservative in her tastes and frequently felt as though Tom were extravagant in the things he provided her. As for him, he had had quite enough of poverty, and remembering the weeks and months he had spent hunkered down in the icy waters of El Dorado Creek, painstakingly extracting the precious flecks that constituted his fortune, he felt he had *earned* his money. And if he wished to indulge his wife, then he would do so. Then, too, he thought the enjoyment of a few luxuries would compensate in part for the time Katrina had spent, enduring her various hardships in Mexico and scratching out her meager subsistence on the beach.

That he loved her, Tom had long since acknowledged to himself, and increasingly to her. Katrina knew that for a country lad from Ireland, for whom the appearance of manliness was paramount, confession of a tender emotion, such as love, did not come easily. She appreciated his words all the more for the difficulty he had in expressing them. In the bloom of his passion for her, he had found it easy to say the sweet things, but it was not a natural skill for him, and though he had intense feelings for Katrina, he would struggle increasingly in his life to express tenderness and affection.

She also was appreciative, however silently, of Tom's apparent willingness to disregard her former marriage and the fact that she had once rejected him as a suitor. Somehow, even in the face of Tom's candid and fervent declarations of love for her, she had not been able to bring herself to tell him that she had loved him all along. Or declare that her marriage to Harold had been one of logic, of propriety, and one born of a desire to follow the counsel of the Church that she marry someone with like beliefs. Though not yet twenty, Katrina had learned one of the most important lessons in life—that similar beliefs are only a *part* of a successful relationship, and that there are other factors that go into the making of a lasting companionship.

Tom provided the caring, the loving, and the concern for other humans which Harold, while devout in his outward religious manifestations, had failed to practice in his daily living. The model after which Katrina, secretly in her heart, hoped to mold Thomas, was that of President George Q. Cannon, who had impressed Katrina as the type of religious leader who combines a basic love for humanity, and a willingness to allow others to come to their own realization of what the Lord would have them do.

Clearly, President Cannon believed what he taught, passionately so, but his manner was not one of coercion. Rather, he was one who practiced tolerance and who radiated a Christlike, unconditional love, which was not encumbered by prescribed expectations. He appeared to follow the Prophet Joseph Smith's formula for inducing righteous behavior. He taught correct principles but permitted men and women to govern themselves, as their wisdom permitted.

The lesson Katrina would need to learn, if she were ever to succeed in following President Cannon's good-natured

345

admonition to "bring Tom into the Church," was that her love for Tom also had to be unconditional, and not tied to the hope that someday, somehow, he would embrace her faith. Without Tom's ultimate acceptance of her Mormon religion, Katrina had no hope of an eternal marriage to this man she loved so passionately. It was a circumstance she had gone into knowingly and willingly, but that made it no less of a concern to her. For now, in the first blush of their marriage and in their early years together, it was something she could live with. The heartache and concern that Tom's failure to embrace the gospel might eventually bring, Katrina had not yet imagined.

By early afternoon the great ship was clear of landfall, and on the high seas. Assigned to First Seating for dinner, their table accommodations were immediately adjacent to the Captain's table, and Tom could not help but reflect on the continuing irony the trip provided, as opposed to that of the earlier trip they had taken in the opposite direction. The ship's First Officer did indeed look at Tom, as had the First Officer on the *Antioch,* but in the present circumstance, with the utmost courtesy, and with a note, delivered by the steward, which invited "Mr. and Mrs. Callahan to dine with the Captain tomorrow evening."

Seated at their table were two other couples, one going to Europe for the first time and a French couple, returning from an extended visit to America. Conversation started immediately, with the Frenchman taking the lead.

"Ah, *Monsieur* Callahan, what brings you to Europe?"

"Purely pleasure, Mr. Benoit."

"Then be certain to see Paris, *Monsieur* Callahan. One cannot consider his visit to Europe complete without having the pleasure of touring the world's most beautiful city."

Tom smiled and Katrina entered the conversation. "It is

346

certainly at the top of our list of places to visit, Mr. Benoit. Any particular recommendations?"

"Every place in Paris is wonderful, *Mademoiselle*. The new Eiffel Tower is a remarkable piece of engineering, the tallest structure in the world and destined to become a great landmark."

"So we've heard."

"What type of business are you in, *Monsieur* Callahan?" Benoit asked.

"Financial. Banking, actually," Tom replied, still a little self-conscious to be saying so.

Benoit coughed and raised his glass. "A toast then, since I thought all bankers were old, crotchety types," he laughed.

Tom accepted the toast, replying, "Too many of those, Mr. Benoit. Thought they could use some young blood."

"And so they can. So then, financially speaking, what do you think of the trouble in Cuba and the Philippines? The Spanish seem to be stretching their legs a bit once again."

"Not certain, Mr. Benoit, but I understand our government is aware of the situation and keeping an eye on things."

"Oh, you can be sure of *that*, *Monsieur* Callahan. It seems the American government keeps its eye *and* its nose, in everybody's business. France has often been required to push the 'camel's nose out of the tent,' so to speak."

"I was under the impression that France is a long-time ally of the Americans."

"So we are. So we are. But then one needs to be careful with nosy relatives too. Well, given the events of the past few weeks, the Spanish require a keen eye, it would seem. Regular hot spot down there—in Cuba, I mean."

Apart from the two occasions when Tom and Katrina

were invited to dine with the Captain, their dinner hour was usually spent verbally jousting with the gregarious Frenchman, who in the end, invited them to be sure to call on him when they arrived in Paris.

One evening, following their first invitation to dine with the Captain, Tom approached a delicate subject with Katrina in the late hours in their cabin.

"What do you think of the Captain, Katie?"

"How do you mean, Thomas?"

"I mean he's, well, he's educated and knows about a lot of things, don't you think?"

Katrina smiled at Tom and came to stand in front of him, reaching up to kiss his lips. "And you don't?"

"Well, not as much."

"How old do you think he is, Thomas?" she asked, continuing to smile at him, and playing with his hair.

"Forty-five, maybe."

"Twice as old as you, perhaps?" she teased.

Tom laughed and pulled her close, nuzzling his face in her hair until she too, started laughing. "I've time to learn, you're trying to tell me, Mrs. Callahan?"

"I think that would be the thrust of my message, Mr. Callahan."

"And at eighteen, you'd be my teacher?" he asked.

"Thomas, life has already taught both of us much more than many people our age. Maybe we should just let it come as it will."

"Aye. Well, I'm only a poor ignorant country lad from Ireland, but with your help . . . ," he said, pulling her close and kissing her forehead.

"Thomas, a country lad, maybe; from Ireland, certainly; but poor, hardly," Katrina laughed.

"Right again, Mrs. Callahan," he said.

Tom spent the final hours of approach to Cork pacing the forwardmost deck space on the ship. Spying land, he put his arm around Katrina and began to tell her of his homeland. During his time in America and Alaska, Tom had put aside his memories of Tipperary, but upon sighting the southwestern tip of Ireland, he instinctively knew that no matter where he lived, Ireland would always be his home.

During their week in Ireland, Tom told his mother that Uncle John had left a will with instructions that his sister, who was also Tom's mother, was to be taken care of by the proceeds from Uncle John's estate. Tom had at first thought of building his mother a new home, but Katrina wisely advised that after a lifetime in one house and community, should the middle-aged Mrs. Callahan suddenly change her financial status, she would most likely lose all her friends and become unhappy in the process. Tom never advised his mother of his personal status, preferring her to think the money had come from Uncle John, as indeed, Tom felt it had.

Their stay in Ireland, then England, with two weeks in London and a train trip through Scotland, was highlighted by an impromptu dinner in Stirling, Scotland, with the young missionary David O. McKay, a man who enthralled Katrina by his warmth and civility. After dinner, D.O. asked Tom if he would meet him the following morning for a brief excursion. Tom agreed, and shortly after dawn the next day, Tom waited as Elder McKay and his companion walked toward him on the street where they had agreed to meet.

"Morning, Tom," D.O. said.

"And to you, D.O. So, what's so important that an extra hour of sleep was lost?" he grinned.

"I want to show you something, Tom. Last night I sensed that you are perhaps, well, the word might be *uncomfortable* with your new status in life. I thought of something I recently came across that has meant a good deal to me. I wanted you to see it."

"Lead on, Mr. McKay. It's your party."

A ten minute walk through the streets of Stirling brought the three men to a stone church, still under construction. "Neither Catholic nor Mormon, D.O.," Tom teased.

"That's right, Tom. But informative nonetheless. Look at the inscription over the entrance."

Tom stepped closer to the newly carved stone, in which was engraved the motto: "What e're Thou Art, Act Well Thy Part."

After reading the inscription, Tom turned back to D.O., who stood, smiling at his Irish friend.

"This applies to me?" Tom asked.

"You're not who you were when we met, Tom. But as you've said to me on at least two occasions, there are those who think you have a purpose in Salt Lake City. Given the significant change in your circumstances, I thought perhaps this little homily might apply and that it would give you something to consider. I know that when I first read it a few weeks ago, its effect on me was profound."

"I see," Tom replied. "It probably applies to all of us, doesn't it?"

D.O. smiled, looking up again at the inscription. "It does indeed, Mr. Callahan. I hope it will be of some use to you as it already has to me."

Tom locked eyes with David O. McKay for a moment, each man feeling the growing bond of friendship, the product of a chance meeting on statehood day in front of an unruly horse in downtown Salt Lake City. "Thank you, D.O. I'll look forward to your return to Utah and seeing what 'part' we'll each be given to 'act,'" Tom laughed.

"Aye," McKay responded. "So will I."

A short North Sea ferry crossing to Norway and visits to all of Katrina's relatives, followed by another ferry ride into Denmark, brought the Callahans to continental Europe. In what seemed short order, four months had passed, with Berlin, Munich, Salsburg, including the salt mines of southern Germany, Rome, and then Madrid, all explored and relieved of numerous artifacts Katrina found "absolutely essential" for their new home. Finally, the Callahans found themselves in Paris, the "City of Lights."

Originally intending to spend a full month in Paris, a telegram from Robert Thurston, received while they were in Madrid, forced a change in plans. No emergency existed, but Robert advised that several prominent western mine owners and operators were planning a meeting of some significance in Denver in April, and if Tom could shorten his trip by just a little bit, he could be on hand to meet them. Thurston thought they might like to meet the Chairman of the Board of Utah Trust Bank, particularly since several of them had expressed an interest in doing business with the new entity. Up against the well-established Zions Bank and other older institutions, Utah Trust Bank would need to put on an impressive face.

News of the disastrous sinking of the American battleship *USS Maine* in Havana harbor reached them while on the train from Madrid to Paris, and the newspapers were speculating that war between the United States and Spain would be the inevitable result.

Tom cabled Robert that he agreed the meeting was important and that in light of world events, they would cut several weeks off their itinerary and return home in time for the April meeting in Denver.

One other change was revealed on the train from Madrid to Paris. When Tom suggested that Katrina consider enrolling in the university when they got back to Salt Lake, she smiled and told him she probably wouldn't have time.

"Why not?" he asked.

"Oh, I'll be busy with the new house and practice with the choir, . . . and with the baby."

"The baby!" he said.

"Yes," she smiled.

For most of the rest of the trip to Paris, Tom gazed out the window of the train, contemplating his new role as father and the burden it would place upon him. Not much time was spent considering how his father had treated him, but a definite decision was made to avoid some of the same mistakes.

Paris, once they arrived after months of traveling and seeing one city after another, was everything Mr. Benoit had described. How the citizens had fallen in love with their city was easy to understand. The Seine, the magnificent Eiffel Tower, resplendent in its night lighting presentation, and the Louvre, all provided a wonderful conclusion to a wonderful honeymoon in Europe.

One week before their scheduled departure, at Katrina's request, Tom had somewhat reluctantly booked seats for a presentation of Puccini's opera, *La Bohème*. Tom's exposure to opera was limited to his attendance once at a performance in Limerick, when he was a boy. He had not been overly impressed, but he nevertheless, agreed to go, "for you," he had told Katrina.

Sitting in box seats to the side of the stage, Katrina watched as the first act progressed and Tom edged ever closer to the railing separating him from the actors below, who were almost within reach of their seats. At the point where Mimi and Rudolfo discover they have fallen in love, language translation from the Italian was not necessary. Katrina watched both the performance and Tom. He sat, totally enthralled by the music and the emotion being portrayed on stage. As the lovers' duet reached a crescendo, Katrina saw tears roll down her husband's cheeks, something she had not witnessed in their brief life together. Seated in their private box, Katrina looped her arm through Tom's and laid her head softly on his shoulder. Without looking away from the stage, Tom reached to take Katrina's hand, fully absorbed by the beauty and power of the music and the depth and intensity of the love story.

At that moment, Katrina felt in her soul that Thomas Callahan was capable of being touched by the Spirit, and that one day, he would embrace the restored gospel. For years to come, that moment would provide the hope and strength she would need to sustain her in an otherwise fulfilling marriage, which lacked only that one ingredient.

That Tom was open to a discussion of what he had felt during the performance was as surprising as his open display of emotion. Back in their hotel room, preparing to go to bed, Tom raised the subject.

"I truly don't understand it, Katrina. The music seemed to reach inside of me."

"I understand, Thomas," she replied. "Why do you think that is?" she said, removing her jewelry and stepping to the door to set their shoes in the hallway for the night steward.

"Katrina," Tom said, "I have discovered so many confusing things about myself this past year, it's hard to understand. The northern lights in Alaska left me enthralled. The music tonight seemed, well, it just seemed to strike a chord in my heart. It's all beyond understanding, really. I come from such a small place in Ireland, have no education, and have always seen myself as, well, sort of a ruffian." He smiled quickly at her, "Sort of like what your father judged me to be," he laughed.

"I'm very confused. It's like I'm two people. Usually I'm someone who brooks no interference. I feel hard, even mean. Other times, such as tonight, things move me. Sitting there, listening to that music, I had the feeling there is more to life than just living. Does that make any sense?"

Katrina came and sat next to him on the edge of the bed, kissing his cheek and stroking the wisp of dark hair that always eluded Tom's control. "It's the Spirit, Thomas."

"The Spirit?"

"Thomas, the Holy Spirit confirms the truth—in all forms. When we hear beautiful music, listen to enlightened thoughts, or hear the words of the Prophet," she smiled again, remembering their good-natured banter about the Prophet and the Pope, "the Spirit testifies to us, Thomas. It's as though God is saying, 'Listen, for I have provided this beauty for your pleasure. It is of me.' Can you understand that?"

"I understand what you told me long ago, that if I put myself in God's hands, he would protect me," he laughed, laying her gently back on the bed. "He has given me the opportunity to spend my life with you, Katie, m'darlin', and *that*, at least for the moment, is sufficient truth for me."

Katrina smiled at him as he bent to kiss her. She reached up to embrace him, closed her eyes, and silently thanked God for the second chance she had to live and to love.

354